"IT'S USELESS," Tatti said, "to build a fort in paradise. As useless, Gordon, as your defense against my love for you. At seventeen, every girl is a woman, and I'm nineteen."

"Quite." Wragby held her hand, but did not look at her. "And I am almost as old as your parents. I have no intention of disillusioning you."

"I'm not under an illusion. You love me too."

"Oh, Tatti, I do." His voice softened. Gathering her into his arms, he put his mouth into the thick chestnut hair at her ear, drawing in the scent of her skin. "To love you would be my final wish on this earth. I'd die should I harm you in love."

"But, Gordon, love does not harm." She pulled free to search his eyes. "I'll go no further. Take off my clothes."

"I shouldn't," he said.

"In love, it's right. Gordon, the Lord meant for us to live."

She raised her hands over her head. Wragby looked at her and saw every hope he'd ever dreamt. He put his hand to the tie at her midriff, and pulled it.

Novels by
Henry V. M. Richardson

The Lady of Skarra
Skarra

Published by
WARNER BOOKS

The
LADY
of
SKARRA

by

Henry V. M. Richardson

WARNER BOOKS

A Warner Communications Company

WARNER BOOKS EDITION

Copyright © 1979 by Henry V. M. Richardson
All rights reserved.

ISBN 0-446-81493-8

Cover Art by Jim Avati

Warner Books, Inc., 75 Rockefeller Plaza, New York, N.Y. 10019

Ⓦ A Warner Communications Company

Printed in the United States of America

Not associated with Warner Press, Inc., of Anderson, Indiana

First Printing: June, 1979

10 9 8 7 6 5 4 3 2 1

Eileen Philomena Haines
Vokes–Mackey
Countess du Bruyère
1893–1977

Eduard James du Bruyère
Vokes–Mackey
1889–1909

Patricia Stuart Hegel Richardson

BOOK ONE
Tempest

I

Tatti McTaggart, home to Scotland for the Christmas season from her English girls' school at Hampton Abbey, had galloped a dozen miles across the Scottish moor toward the River Deveron. Peter would be waiting for her on the Deveron. Peter, her childhood sweetheart and friend, who had built the rock pools along the creeks with her, and sat in the heather on the banks, eating macaroons, while they watched the salmon break clear of the ripples in short bursts of wriggling speed, to pass the stones and enter the pools to rest, and then swim upstream to spawn. It was Peter who helped her tuck up her voluminous silk skirts and petticoats, after she had slipped off her pantalettes so she could wade bare-legged beside him as he cast his fishing pole, but that was never at spawning time. Peter Frobisher-Barrett was such a sportsman he would never fish at spawning, and he always threw back the egg-laden "hens" anyway.

In fact, Tatti had worried at one time that Peter liked fishing better than he liked her. Yet when they had grown beyond childhood, and Peter's voice was changing, she felt him catch his breath when she put her bare foot out of the water to stand on a moss-covered rock where they were fishing, and she saw the look in his eye when he glanced up at her to see if she'd heard it. Tatti had said, "I do believe you'll catch a marvelous fat trout." She gestured at the dark sheen that lay on the pool, and Peter cast his line toward the shadow of a tree along the bank.

Tatti reined in her Thoroughbred when she heard the English fifes piercing the cold morning air. "Whoa," she said, and patted the horse's neck while searching for the soldiers. She saw a platoon of redcoats in gaiters marching up to and past isolated cottages. She ran her eye along the road where they marched, and the cottages seemed to dissolve into smoking shambles and spread their white-clothed innards into distant walled gardens.

"No!" Tatti screamed, forgetting Peter, and whipped her horse into an explosion of hoofbeats. "No, you cannot clear our cotters!" Her voice was lost in the chill air as she raced to head off the English. They were clearing people off the land to make room for grazing sheep. "The Clearance Acts of an English Parliament! Never on Skarra!"

Ahead was the cottage of Cora Lundee, who lived south of Skarra on the Firth of Fovern, and had been her childhood nurse from Tatti's earliest memory. The Lundees were distant kin, as was all of Scotland, and Angus, a bearded old man who was Cora's father, had the keep where Lord Skarra's red deer wintered.

English soldiers thronged the yard and cottage of the Lundees as she galloped in. "Stop!" Tatti shouted, leaping from her horse among the redcoats who scattered as he galloped through. Then she saw old Angus.

Angus Lundee lay on his back, the body stretched out on the brick pavement, his shirt ripped open to show a mat of coarse white hair, thick on his chest and hiding his navel. The white beard wafted gently in the morning light, and his bare toes were so naked and quiet. His blue eyes were fixed on the well-hoist. His bald skull had been crushed; but not deep enough to kill him, it seemed.

"Angus?" Tatti whispered, while English soldiers moved briskly in and out of the cottage, carrying out the soft furnishings to feed a fire they had started.

"Old coot's dead," said a man who watched her. "He fought the King's law."

"Cora!" Tatti shouted, running to the cottage doorway. "Cora!"

A large redcoat with a white wig heaved her backward, and she fell on the flagged paving. Getting to her knees, she saw the herd-boy, Craig. He was lying across the garden manure pile, his head down, bleeding from his nose. "Craig?" Tatti called uncertainly, and was glad to see the boy move an elbow over his eyes and hear him groan. "Thank God, they didn't kill Craig," she said.

"Into the manure pile with 'em, boys!" the large soldier with the wig said.

"Damn you!" Tatti shouted and darted into the cottage. Her childhood nurse, Cora Lundee was hurling herself at the soldiers, seeking to stop them. "Tatti, the English!"

"How dare you?" Tatti stepped in front of a sergeant.

He flung her through the door, into the yard.

"Stop!" she screamed. "Lord Skarra declared that our cotters were loyal!"

The soldiers paused and looked at her.

"Lord Skarra's word! Where are your officers?"

"We have a higher law," said the sergeant, and the men went back to work.

"I command you! Cease! In the name of the King!"

"Never her mind, boys."

"Damn you, sergeant, I'm Lady Tatti of Skarra!"

"What's a lady these days?"

"Goddamn the English!" The half-grown boy sprang at the large Englishman, knocking Tatti aside as he tore off the soldier's mitered hat and turned his wig sideways over his eyes, so that he looked like a long-haired goat.

"Good boy, Craig!" Tatti shouted, as the soldiers stopped to laugh.

"Fight in the bitch, eh?"

Tatti had her crop in her hand, circling the Englishman with the Highland boy who was wet with manure stains from his matted hair to his bare calves. The boy had his fists balled and was grinding his teeth.

"Trouble with Scots is they don't know when they're beat." The sergeant's faded blue eyes danced with cruelty as he turned to face Tatti, drawing a short sword from a white baldric.

"Would ye kill 'er, Sarge?" a man said.

The petty officer showed his teeth and swallowed as he toyed his saber point at Tatti's skirt. "She's mine, boys. Never raped a lady afore."

Tatti kicked his blade and leaped past his guard. Her crop cut a white groove down the side of his jaw and skull, splitting his lips.

"Good blow, my lady!" Craig shouted, grabbing a milking stool into his hand.

"Seize them, men!" The sergeant felt along his bloody split lips and lunged awkwardly forward with his sword.

Crunch! The stool's oak seat caught the sergeant across an eyebrow. One eyeball sprang from its socket and hung on its pink muscle, and he screamed in pain.

She felt herself kicked and flung about the cottage yard. Soldiers came into and out of focus, bricks and boots and white gaiters passed her face, and Cora's wooden churn was smashed to splinters before her eyes.

She lay still then for a long time, her face quiet against the cool manure.

"Tatti?" Cora whispered.

"Cora, I can't see." She felt her nurse's hand go over her neck and stop across her eyes.

"They killed the lad, and they wanted to kill you."

"God, poor boy." Tatti's eyes swam with tears.

"They did not rape you because you were a India rubber doll in their midst, aflopping over your own bones."

"Oooh, I hurt."

"Shh. They flung us in the manure pile, and they're takin' us to America."

Tatti fumbled through the manure for her friend's hand.

The week passed like a nightmare for Tatti. After a half-day's march through the wet night and across the mud-caked moor, Tatti looked no different from any other prisoner on her way to America.

"We killed the King's sergeant," Cora said, "and they'll not listen to reason."

"They killed two of ours," Tatti said, wiping the droplets of fog that condensed on her eyelashes and lips.

"Bond servants, they calls us," said a man who was coughing into the cold night as the prisoners were herded down Princes Street toward the quays of Edinburgh, where the ship lay in wait for them. "Slaves we be."

They passed Fendrath Hall, the town house of the Barretts, where she had stayed a thousand nights. She remembered how their childhood shouts had been muffled on the thick Turkish rugs, and recalled the Italian vases filled with wildflowers from the Scottish moor.

"Cora," Tatti said, taking the older woman's hand, "my father's a royal counsellor, and my grandfather's the Earl of Skarra. Things like this don't happen to us."

"My lady, 'tis a hard way for the common folk."

"We forbade it on Skarra."

"Child, they did not kill you. Now be still." She slipped her arm about Tatti's waist.

The warmth of her friend's body buoyed her, and she saw Cora's freckled nose in the flare-light. The wet air was cool on her lips and Tatti tried to comfort herself with the memory of the warmth within the manor house of Fendrath, the fires that lit the bedrooms and threw warm shadows across the canopied beds, and the plush curtains that were drawn behind the paneled shutters, to hold out the night and keep the fog away.

"Peter will come," Tatti said.

"Aye, he'll scour the moor, but we'll be gone." Cora snuffled.

"Peter will follow."

"Aye, ye were both stubborn children."

"Peter," Tatti said to herself. She had grown to love Peter unconsciously, much as a light fog seeps down the moor and swallows the river from sight, then fills the glen with peace. Peter had surprised her; one day he was a slender boy with quiet gray-blue eyes and blood red lips who chased beside her pony, laughing and hanging onto the pony's tail while she laughed and the pony tossed its mane, and they spilled their picnic baskets across the moor. Then he came home that time, almost an awkward stranger, who could not look into her eyes without swallowing openly in his gullet. She knew then he loved her and that she would never love another.

Peter Alexander Frobisher-Barrett was his full name, and he was the third son of Lord Fendrath, Earl of Kindok. Peter's mother liked the idea of his marrying Tatti because it allied old Scottish estates, "with a proper merging of old money," she would say, compressing her lips. Yet Lady Beth never quite understood her son. Peter seemed to lose himself on the moor among ancient whiskered Scots who lived in rock huts warmed by shaggy cattle, delighted with them as a whole world to himself. When not on the moor, he wandered free among the servants of Fendrath Hall, speaking Gaelic with them. If not following an old gillie to fish or net birds, he led Tatti and her gray dappled pony, Daffodil, on day-long treks to the sea coast or along the River Deveron.

"Thank the Lord for Tatti," Lady Beth would say. "I thought we'd lost him to the servants."

Peter adored Tatti. She was everything he loved about the moor and Scotland, but it was the slender knee and fragile tendon beneath her white thigh and her elegant bare foot stepping across moss-green rocks that had fired his soul.

Tatti limped when she stepped atop the sheening cobblestones, wet beneath old Edinburgh Castle. The great ramps were lowered, and flares pushed through the mist in a row of lights of the great hall where she had danced a hundred nights with the Royal Scots Greys and the Highland regiments. The men's eyes had filled with lights when she looked at them and spoke, and she knew she had power over them. Her flesh was fair and body full, and her chestnut hair fell to her waist; yet it was her voice and mouth and hazel eyes that turned men to her.

"If only Lord Skarra were here," Cora Lundee said from her reverie, and Tatti thought again of her family. She had been named Tatiana for her Russian grandmother, but became Tatti to her Scottish nurse; and her grandfather, old Lord Skarra, had said anything grown in Scotland was Scottish, "no matter her father, that clever Edinburgh lawyer, is English."

"Peter will find us," Tatti said. "Father's in London at Westminster." She knew her father, Sir Jonathan Hogarth, could free her in a moment, if only they could contact him.

"Step lively, dear friends!" said an assured voice, rich with the melody of command. "'Tis a sound ship for America!"

The varnished yardarms towered over the quay, looming in the flare-light like slick winter tree limbs suspended in the fog. Cora shrank back when she looked up at the ship. "'Tis unnatural a thing to go upon the waters," she said.

"Board the *Daphne!* Feather your feet!" A man wearing a shellacked black hat and dressed in cutoff canvas trousers was standing

17

on the rail and calling out through a speaking trumpet.

"A East Indies ship," said the prisoner who coughed at Tatti's side. "They'll bury me at sea."

"Not unless you die," Cora said, wiping her dripping nose with the back of her wrist.

"I'll die out of grief for the glen."

"Nay," Tatti said, dismayed by the man's resignation. He had a gentle, lined face. "Ye'll live, and not accept more than ye can bear. Nobody needs to die."

The man looked away, and Cora hesitated as she and Tatti lifted their skirts to step up on the gangplank. Tatti could see the prisoners streaming onto the deck of the ship through the open gangways.

"Step lively, ladies," said the man in the varnished hat.

Tatti caught the rough approval of her beauty in his eye. Fog glistened on his muscular cheeks.

"He's bosun, called Stowell," a woman said. "A wencher, but not mean."

There was a roll of snare drums on the quarterdeck, arresting the shuffling of the prisoners who were stumbling over manila hemp and falling against the ratlines, their hands clinging to the rails and lifelines on the cluttered deck.

"The Captain!" the bosun roared as the drum roll stopped.

An elegant officer stepped forward and looked tolerantly down at the bond servants, his hands clasped behind him. He was wearing the blue hunting livery of the Duchess of Beauford, and Tatti saw a touch of gray hair at his temples.

"Dear friends," the Captain said, "we expect a quiet crossing. Six weeks we might hope, but ten weeks more likely. We shall steer for the warm latitudes to avoid the cold, and let us try to be friends in our hour of travail." He smiled benignly at his own sense of melancholia at having to distress the hapless, uprooted emigrants.

Cora nudged Tatti, and nodded into the yardarms and rigging over their heads. Sailors were all through the masts and forest of lines that dropped out of the fog, the whole length of the ship.

"Parade arms!" A platoon of red-coated marines slammed the butts of their muskets to the deck.

The well-deck was crowded with prisoners, who stared in silence at the six naval officers who stood by the side of the Captain, each in varying livery of hunting blue, and wearing plush velour hats with turned-up side brims, and cockaded plumes caught in sterling clasps.

The bosun stepped before the officers, holding a forelock in his hand and bowing. The Captain nodded and turned away toward the bright lantern over the *Daphne*'s taffrail, and which lit the whole quarterdeck and massive double steering wheel.

"Cotters, you'll not be harassed," said the bosun. "You're not criminals, you're just enemies of the King."

"Harrumph," said an officer with a grog-swollen face and bloodshot eyes.

"Begging your pardon, sir," said the bosun, nodding to the officer. "Friends, it's politics and not thievery that we're takin' you to America, so you'll not be locked in irons, but you must stay below deck, to your own company, unless you be takin' the air." He paused and looked at the officers.

"Very good, Stowell," said the Captain, approaching the line of officers once more, and staring quietly at the throng of men and women and children.

Cora gestured to the sixth officer in line, a tall young man with a high forehead and fair mouth, an Italian spyglass tucked under his armpit. "Blue eyes and strong hands," Cora whispered with approval.

"Now be so good as to go below and make yourselves comfortable, as guests of the King," the Captain said, spinning away from them on his heel. The cotters stared at the officers for another moment.

"Avast! Below!" roared the bosun, causing the civilians to shrink backward in a shuffling, herdlike motion.

"Mister Stowell," the Captain said, spinning back, "on this ship we never raise our voices."

"My lord." Stowell caught his forelock again.

"Very good. No ill temper, mind you."

"My lord."

"A quiet ship is a happy ship." The Captain smiled indulgently at the cotters, who began easing their way up the main deck and down the hatches into the gun deck and first deck.

II

The ship was underweigh on the ebb tide. The lights of Kirkcaldy across the Firth of Forth moved in golden streamers on the slack water. "Lord, we're shut off from land," Cora said.

"Aye, our own universe, this ship," Tatti said, stooping to look out a gun port. "A floating world. Peter loved sailboats. His family bought him a commission in the Royal Navy."

"I wish Lord Peter was on this ship."

"Peter will come."

The whole length of the gun deck was alive with people, bedding down and moving about in stunned silence. Some of them were going up and down the double ladders to the galley fires on the exposed main deck to cook their porridge and prepare tea billies. Cora found a Highland family from Kildrumy to share their sleeping space. They had seven children, half grown and smaller, with whom Tatti and Cora shared an instant liking.

When Tatti spoke, her accent gave her away as a member of the ruling class. "A lady in bondage?" said the mother. "How can such be?"

"A mistake it was," Cora said briskly. "My lady was mistaken for a cotter by the English soldiers. Fearfully ignorant they were."

"Ah, poor thing," the woman said, her voice soft as she paused to lay out her children's pallets.

"There are English gentlemen coming to rescue her," Cora said, with a quiet optimism that was amazing in a Highland woman whose home had been destroyed and father slain.

"Such a kind man is the Captain," the mother observed. "A Christian gentleman, he likes quiet. Aye, a true gentleman."

"Aye, there be good in all," Cora said.

Christopher Harrow swung down the ladder from the quarterdeck. Cora recognized his muscular thighs and white silk stockings. "My lord, a terrible mistake has occurred," she told him. "We have a lady in our midst, a friend."

"A friend, surely not."

"Aye, my lord, Peter Barrett's bespoken."

"Lord Peter? A bond woman?"

"A lady."

22

In less than a quarter hour Tatti had proven her identity, had shocked the English naval officers with "the stupidity of the British army," and had caused the Captain, Gordon Wragby, to personally apologize. "My dear girl!" He took Tatti's hand into his. "We crave your indulgence for an upheaval that appalls all gentle folk.".

"But you won't put back to shore with me?"

"Alas, once under weigh, my orders forbid it." His voice was soothing, but she broke down and sobbed into Cora's strong consoling arms.

"But I don't want to see America, no matter for a single day!"

"My lady, the cotters have lost their homes forever," Cora whispered. "Don't let them see thee cry."

Tatti nodded her head and dried her eyes into Cora's rough shawl, lest the cotters see she'd been sobbing.

When the *Daphne* had cleared Tantallon Castle two miles to starboard and had shaped her course under full canvas for the Orkney Islands, Tatti knew they were in for a long voyage. "Coffin, the paymaster, has true cause to regret us," Cora said. "We have been given his cabin."

Tatti ran her eyes over the small but delicate cabin in its varnished and carved woodwork. It had two bunks and a small folding table and commode, as well as an armoire. They were comfortable and the officers had given them apparel bought for wives or sweethearts, so they were well clothed. Tatti was not content, however.

"Peter and the moor and the salmon in the River Dee, that's what I want," she said.

Crowding her masts with all canvas she could carry, the *Daphne* sailed north along the coast of Scotland, schooning the sea in a swift rush of days. Salt spray was flung over her bows at every plunge. Tatti wrapped herself and Cora in an eiderdown puff and watched the headlands of Scotland fall away and vanish, as the ship set sail into the Atlantic.

"Look on our voyage as a pleasure jaunt," Christopher Harrow said, coming up behind them.

"There's no pleasure in leaving home," Tatti said, "especially if one may perish at sea."

"Oh, dear girl, this ship's a bit of England," the young man said affably. "Stout as the English oak."

"We are not English."

Christopher was quiet and fingered the embroidered frogs along the front of his great cape. His eyes glanced uncertainly into Cora's. She saw his quandry but let him search the silence in his embarrassed failure to please.

"That is our home." Tatti gestured at the rough banks of gorse that were falling out of sight. "Our hearts lie on the moor."

"Certainly," Christopher said, leaning toward her.

"Why then the deception?" She still refused to look at the young officer.

"Because 'tis inevitable, and I'd not have you grieve."

"Thank you, Christopher."

Christopher Harrow waited a few moments at their side, his cape blowing against the women. He knew Tatti felt the warmth of it and of his presence and, in fact, was pleased at his attempts to ease their captivity aboard ship.

"The ship is our mistress and we her slaves, yet if we are true to her, she will never betray us." His voice had a full, rich sound.

"Thank you for our quarters," Tatti said, turning to him and putting out her hand through the folds of the eiderdown. He took it and smiled, his mouth and eyes delighted.

"To be enslaved by beauty . . ."

"Oh, Chris, I'm Peter's slave already," Tatti said.

"No chance for me?"

"He took me fishing and I fed him macaroons. No man can top that."

"I'll see you at breakfast," he said, and settled his plush officer's hat, and turned to study the binnacle and helm, and looked up into the evening stars.

In the days that followed, Tatti spent hours on the raised poop deck of the *Daphne,* watching the graceful ship bowl along under a staggered tier of sails. Only the wind brought her any sense of comfort. It was wild and barbarous in its indifference to them on the deck of the ship, yet it drew against the sails, and drove the ship headlong across the long swells in the sea.

25

Cora was usually at her side, seldom speaking, as both gazed up at the sails which rose along the *Daphne*'s three masts.

"'Tis beautiful, this ship," Cora said, "but 'tis unnatural. If we was meant to go upon the waters, why we'd have wooden legs and arms a-stickin' up, and big ears for sails."

"Oh, dear Cora, I love you." Tatti snuggled into the eiderdown puff, and felt Cora hug her waist tightly. "I'm so glad we're together."

"Aye, just as we were when ye was a wee one and I a lass."

Tatti glanced into the russet eyes of the handsome woman, and onto the pale sandy lips that spoke in soft deliberation. "Love me, Cora, as you did when I was a little girl and you took care of me."

"That was then, Tatti. Now you're grown."

Together they watched an emigrant woman holding a drab shawl about her shoulders scuttle across the windy deck with a saucepan. "But we're all of one spirit, child or grown, and I suppose I crave to go back."

"Aye, lass." Cora touched her hair softly.

Several times each day Tatti moved among the emigrants who were spread the whole length of the gundeck of the ship. The decks were low, and the length of the ship was like a long, shadowed cave, in which many men and women were crowded, where the cries of children never ceased, and babies wailed night and day. Cora and Tatti encouraged the women with milk in their breasts to share with women who lacked the milk to suckle.

26

"If we stay with them, they'll do it," Tatti said, as she settled amidst a family of dark-haired children. "They can't live as lonely islands."

As the first weeks passed, Tatti noticed she had a quieting effect on the uprooted cotters. The men were respectful to her, not because of her class but because of human need, and were unguarded in a frightened, rude manner, with their future in America uppermost in their minds.

"With a sense of God, I think our lives'll always have a purpose," Tatti said, looking away from the trusting eyes of the cotters who wanted to believe her and hung on her words, and she wondered why they could believe so openly when she herself was so unsure.

Captain Gordon Wragby often met Tatti when he strolled the main deck, or visited the galley to sniff "the fresh nourishment" in the emigrants' stew and porridge kettles, which steamed all day on the open deck.

"Lot of tommyrot, calling our strongest and finest blood criminals," he would say, and then glance nervously into the rush of white clouds that chased on a rising wind.

Gordon Wragby was a typical slender English aristocrat of modest means who appeared inept as a matter of good taste, and who dabbled in metaphysical poetry. Tatti learned from Christopher that, as a young man, Gordon Wragby had adored a succession of beautiful women without fortunes, until the day came

27

when he realized his youth had vanished and no woman remained to arouse a fire of hope within him nor had a fortune large enough to buy his life. Now the Royal Navy, his retired pension, and his sister, Lady Nellie Rush, were to be his final consolation in life.

"Lamb stew, every third day," the Captain would repeat while the cooks held their hats in respect. "Give the cotters all they can eat. I'll command no death ship of prisoners."

"No death ship, the *Daphne*, my lord," the grog-cheeked first lieutenant would repeat.

During the third week, Chris came up onto the quarterdeck in the evening twilight and slipped a long cloak over Tatti's shoulders. "Caught you alone, and without an eiderdown," he said.

Tatti pulled the cloak about her throat and smiled at the tall young man. "Thank you, and will you accept my apology for being so rude so often?"

"You were hurt."

"Aye, helping the emigrants has eased my soul. Poor people, they go to an unknown land, they cannot read nor write, and they're impoverished."

"All they have to sell is their bodies." The young officer's voice was subdued at the glimpse of cruel reality. "Oh, I know it's all wrong," he said, "but you shouldn't think about it."

"Not think about it! Lord, they're my own people, my kin!" She pulled back to stare up into his well-bred face.

"Please don't think about it, please." He protested, pulling her close to him. Then he tipped her face up and kissed her lips, and she felt his heartbeat jump in his chest and his breath explode when she pulled her mouth free of his to breathe again from the kiss.

III

The wind gathered strength as the days wore on, and Tatti could see the sailors of the watch had shortened the sails on the foremast and mainmast, and the canvas on the mizzen-mast fairly strained over the quarterdeck and wheel. The *Daphne* laid into the sea, and took the waves in long plunges, as though frisking in her exuberance as a thing alive upon an ocean that she alone could master.

Tatti noticed that the crew seemed spritely, that the rising wind brought excitement. Below, on the gun deck and maindeck, the unordained preacher, Josephus Byles was everywhere among the emigrants.

Byles was a bald-headed man with large arresting brown eyes and a boyish smile. His

31

jaw was coarse, and his mouth never stopped exhorting the cotters and sermonizing as he smiled. He had come aboard the *Daphne*, he explained, to "follow his flock and help lead them to the promised land, as Moses led his people out of bondage." He smiled quietly and searched the wine-plump features of the naval officer, who cocked a skeptical eyebrow at him.

"Harrumph. Garbage for the common people, God help them," the officer said, turning away from the preacher.

Byles smiled at the insult and was content to watch the officer out of sight. "We humble servants of the Lord must expect our thorns," he said, returning to where he was haranguing a handful of emigrants who lounged about the mainmast and listened to the long swish of the ocean down the flanks of the onrushing ship.

Cora put her hands to her hips and spoke quietly behind Tatti. "He's too eager to help not to be hateful."

"Oh, Cora!"

"He turns every word to his own advantage. You cannot insult him."

"He's a preacher," Tatti said.

"Aye, and what gospel does he preach?"

"There is but one." Tatti arched her eyebrows, and turned to Cora.

"Aye, so 'tis, and how many have we murdered in Scotland over the one?"

"Oh, tush, he's harmless." Tatti laughed outright and clapped her hands on the arms of her nurse. "We have Royal Marines, sailors, naval officers. He's a diversion."

"Aye, but he don't know it, my lady."

"Cora, I'm ashamed of you." She hugged the woman who towered over her still.

A day later Tatti noticed a wild green sea roiled away to the horizon on all sides, though the sky was clear blue, broken only by the rush of soft white clouds that streamed aft. The ship seemed to skip across the ocean, and the sailors scampered up and down the ratlines, setting the sails to the screaming pipes of the bosun and his mates, who filled the main deck with cries of the weather.

"It's so exciting," Tatti said, watching the two men spin the large spoked wheel that steered the vessel. She saw the waves crash on the windward bow and explode into a cloud of spume that caught a rainbow and vanished over the lee deck.

"You'll love the navy yet," Chris said, coming up beside her.

"So clear, and a warm wind at last."

"Aye, Captain Wragby steered into the southern latitudes to find warmth for the emigrants."

"What a kind man he is," Tatti said.

"Too kind, perhaps. He lacked the grit for the ruthless climb to admiral."

Tatti turned to Chris. His face was preoccupied with the mercury glass of barometric pressures as well as gauging the direction of the speeding clouds and wind. "No flag rank, no title, no knighthood, no money." He spoke without looking up. "Poor Gordon Wragby."

"He's just a good man." Her voice was touched with ironic humor.

33

"Yes." Chris laughed outright and swung her into his bosom. "Could you marry me?"

"Oh, Chris, what would we do married, with no house and no prospects and not even grown up?"

"I'm twenty-two, same age as Peter."

"Well, I didn't marry Peter." They laughed and held each other as the graceful ship pitched her bows in the seas and her stately masts shivered in the ecstatic humming of her taut shrouds, and they listened to the wind whine as it cut across the forestay.

"I think the Captain may have got us so far south we're verging into a hurricane," Chris said.

"Oh, Lord." Tatti slipped her arms about his waist to take comfort in the strength of his body.

That night they dined in the Captain's cabin with the officers of the *Daphne*. It was quite gala. The salon was radiant in the candlelight of the Portuguese chandelier and along the paneled walls elegant weighted silver sconces held their candles upright as the grand salon followed the sea with the ship.

Tatti entered the salon in a green moiré gown that sculpted her torso and held up her breasts, her white rounding flesh luminous against the green.

"Lovely," said Gordon Wragby, lifting his glass of Madeira. The officers rose, as if one man, smiling and watching her hazel eyes dance at their admiration.

"My mother would whip me if I wore a gown like this in Edinburgh."

"It's all I had," said Coffin, the Paymaster. "And I'm glad I did."

"Exquisite," said the Captain, sitting down. She settled herself on his right.

Cora was in deep beige taffeta, and crushed a sachet hanky in her moist hand, not at ease with the extravagant compliments of the officers.

"Harrumph," said Leghorn, the first lieutenant, at Cora's left. "Not often have these jolly savages known such good company, my lady."

Cora stared at him, her russet eyes riveted on the red-flecked face. "Sir, I was the lady's nurse."

"Ah, then 'tis you we must thank for such grace."

"Nay, good sir, the lass is the Lord's handiwork. And who are the savages, my lord? I do not understand you."

Leghorn sipped noisily at his wine goblet to regain his composure, and laughed. "The King's officers, savages all."

The table laughed in masculine good nature.

"Aye, we know the English," Cora said, settling herself. "You spoke right. Savages."

"Bravo!" said Coffin, a short man with white puffy cheeks and wet eyes, and the naval officers sipped their goblets to the impromptu toast. "Savages."

"We crave beauty in the navy," Gordon

Wragby said, his face delighted as he stared unfocusing across Tatti's neck and eyes and bare shoulders, avoiding looking directly at any part of her body, to keep from embarrassing the girl. "Sailors are great company, but the sea makes us especially fond of that sublime half of the human race."

"Hear, hear!"

"Well spoken, my lord," said Leghorn.

Tatti flushed in the open admiration and licked her lips quickly, and lifted her wine goblet to sip. The wine dizzied her and filled her with warmth.

"Chris, you're quiet," said Coffin.

"It's enough to listen and look."

"There's a little devil, 'look,' he does." Leghorn gestured at Tatti

"Alas, you flatter us unfairly," Tatti said. "We have no defense."

"When do we get to America?" Cora said, to get the conversation practical once more.

"America, another chance for the race of man," said Gordon Wragby, with the lost look of a middle-aged man who knows he will not have another chance passed behind his eyes.

Tatti saw the look and said, "Wragby Hall is lovely, I hear, especially the lilacs."

"Aye, my sister loves them. Lilacs and roses."

"Mother loves roses."

"Will Lady Skarra ever forgive me for stealing her prettiest rose?" the Captain said, his face alive with admiration again.

"We'll not stay in America, the Lord willing," Cora said.

"To the King!" said Captain Wragby.

"The King." "The King." "The King." About the table the officers repeated the toast, and raised their glasses to sip.

"He's a Stuart," Cora said, and touched her tongue to the outside of her goblet without drinking.

Two Hindu mess boys served dinner, while a cotter played soft Low Country airs on a dulcimer. Course by course, in the bright candlelight, amid the naval officers in hunting blue, Tatti was swept away into a heady fantasy that she at last understood men and could hold her own in the adult world. Once or twice she returned a compliment, bold as it was given, causing Cora to frown at her.

After dinner the Captain escorted her across the saloon to sit upon the elegant cushioned bench that ran athwart the sterncastle of the ship and to stare out the fine slanted windows. They watched the sparkling light thrown down across the stern of the ship from the large taffrail lantern.

"What a lovely golden veil it is, to play on the waves each time one looks out," Tatti said. The waves rushed in at each other in a quick froth that flooded the wake of the fast sailing ship, leaving a white confusion that eddied just under them and chased the ship through the night.

"'Tis a cold sight," Cora said. "Too much water and not enough of us."

"'Tis a stout ship, and she rides the sea well," said the Captain.

After sipping Moorish coffee while the company relaxed in good humor and pleasant conversation, Gordon Wragby showed Tatti to the open deck. He wrapped her in his long cloak and they stood together and watched a half-moon breaking through the low rushing clouds. The moonlight fell in mottled white illumines, reflecting from a sea that was growing white under the wind.

"An enchanted evening, my lady, that I never dared to hope for." Wragby spoke softly, drawing his cloak about her body with his encircling arm, but not touching her.

"What a gala evening," Tatti said.

"This is my final voyage, then retirement —the Lord indeed blessed me with such beauty."

"Me?"

"Aye, my lady."

"Please, call me Tatti."

"As you will, but my temples are gray and you are a girl."

"My father's temples are gray."

"Oh, yes, Sir Jonathan Hogarth." Wragby dropped his hands from about her. "I'm sorry."

Tatti turned quickly and saw the hurt in his eyes, and flushed in embarrassment at her youthful disregard of his sensibilities, especially when she saw the detached smile that hid his feelings.

"Forgive me."

"Forgive perfection, my dear? Indeed, it seems the higher one rises in his station, the deeper the folly he floats upon."

Cora came across the deck and looked

solemnly at the Captain while Tatti squeezed Wragby's hands. "Oh, Lord." Wragby dropped his arms. "I'll bid you ladies a good night as you take the air." He waved his arm across the moonscape of the ocean. "We may have a bit of a blow on the morrow, but she's a good ship." He bowed and was gone.

Cora stood at Tatti's side until the moon cast a bright glow across the deck. "I'll have your bed turned down," she said, and went to the hatch door to their cabin.

IV

Tatti woke in a start and sat up quickly in her bunk in the morning light. Her cabin was leaning at a cozy angle. Although she was still snug in her bedclothes, the whole ship had trembled about her.

"What was that?" she said, but Cora's breathing did not stir in the bunk over hers.

Whooomp! The ship thundered and Tatti heard a labored tremble as the *Daphne* lifted her elegant bowsprit once more, and she looked out the varnished casement window to see a wild sea, tormented under sheets of low-flying white spindrift, though the sky was still a clear blue. The sunlight cheered her.

Whooomp! A mighty concussion shivered the timbers of the vessel. "Cora!" Tatti cried, and jumped out of her bunk to the cabin deck.

"What is it?" Cora said.

"The sea, I think. Chris said we'd got into a hurricane, but no danger."

"A body'd best be dressed," Cora said, slipping out of bed and handing Tatti a sponge and towel.

Tatti dipped into a basin and wiped her face, while looking out the port. "Hurry." In a moment she and Cora had washed and dried their bodies perfunctorily, and shifted into a series of petticoats and pantalettes, Cora helping her with the spare hand that was not dressing or drying her own body.

"Oh, I forgot the commode," Tatti said, lifting a mass of skirts to sit upon the chamber pot.

"Reckon the Lord don't send His torrents at suitable times," Cora said. "Hurry, child."

Tatti could feel the vibrations of the ship carried through the round seat of the tall elegant china pot to her bare bottom. "Oh, I can feel the ship underneath me."

"Dare say the officers are about," Cora said.

Tatti stood clear of the commode, pulling up her pantalettes and flouncing out her petticoats beneath her skirt. " 'Tis a brisk wind, I know." She pulled open their door onto the quarterdeck. *Wham!* The wind hit her in the face, tearing the door handle from her hand, and blew her backward into Cora and sent the hand basin clattering to the floor.

"Good Lord, such a wind," Tatti said. A note of fear echoed in her voice, and Cora looked at her quickly.

The ship was close-hauled on a light canvas, taking the seas on her port bow and holding into the rolling clouds of the hurricane. Tatti seized the ladder to the quarterdeck and felt her skirts blown wildly over her head.

"Here!" Chris shouted, grabbing her arm and swinging her to her feet on the deck, where the paymaster had already pulled Cora.

Tatti was at ease when she saw the officers had no fear in their faces.

"We'll ride her out, our bows into the sea, veering astern on our drogue and our free hawsers."

"Terrifying it is," Tatti said. "We're so small —and look!"

The horizon had closed upon the ship on all sides, and rain was slashing the decks and spraying the seas aboard in swarming waves. The officers slipped lines about Tatti's and Cora's waists and tied them to the cleats of the masts. The two helmsmen were lashed to the massive wheel, drenched in spray and staring into the clouds and seas as they held the ship into the rising wind of the hurricane.

"Nothing like a bit of weather!" Chris shouted, his voice filled with boyish glee.

"Oh, this scares me," Tatti whispered, chilled by Chris's defiance of such a terror.

Tatti saw Gordon Wragby standing forward of the wheel, his hand resting lightly on the rail abaft the quarterdeck, his plush hat wet but caught under his chin by a strap, leaning with a single line caught under his thigh to hold him upright. He watched the darkness that settled over the day. The white clouds seemed to swell into ugly masses that hovered over the ship like shapeless giants, and Tatti felt the ship no more than a chip of wood.

"Forgive us, O Lord, our trespasses." Cora prayed spontaneously as they saw the water rise up out of the ocean to join a dark movement that fell down out of the sky to smother them in rain and suck the breath out of their lungs. The ship was lost out of sight under water before her, and they heard the sails torn from the cleats. Tatti saw them festoon the masts like spent banners, and the *Daphne* began to labor in the sea.

"Let us live, O God," Tatti said, clinging to Cora, wondering where the officers had vanished.

Green water rolled down the main deck of the ship. Tatti heard the oak doors smashed in as the seas swept through their cabins and out the windows under the taffrail astern. She felt the storm rise high, pitching down the bow to slide under water again.

"She'll hold!" Chris shouted, and Tatti knew he had been with her all the time.

"The emigrants, where are they?" she shouted into Cora's ear.

"Below!" Chris yelled.

"They must be terrified! Can't I go down and help them?"

He shook his head at first, licking the water off his lips, then nodded. "Hang on!" he shouted, and slipped her out of her bowline.

"Tie up your skirts!" He swung her by her arms to the scuttle-hatch leading down through their quarters into the covered gun deck. They were climbing on hands and knees in the dark, and for the first time Tatti was able to hear above the roaring of the wind.

He pulled her out into the low cavern deck which lurched and rolled in the rushing water where they could hear flooding the deck overhead and crashing against the hull.

"We're under water half the time, I dare say." He spoke with pride and awe.

"Lord, we're soaked." Her layers of petticoats were clinging against the backs of her legs and hindering her knees.

Chris watched her struggling in the dim light as they made their way forward, past the heaps of loose gear, cordage, tackle, ropes, powder buckets, and gun swabs.

"Pull them off," he said. She unbuttoned the waistbands of four skirts which clung to her legs, and he stooped to pull them down so she could step free.

"Lord, this hurricane is a pure terror," she said uncomfortably.

"Nothing matters as long as we stay afloat," he said. He led her forward where they could hear the frail notes and voices lifting in a hymn.

Eternal Father strong to save,
Whose arm hath bound the restless wave,
Who bidds't the mighty ocean deep,
Its own appointed limits keep.

The cotters were crouching in a mass of frightened men and women and crying children. Tatti heard the notes of a dulcimer rallying a sweet sound that was astonishing in its bravery, and rose above the endless roar of the ocean about them.

Oh, hear us when we cry to thee,
For those in peril on the sea.

Tatti let her lips form the words she had sung a lifetime in Edinburgh Cathedral, but did not sing. She waited with Chris. If an Almighty would save them and the ship, it would be done by the terrified cotters and the Lord alone, without her trespassing among them in their grave hour. In their time of desolation, Tatti felt the emigrants were far stronger than she, and she was suddenly more fearful in her loneliness than she was of the storm.

"Lord, save this ship and spare these people," Tatti said, dropping to her knees. "Lord, save the children!"

Chris stood at her side, and she felt him watching her in her soaked undergarments. "The Lord hears us," he said, dropping to one knee and touching her shoulder. "But the ship's sound."

"I've never known where God is, and maybe they know the way," she said standing up. Then she noticed Cora kneeling among the mass of cotters, a small child standing between her arms, singing the ancient hymns of deliverance from peril and death.

"Here, my lady," said a woman, sweeping a Stuart tartan over her bare shoulders.

"They say the ship will float," Tatti said, adjusting the tartan, "but we must pray."

They heard a different noise as the ship heaved up its bow, felt a turning motion rotate the deck, heard the overhead boards strain under the sea, and saw water pour through a

46

thousand cracks upon them. The emigrants blanched in terror, the hymn faltering and a woman screamed.

"She broached, but she'll hold!" Chris shouted, ducking.

"We must suffer our faith for a living God." It was the resonant, persuasive voice of Josephus Byles, the preacher, calming the emigrants. "The storm is our woe, God's test of our faith in our fathers." He smiled confidently in a deliberate pause, both to gain their attention and to dominate their confusion.

"Simply a divine chastening to purify us for our new world, a world without aristocrats, a world of common, godly spirits. " Byles flung out his upturned hands and shook them, his smile as warm as his voice. He picked up a child and walked among the people.

Tatti shivered, a convulsive chill making her wrap the Stuart tartan snug about her body. She stayed with the emigrants, drenched as they were under the pounding that tons of water poured over the laboring ship. She slipped her arm around a woman while Cora held a child to her bosom.

"Do you think the Lord will spare us?" she whispered to Cora.

"I don't know." Cora shook her head quickly.

They felt an easing of the seas, where the wet thunder on the hull softened, and left only bows to pitch and stagger the timbers.

"Maybe we've escaped," Tatti said. "You stay here!"

Tatti made her way aft over the debris,

wading in water up to her knees in the scuppers. Climbing the scuttle-hatch once more, she darted out onto the poop deck, and ran forward to the mizzenmast in the moment when the ship hung poised before plunging her bows.

"Oh," she shouted as the wind snatched the tartan off her shoulders and tore the short sleeves of her camisole; but she felt free of impediment as she clung to the mast rail, her hair streaming loose in the wind.

"Great Scott!" Chris shouted, lashing her against the mast. "You should've stayed below!" He gestured across the sea. "We're in the eye!"

"The eye?"

"The eye of the hurricane!" He was lashed to the quarter rail, and the other officers were lashed about the wheel and quarterdeck, watching the seas and the storm, every man soaked to the skin in breeches and shirts and soggy blue jackets.

A figure sprinted into their midst, naked except for wet canvas trousers. "Four foot of water in the hold, my lord!" Bosun Stowell cried to the Captain.

"Start the pumps," Wragby ordered, and turned to Leghorn, who ducked into an escape hatch to the hold.

"Aye, my lord!" Stowell seized the line about his wrist, swung his legs over the quarter rail, dropped onto the main deck between rushes of green water. He disappeared at a run up the deck to the forecastle, blowing his shrill bosun's pipe.

V

When the confusion of waves vanished as
they passed out of the eye of the hurricane, the
wind struck again, broaching the ship under
heavy water four times and rolling her main
deck vertical so that her masts whipped the
surface before the bow caught up on her free
hemp line, dragging from the hawse, and drew
her bows into the weather once more, and she
rode the sea.

"She's easier!" Chris shouted to Tatti as
they saw Leghorn reporting to the Captain.

"Land ho!" The strange cry pierced her ears,
and she saw the officers snap upright, as though
jolted by a stunning blow.

"Where away?!"

From the crow's nest she heard voices crying out in excitement. Gordon Wragby slipped out of his bowline and stepped to the taffrail, and Chris seized the halyard and climbed swiftly to the boom.

"One point abaft the port quarter!" Stowell was in their midst, pointing over the ship's stern, and barefoot sailors tore past them, dragging ropes.

"Breakers, my lord!" Leghorn cried, and they could hear the faint thunder of a driven sea crashing upon land.

"My God," the Captain said. "We escaped death for this."

"Bermuda, my lord, the Outer Banks."

"It can't be!" Gordon Wragby ripped open the large vellum chart and stared at the smear of ink and pencil marks. "Goddamnit, it can't be!"

"The best chart we had, my lord," Leghorn said, as Chris joined them, to stare at the distant surf, then back to their navigation chart.

"Goddamn the Admiralty!" Gordon Wragby cursed. "Tea-sipping admirals! They can't draw a chart any better than they can fight!"

"Useless as tits on a boar, my lord." Leghorn spoke matter-of-factly.

"We must sail her off!"

"In this gale, my lord?"

"That or die. We have no choice." There was a calm to the Captain's voice as though one might measure death with a plan. "Beat to quarters, if you please."

The bosun's pipes shrieked all through the ship and in the ratlines and yardarms where sailors had tied themselves. On the wind its piercing wail was snatched away.

"What is it?" Tatti whispered to Chris. The sea was easier.

"Very bad."

"Bad?"

"The worst. We can't sail into the wind and we're being driven against the shore."

Tatti gagged in fear when she saw the distant breakers.

The seas were spilling over the ship in a lighter froth as they neared the land, and Tatti could see the long swells suck back from the shore where the ocean gathered its strength, carving deep valleys in the sea.

"The spanker!" "The flying jib!" "The staysail!" Leghorn's cries were carried up into the masts where sailors worked frantically.

Wet sailors scampered into sight as the big wheel creaked and began to spin, and all eyes watched the bow and the masts and looked fearfully astern where wreckage lay for the ship.

"We have weigh!" called out the helmsman.

"Underweigh, my lord!"

Gordon Wragby nodded and watched the jib topsail drop into its cleats and felt the ship lay urgently onto her port beam, green seas flooding into the scuppers.

"Oh Lord, let her sail free," Chris prayed.

A massive wave rolled up against the bow, flinging high the gilded bowsprit, and rolled the ship. The sails went down into the ocean, and Tatti clung to Chris and the mast. "She'll right herself," Chris said. "If only land weren't there."

Tatti stared at the shore. It *was* there. "Chris, we'll swim."

Against a wind that drove the sea white before them, they watched the ship right herself, the masts trembling in their straining shroud lines and the small white sails lifting high into the storm.

Craaash! Tatti heard a tearing sound of wood as though a tree were splitting apart in a forest.

"The foremast!"

In a moment the foredeck of the ship was entwined in a mass of tangled lines that dragged yardarms in the sea, among large splintered beams.

"Douse the spanker, and prepare to anchor!" Gordon Wragby shouted.

"Stand by the anchors!" The sailors with bare torsos and skin-wet trousers swarmed over the wreckage toward the bow and then clustered at the chains to drop the anchors.

Gordon Wragby looked pensively astern where a wall of white sea thundered in wait for his ship. "Get the emigrants on deck and splinter casks and cordage for flotation."

"Oh, Captain, will the anchors hold?" Tatti asked, understanding Wragby's grave awareness of the peril. She stepped to his side and grasped the rail.

"Only God knows, little one." He touched her hand and nodded as the ship dropped down into a trough as though to sink amidst the running swells. In another moment she rose over a swell that picked her up and rushed her backward at the shore.

"Let go the lee anchor!" Wragby's voice floated aft on the wind. "Let go all anchors!"

Tatti heard the shrieking bosun's pipe and saw Stowell's wet body among the sailors as the anchors splashed into a froth."

"She's snubbing, my lord!" Leghorn cried, as the ship eased her rolling and the anchors quieted her bow.

"Aye, we're slowing." Wragby watched the taut anchor cables. "Not likely to break, if they'll only dig in and not drag."

A calm settled about the ship as the anchors took hold. She was being dragged backward, stern first toward the islands through immense green seas that rolled down her flanks. The Royal Marines were drawn up on the quarterdeck as if on parade and Tatti heard the drummers rolling their snare drums and rattling their sticks to the notes of the fifes.

"But the ship's holding?" Tatti said, when she saw the emigrants move uncertainly into sight, staring aft at the raised poop deck where they stood, at the marines and drummers, at the chaos of broken masts and lines, and at the sailors who were chopping up barrels and staves.

"I want them on deck, if we're driven ashore. Not trapped below." Wragby looked into the distance astern, where the surf roared at the beach in a white crescent.

The emigrants shrank back and held each other when they saw the wreckage and sensed what might lie ahead. "Those poor, desperate people," Tatti said.

"Our anchors are dragging!" It was Leghorn among the sailors on the foredeck. The ship was moving backward toward the beach.

"Play out all line—it may hold," Wragby said, and Chris jumped down onto the main deck and raced forward with the order.

"We've slowed, my lord!" It was Stowell, his blue eyes as dark as his sparse chin stubble. "But we can't grab bottom to hold."

"Thank you, Bosun. Strip the women of their skirts."

"Aye, my lord," the bosun cried.

"I'm going to the people," Tatti said. Slipping her bowline, she darted over the rail and down the deck, clambering over and ducking under the wreckage. In a moment she was surrounded by men who were blanched and speechless and crying women who clutched children's hands and arms with white-knuckled fingers.

Half-naked sailors smashed up pieces of wood and pressed them into the hands of men and women, who stared at the timber, refusing to take it, as though by accepting it they would confirm their danger.

"Take it!" Tatti screamed, wrapping a man's arm about a timber. "And hold on!" The man stared down at her.

Cora was at her side as Stowell darted up, his bosun's pipe lying in the mat of black hair on his chest; and Chris went by, leading a band of sailors dragging a long rope.

"Get the women's skirts off!" Stowell bellowed, his eyes darting over the emigrant women. "They'll only drag them down." He looked at Cora's wet skirts and at Tatti's pantalettes. "Get them off your legs, you'll drown!"

The women stared at him. His face was drenched with water and his jaw worked anxiously.

"Get them off, my lady!" He reached forward and tore Cora's skirts from her, tipping her over as he did. In a single sweep, he ripped Tatti's undergarments from her torso and snatched off her pantalettes, leaving her naked.

"Strip the emigrant women," he ordered the sailors about him. "And get the men's coats off!"

He jerked Tatti up by her wet hair. "Lady, all you have is your life! Hold the children by the hair!" He drove his hand back and forth, holding Tatti by the hair of her head for the emigrants to see. "When you swim, hang onto the child's hair." He balled his fist in her hair. "The hair won't slip outen your fingers!"

"We have to drag the children?" Cora said.

"If the anchors don't hold, we do!" He reached over and snatched Cora naked.

"The Captain said the skirts, not everything," Tatti protested.

"Aye, my lady, so he said. But if you be naked, we might get the skirts off the common folk."

Tatti heard the old hymn rise on the voices of the emigrants accompanied by the dulcimer:

A mighty fortress is our God,
A bulwark never failing;
Our helper He amidst the flood,
Of mortal ills prevailing.

Around her the people prayed on their knees. Children wept and clung to their parents as the wind scudded the wave tops across the open deck in stinging salt and mist. Some of the women had stepped out of their skirts, but most were too dazed to grasp the enormous desolation about them, and clung to the bodies of their loved ones.

"She's draggin' even!" a sailor shouted, one of a handful tearing the soggy wool garments off the emigrants.

The ship was being borne slowly backward to the white wall of noise and breaking seas at the beach.

"Friends, brethren, we can walk on the water! With faith!" Josephus Byles was strolling among the weeping emigrants.

"The storm is but a test, a visitation of the Lord to see if we be fitten for the promised land." He walked boldly as his voice rang out over their heads, the words surprising for their clear force.

"A child is innocent, dear friends, 'twill walk on the water." He smiled, stretching out his arms among the emigrants who stared up at him.

Some people turned their heads but nobody moved, and Byles smiled boyishly at Tatti, glancing at her naked breasts and thighs, then at Cora, who was transfixed by the storm, the wreckage, and the madness about them.

"Chris!" Tatti looked to where the red-coated marines stood rigid as if in a tableau, and she heard the snare drums rolling with the storm and piercing fifes defiant in iron discipline. Gordon Wragby was at the wheel, Chris was tying a rope around his naked waist as he searched the shore.

"Too far!" she screamed, but her voice was swept away.

"Suffer little children to come unto me," Byles's voice caressed them. "Let me have the child, sister."

The woman gave up her child, her hands going out to the preacher.

"A child will lead us out of corruption." He flung the child into the flying scud, and Tatti ran to the side to see it vanish into the foam. "A rebirth in innocence." He smiled assuredly.

"My God!" Tatti screamed. "He threw that child overboard! Gordon! Captain!"

"Lord God, stop him!" Cora pushed through the huddling people, shivering and praying and singing, shattered by the calamity, and onto Josephus Byles.

"Hypocrite!" She pummeled his chest.

He brushed her aside, crying, "Abraham had to sacrifice Isaac. Brethren, God demands atonement!" His full, rich voice rolled on. "This is our punishment!"

"Monstrous evil!" Tatti shouted, running and falling and skidding up the deck, clambering under ropes and across canvas sails. "Marines!" she screamed. "Gordon!"

The Royal Marine sergeant's eyes rested on her face, at attention, drawn sword by his ear. "He's killing the children!" Tatti beat the marine's chest, and looked up at the Captain.

"Lord Gordon, the children!"

Gordon Wragby's eyes fixed on her, his hair streaming loose about his head, his satin breeches and silk shirt stuck to his skin.

"God is angry, the storm is proof of our evil!" Byles's voice struck their ears.

They watched Byles pick up another crying child, who stared over the adults in a hushed terror, and walk to the gunwale. He tossed the child into the wind and scud. The child's face looked back in wondering silence then vanished into the sea and foam. "Woe unto the world because of offenses!"

"Murderer!" shrieked a woman, rising up, and they saw Cora's muscular shoulders and wet buttocks as she grabbed the man by the neck and screamed, jerking him off his feet.

"Sergeant! Bosun! Deep-six him, goddamnit!" It was Gordon Wragby's voice roaring down the deck.

"Overboard, damn ye!" The marine sergeant ran forward, his sword pointed awkwardly ahead of him.

"Hurry," Tatti shouted, darting past the marines.

"Throw the bastard into the sea!" Stowell swung into their midst on a halyard.

One sailor thrust his forearm through the preacher's crotch, his hand in a fist, which an-

58

other sailor caught and lifted. Byles was elevated head and shoulders over the people.

"No!" Byles's voice was a piercing cry on the wind.

"Let's see you walk on the water!" The sailors rushed Byles to the gunwale rail, kicking wildly and thrashing his arms as he saw the wild ocean before him.

"Tell God about your virtue!" Stowell shouted while the others laughed.

"Jump, you sonofabitch!" another sailor shouted, as the sailors flipped him end over end into the sea. They watched his startled face bob once into sight, his mouth spewing brine and foaming, the soft eyes aghast in a flaring insight at reality.

The seas were higher than the deck as the ship struck bottom, then lifted wildly atop a rushing green hill of water.

"Chris!" Tatti screamed, seeing him plunge into the ocean, leading a rope that went down into a slack eddy, his arms and legs flailing.

"Disband!" Gordon Wragby shouted at the Royal Marines, and began to slash the helmsmen free of their bonds.

Tatti ran toward the sailors, watching the frail image that thrashed on the surface, the rope about its waist. "Chris!" she shouted, jumping up onto the poop deck to see better. About her thronged the disheveled sailors.

"Why did you let him?" she shouted into their faces.

They shook their heads and watched the young officer swim for the beach. Chris was picked up and rode forward at the speed of a hurdler, his torso and arms well clear of the water, then vanished out of sight under water, as the wave swept past him. The sailors groaned.

He reappeared. "Hurray! He'll make it!"

Gordon Wragby came among them, his slender face aged in lines, far older than his years. "Brave boy," he whispered.

They watched Chris until he no longer appeared as a thrashing ripple, and the rope lay slack. The sailors avoided Tatti's eyes.

"I knew his parents and his grandparents," Gordon Wragby said. He looked at the wreckage strewn the length of his ship. "And I lost my ship."

"What does he mean?" Tatti said to a sailor.

"We're going to die!"

"Prepare the ship for beaching!" Wragby's voice regained a note of strength.

The ship was enveloped in a chopping sea that boiled up as a mist where the shallow water lifted out of toiling waves. The deck was in and out of sight, as Tatti saw for the first time the massive wall of surf that hurled itself ashore. It was less than a ship's length away. "Cora!"

Tatti turned to Wragby, who watched the shore in a trance. "This ship is England, and I lost it." His words were more to himself.

"Gordon, take a child!" Tatti screamed.

"I must perish with my ship." He spoke gently.

"My God, enough are to die." Tatti shoved a child toward him.

"It's my life's honor to die. This ship is England."

"Rubbish!" Cora's eyes flamed as she faced the Captain. "This child is England. Take it by the hair. It's your only life, even if you ruined us on the moor!"

Gordon Wragby's eyes focused of a sudden at the fierce purpose of the naked woman and the crying children.

"Lord Gordon, life's in the living—the ship was more than we could save." Tatti was crying as she watched to see if Gordon Wragby would come forward to live again.

He looked at her and smiled. "Of course. I was mistaken." His elegant fingers slipped through the thick mat of the child's hair. "You are very beautiful, and so is the child." He put his lips to the side of the child's neck, then kissed Tatti's breast. "Thank you for reminding me."

"Hold 'em by the hair!" It was Stowell, shoving a large wooden grate into their midst. Their arms and hands went instinctively into the open squares.

"She'll rear up by the bow!" Gordon Wragby called out. The ocean had risen to a huge roar, just over the gunwales.

Tatti moved a leg about a child's body, getting it securely between her knees, as Cora had done.

"I love you, Cora," Tatti said.

"And I thee, child. Now hold your young'uns!"

Cora cried as the wall of green water climbed over the rising bow, and they were plunged down. The child's luminous eyes were huge in its gaunt face, and Tatti strained every sinew and muscle of her body as the massive sea smashed down in a wall where everything disappeared.

She felt herself spun madly. A thousand blows struck her body in a wet darkness, the salt brine filled her nostrils and her feet turned wildly behind her where she locked her thighs on the body she held. Down they spun, her eyes burned shut in the sea, and she realized that she could feel, that she was off the ship, and that she was not dead.

In gladness of life, she wrapped her hand more firmly in the child's hair and gripped her thighs tighter, clinging to the grate with her free hand, knowing if she could hold, the Lord would set her ashore. The grate floated under a surging sweep of waves, and Tatti felt free air on her face. She was at the surface. She dragged the limp child's body before her and raised the one she held between her legs.

Other children were on the grate, coughing in wet strangles and crying, their stomachs heaving. She heard a woman screaming somewhere off over the dark waters.

"Tatti!" It was Cora.

"Right here, Cora." Cora was across the grate.

"Did you keep your young'uns?"

"Aye, and thee?"

"Aye."

"Lord Gordon?" Tatti tried to fix her eyes on a solid shape as the waves washed over their heads. "Gordon?" she called.

"Yes, my lady, and I kept my child." She

heard his cultured voice. "Such a pretty child, worth a ship indeed. Alas, the poor *Daphne!*"

Tatti looked back to sea and saw the ocean breaking over the *Daphne,* rolling her masts toward the shore, her battered white sails beating through the air like wild flags. Then she saw the trough suck under the ship, drawing her back to sea. The ship rolled her deck vertical on its side, away from the beach, revealing her broken keel and the splintered boards of her hull.

"She fought all the way for her life," Wragby said.

Water poured over the wreck again, driving her once more onto the beach; and again she rolled, the masts waving the torn remnants of her sails like banners. Each time she rolled, she was driven more helplessly ashore.

The breakers at the beach picked them up, and Tatti felt them speed up toward the shore. Sand blasted her naked body, burning her nipples and grinding in her teeth, as the ocean sucked up the land in its great waves.

Tatti felt something swirl past her feet. The grate paused, sucking backward, and she was fearstruck they might be swept to sea. Suddenly the sea rose under them, and the grate shot ahead. She heard a child scream in front of her. She pushed the child back, and felt land under her feet.

She lay on the edge of the shore so tired she could feel every pore of her skin drain strength. She held the children, listening to Cora's thick, heaving gasps for air, and felt the waves float them foot by foot up the beach. She kept her eyes closed, because she did not want to see the nightmare in the faces of the children she'd saved. More of them must have died than lived.

"Cora, what about the rest?" she whispered in a croaking voice.

"If one lived, 'twas a miracle." She could hear Cora crying in the dark among the spent waves that broke over them.

"One thing good from this whole sorry loss." They heard Gordon Wragby's hoarse retching, as he wept on the edge of the sand.

VI

A dark shadow hovered over them and
Tatti awoke to a harsh cry by her face. She
looked up at a large, strange bird staring at
her with amber eyes, and she raised her head
quickly. She squinted in the glaring light and
felt its moist heat on her naked flesh. Then she
remembered, just as the bird made a guttural
call and flapped away from them. The shipwreck.

She got to her knees and looked along the
beach. Quiet bundles of clothing were strewn
upon the sand a hundred yards from the surf
in a haphazard row for a quarter mile. The sea
birds were hopping about them, some pulling
at the bundles, and she saw two birds tugging
a small white hand, while a third pecked at a

child's head. She screamed. It was the nightmare of the wreck, now carried into daylight.

"What is it?" Cora raised her head, and a child whimpered in front of her.

"They're eating the children!" She gestured down the beach.

Cora got to her knees, wiping sand from her lips with her arm. "Lord God, child, are those the dead?" She squinted.

"I don't know." Tatti laid her hand on Gordon Wragby's slender back and felt his ribs move, but he did not raise his head.

"Gordon? Lord Gordon?" Tatti saw his crimson face and slipped her hand across his mouth and felt a high fever. "Cora, he's sick."

"They can't be dead." Cora got to her sturdy legs, sand showering from her thighs and belly. "Not *all* of them!"

She ran toward the bodies, waving her arms and shouting, and lifting waves of gulls and cormorants that wheeled and circled overhead.

"Halloo!" Tatti heard men calling and saw sailors coming through the saw grass, led by Stowell, carrying rolled canvas and boards from the cedar forest.

"Oh, Stowell, did they all die?" She ran toward the men, who had heard their shouts and the cries of the birds.

"Sixty-four lived, my lady." As the men came nearer, Tatti saw that Stowell's hand had been crushed, and his chest laid open in a wound, but his blue eyes shone as confidently as ever from his stubbled face.

"Out of hundreds." She gestured behind her.

"All dead, my lady."

"The officers?"

"Only his lordship." The sailors glanced at the Captain, who lay on his face, his hair buried in the sand. Six children whimpered about the wooden grate at his feet.

"He's full of fever," Tatti said.

Stowell rooted about in a bundle of canvas clothes and drew out a pair of white trousers and a sailor's shirt. "Begging your pardon, but you'll need these."

"Yes." She took them and pulled them onto her legs and slipped the loose shirt over her head. "We need water." She spoke matter-of-factly as Cora came up.

"To my dying day on this earth, I'll never again see the like," Cora said, her russet eyes red-flecked in the white.

"The world turned upside down, Cora," Stowell said, holding a jumper and trousers for her.

"'Tis a cruel mistress, the sea," said an old man in canvas shorts who was with the sailors. He had a white beard and wore a straw hat, and was so skinny his spine showed between his shoulder blades.

Tatti held the trousers for Cora to step into, brushing the sand from her knees and loins and about her waist. She ran her hand across her nurse's bosom to loosen the sand and slipped the jumper over her head in a fluid motion. "Cora, we're sunburned bad already."

"Aye, lass." Cora gestured confusedly down the beach at the bundles.

"Later," Tatti said. "We need a tent for shelter and shade." It seemed she could think well enough for the humble needs of desolation; yet in her own heart she could feel nothing, not for Scotland, nor for outrageous cruelty, nor for the storm, nor for the shipwreck.

"We've hoisted a tent in the trees, my lady," Stowell said.

"Good, and how does one bury the dead?" She gestured down the beach, taking a child's hand in hers.

"Too many, my lady. "We'll put 'em to sea."

"To sea?" She did not look at the sailors, who stepped back when she turned.

"Off the spit, on the ebb current. The tide takes 'em out."

"And the sea shall give up its dead." She spoke more to herself, feeling nothing in her soul, but tasting the tears in her nose and on her tongue. "We'll bed down the children and the families, what's left." Her voice had a lost sound.

"Aye, my lady."

"And Stowell, bring the Captain."

"Fetch his lordship, men."

The six sailors lifted Gordon Wragby, and turned him on his back. "He don't need sun stroke, no he don't," the old man said as he laid his hat on the captain's face.

"This here's Noello, the hermit," Stowell said.

"Aye, Noello. I be on these islands nigh forty year." His soft eyes glowed as he cocked his head and put his hand out and touched a child's head.

The child looked solemnly at the old man and went gravely to his side and gave him his hand.

Cora walked beside Tatti as they led the children and sailors carrying Wragby, with Noello and Stowell showing the way, to the shelter.

The island had more to offer in shelter than Tatti could have hoped. There were palmetto groves, and the pungent scent of the distant cedar groves came with the shift of wind. The sailors rigged a broad tent amid the trees, into which they carried the kegs and boards and debris that were scattered along the beach. Nothing was left on the shore, as plans were made to salvage the damaged longboat, so that they might board the *Daphne* later.

"Water," Tatti said to Margene, a tall woman with high cheekbones. "And oatmeal. Get them fed."

"Aye, my lady," the Highland woman said. People squatted silently about the tent as though total strangers to each other. The children never stopped whimpering for their lost parents and shattered families.

"Put Captain Wragby in the palmetto shade, Cora, and cool his fever."

Tatti watched until she saw his temples and forehead bathed in sweet water cloths that Cora wrung out and changed as she knelt by Wragby's head.

"We can wade out to the *Daphne*, my

lady," Stowell said. She lay just offshore, on her starboard beam, the gilt bowsprit raked high toward the sea, and down by her stern-castle. The water was calm under her hull, and a light wind ruffled her spent sails.

"Nay, not without the longboat," Tatti said, distrusting the water even for wading.

There was an elegant despair about the wreck, but it no longer interested Tatti. She felt a strange detachment remove her from any words or thoughts on how they were to survive. It was to her a fact that they would survive, and her duty to see that it was done. "No family is complete, and no man and wife survived together," Stowell had said.

Tatti counted the seventeen children and thirty adults, over and over, dismayed each time she did at the number of unburied dead waiting along the beach.

"We can't leave them in the sun another day, my lady." Stowell spoke gently as the dozen sailors and single marine waited for her to say something.

"Aye, bury them." Gordon Wragby was sleeping quietly, and Cora walked with her as they went down to the beach. The men seemed disoriented, and she knew much of the burden of their survival lay on her.

Tatti walked along the beach where a hot sun had beat upon the dead half a day. Flocks of sea birds rose before her.

The gulls had pecked out the lifeless eyes of the dead children, so that each child's body had a skullish set of empty eye sockets, like small open mouths in a startled scream.

"I shall never believe there's a God after this," she said calmly to Cora as they walked. "Stowell, take the dead to the spit, and tell the sailors to carry the children gently."

"Most gently, my lady," the bosun said. "Our sailors never had children to touch before."

Tatti watched the sailors lift the small stiff bodies out of the sand, the fragile limbs open, a clean palm up with exquisite fingers curled. The men brushed loose the rivulets of sand from the pale skin, and puffed on the grains to free them.

"I never thought I could live through such a thing." Her eyes flooded and her nose ran while she watched the children carried out on the long spit of sand, and saw the sailors wade out to their chests, to set each child's body free to drift off in the tide and disappear.

"We saved seventeen, my lady," Cora said, breaking the silence in the afternoon sun.

She watched them struggle by twos and threes to get the hundred and more adults to burial in the tide. Toward the ship the men waited around one body, and she knew it was Chris.

"Chris," she said, laying her hands on the rope burns about his flat belly, and feeling no resilience in his flesh. "Oh, Chris." She put her forehead on his chest and tried to cry, but no tears would come. She knelt upright and touched his thick hair that yet had a buoyant life to it, and placed her hand on his bare thigh. "You weren't Peter, but I could *have loved you to have saved you.*" She burst into tears

71

and flung herself backward onto the sand, and sobbed on her forearm.

When she had regained her composure, she whispered, "Cora, tell the men to take him to the spit, please."

She got to her feet and watched the sailors carry Chris's body out into the tide, and set it adrift among the children and people he'd died trying to save. Cora slipped her arm about her waist, and Tatti felt the strength of an old friend assure her in the silence.

VII

Their quarters were very commodious under the broad open canopy of outstretched sails. A breeze from the ocean passed through the cedar trees on the knoll, where they had pitched the tent, and cooled them night and day. Water was found a quarter mile away, along a path through a soft palmetto glade. The water was sweet, with an herbal taste, and clear.

The first four days seemed unending as the sailors, under Stowell's direction, rowed out to the wreck and salvaged rope, timber, whale oil, lamps, rum and whiskey, barrels of flour and oatmeal, carpenters' tools, and the surgeon's implements.

Gordon Wragby sank into a fever that

would not come to a crisis and break. Tatti had him placed on a rush and canvas pallet by her side, and nursed him through the night, cooling his fever; and Cora waited and watched him through the day.

On the fourth day Tatti noticed that a grave lassitude had settled over the survivors, particularly the cotters. Of the seventeen children who lived, three had pneumonia, and two died who had apparently been well. "It's as if they were carried off by grief," she said to Cora.

"We're going to have to doctor these people, if they're to live," Cora said, kneeling among the sick.

"Never touched his knives," Stowell said, bringing the surgeon's lacquered medical chest to Tatti. The nickel clamps, sutures, scalpels, and steel probes lay in their velvet trays. "The ship's surgeon was to saw and cut in battle, and a battle we never had."

"Thank you, Stowell." She reached for his sling. "May I see your hand?"

The bosun looked down at his sling. " 'Tis healing, my lady."

"I'll see it, please."

He held the limb forward, lifting it and she slipped it out of its sling, seeing the dark clotted blood on the bandage, and gasping at the smell of rotting flesh. When she had unwrapped the wound, she saw the white bones of his hand and wrist were thrust out the skin, and the flesh had a gorged red color, darkening to black.

"Stowell, if it doesn't heal, you'll lose your life."

"Aye, my lady."

"I'll look at it again tomorrow."

"Aye, my lady. Will you take it off?"

"Yes." She did not look at him.

" 'Twas a loose cannon on the gundeck. As the ship rolled, it drove like a battering ram into the hull." He stared at the bones laconically. "I got a line caught in its wheels, and it crushed my hand."

"I'll see it tomorrow."

The old hermit, Noello, was a great help to the sailors. He brought armloads of fresh tropical fruit, and led them to fresh water. The sailors had so far managed to salvage three muskets from the wreck, and a keg of powder; and with Noello as guide, they hunted the feral hogs loose on the island.

Tatti was glad the sailors had such enthusiastic resolution to every problem, because the cotters had lost all purpose to their lives, and could barely cope. Of the sixteen women, only three would tend the basic rudiments of their children's needs. Cora kept a vast pot of oatmeal stirring under a fly tent. When the sailors brought in a goat, she said, "It's not lamb, but it's stew."

"I wish we could reach their spirits as easily as we can reach their stomachs," Tatti said.

On the fifth morning, after a night holding three children to her, she heard from Brighton, the gunner with tight curly hair, that two adults had vanished into the sea and a third had died. "Twenty-seven cotters is all that's left, mum."

75

Tatti nodded. "But we didn't lose any more children."

Stowell slipped into a raging fever on the fifth day, and raved on a canvas pallet in the tent. His wrist had swollen to twice its normal size, and Tatti wiped powders from the Turkish poppy into his mouth and tongue to ease his pain. The fever did not fall, however.

"My God, I don't want to cut it off," she said to Cora as they knelt by his side.

" 'Tis death as it is."

"Aye, but I have no stomach for it."

"We have no choice, Tatti," Cora said, catching her eyes with a glimpse into her soul.

"Aye, call the sailors, and put whiskey in his throat. The poppy does no good."

While the men held his body and legs and free arm, Cora stretched out the broken arm and hand, gripping the proud flesh that began to ooze dead blood. Tatti got the elbow between her knees, after putting on the tourniquet to stop the blood. She drenched the scalpel and saw in raw whiskey as she'd seen done on Skarra to purify, and stared at the arm. There was a certain integrity to the flesh, even if grossly maimed. It belonged to a man she deeply respected, and she was about to maim him forever.

"He has no choice," Cora whispered hoarsely, sensing her thoughts, while the sailors breathed in anguish behind her.

"Aye."

She held the scalpel firmly and cut deep and across the back of his forearm, feeling the bone chunk against the blade. She cut lightly on the sides of the flesh, as blood ran all through her fingers and over her hands, drenching her trousers. Setting down the scalpel at her knees, she carefully eased the flesh up and down the two bones, to expose them, and when she could feel the bones clearly in her fingers, she felt for the blood vessels.

"I must find the veins and blue things that bleed," she said, carefully searching in the flesh for the blood channels to clamp, and clamping them.

"Get the cauter-iron ready. The bones are in the way." She reached for the saw and sawed each bone in turn, and was astonished to see the darkened forearm fall loose in Cora's hand.

"The cauter-iron," she said, reaching toward the sailor who stared with dumb eyes at the detached hand and arm lying between the two women.

"The cauter-iron!" Cora said, looking up, her face blood-speckled. She blinked her eyes to clear them.

Another sailor jumped to the fire and handed the iron to Tatti. "'E's got no grit for blood, my lady."

She set the cauter-iron to each rubber-stretched vein and artery that she'd clamped, turning the blood to steam that boiled up with the acrid scent of burned flesh. The blood vessel curled up into a twisted black scab that would not bleed.

"My hair," Tatti said, not looking up.

Cora knelt upright and pushed it behind

her head, and spoke to a sailor. "Hold it out of her face."

When she had cauterized what would bleed, she released the silver clamps and cut loose the forearm entirely, and set aside the scalpel. Using her two hands, she gently milked down the flesh over the bones and veins of the stump she gripped between her knees.

"We'll bind it, but not too tight." She took the whiskey-soaked silk to sew the flapped skin together. The needle kept slipping backward through her blood-wet fingers. Cora reached between her hands and pressed a thimble against the needle's eye, and they sewed the flap of wet skin against the skin.

"It's got to drain itself," Tatti said, setting boiled bandages lightly over the stump. She eased backward to see her work, feeling his shoulder under her rump, and blowing the blood-stuck hair from her lips. "My God, when I saw that done at Skarra to a poor smithy, I never thought I'd have to do it myself. What we have become, Cora!"

"And look at us," Cora said.

Tatti was blood-spattered from her waist to her knees, and Cora had blood smeared all across her face where she had wiped her eyes with her blood-slick hands.

"Hold him till he sleeps sound," ordered Tatti, getting to her feet and ignoring the men, who averted their eyes in deference.

Two of the children started to cry when they saw her gore-smeared lap and waist. "Come on, Cora, bring the whiskey and we'll go bathe," she said.

Tatti crossed the wide tent and looked down at Gordon Wragby, who lay wrapped in wool blankets to keep off a chill, and nodded to a small woman and the marine who changed the fevered cooling cloths they kept on his forehead and temples. The Captain's face had eased in his long fevered sleep, giving him a gaunt lost-child look. "If he'll only wake." She looked to Cora.

"I 'spect he's sleeping through the notion he died with his ship," the woman said.

"I hope so," Tatti said, leading Cora out of the tent.

She floated naked on her back in the fresh water of the pool below the spring, balancing the whiskey bottle on her bare ribs. "Delightful, Cora, delightful." She heard her own voice clear and light. Each guzzle of whiskey burned her throat and warmed her body with fire. She saw Cora in the vague haze, still moving sedately through the water up to her waist. Tatti laughed, and dipped her face in the water and drank.

"Try it, Cora. You don't get drunk till you drink the water."

Cora stared about her, the russet eyes bleared and out of focus. "I don't think we need all that whiskey, my lady."

"Oh, have another drink." Tatti handed her the bottle, and tipped over on her back and paddled with her fingers, squirting water out of her mouth, trying to hit her breasts and navel.

VIII

By the seventh day after the shipwreck, Tatti had forgotten everything she had known in her life before. Fourteen women and eleven men were left of the emigrants, and they were down to thirteen children. She knew there was no way to reason the survivors out of a surrender to death, but she knew the children could be reached.

Gordon Wragby's fever had broken, and he smiled and sat up to take some soup. The people scattered through the tent seemed beyond his understanding, and he looked softly at Tatti and said, "Thank you."

"Oh, Gordon, you'll live." She took great hope in his apparent recovery, and her mind turned again to the children.

It was in a large pallet bed that she felt she might be able to save them, if they could feel her body at night. She had discovered the routine on the third day, that the children wanted to cling with their naked bodies to hers, and she bedded all thirteen of them with her and Cora on the sixth night.

"I don't know why," she said to Cora, "but it's to us they want to crawl and cling."

"We've got no time left for conjecturing," Cora said, nodding.

The calamity had been too much for the women who had survived, and with the strength of the ruling class who had never known failure, Tatti was determined that she could save the cotters so that the bloodline would not die. "We must not perish," she said.

Thereafter Tatti slept at night with small and half-grown naked bodies pressed against her flesh, hearing them whimper through the night and feeling them reach for her and one another with frail limbs. Often she heard Cora roll them into herself to spare her waking.

"I think it's wrong," said a buxom young woman called Sheila, who had no children of her own, but had lost her husband. "Being naked with young'uns ain't right."

"Young'uns are born naked," Cora said, kneeling in the middle of the large pallet. "And they suck naked."

"You could join us," Tatti said quietly. "My body's not so womanly as yours."

"Oh!" Sheila said, crossing her forearms over her bulging breasts and flaring her nostrils. "The very idea, for a decent woman."

"Decent woman! Help us or leave us be," Cora said impatiently, dragging on a pair of canvas pants. "We ain't got time for carping."

"Aristocrats got no morals."

"I'm a crofter. Begone!" Cora glared through her sleep-tousled hair.

As the tropic nights passed, Tatti felt she was winning the children back to life, particularly when she woke at dawn and found small frames of bare skin and quiet breathing heaped across her breasts and arms and thighs and belly. It restored the children to a sweet wish for joy at waking; and she looked forward to sleeping each night as a time of refreshment of her own desire to live.

There was an enchantment to Bermuda, and Tatti began taking long walks through the broad savannas, and exploring with the children the palmetto groves. Rich mangroves grew along the swamps, and she delighted in the mockingbird's repetition of the children's calls and whistles. Often they carried mangoes to the pool, to eat until gorged and smeared yellow from the wet flesh, from ear to ear and to navel.

In the pool they bathed and she held them as they thrashed and floundered to her, all clinging in a mass of water-slick bodies, and laughing with her. The water seemed to lighten them with a new image of life, as it bathed away the ache, and filled their minds with a need to paddle and breathe. It was Tatti's first experience with a tropic isle, and the moist warmth gave her a hope they would all live.

"It seems easier with the children than the

grownups," Tatti said, returning one afternoon.

"They've got less to remember, and more to hope," Cora said, supervising the steaming laundry cauldron set under a thatched lean-to outside the broad tent.

Tatti ducked into the tent where Stowell mended slowly, lying in his pallet by the fire. The wound healed without festering; however, Stowell slipped into a profound sense of despair when he realized his right arm had been cut off.

His despair and gaunt helplessness seemed to bring out a surge of affection for him among the emigrant women, who remembered him as the assured masculine bosun. His voice had sung out the whispered orders of the officers; his silver pipe lying on his hairy chest had shrieked to send the sailors into the tops and out the yardarms; and his tireless courage had filled them with hope when there was no hope. Now he sighed at their feet, mutilated and haggard, and they listened for his every whimper to tend him, driven to restore him to his full masculine grace.

Tatti walked to Stowell's pallet, and the woman who had been feeding him crouched aside.

"I'm glad to see your fever broke." She set her palm on his forehead, carefully avoiding the dark blue Yorkshire eyes. She saw the haunted love in the man's face for her.

"My lady," Stowell whispered.

"A pretty island awaits you, sir."

The eyes searched for hers as they looked

up, but Tatti turned to the small woman who nursed him. "What a wonderful recovery."

"Thank 'ee, my lady."

"And you must eat all your porridge." Tatti smoothed the oatmeal crumbs from the hair around his lips, still ignoring the questing eyes, then stood and went to the Captain.

At nineteen Tatti knew enough about men to know they would love any woman who would care for them, and live for the hope they might have her. With her duty to the survivors, her personal life could not even be considered.

Now Gordon Wragby began to eat regularly, to sit up on his pallet, and asked for his razor and any books they might have found. Tatti was delighted.

"We'll go for a walk tomorrow."

"Splendid." The elegant corners of his mouth turned up. "Need to get on my legs."

"I'll come for you, my lord."

"Alas, I shan't sleep a wink tonight." He chuckled to himself.

The next morning Tatti walked slowly along the beach with Gordon Wragby, followed by the marine and Leslie, his nurse.

"Bit wobbly, but I like to feel my muscles strain." He held her forearm while a rousing surf filled the morning air with cheer.

"Glad we found your sea chest," Tatti said, drawing the collar of his blue coat snug about his throat. "You are the Captain."

"Not really, Tatti, I've seen the wreck."

"We are not to question our estate, nor our misfortune, Gordon."

"You make me feel better, and I can almost believe you."

"You can't believe the beauty of these islands—and we have an old hermit."

"A hermit?"

"Yes, Noello, dear little man with great soft eyes."

"You've done wonders." He laid his slender fingers across the back of her hand.

"This place is paradise." She waved her arm toward the long green savanna, framed by trees, that followed the creek to the small cove in the beach.

"To be in paradise! Indeed, I'd never expected as much so soon, and with you."

"Oh, Gordon, do stop joshing, 'tis real."

Gordon Wragby nodded his head slowly. "Forgive my mockery of myself. Thank God we lived. We're indebted to each other as people. To you and your nurse, I owe my life and my sanity."

"No, that's too much."

"I must mock myself or weep."

"Stop, you'll make *me* cry."

"Alas, I'm hopeless." Gordon Wragby laughed.

"You laughed," she said. "It is a beginning."

"Aye." Wragby ran his eyes along the grass-matted knolls, and the trees in which the broad white tent nestled at the edge of the rich earth.

"Tatti, we must build more permanent

quarters. A thatched roof, a pavilion, per-haps. The flax tent will rot soon enough."

"A thatched pavilion?" She caught his blue eyes.

"Aye, put the people to work building. 'Twill hearten them and restore their souls, and ease their grief."

"Oh, Gordon, do you think so?"

"Aye, let them work for themselves with a common purpose, like a ship."

"Or one of our Scottish clans?"

"Aye. You've saved the children, you and Cora, but you need a common hope to lift the sorrow."

"Oh, wonderful!" Tatti hugged Gordon Wragby's forearm to her cheek.

Wragby nodded, and Tatti saw how pale he was. She gestured for the marine and Leslie to take his armpits, and they went toward their tent.

IX

At supper that night, while they watched a tropic rain pour down the eaves of their broad tent, dripping small clumps of moisture that pattered onto their arms or caused a face to look up, came the moment Tatti had awaited.

"Thatch, thatch is what we need," Tatti said, smelling the brisk ozone roll in with the rain. "We won't be dry till we're under a thatched roof."

"Thatch, on a tent?" someone said.

"No, I want a thatched roof set on a wide pavilion, with open sides." Tatti stared quietly over the heads of the eating company, who had fallen silent.

"I want something we can live in when the winter storms come."

The sailors and the emigrants who were eating goat stew glanced about at each other, and one man with a beard set down his cup and licked his stubby fingers in slow deliberation, his blue eyes fastened on Tatti. He got to his feet, as though astounded both with the thought and its coming from a woman little more than a girl.

"What did you call that thing, ma'am?"

"A pavilion," Tatti said. "I want it right here on this knoll." She gestured out to the forest of cedar and palmettos beyond the bright savanna of grass. "There's timber, just waiting for you, and we need this place. So cool at night, and healthy through the day, and the view of the ocean and the green island is lovely." She clapped her hands together and laughed. "I want no sides, so I can look out, and the children can run in."

"No sides, it is, boys," said a sailor.

"But a house."

The men rose purposefully to their feet, setting aside half-eaten dishes and cups of food, all talking at once; and the women began to gesticulate and point and stare about.

"The stove goes here," one said.

"And the laundry house there, or whatever her ladyship called it."

"A pavilee, Eyetalee it is."

"And a privee, to leeward," said the pock-marked sailor.

In the days that followed, as though by some primordial command, the thatched pavilion seemed to unlock the wellsprings of life once more. There was constant talk of angles, eaves, gables, drainage, wind shelters, and where to put the garden. A note of laughter rose from a woman's throat.

"I think we have a purpose," Tatti whispered to Gordon as she sat by his pallet that evening.

"Aye, a purpose to stand, then to walk." He took her hand into his. "The purpose of life is to love it," Wragby whispered hoarsely.

"And why didn't you love enough to marry?" Tatti spoke gently.

"I loved my sister, but we were poor, and Nellie had to marry Lord Rush to save Wragby Hall. My mother's lilacs and roses."

"Oh, I'm sorry," Tatti whispered.

"Lord Rush was a brute of a man, not just a stallion, but cruel. But Nellie saved our home."

"What an awful fate, to marry for money," Tatti whispered. "Oh, Gordon." She squeezed both his hands in hers and held them in the gloaming shadows of the evening.

Tatti watched from the grass knoll while the men crossed the pleasant savanna to the cedar forest, and she could hear the ring of axes chopping on the clear air.

"Cedar won't need curing like other wood," said a gaunt man who had lost three of his four children and his wife.

Once she had drawn the actual dimensions of the pavilion in the earth, and sketched the side and front view she wanted built, Tatti thought it would be better to let the emigrants and the sailors settle the details among themselves. "I can never know more than the people themselves," she said to Cora, "once I've got the notion and plan in their heads."

"And in their hearts," Cora said, a scrub towel in her hand.

"It was Gordon Wragby who put me onto it," she whispered.

"Aye. Pity a good man could know how to live and yet not be able to make a life."

"How does one tell a living from a life?" Tatti looked at her nurse.

"Living is feeding, and life's a bliss that makes a joy of every day." Cora's eyes searched into her soul. "Look at them."

They stared at the busy movement of people working among the shadows of the distant forest trees.

"They sweat for the joy in their own lives. 'Tis a bliss to work, even to swing a hammock." Cora touched Tatti on the shoulder and walked back to the tent.

Tatti waited until she could hear the fall of trees, and the slashing blows of the axes trimming the limbs before she allowed herself to be among the people, despite some of the children who tugged at her to go across the savanna. "Bye and bye, we'll go see. Now we must stay close to home."

"The Eyetalee House," as the cotters called it, consumed the people. Even after supper, impassioned discussions broke out that had to wait until sunrise to be resolved.

"I'm dying to see their work," she whispered to Wragby. "Lord, they have all the fun, and I have to stand on a knoll and pretend I'm not excited."

"Your image is their life." Wragby nodded his head.

"One woman?"

"Aye, one woman, but the right woman." His eyes caught hers. "The shipwreck cast you in the role they demand."

The woods were aromatic with the pungent split cedar that Tatti loved so well. She moved quietly along the edges of where the men worked, until she found a broad stump. She sat down and drew her knees up under her chin, and watched in silence. The men knew she was among them, yet nobody looked at her. Somehow, each man was able to do something that she could see, where moments before they might have had a half-naked, straining back to the forest where she perched. Tatti stayed in the forest all day, alone, accepting tea and lunch with Cora.

Tatti came and went each day, sometimes accompanied by one or two children, and often with Cora and an emigrant woman who would return the lunch basket. Tatti noticed that the women now were able to speak in full sentences as they talked to her, which they had been unable to do the first weeks after the shipwreck. Then a vacant stare had lain behind their eyes as they spoke, and often one would stop under the memory of a child lost in the storm.

Tatti marveled at the timbers squared with an adze by hand, so that they had the

93

purlin and joists and plate rafters chopped out in the woods. What quixotic fortune had brought an ax, a saw, and a carpenter's square through the storm on shipboard to be found intact by the sailors as they explored the wreck, and decreed so many human beings should not survive?

"I never lived in a house without sides," said the small woman who had brought the breadfruit cakes.

"In the tropics, one must acclimate oneself," Tatti said.

"Aye, my lady." The woman dipped in a slight curtsey.

Tatti knew she must play an iron role of discipline and absolute duty, or the whole band would degenerate to a squalid mob of castaways. They all looked to her, as Gordon Wragby had said. She was grateful she'd seen her mother and her Russian grandmother rally mansions and vast farms of people to duty and to life. Tatti knew she needed every advantage against the odds.

"I want the longboat seaworthy," Stowell said the next evening, causing a lull among the score of grownups who were waiting to have supper.

"The longboat?" a woman said who cooled his fever with damp cloths, and held him in his deliriums.

"Aye, woman, we've got to get home, one day."

"Home? How?"

"By the longboat."

"Oh, no, not the waters again." She put her face down on his chest and moaned.

"No, Mister Stowell," Tatti said, walking through the people to Stowell's pallet. "This is not the season for boats with hurricanes about."

"My lady, it takes a seaworthy boat, and besides——"

"Nay, no boat. Now's the time for calm and decent quarters to live, and hope to be restored."

Stowell sank back into his pallet, half smiling and sighing. He glanced self-consciously at Tatti, but she walked back to the kettle where Cora worked.

"I say, the bosun's right." It was Gordon Wragby, who had got to his feet from the small corner reserved for the Captain. "We do indeed need a seaworthy boat. Tatti, I haven't visited the *Daphne* yet."

"No!" Tatti's word cut him off as he walked toward her. "No, you'll not visit the shipwreck."

Gordon Wragby looked startled, his quiet blue eyes seeking what wrong had caused Tatti's emphatic denial. "After all, my lady, a captain should visit his ship."

"That ship ain't a ship no more, my lord," Cora said, coming to Tatti's side. " 'Tis a wreck."

"Gordon, we almost lost you to a madness in your grief for that ship." Tatti spoke softly. "Now we've come too far to lose you."

"But I am the Captain, and that is the

King's vessel." He drew himself up straight, and the cotters withdrew a step, leaving him to confront the two women.

"Gordon, you fainted when you saw the wreck."

"Well, I'm feeling stronger." He settled his blue jacket at his ribs, while the people watched.

"My lord, you wanted to drown on that ship," Cora said, pointing to the sea with her wooden spoon. "And we put a child in your hands, and the Lord gave you the wit to live."

"Lord Gordon, you are the captain of this whole company," Tatti said. "This island is England's and yours to command. But you must not touch that shipwreck." Tatti's voice filled the tent in its bell-tone clarity. "I forbid Lord Gordon to go near that ship!" She searched the cotters' and the sailors' eyes.

"Aye, you're not to tempt the Lord," said Margene, sucking her hollow cheeks over her toothless gums.

"Better a live dog than a dead lion," said a cotter with stubby hands. "Your lordship, you ain't no dead lion because them ladies fought for you, and I say they be right, eh, folks?"

Men and women nodded instinctively, agreeing. "No boat for the Captain!" "His Lordship can't go upon the waters."

Gordon Wragby listened to the words of agreement with Tatti, denying him the longboat. Tatti walked to him and took his hand, easing the confusion in his eyes. "I will visit the *Daphne*."

"You, my lady?" said Brighton, the curly-haired sailor.

"Yes, you may repair the longboats after we get the pavilion well started." Tatti turned to the bosun. "Mister Stowell, later you may take me out to the wreck. Alone with your crew."

"Aye, my lady," Stowell said.

"We was rescued out of perdition for some purpose," Cora said, eyeing the bosun. "And dry land put under our feet, and until we see otherwise, here we're waiting for another sign." She turned back with her spoon.

The work felling trees and shaping logs by hand held the minds of the survivors and sustained their spirits. And the strange vegetables and herbs fed them.

The Scottish cotters and English sailors had balked at eating breadfruit when old Noello, the hermit, showed them how. Tatti had smacked her lips, kneeling before her plate. "Thank goodness some lost soul planted that delectable breadfruit on this island," she said. "It smells divine." She burned her finger in the hog fat they'd fried it in and scorched her tongue, not knowing how to eat it. "Why, it tastes like roast grousel"

One sailor gagged, and a cotter rushed outside to vomit, but the others began tentatively to eat. Cora chewed and swallowed hers, her eyes watering, licking her fingers to hide her tears. "Now we won't be likely to starve to death when the oatmeal and flour gives out," Tatti said. "We can save it for emergencies, and wait for our rescue."

X

Old Noello had been abandoned by a French corvette many years before, and he had adapted to the wild goats and pigs on the island, capturing some to domesticate, and snaring others to butcher for food and to skin for leather garments. He was entirely self-sufficient.

With his large brown, circular eyes and the soft puckered skin bags under them, Noello had a goatlike appearance. Tatti half-expected when he spoke, that he would bleat and bound off in terror.

Noello had been transfixed by the children, and they had sensed he had become a firm friend, though he had refused rescue from the islands by other ships on several occasions.

"No, I'll take my goats to rescue. Why, I've got so many hiding places on this island, nobody can find me." He blinked slowly with a sly boast. "I just turn out my wildlife, and they skeedaddle, till the strangers sail away, and then I call them up. Like that." He bent over suddenly in gasping spasms of shrieking laughter.

"Reckon a body needs a body to ladle out his madness," Cora said out of earshot to Tatti. "Otherwise he goes plumb crazy alone."

"Poor little man," Tatti said.

"Crazy or not, he is our best friend."

"Maybe these islands are the best place for him," Tatti said, realizing that perhaps Noello did indeed have a depth not immediately apparent.

Tatti never let the cotters or sailors lose hope of rescue. When ominous periods of silence fell over the whole company, and Tatti knew the terrible thought they were doomed to be forgotten forever, she would shake back her hair and say firmly, avoiding the wondering eyes that searched hers for reassurance, "The Royal Navy never gives up. Lord Peter Barrett'll come looking for us."

"Even with the wrong charts, my lady?"

"Of course. Lord Peter is a brilliant navigator. He has the finest Admiralty Charts of Greenwich—he told me."

"Aye, Lord Peter." They would nod and go back to work. "He'll find us."

Tatti was careful to avoid Stowell's eyes when she made declarative statements that were more passionate hopes than reality. The bosun knew she was frightened and as lost as the others and that she was playing the game to make them live against very heavy odds. Her face might betray her if she saw him look into her desperation.

"You carried it off beautifully," Gordon Wragby said, after hearing her intrepid certainty.

"Did I?"

"Aye, you're doing far better than I could ever do."

"Stowell knows we're desperate."

"No matter. He's loyal."

She glanced at the Captain.

"Oh, a loyal man'll keep your lie to serve a truth." He patted her hand. "Tatti, men are often far greater than they ever know."

It was sometime after they had been on the island well over a month that Tatti followed the men across the bright savanna with an adzed and tenoned beam. It perched rigidly on their shoulders, rather sedate it seemed above their struggling legs all in a row.

"What a grand purlin 'twill be," Tatti said, and ran across the field to make her hair blow in the wind off the ocean.

All day the survivors carried the timbers out of the woods and toward the edging of grass and cedar knolls which girdled the black earth from the broad sand beaches. Massive timbers were heaved in unison by stooping men, with the delicate chopping of small axes adjusting the edges and projections, soon to be joined into a building.

Gordon Wragby stood among the throng,

his auburn hair tied back in a neat club, reaching here and there to hand a tool to a gnarled hand; and sometimes he pushed on a beam that heavy men grunted against with his elegant, slender fingers. Tatti noticed how respectful the emigrants were, never looking into his eyes. He seldom imposed himself by speaking to them.

"Splendid beam, so true," Wragby would say, letting his fingers and thumb feel the sharp right angle of their craftmanship, and he would pat it, talking aloud to himself.

As the pavilion took shape about their legs and under their bare feet, Tatti noticed how festive the atmosphere became. The strength of all the men and women was needed to raise the beams, which had been mortised and driven into tenons by a huge wooden hammer. After the bays were trued up and square to each other, lying flat, the foot plates were scotched in place, and the tops were lifted by iron pikes, salvaged from the shipwreck.

Tatti ran down toward the beach, shouting, "I want to see it in perspective, how it sits across our knoll."

She stood at a distance and watched the cotters and sailors heft the long ridgepole by sling, and winch it into place atop the purlins. Set on vertical center poles for balance, the rafters were quickly passed up to the laughing men who jostled the heavy beams into the notched joists, and she heard the sharp blows as they nailed them for added security.

The timbers bridged across the skyline, seeming to tie the warm knoll-top to the thick grass on the one side, and the copse of cedars on the other. "We'll thatch it!" she cried, hearing her voice alone.

When Tatti got back to the pavilion, she felt the joy among the people at having raised a house by their own strength and ingenuity. Women were bringing in large bundles of dry savanna grass to tie into thatching, and it amazed her to see the first course of grass take shape along the eave of the windward gable.

"The further we go, the faster we seem to work," said a cotter.

Some of the women had kept food cooking over a kettle and skillet all day, nourishing the common purpose. It was the first day Tatti noticed that everybody spoke and laughed. The children were everywhere underfoot; and, for them, there seemed to be a common caring.

The sailors were particularly exuberant, and this surprised Tatti for she had supposed that mariners, having followed the sea, might have lost their sensitive passion for home. Yet the opposite was the case. Any task, the smallest detail, was enough to excite the mariners, who had loud discussions about how each portion of the pavilion was to serve the company as their home, and to send them scrambling perilously amid the rafters, beams, and thatching, often disrupting the more cautious emigrants.

"They never had a home," Stowell said, coming up behind Tatti, and sensing the childlike joy in the sailors. "Most were pressed off the street as urchins."

"The world I never knew," Tatti said.

103

"If you say it's home, then it's gospel."

" 'Twill have to do till rescue."

On a sunny patch of meadow they had turned the earth for a large kitchen garden. In the moist, warm climate Tatti reckoned a garden would augment the wild fruits and vegetables, particularly if planted with the tropical flora they had discovered through Noello. To protect it from the wild pigs, they had driven a pale of sharpened sticks about the garden, woven with vines from the verges of the mangrove swamps.

"With the breadfruit, I think we could live here as long as we pleased," Tatti said.

After Tatti had the pavilion and a laundry house erected, and had supervised an oven for Scotch bread and baking, for which she had saved the flour, she considered visiting the ship. The wreck of the *Daphne*, which lay just offshore a mile down the beach from the pavilion, was a towering reminder to the survivors of life as it had been.

Tatti waited for Gordon Wragby in the evening twilight, content in the warm bulwark of the home they had built in an unknown paradise. In the distance, the ship lay tilted awkwardly on her side, locked in the sands and reflecting her topsides in the shallow water surrounding her. It was a shambles of splintered mast and gaunt poles abaft the jagged stub, leaning out over water, but not falling, and trailing the torn white sails that moved idly on the breeze. The Union Jack still flew, adding a note of color to the bleaching wood and rope. She did not like it, and looked away.

"'Tis not a pretty sight," Gordon said, sensing her mood as he came up behind her.

"Aye, to have a wreck be our only link to home."

"Tatti, have you forgotten our pavilion? This is home." He gave her a quick hug about the waist as they stepped off together down the beach.

"Aye, we built a home, only when we had no care of time nor place."

"But only you were able to turn your back upon our past."

"When the world turns to water, you've got to start swimming." Tatti caught his quiet mood.

"We're all so torn, I suppose," Wragby said. "Not knowing whether to keep the old or the new, nor what to destroy, nor what to love."

"We let the storm and shipwreck decide it —life or death."

The *Daphne* loomed in light profile on the beach as the sun set, and the moonlight fell across the quieting ocean.

"Why didn't you ever love?" Tatti said, glancing at Wragby, who looked down at the rivulet of beach foam they skirted.

"Real love?"

"Aye, love that binds two people into bliss, and through grief, right on beyond death."

"Where would you learn of such a thing?" He glanced quickly at her.

"From a houseful of parents and grand-parents," Tatti said evenly.

"Aye, the Scots, they are family, indeed."

"Family, that's all we ever were, and the English never understood us."

"Perhaps we envied you, and resented you out of it."

"You?"

"Good Lord! No!" Wragby shook his head. "I may be an Englishman, but I do tell the truth, even about England." He took her hand. "Oh, what I loved was England, the trees and the soft rivers that lay through the quiet summer meadows, and the hedgerows along the gentle roads. The cottages, the people, and old Wragby Hall, our home."

He stopped speaking and they could hear their footsteps squish on the wet packed sand.

"But the ships? The Royal Navy?"

"Oh, that was talent and grace, and no money." He shrugged his shoulders. "A career to survive, no more."

"They say you were a good sailor." Tatti heard an honesty that might hurt him, and sought to ease the moment.

"Oh, yes, I grew to love sailing, it's sort of scooting over the waves on God's breath—no human evil, and I was gentle with my sailors, so they made me a grand name out of their heroic exertions."

"Chris said you never flogged your men."

"Poor brave boy."

"And that all the admirals were cruel for ambition's sake."

"Aye, Chris understood. Well, what would I have had as an admiral that I didn't already have? A title? I have one. Manhood? I am a decent man. No, I'd rather retire to Nellie's rose garden than the Admiralty and Whitehall."

"But why didn't you love?"

"Oh, we all loved. The elegant young officers who seduced married women, and kept a score of ravished bodies and broken hearts. Those who seduced the sisters of their friends, and did not marry those without a dowry, or who could not help advance a career. That was rollicking, casual, utterly selfish love, fornicating as a contest, measured by wreckage and laughter and gossip, gossip, gossip—I lived through that until I was sick of it."

Tatti nodded. "I danced all night with half the officers in Edinburgh and London."

"And may I ask?" He caught her eyes.

"Yes, you may, my lord. I am still a virgin."

"Alas, if I'd have met you, I'd have courted you until I perished."

"You'd have married me, or nothing."

"Alas, too late for me, you see."

"Oh, Gordon." She hugged his arm into her side, and released it, remembering Peter.

"Nothing ever held me as true after I left Wragby Hall and the countryside. When I met a woman with money, whom I respected and could have loved, she thought she'd bought me, and this revolted me. And if she had no money, 'twas carnal to her, or my threadbare title that couldn't feed us. So I grew a passion for sailing and walking the English meadows, and talking to strangers who toiled in the earth."

"Why?" Tatti stopped, seeing their double shadows suddenly fall as they faced each other.

"Oh, there's a lack of pretense when the

human species stands in manure to its knees." He saw her lips half parted as she smiled, and he slipped his arms about her ribs and drew her to him, and flooded with a desperate bliss when he felt her yield to him. His mouth tasted the fresh breath of her lips, and he felt her sweet tongue inside her even teeth, and he gasped in a hope he'd never dared feel.

"No," he whispered, setting her back from him. " 'Tisn't fair. I'm taking advantage of a girl . . . ."

"Oh, Gordon, dear Gordon." She set her hands along his temples. "I'm not a girl, virgin or not."

"Well, I shouldn't."

"Very well, you may hold me." She slipped her arms about his waist and laid her head on his chest and listened to his heart thump under her ear, its rhythm mingling with the surge of the calm ocean rollers, upon the sand.

XI

When the pavilion was so successful that they were extending the structures in small additions and a compound of loose thatched cottages, and it was clear to Tatti that they would survive, she agreed to visit the wreck of the *Daphne*. She had hesitated, not only for the obvious reason that it reminded her of loss and grief, but also because it would take her to Gordon Wragby's ultimate failure—and she loved Gordon Wragby. She had brought him out of despair to life, to forgetting all past misfortune, and she wanted no part of what could distress their growing love. It was also clear to her that Wragby did not realize he loved her, and that he had been so wounded, he might take refuge behind his middle-aged years if she were to hurt him.

She had seen Gordon Wragby beaten, had held him in his delirium when he raged his orders against a storm on a doomed ship, and she had cooled his temples and held his arms in her knees to calm him. The man who had stood upright after he had crawled drew Tatti. In Wragby, Tatti saw a grandeur that Peter was too young to have gained.

"I love him," Tatti said to Cora while they stood on the beach and waited for the sailors to bring the cutter down the shore from the tree-lined cove where they kept it, to take them to the wreck.

"Any man or woman with eyes can see it." Cora watched her. "Except him. Gentlemen are blind to start with, and in love, they don't have a wit in their head."

"Fortunate for us."

"Wish he were younger, his lordship."

"He wouldn't be the same." Tatti raised her hands to run her fingers through her loose hair.

"Leastways, he ain't going to take advantage of you, so I'm content." Cora watched the cutter plunge through the rolling breakers, under a taut lugsail.

"Ahoy, my ladies!" a bright voice called out, as the boat ran her bow upon the beach, and happy sailors leaped clear of the gunwale, and came splashing through the surf to their hips.

"Hold her, lads!" The men steadied the small vessel on her keel.

Tatti waded out with Cora, glad they wore

sailors' canvas pants and jumpers which could be rolled up and wind-dried.

"Shove off!" Stowell bellowed after he had seated Tatti, and the sailors heaved the cutter off the beach·through the light rolling breakers, and flopped up over the gunwales as the lug-sail caught the wind, and the cutter heeled on her side and schooned into a bright sea.

"He's terrified," Tatti said, nodding toward the huddled figure of Noello, who was hunched down onto his knees at the bow, his eyes on the ship.

"Noello says we should burn the hulk," Stowell said. "It only attracts pirates."

"Aye, yet 'tis Crown property. The King's ship." Tatti knew the other, greater reason to spare what was left of the *Daphne:* to burn it might be the final blow that would destroy Gordon Wragby.

"There's yet much salvage to her." Stowell nodded his head.

The sailors were forward of them, and Cora leaned against the mainmast and seemed to enjoy the wind as the cutter sailed down the shore toward the wreck of the *Daphne.*

"My lady, it may be years till rescue."

"Then we'll wait." Tatti heard an urgent note to Stowell's voice. She also knew the ship-wreck would attract both the good and the bad. She reckoned she had to chance it, for the immediate danger was neither pirates nor starvation, but the lassitude of despair. The shipwreck was visible evidence of home, as well as a beacon to other ships and rescue.

"Could you love me, my lady, if I wait?"

111

She looked quickly at him and saw the passionate hope in the bold eyes that searched hers fearlessly.

"Mister Stowell, love is the last thing I could indulge in, with my responsibilities." Tatti gestured toward the shore and the pavilion that clustered in a thatched image on the savanna.

"You saved my life." He glanced at the stump of his right arm, handling the tiller with his bare foot and single hand.

" 'Twas my duty."

"Duty, no more than duty, my lady?"

"Of course, I fought for your life. Why wouldn't I?"

"I love you."

"You have a passion." She looked away from him.

"Oh, Tatti, please, we could love. Lord, life's not for death." His voice tightened. "Oh, God, I love you."

She set her hand atop his nut-brown sinewed hand on the tiller, feeling his fingers coiled like steel about the steering post.

"No, you don't love me, because you don't know me. You have a fantasy of me."

"Lass, dear God, I've watched you day and night, listened to you breathe, stolen glances of you in your bath and longed to touch your hair . . . ."

"No more, you're driving yourself mad." She put her face into the wind to avoid hearing his words, and set her hands on the seat.

"My lady, you are no fantasy to me—I love you, flesh and blood and breath."

"No more! Please!"

He shrank back into himself, watching the sail, and drawing in the sheet to ease the luffing, while the sea lapped on the gunwales.

"Am I wrong? To love you?" His voice was composed.

"No, nobody is ever wrong to love, but you must not say it, for my sake as well as yours."

"That I slaver in my mouth so I can taste it when I see your naked body . . ."

"I'll be obliged," she said, catching his eyes, "not to arouse a useless torment."

"I owe you my life."

"You owe me nothing." She moved away from him. "We have to examine the shipwreck."

The longboat came in under the lee of the *Daphne*, luffing its sails in the wind and coasting under the overhang of the stern. The gilt pilasters decorating the sterncastle were salt-glistened, and the elegant casement windows were blown out. In a moment Tatti was clambering up a ladder held by the sailors and onto the deck with Cora.

" 'Twas unnatural to go upon the waters," Cora said. "The earth gets us all bye and bye."

"The sand, in this case." Tatti held onto the quarterdeck rail and went down the tilted ladder to the main deck.

"No, we thought we were bigger than life." Tatti walked forward along the deck where she and Cora had scrambled the night the ship foundered. All was disarrayed in lines and halyards and cordage, though the sailors had worked for weeks, prying loose eyebolts and iron rods, and stacking planks torn from the deck and hull.

Stowell motioned for them to follow. They climbed down into the covered gun deck and saw the bright sunlight playing across the gloom where the cannons had torn loose and gone careening through the rolling hull.

"The water drove through here like a syphon on a plunger."

Tatti nodded her head slowly.

"And her back's broken. Eight foot of water in the hold."

The ship depressed Tatti. It was a relic to taunt her, of elegance and human courage and defiance of death, virtues that had failed so many, when she'd been taught a lifetime such virtues would triumph. All about her she heard the shipwreck creaking, gently nudged by the sea that played around it, as the sand held it.

"We weren't ready to die," Tatti whispered to Cora.

"Aye, a few lived, and enough."

Tatti nodded, and Stowell escorted them to the ship's safe. They entered the saloon where the safe stood, still unopened, a symbol of legality. She hesitated when she saw the ruin. Saltwater had scoured the paneled room of it's enamel and gilt, sanding it down to bare wood, and the smell of dark sea mold cloyed in her nostrils.

At Stowell's nod, a sailor pried off the lock with a crowbar, and the iron door swung open. The man reached out a varnished case. "The chronometer."

"Rusted." Stowell spoke.

"But the charts," Tatti said, taking the portfolio bearing the Admiralty crest.

"I don't read, my lady."

"No matter, I do, and America is west."

"America, my lady?"

"The wind blows west, and America's west."

The bosun glanced at Cora, astonished at Tatti's understanding. She tucked the charts under her arm. A sailor handed her a gold ring from the safe. It bore the signet of a bee and hawthorne trees.

"Chris." she whispered, and slipped it on her thumb and closed her fist over it. "He died to save us." Her eyes swam with tears and she stumbled over the hatch-combing as Cora guided her out of the saloon.

When they were seated in the stern of the cutter, Stowell spoke quietly. "My lady, a ship's safe as long as she's afloat at sea. It's not till she grounds, and changes to land, that she's pounded to death."

"Burn her," she said.

"Nay." Cora set her hand on Tatti's knee.

"Don't touch her, then, save for salvage." She kept her eyes closed to hide them from the bosun, whom she could feel watching her.

"Aye, my lady. 'Tis Crown property."

That afternoon Tatti slept in a hammock under a thatched lean-to, while Cora kneaded a dough pounded from a native barley, and waited for her to wake. The sunlight fell across her bare legs, and she felt the warmth ease her mind out of its deep swaying peace.

As the dreams pulsed in and out of focus,

Tatti woke, knowing she could never turn back from Gordon Wragby, or ever satisfy the gallant Stowell.

"Cora, I want to walk with you, alone on the beach." She put out her hand and touched the strong shoulders of her nurse, as Cora knelt and kneaded the dough between her knees.

The sunstruck beach was theirs alone, and Tatti walked through the rolling crests of waves that followed each other against the shore. The water played about her knees and thighs, and she sank down to her neck to feel her skin enveloped in a cool wash, and stood to feel the air chill her and make her flesh crinkle all over her body.

"Oh, I love it, Cora. The water washes off everything, and for a moment, I can forget."

"I'm not sure I want to forget all that much," Cora said, standing and wiping salt spray from her eyes. "But a good bath never hurt a body."

"I don't understand men," Tatti said. "I cannot see how they can be so cruel to one another and to helpless women and children. Oh, Cora, whenever I know a man and feel I could love him, I want to go back to the security of women."

"A wise notion, lass. Men are the trouble we was born for, and no woman goes willingly."

Tatti waded toward Cora in the shallow water. "I don't see how anybody can ever love without being terrified."

"Remember, Tatti, when you was little?"

Tatti swept her arms about Cora, feeling their water-quick flesh slip together as one human being in their hug. "I'm ashamed of my terror." She began to cry. "I'd forgotten what it was to hold my mother—the pure life you weren't afraid of."

"Now, now, little one, no need for that— I ain't Lady Frances, but I'm next to her, and near as good. Old Cora."

"You're not old—Lord, without your strength I'd be dry grass." Tatti wept in relief against Cora's shoulder.

Cora hugged her until she stopped, and they walked slowly out of the surf to where they had left their canvas jumpers and trousers. "One day we'll get back to Scotland, where up's up and down's down, and light's light, and you'll laugh about men."

"But not Gordon," Tatti whispered.

"Aye, he's different." Cora spoke pensively as she handed Tatti her clothes.

XII

The Bermuda summer had come, bringing a warm earth into paradise under the wet ocean air that moved over it, cooling the beaches and enriching the savannas of grass, making their tropic vegetables leap into sight as if by magic, and filling the cedar woods with birds that always sang.

"What a thing is this island," Tatti said. "If we're hot, we're cooled, and if cool, we're warmed."

"Never saw the like of our vegetable garden," Cora said.

In the garden, and in putting up a loose arrangement of grass-thatched, open-sided cottages, Tatti realized she had her mind and body fully occupied. And as long as her days were thus filled, she could postpone any commitment to Gordon Wragby, and let her love be quiet, to grow as it would.

In the evening she loved walking alone on the beach with Cora. The ceaseless stir of the waves, slipping into the faint illumined sand before her, eased her mind. "No matter what the day, the beach at night puts me to bed," she said.

"Aye, and there's turning back on the beach as a body fancies," Cora said.

"Which is not so in love, I know, Cora, as you've told me."

"With a man a woman can never be forgetful, leastways till he dies."

"Oh, how somber, Cora."

Tatti looked back at the pavilion that glowed in soft thatch-work in the gentle light of their fires. The pavilion had grown, and in the shadows it looked like a village of native huts. As they felt the primordial voice of the ocean wash about their toes, Tatti could hear the hymn-singing. The emigrants filled each evening after work with a spontaneous worship that took the form of hymns. She had heard the first fragile notes three weeks after they had thatched the roof, and after they had repaired water-soaked dulcimers and found the marines' flutes, their confidence seemed to return.

At least once a week Tatti entertained the children with an Italian puppet show in the evening. It seemed to put an air of brightness into their island captivity to fashion a mouse and a frog and a bumblebee out of sawgrass and painted canvas, and have the whole puppet menagerie sing and dance and talk.

There was another, more poignant reason: Gordon Wragby, who had moved into his own small quarters, had grown remote from her, in response to the mutual need each sensed to love. It's out of the question, Wragby's eyes said, and avoided hers, once that mystic chord was struck at first glance into each other's eyes.

Yet Gordon Wragby would join the whole company inside the pavilion, alight by the embers of the fire in its center that vented through the roof. And Tatti would slip the characters of "Froggie" and "Missie Mouse" onto her hands and sing in a clear lilting voice that floated over the people's heads, her eyes on every face, except the slender one of the man she loved.

> Froggie went a'courtin', and he did ride,
> Uhhmm, Uhhmm.

> Froggie went a'courtin', and he did ride,
> Sword and pistol by his side.
> Uhhmm, Uhhmm, Uhhmm.

> Missie Mouse, will you marry me?
> Uhhmm, Uhhmm.

> Missie Mouse, will you marry me?
> Not unless Uncle Rat'll agree.
> Uhhmm, Uhhmm, Uhhmm.

The firelight fell across the faces of the delighted children, who would soon sway in unison, singing with Tatti stanza after stanza of the old Scottish ballad. They improvised new animals and fanciful situations, which Tatti would be obliged to portray in puppet image

121

before them, keeping up to the new words, until they fell behind; and the children would break into laughter and roll over each other in glee at the confused gyrations of the animal puppets.

Many of the adults joined in from the background, particularly the sailors. Several of the emigrant women, however, those who had suffered the most, remained dour, their arms folded under their bosoms, and their mouths compressed in disapproval.

"I don't care," Tatti said when Cora had pointed it out. "If the children will laugh, we can laugh again ourselves, and be their parents, even though we're all grief-struck."

"Aye, but all they can taste is their grief and envy for your grace," Cora observed. "The joy arouses spite."

"No matter." Tatti dismissed the problem, certain the risk was small to the end gained.

"Now Miss Tatti will answer bold Froggie!" Tatti would cry, evoking wild cheers and applause from the audience. Hitting her Spanish tambourine on her knee, she would sing:

> Mister Froggie, you frighten me.
> Sword and pistol by your knee,
> Uhmm, Uhmm.
>
> Mister Froggie, you frighten me.
> Little bittie mouse was scared of thee.
> Uhmm, Uhmm, Uhmm.

Dancing in pantomime of the courtship of the animals of the nursery, Tatti found a buoyant release that captivated the children and drew her audience into one family bound by a common joy of childhood fantasy; and she saw the gentle ray of love alight the slender man she loved, who'd fled from her, except in those moments of innocence.

It was these evenings, as the dying fire threw shadows across the happy faces of the whole company, when laughter was everywhere and the stars rested in tender light on the ocean, that Tatti knew they would live.

BOOK TWO
Ravendale

XIII

The girl had grown to be an obsession that he very carefully pushed away from his mind. Gordon Wragby, the Marquis of Ravendale, was disciplined to his fingertips to play the role of a naval officer; and in his middle years, he was determined that Tatti would mean nothing to him. Bred never to show emotion, he was ashamed that he had fainted in front of his subordinates when he had seen the wreck of his ship. "Alas, she was such a beautiful ship," he'd say.

Wragby had seen the inside arch of Tatti's bare foot, when she knelt at his head in his fever. The sole of her foot was soiled from the earth, and the tracery of dirt in the folds of bare skin enchanted him. He was swept with an insane fantasy to kiss her foot, and he thought he might have, if the fever hadn't weakened him so. Now he blamed the fever for his rage to look at the smooth flesh behind her ear, and to stare at her lips, seeking to see her tongue brush into sight behind her white teeth.

"Absolute madness," he said to himself, "can't have it. After all, I'm middle-aged, and Tatti's a girl. Besides, I must be an example to my men."

He was dismayed by this thought, for Gordon Wragby never really believed there ever was "my men," and was always mildly astonished when they obeyed him, though it also never occurred to him they would not obey him. Now, in fact, the sailors belonged more to Tatti than to him, which somehow relieved him.

The fact that Tatti had the allegiance of the sailors and the cotters captivated him, and he was immensely proud of her, as a parent might be proud of a child. His obsession to see and hear and to be near Tatti was a torment he bore in quiet determination to endure.

The fact that he loved Tatti, and could not have her, that he would deny himself, was a continuation of the pattern of his life.

In Noello, the old hermit, Gordon Wragby found a kindred spirit of human courage to endure and surmount impossible odds, and still to carry on. Wragby liked Noello, and exploring the island with the lost little man in the straw hat gave him an excuse to be away from his obsession. "If I were ever to love her, I might hurt her, and I can't have that," Wragby would think as he pulled on his boots, with the aid of Leslie, the Highland woman.

"Good morning, Caruthers," Wragby said, striding out as his marine orderly came to attention, his uniform and kit as bright as could be made, considering the hurricane loss.

"My lord!" the marine saluted.

"Now where shall we amble today? First, we'll find Noello, and dine with him, while of course planning to fortify our encampment."

"Aye, my lord."

Gordon Wragby had always taken long walking tours through England and Scotland. His friends had accepted these extended disappearances as a part of his personality that made him even more attractively different. Wragby always dressed well, in greased, waterproof boots and a vast redingote, that turned the rain. He'd set off directly into the Lake Country, or into the wildest moor of Scotland or Ireland, always on foot.

The secret Gordon Wragby shared with no one but his sister, Nellie, was that he liked to talk to ordinary people who did not know who he was. He could lose himself in their lives, and admire their robust courage to say and do as they saw fit to do, something he had found denied himself in his naval career, and in his duty to barter a threadbare title to an heiress.

His cultured accent always gave him away, but his genial good humor and adequate funds assured him a warm reception wherever he tramped, and in whatever country.

Life slipped by this way, broken by grand hunts, wherein he found himself in love, often as not, with his horse. The courage of his horse as it hurled itself over wide ditches, and leaped walls and fences in a storm of noise and mud and hunting horns was more true than the other riders who fought to stay ahead of each other as they rode their hunters to death in perilous jumps.

There were often beautiful girls and ladies to see at the hunts, cocked up on their side-saddles, and brave as grenadiers as they sailed past him, trailing lace and satin skirts. Frequently, they were as rough as their horses and repelled him when he got to know them.

Thus Gordon Wragby's life had passed its way. As a gentleman he found a stoic joy in sailing, and his mother's flower garden at Wragby Hall. Now that his brother-in-law, Lord Rush, had been thrown by his horse to his death, Gordon had his sister, Nellie, to console. He had found a purpose to retire to.

All that changed with the shipwreck and he dare not think of it. Tatti was a mad obsession; it was as though he'd lived a whole lifetime preparing to fall in love with this beautiful girl. "Impossible, quite out of the question," he said to himself.

"I beg your pardon, my lord?" said the marine who followed him across the savanna toward the woods.

"Oh, nothing, Caruthers. I talk to myself—rather eases one's folly."

The marine hurried to keep up, not understanding his captain and afraid he'd misheard him.

Gordon Wragby crossed the savanna and passed into a scented woods of cedars, and came out onto a shallow glade to enter a cool thicket of palmetto.

"Noello, halloo!" Wragby called, waiting for the hermit to appear. "This island's like the palm of his hand," he said to Caruthers.

"Likely, sir, if he's been marooned for forty year."

They heard brush stir behind them, and turned to see Noello.

"Ah, Noello." Wragby smiled when he saw the wispy beard under the round soft eyes with their baggy pouches. "We've come to see your tree house, as you promised. And I must build a fort."

"A fort?" Noello's eyes blazed in a pure terror.

"Oh, no danger." Wragby waved his open fingers. " 'Tis my duty, however."

Noello nodded his head. "I can hide, but not so many women and children."

"Right-oh, just a precaution."

"No fear, then." Noello's chest heaved with relief and his soft eyes were self-assured again.

"None," Wragby said.

Noello gestured for them to follow, and led them along a mangrove swamp, out into the high sunlight; and feeling with his feet, he found an underwater bridge that crossed quicksand.

Perchunk! Wragby stopped. Then he saw that a large bullfrog, tied with grass string, had plopped out into the swamp from the bank, and croaked aloud.

"My sentinels," Noello said, and broke into a shiver of laughter. "I have froggies tied up and down the whole swamp, 'deed I do—'deed I do."

"Well, you don't have to change the guard." Wragby sat down to let Caruthers pull off his boots so he could wade.

"A bit balmy in the head, my lord." The marine spoke under his breath.

"Regardless, an enchanting soul." Wragby walked to the bridge while his orderly carried their boots under his arm.

They waded the hidden cedar bridge, until they reached a steep bank, up which they crawled, and into a forest so deep it was shadowed with dusk. Suddenly, Noello began to climb rapidly upward, his fingers and toes caught into bark notches on a tree trunk.

"By Jove," Wragby said, following. In a moment he was lost in a maze of cedar limbs and massive clouds of greenery. The sight of the forest floor had vanished the first time they looked back. In a moment Wragby stepped out onto a roofed platform of palmetto fronds and edged with cedar buckets filled with scented flowers and Cape jasmine.

"Gardenias, the Spanish call them." Noello set his hand palm up at the side of a blossom.

Wragby looked out from under the palm-frond roof, and saw the ocean lying in a blue distance.

"My word, what a stunning view."

Noello clapped his fingers together, and

fluttered all about the side of the roofed house, darting out along the limbs, hopping over jasmine and gardenias, his thin hands caressing each stalk of greenery, rather like a human hummingbird.

"I've hid here a lifetime, my lord."

"Dare say you've had splendid company." Wragby set his elegant hand at the edge of a double gardenia.

"Ah, I've loved it, oh, I loved it." Noello hopped back up to them.

The Royal Marine's astonished eyes traveled from his Captain to the hermit and back.

"It's all right, Caruthers." Wragby nodded assuredly.

"I loved my solitude. Every day was eternal and every flower infinite, oh, I read all my novels—'twas grief." He waved his hand at a shelf of French and Italian books with rich vellum pages.

"Until we invaded your island," Wragby said, taking a cup of herbal tea, and sitting on a small stool, nodding at the marine to do the same.

"Nay, my lord, you didn't invade this island, no indeed. You were all flung ashore, right out of death you was snatched." He crouched and snapped his fingers. "I watched your ship break up, and I knew I'd lived forty years to save you."

"Did you?" Wragby said.

"Aye, I just knew I had a grand purpose, and you know what?"

"Do tell."

"Waiting for folk in need. Took near forty year."

"Well, here we are." Gordon Wragby threw his hands apart and clapped them on his knees.

After a lunch of split palm hearts and fresh mangoes, Wragby walked out of the forest. He sent Noello on to the emigrants, whom the hermit liked to sit amidst and watch the women and children. And he dispatched Caruthers alone back to their open quarters. "We'll have to see to the weapons." The sailors had salvaged thirty-eight muskets and five blunderbusses, as well as a stock of cutlasses, knives, and grenades. "I want those grenades honed out, and reloaded with fresh powder."

Caruthers nodded firmly, staring at the bouquet of flowers from Noello in Wragby's hand.

"And tell Stowell to try to find a small cannon, something we can carry onto the savanna."

"A small cannon, my lord." The marine's eyes lit with understanding.

"Yes, something very portable, rather larger than a blunderbuss, but not clumsy."

"I'm sure we can find the very cannon, my lord."

"Good, now I'll just take a nice stroll quite alone." He nodded and saw the marine off, glad to be by himself.

Gordon Wragby walked along the edge of the shaded creek, the savanna lying off to his right, and exulted in the pure joy of being absolutely alone, yet knowing somewhere not far ahead were people whom he cared for. "Aye, and folk I love," he said to himself, and raised the bouquet to his nose and inhaled deeply. The creek ran softly about the roots of massive trees reflecting their cool green images. He sat on the bank, and set his slender feet into the mud, and wriggled his toes.

Then he got to his feet and walked away from the creek, out onto the savanna, and let his eye cast across it, looking for a knoll, not far from water and yet clear of the trees, to preserve an unobstructed field of fire. "There must be an ideal place to situate a fort."

The long grass brushed under his bare feet as he walked, seeking to gain an elevation and calculating distances. No place seemed to meet all requirements. "No matter, I'll walk out in the morning. We must be able to defend ourselves."

XIV

Life on the island had become a delicious trance to Gordon Wragby, where he had lost all sight of time, and where people lived out of the simple delight to stay alive and there were no quarrels for him to settle or even to know about. And there was Tatti. His soul leaped into his throat, just to hear her talking to Cora, or calling to the children. Slowly, Wragby had come to realize he was absolutely happy, perhaps for the first time in his life, and time was the last thing on earth he wanted to know about. "I don't want to change," Wragby would say to himself, and dig his fingernails into his palms to be sure he was truly alive, and not in a trance or dream of bliss.

Gordon Wragby had never thought much

on God, as a matter of taste; in fact, it was a subject a gentleman would avoid, in order not to have opinions, so he would not offend anyone, and certainly no gentleman would discuss the Almighty. As an immensely sophisticated man, it came to him as a surprise that his happiness might well suggest a divine bliss did exist, and that it was the girl whose image haunted him with a joy he dare not savor.

Cora kept a very logical, sequential reckoning of the days as they passed, and with Stowell, had carefully noted the dates and months. "Four months, three weeks, two days, and one hour past dawn," Cora said, marking the "calendar board."

Tatti marveled at her nurse's determination to keep everything exactly straight, and really had no care of each day as it came and went, yet instead looked upon the rush of them as moments out of eternity, if they could but live; and in this way, Tatti measured time by days of laughter, bodies that filled out, pavilion bents raised, children who smiled, and the day Stowell walked.

"Gordon told me this morning that he wanted to canvass the savanna," Tatti said, as she rolled to her feet from her hammock, having napped after lunch.

"Aye, we'll have supper one hour before sunset," Cora said, glancing out at the mid-afternoon.

Tatti splashed water in her face and combed back her tousled hair, then walked deliberately along the edge of the knolls and through the narrow belt of trees, a half mile from their pavilion, until she heard him call. "Tatti, over here."

When she saw Wragby in his open shirt and short linen jacket, wearing tight pantaloons but barefoot, she shouted, "Gordon, you've gone native!"

"When in Rome, my dear." He came to her, his thin face lined about his fragile lips and thin nose, his hands outstretched to take hers. He hugged her to his chest, smelling the rich scent of her hair in his nose, and set her deliberately away, at arm's length. Then striding briskly out into the cooling savanna, he said, "I must build a fort, and I haven't found a place . . . ."

"A fort, Gordon, what for?"

"Defense, my love."

"In paradise?"

"Useless." He stared evenly about the rolling field of green, blotched here and there with small clusters of trees.

"Aye, useless. As useless as your defense against my love for you. At seventeen, every girl is a woman, and I'm nineteen."

"Quite." Wragby held her hand, but did not look at her. "I have no intention of disillusioning you."

"That's not fair!" She stopped, tugging him around to face her. "I'm not under an illusion. You love me, too."

"Oh, Tatti, I do." His voice softened. "I love you like the sunrise, I love you as the dawn that lifts my soul of what I lost a lifetime—

139

your voice is all I can hear, and your laughter rings in my ears as a chime that wakes a valley. Your face, the mouth I see that frames your breath, while your eyes are in mine, wherever I look." He saw past the stillness that gripped her as he spoke, and knew he'd touched her soul. Taking her into his chest, he put his mouth into the thick chestnut hair at her ear, drawing in the scent of her skin and her rich breath that enveloped his face. "To love you would be my final wish on this earth, and so much do I yearn to lay my hands upon your whole body, touching what I dare not, kissing all that you are in your purpose as a woman, that I could not. There is nothing more."

"Nothing more?" Tatti spoke uncertainly.

"Aye, the dream of God and bliss would be fulfilled in thee," he said in the divine passion of intimacy. "And often the dream fulfilled is the nightmare come true. I'd die should I harm you in love."

"Dear Gordon, love does not harm. It restores. My parents' love gave them strength." Her wide eyes searched his.

"Tatti, my love, I straddle the years, of both you and your parents, with all the desolation of wit tempered by wisdom. I dare not hurt you, even if I can taste you on every nerve of my tongue, and would kiss you with my mouth in every way that I could."

"Well, I think I saved you for that very purpose." Tatti spoke evenly. "I had a feeling about you, when you were kind to the emigrants."

"Tatti, I'm a disciplined gentleman."

"It's time you changed. I can taste your tongue, same as you mine."

He tilted his head in a quandry.

"Later, we'll find a knoll for a fort. Now we're alone."

"Come, let's walk on." He took her hand in his, and they walked slowly across the broad field, not speaking or looking ahead. In what seemed moments he was leading her through the soft shade of the small palmetto grove, one of many scattered across the wild savanna.

"No, I'll go no further." Tatti stopped, facing him. "Take off my clothes." She put her hands over her head, and searched his eyes.

Wragby looked at her and saw every hope he'd ever had. He put his hand to the tie at her midriff and pulled it, and felt himself swallow the dry taste in his throat as her loose pantaloons fell free of her hips and slid to the punk, baring the feathered shadow hair at the joining of her thighs to the slender cords at her bare feet.

"I shouldn't," he said.

"In love, it's right."

His hand trembled as he reached to touch her narrow waist.

"It's why the Lord put us here."

His hand lay along the firm flesh of her rounded hips, and he ran it down her smooth thigh, to see her fine knees and feet before him. He slipped his fingers under her blouse and lifted it until she was nude.

"I crave to see and touch you." His voice

was strange to him as his hands set along her rib cage, and his breath caught when he saw her smooth breasts just before his face.

"You kissed me on the ship," she whispered.

"I thought we were dying, and I thought it was the last decent thing I could do."

"Gordon, the Lord meant for us to live." She raised her hands over her head and turned slowly before him.

Gordon swallowed at the bounty of her full thighs and flat belly and small waist, topped by the delicate breasts, all quite openly before him.

She faced him, her eyes catching his, and held him in their grip, her arms still overtop her head, and refused to look away.

"I'm at your feet, Gordon." She flung herself into the dry punk.

"Good Lord, get up, Tatti."

She put her mouth to his foot.

"Tatti!" He lifted her by her shoulders, marveling at the swelling symmetry of her buttocks, and felt his heart sing with a mad pleasure that he had something exquisitely beautiful, all for himself, when her small red nipples came up before his face. "Ah, so utterly, utterly lovely." He held her fine-boned hand which was grimed with sap and dirt. " 'Tis madness to not love." He could barely speak for his hoarseness.

"It's why we lived," she said as he enfolded her into his chest and taut body.

He encircled her slender form with his

arms and struggled to ease his breath in his throat, that seemed to flood with a wet desire so that he could not breathe.

"Aye, we'll love," he whispered. "Come to my quarters at dusk."

"Oh, Gordon." She lay her head on his chest.

" 'Twill be right to love, only if we bind our immortal selves, our souls into one being out of eternity, and live beyond the flesh through the passion of our bodies—that is love."

"I'm so glad you know."

"I don't know, I just know the flesh is fulfilled too quickly."

"But I feel we must love." She looked into his eyes, and began to weep.

"Lord, yes, yet we must feel beyond what we touch, and that is love."

"Oh, that's fine." She pulled her head back, drying her eyes. "If I can't hold you and feel you, I won't know I've loved you."

"Certainly. One must touch to share one's soul."

"Yes." She laid her head against his chest.

He held her quietly as he got control of his passion.

"Now you must dress. I'll help you. Tonight at dusk."

She took the back of his hand and kissed it as he ran his fingers through her thick, moist hair. "Oh, I love you."

He knelt and held her pantalettes to step into, charmed as she rested her hand on his shoulder, standing on one leg at a time. And he stood, and slipped the jumper over her head, and caught the abundant hair, and drew it out over her broad white collar that lay across her back.

That evening Gordon Wragby sat in a folding campaign chair and watched the sun settle toward an untroubled sea, highlighting the straight horizon. Soft clouds tufted overhead in the twilight, and he could hear the broad pavilion throb with the voices of the emigrants, both jolly and tired from a day at work in their expanding garden.

Gordon Wragby knew Tatti would come to him, and he knew he would do what he would never have done before. He would love her out of love, and love alone, with no thought or care for tomorrow. In Tatti was the living proof it was not too late to change his life, and in their isolation on the island, there was no tomorrow nor yesterday, only today, and it came each dawn.

When the dark had settled, he lit the small tallow lamp at the rough desk where he wrote, and dropped the woven screens along the sides of his quarters. The small thatched room glowed with a soft gold light in the reflection from the palm fronds, and he set aside the last of his supper.

"I shan't eat any more," he said to Leslie, "and I won't need anybody until after dawn."

"Thank you, my lord." The woman's figure was composed as she crossed before him.

It was late, and he sat outside and waited

for Tatti to come from across the compound where she and Cora lived.

"That's no sleeping jumper," Cora had said when she saw Tatti pull the long flowered nightgown over her head, and begin tying the bows at her throat. "You wooed him, lass?"

"After dark." Tatti did not look at her nurse.

"He's consented?"

"We might be here for years."

"I'm not faulting you, Tatti."

"I love him."

"Go, then, lass, only I want it writ in the Bible." Her russet eyes were feverish in the dark.

"The Bible? Not at a time like this."

"Bye and bye, I want it writ out, that you and the man became one in the spirit."

"All right. We'll write it."

"And where I say."

"Where you say, as you say." Tatti faced her nurse. "Oh, Cora, I love him so. Kiss me."

The strapping shoulders swooped her into the bosom she'd loved a lifetime, and she felt the awkward arms jerk her frame into the body; and Tatti was astonished at the breath and mouth that kissed her neck, her shoulder, and then her mouth with a vehemence that hurt her lips. "I love thee, girl, and I have loved thee all thy days."

"Cora." Tatti set her hands on the shoulders and arms to calm her.

"He's not one of us; he's English, but he'll do."

"I love him."

"I'll sit up all night."

"Likely I'll stay."

"I'll sit up all night anyway." Cora turned her toward the door and pulled aside the palmetto screen.

XV

He saw Tatti come into sight along the swept sand path their mason had lined with split stone. He saw the moonlight free itself of a passing cloud, and cast a soft haze onto the nightgown that brushed just above her tan feet.

"Tatti," he whispered, and walked softly to meet her.

"I'm so excited I can barely get my breath." She clutched his hands in hers.

"Now, now, we must be slow." He girdled her waist with his arm and led her to the gentle warmth of his quarters. "We have a lifetime, you know."

"Gordon, we have to start somewhere." Her eyes were moist and luminous in the golden light of the lamp, and reflected immense, both in her fear and her excitement.

"Well, of course." He searched her eyes, and read the quandry and the passion. "We mustn't do anything to frighten you."

"Good Lord, Gordon, I'm scared to death."

"Tatti, at my age, I'm not altogether sure about anything, except that age has made me a coward."

"A coward? You?"

"My word, yes."

"We mustn't talk about it." She swallowed and searched his eyes.

"Ah, Tatti, 'tis thee I adore, and I wouldst have thee, or die." He spoke the words deliberately in his spiritual intimacy.

She waited, catching her breath, and he leaned forward and kissed her lips, and of an instant felt the moist life pressed into his mouth. He swallowed. She seemed to move against him and he drew her to his body and slipped loose the ribbons at her throat, so that her gown was free.

"I love you," he said.

"Life without thee wouldst be death."

He raised her nightgown over her head until she was aglow in her bare skin by the soft lamp light.

"Ah, such elegant beauty," he said, and averted his face for an instant, stricken by the beauty in his arms.

"Gordon?"

"I almost can't look at you."

He drew her to his chest and kissed her small breast until he felt its nipple crinkle as a tight bud, taut under his breath. He dropped his head and kissed her navel and drew her down onto her knees and turned her backward over his wide bunk, until she lay outstretched before him. He pressed his mouth to her belly, and touched her thighs and kissed the flesh until it became sweet, and he heard himself gasp and seek to cram her whole body into his mouth, and he heard her sigh, "Oh," and squirm in his grasp.

"Alas, I didn't mean to frighten you." He knelt back, seeing her arm flung away from him as though to flee and her body twist toward the screen.

"No," she said, rolling toward him. "Gordon, you've driven me wild, don't stop now."

"I don't want to hurt you."

"Oh, God, Gordon, I'm terrified and ecstatic—don't stop!" Her hands caught his shoulders, and drew him down to her.

Her smooth flesh against his bare chest sent a mad surge of life throughout his body, and he pulled back to free himself of his shirt and tore at his pantaloons to get them off.

Against his naked skin the whole flesh of her drove him into a passion to hold her and envelop her and to penetrate her, as well as kiss her, and want her all over as a part of him. Her breasts were at his palate, and her belly to his lips, and the fine hair in her armpits tasted sweet caught in his tongue, until he felt her legs shift, and he slipped his knee between hers.

"Gordon?" Her voice was uncertain.

"Let it be, I won't hurt."

"Yes."

He tasted her mouth, deep with his tongue, until he felt her knees rise and heard her breathe. He knelt back and laid his hand inside her thigh, until she parted her legs and he slid his hand to the fine hair, and put his mouth down the skin of her thigh, kissing it until he kissed the gossamer nest of filament where his fingers lay, and felt her move, and he went up her body to her breasts, and settled between her knees, and held her shoulders in his arms.

"Gently," he whispered, searching past the fear in her eyes, to the impossible desire he had aroused in her, and he pressed slowly until he felt her loins yield up to him, and the lips gently part, and he slid in a trifle. He felt her stop breathing, and he stopped.

"There," he whispered, and held.

"Oh, Gordon." She grasped him in relief. "Oh, Gordon, I love you." She flung her head from side to side. "It doesn't hurt!"

"It shouldn't."

"A little more."

He eased himself up and down her loins until he felt a small passion of delight sweep her belly as her thighs raised to grasp him about his waist.

"A little more." Her fingers caught his shoulders, and he could feel her shiver in his arms.

"Tatti, I love you." His eyes went out of focus in the soft light and he felt her ease into a passion while his skin and body pulsed in bliss.

"Gordon!" Her voice was low, as she felt

the quiet confidence invade her whole body and a sense of bliss that radiated out from between her legs where she held him until she knew she had devoured him in absolute purpose. She trembled at the peace and triumph of a gentle passion, rising in waves across her belly to her every quaking nerve, delighted at not being afraid, and felt him shuddering between her thighs, and fluttering his limbs in her grasp like a bird caught in her hands.

He rested atop her, spent except for his breath, and she ran her arms up and down his fragile body, assured in her delight. "Gordon, we must try again," she whispered.

He nodded, unable to form his words. When he had swallowed, he could turn his head. "Tatti, we must go gently into love, so that we go far."

"Oh, certainly." She spoke vigorously.

"Alas, I can scarce speak." He felt the strength drained out of every fiber of his body by the ecstatic bliss that had seized his spine and pulsed out his nerves until he thought he had died. "Oh, I feel I died and came back to life." His head rested into the pillow. "And in your arms." He heaved for breath, and felt his hands exhausted, the fingers unable to bend or move where they were caught about her.

"Gordon," she whispered, glimpsing her triumph and relief at the expense of a man she respected. "Are you all right?"

"Yes, spent, quite more than I expected."

"Love, holding you is a peace I never dreamed of." She gently clasped him into her body with her arms and legs.

"Tatti, I couldn't raise my hand or head if you turned me loose." He let his whole frame slip into the bedding about them, and felt his mind free itself of trouble, and his body waft into rest, drawing his spent legs and soft breathing into sleep with her.

In the days that followed, Gordon Wragby felt his years drop away and all care vanish. His every thought was of the girl who dazzled his eyes and enveloped his soul in rapture; and he wondered many times why he had had to wait so long to find her. He knew he would cherish her as the ultimate gift of life, and savor her in gratitude for this unknown delight. He was absolutely staggered by his discovery.

"Come, we'll roam the islands," he said, "and wade the beaches, and picnic on the cedar knolls." He took her hand and strode out briskly, as Leslie and Cora handed Tatti their wicker picnic hamper.

Tatti saw the startled eyes of the cotters and the sailors who moved busily about the compound after breakfast each morning waiting to see when Gordon Wragby would turn again to his duties.

"The cannon, my lord, we found the very cannon," the marine said, and six sailors heaved a robust cannon to their shoulders so the Captain could see it.

"Oh, yes, the cannon, yes, we'll need it." He did not let go of Tatti's hand while he ran his eye over the verdigris-smeared weapon.

"And we have powder, my lord." Stowell

smacked his hand atop a keg of powder, avoiding Tatti's eyes.

"Good. Keep everything." He clutched Tatti's hand to his waist and strode through the people.

Cora watched them walk off along the beach toward the cedar copses and the distant woods. The women about her were silent, knowing she had been Tatti's nurse. Cora shook her head. "When a man falls, it's dangerous, unless a good woman gets him." She turned toward the pavilion. "Bye and bye, we'll get them back."

Wragby lived in a haze where nothing lived or breathed or moved except the girl. Tatti was life, and he meant to have her and life as a drowning man pops to the surface, clutches a floating branch and clings to it in passion and hope.

Tatti arranged their picnic in the shade by a quiet pool along the creek, where they could still hear the surf roll in the distance.

"Ah, yes, tea." Wragby would lie on his back, looking straight into the treetops, where the limbs sheltered his sight from the clear blue sky.

"I love being your slave, Gordon." Tatti knelt to fix the tea.

"Nay, lass, I am the slave." He sat up to take his cup. "In slavery is freedom and in freedom bondage, when one is slave to life."

When they had rested he touched her slender neck and drew her to him. Her lips

153

filled his lungs with an urgent scent of moving flesh that he ran his tongue through, then plunged into her soft mouth. He felt her breath sweep about his ears when her tongue seized him, so that his eyelids fluttered half closed.

"Oh, Gordon." Her head fell away from his mouth, her hands loosening her ribbons at the waist of her light summer frock.

"Here, let me." Gordon's hands slid about the satin ties until she was free of her binds, and he could lift the delicate impediment of her clothing from her, so he could once again see and feel her as she really was—the way he loved her.

He buried his face into her armpit to lick the tart hair and smell the wet odor, then set his mouth to the small breast that rose against her slight body. In moments he could feel her flesh twist against his body from her neck to his thigh, which he pressed to part her knees, and felt her encircle him with her arms and limbs, and heard the moist grass wet beneath them as he rolled their bodies into one flesh he could grasp to his chest and loins, and draw down into his mouth.

When he had torn loose his light clothing, her body enveloped him in urgent flesh that he could feel alive in twisting muscle which burned his skin in an endless passion, as if all life and all God lived at that instant and in her body. Her breasts swelled against his tongue, and he tasted the fragrant nipples in his nostrils with his breath.

"Gordon, there is no other god." He

heard her gurgle in ecstasy as her fingernails caught his ribs.

"I think there's another," Wragby gasped, "but I don't really care just now."

He had her flat belly to his mouth, lifting the hips to smell the tender hair at the union of her thighs, and to taste the pungent salt of life at her secret places, where life sprang to enrage the earth smells of eternal hope, like a rain wetting a parched soil.

"Gordon, dear Lord, Gordon."

He felt his iron pestle clasped to the soft wet folds as her arms and legs engulfed him, and her body rose into his loins, and he drove his trembling body into the gossamer hair and fine lips between her thighs, while she drew the life out of his throat with her tongue. He trembled through eternity as the ecstasy pumped its way through his body on bare nerves. He gasped for life as she held him; he was swept in tender spasms that drew past his knees up through his spine to his skull, and he drifted off toward oblivion.

Often Gordon Wragby drew Tatti's face across his arm while they lay back in a mild shaded copse, the surf playing in the distance upon the beach. "I really never thought it of myself."

"That you could love?" Her mouth was soft. "Oh, Gordon, you were wasted in society."

"Aye, 'tis such a folly to be measured by others, and not ourselves."

"And you were wasted at war."

"I never felt warlike, it was just my duty."

"To be warlike."

"Yes, but I made it a game. Any gentleman knows war is a vile expression of common arrogance, so we make it a game."

"Gordon, the common people were torn loose from the moor, and 'twas no game to them." Her voice was gentle in reproach.

"Ah, yes, no gentleman ever uprooted wickedness. We live with it."

"Love is the only lasting value that transcends life itself, to prove life divine." He set his hand along her cheek. "I wouldst love thee, defying all gods to discover the Almighty in one final desperate wish."

She searched into his soul, and saw the pathetic composure of a man who had glimpsed himself for the first time at middle age. It both warmed her and shamed her that she could mean so much to him, and that he had been denied by life so long.

"Gordon," she whispered, "love me, love me so I can love you, and we can prove that life is true."

"Aye, I love you so much I'm absolutely indecent."

"I love to be indecent." She rolled atop him, her hands playing in his ruffled dark hair and her breasts under his chin.

"Too much of a good thing may tempt the gods," he said, rolling her free and pulling her to her feet.

He led her to the bright creek and lifted her shift until she was nude. Wading her out by the arm, he stopped and lifted water in his cupped hands, to let it bathe down her skin to see highlights play over her flesh in rivulets, slipping round her breasts and down her flanks to her wide thighs.

She watched him and turned up her face, so he could dash water against her nude body and slide his hands along her flesh, beside himself with intoxication at her beauty.

"Your breasts, I must kiss them." He put his mouth to her nipples and felt his lips and tongue gorged with her wet, quick flesh. "I had no idea I'd go so mad to kiss you, to kiss you all over until I ached."

He pressed his face into the fragile hair that rubbed gently in his nostrils, and tasted the parting folds, until her thighs stepped open and he felt her loins tilt up to him.

"Gordon, you've killed me with love," she whispered.

"Aye, lovers both slay and are killed in love."

"I'd not die another way." Her hands were on his shoulders.

He was lost to her knees and ankles, her supple waist, the strong symmetrical toes he held to his face—it was the supreme moment of fantasy that care had vanished, and he had found eternity in a woods sylph of flesh and joy.

Tatti was the living fantasy of perfect love that every man hopes one day life will bring him, that sustains his sublime dreams of love and exquisite bliss in a woman's soul and on her breath and smile, and whose voice carries his purpose on earth. Gordon could not believe that he had at last reached that insane point of bliss in human life, when ecstasy of the flesh becomes the soul in its purity.

"I cannot stop," he said, resting at Tatti's side. "I suppose if you're parched for water, each drink itself is another taste to remind you you didn't perish."

"Love is witless, Gordon, or one couldn't love." Tatti lay on her back, a wet stalk of sweet briar half munched in her teeth.

"Perhaps, and one also measures love against grief."

"True, if we could not die, we would not live." She rolled up onto her elbow.

"Oh, Tatti, the brave die every day," he said, "and know it."

XVI

Bye and bye, Gordon Wragby began to come out of the fogged haze that had engulfed him. Tatti was at his side, morning and night; but she had begun once more to spend some of her daylight hours with Cora, rather in silence, for the fourteen women had worked into a daily routine of house chores and garden cultivation. There was little needed of her, once she had rallied the emigrants to their duty to live after the shipwreck, and her mind was now filled with the hope and bliss of her love. The children were a joy to her. They all could run and walk, for the storm had drowned all the babes in arms. One woman, Caroline, had survived in a pregnant state, and was to bear a child any day.

"Cora wants to have an engagement and wedding feast," Tatti told Wragby one evening.

"Splendid."

Gordon Wragby was moved by the idea of a fête, sharing the rising sense of roots and strength put down by the castaways. "We'll get that fort up in no time," he said to Caruthers and the sailors. "Right now, let's get on with childbirth and a marriage."

The ruddy company of sailors and the marine seemed relieved, and were swept away again more eagerly than the emigrants. "Jolly good notion, my lord!" cried Caruthers. "Three cheers for the Captain."

"Hip, hip, hurrah!" the sailors shouted.

Tatti was proud of Wragby's reassertion of leadership, and avoided Stowell's piercing dark blue eyes as he stood among the seamen and watched her, while she waited at the side of the man she loved.

"Oh, Gordon." She took Wragby's arm as he nodded to his sailors once more, his hat in his hand out of respect for them.

"What a grand race of men we grow in England," Wragby said, walking into their quarters with Tatti.

"Gordon, it's you they love. Any race loves a good man."

"Tatti, I was always a failure."

"That's why we love you."

Tatti was swept along on the mood of expectation among the women as Caroline, a slender woman with pale skin, went into her confinement. The pavilion had been screened off into sections, and one was reserved for Caroline's final days before childbirth. It was a pleasant, hopeful travail that seemed to unite the women as a single purpose. "Birthing is always a reassurance," Cora said. "It has a good purpose."

Outside the pavilion, scattered about the compound enclosure, were cannons, kegs of powder under canvas, carpentry tools, and something of a village life.

"It would be nice if we could hang Japanese lanterns among the lower limbs of the trees," Wragby said.

"What kind o' lanterns, my lord?" asked a lean, bald-headed man.

"Japanese," a sailor said. "Off the coast of old Cathay."

"Aye, for the wedding," Leslie said, her adoring eyes on Wragby's form.

"Well, we could light the lanterns every night. 'Twould be a warm reminder of our gentility," Wragby said affably.

"His lordship's right. We need them lanterns every night." The bald-headed man nodded gravely, amid small words of assent, as the people returned to their work.

Noello became so excited at the idea of a childbirth as well as a party with lanterns hung in the trees, that his chin jibbered in silence, trembling his wispy beard; and he darted off across the savanna, shouting in Portuguese and French. They watched him out of sight, his thatch of white hair and bony legs scampering through the long grass, where at the woods they heard him begin to laugh in hysterical delight.

"Poor man, we'll be nursing him before it's done," Cora said.

"I dare say not, dear Cora," Wragby said. "That's one human spirit that must be free or altogether perish."

"That little man, my lord?"

"Aye. Now where am I going to hide our arsenal since you've run off Noello?" Wragby took a cup of herbal tea from Leslie and raised it in a delicate motion to his lips to inhale the bouquet. "Ah, not Pekoe, but still exciting."

"Thank you, my lord." Leslie's eyes feasted on him.

"He'll be back to sup, my lord."

"Thank you, Leslie." He walked toward his quarters, knowing Tatti was resting in a hammock after a bout of morning sickness.

Gordon Wragby was as content as Tatti at how events on the island had progressed. He felt he had chanced upon a secret door which opened onto a world he'd lost. He wore his short naval jacket, trimmed in gold lace, as an emblem of the authority he carried as a naval officer. Yet his cutoff pantaloons and bare feet, topped by the broad-brimmed straw hats that both he and Tatti wore, were his natural state in his newfound freedom.

Still, Gordon Wragby was aware that both he and Tatti played a role of maintaining values, as to what was truly important in life, and of living out those roles in public. Tatti had given up her jumpers and pantalettes to wear light smocks and a petticoat, despite her bare feet. "Whatever we do, we must always support the decent, simple life of virtue," Wragby had said, "and always in public."

"Nothing less," Tatti agreed.

"Pregnancy is an act of God, and courteous folk never discuss passion."

"Fortunate for passion," Tatti had said.

"Yes, there's an innate wisdom in simple living, as a cure for life."

Tatti nodded, and did not answer Wragby when he sorted out his mind.

Another vague specter stalked Gordon Wragby. He alone seemed aware he had to arm his company for their defense. Pirates and buccaneers had used Bermuda for years, and though impoverished of worldly goods, men and women who had come upon misfortune or calamity were frequently made slaves when discovered by "infamous rescuers."

Gordon Wragby was a good soldier and able sailor, and he knew he had not only to build a fort, but he had also to cache weapons in handy locations, where he could fall back and rally, or counterattack if defeated—and he had to do all this without alarming the cotters or Tatti and Cora.

It was to Stowell, his bosun, and Caruthers, the marine, that he divulged his compulsion to secrete arms, and to Noello. "Oh my, such wisdom, my lord. Pirates would ravish this flock by sea like wolves in a fold of sheep."

"Aye," Wragby had confided to the three of them. "I want the grenades charged with powder and primed, and hid, along with a supply of muskets and black powder."

"I have the hollow trees," Noello said.

"Good, and we'll have the fort as well—but we must never betray our fear."

"Never, Lord Gordon," the marine said, and Stowell and Noello nodded.

"We'll have a grand party," Tatti said, waking in her hammock at his side.

"Grand, indeed."

"Cora says you can marry us. And she'll sign her name as a witness."

"All women share a need to see other women triumph in marriage," Wragby said. "Your nurse will never fail us."

"I think you can do anything as long as you have your family behind you," Tatti said.

He stroked her hand in his slowly, as if to move too fast might miss some secret of her palm and fingers. "Family is life, and life is all we have." He lay looking up into the thatch above his hammock, where they rested in the cool afternoon air. "It took Cora and you to teach me that, in my middle age."

"No, Gordon, you always knew it."

"Perhaps, but the hardest thing to learn is what you always knew."

"Some people never learn." She took his hand.

"I lost my ship, but gained my life."

"Nay, you're a good sailor. The charts were wrong, and you were afraid to live." She stood and put her hands about his temples.

"Aye, the noble coward." He sighed. "I can only say I did not shrink from my terrors."

She set his hand on her belly, just under her navel. "It takes a brave man to put a child in a woman—our child."

He smiled. "I can't believe it, that we're to have a child." He drew her down atop him in his hammock, and felt her ribs against his, while he clung to her, and breathed in deep contentment.

All was hubbub about the compound, with men bending and tying reeds, to glue with barley flour the dyed canvas for the lanterns. People were up in the trees, arguing with those on the ground. Women moved purposefully from pots to examining articles of clothing against their outthrust legs, murmuring disapproval and looking to other women, who always disagreed and said, "It looks lovely."

While Tatti lay in the wide bed where they slept together in the cool night, Gordon Wragby slipped away with Stowell and his marine. The sun scorched his forehead as he tramped the savanna searching for a site for the fort, and he saw Noello come out of the forest, followed by a wild sheep.

"Hallo, my lord!"

"Noello!" Wragby waved his arm, and saw the sheep jump aside from a muddy bog and bound up a rise.

"Why, it's a spring under a knoll!" Wragby exclaimed as he ran forward. "Water and a field of fire! A perfect fort!"

"Why, the very place, my lord!" the marine said.

"Aye, we could fight from here forever, Captain." Stowell stood on the knoll, looking down at the bright spring that flowed in a short run to the wide creek, which divided the savanna from the woods of that place.

Wragby was swept with a sense of relief that he'd found a rise of earth that could encompass a pallisade, as well as a source of water. "Well, after our festivities, we must build a redoubt and keep."

"A stockade and blockhouse, they calls such in our colonies, Captain," Stowell said.

"A paling? Or stockade?" Wragby shrugged as his eye traveled the sloping ground from the military crest of the hill. "We'll build it under the skyline. Can't allow it to be silhouetted."

"Never, my lord." The marine's blue eyes glared across the empty savanna, as though measuring an immediate attack.

"Aye, time enough." Wragby grasped a stem of wild rose by his ankle, and walked toward the distant beach, where a party was awaiting him to honor his marriage.

XVII

The ethereal music of the dulcimer floated on the night air as a zephyr that cooled Tatti's mind. She heard the old English country melodies that often trilled in fluttering notes of the nightingale she had fallen asleep to throughout childhood. She knew that waiting for her outside their quarters were the cotters and that hope which the fifty-two men and women and children shared to bind them together. They had managed to arrive at that point in seven months as castaways and could laugh in joy at a wedding. Tatti lay in her hammock, staring at the shadows on the thatch. "My God, marriage? For me?" She sat up, calling, "Coral"

She lay back, waiting for her nurse. All had seemed plausible. She had fallen madly in love with Gordon Wragby on an enchanted island in a never-ending springtime. "Caution, who cares?" she'd said. "A child? I'm proud to carry his. In pure love." As long as it was their secret, Tatti could live it.

But they waited now to celebrate in public—and she wanted the nightingale, her childhood bed, Peter, dear Peter, and her pony on the moor, eating macaroons, on the banks of the River Deveron.

"I don't want to marry him!" She clutched Cora by the shoulders, when she came up.

"Why not, lass?" Cora settled her back.

"I don't love him."

"Said you did."

"I was crazy. A mad fantasy."

"They call that love—just that."

"It's not fair. I don't know him."

"I've seen 'em a lifetime, and he's far and above most."

"But don't you see? 'Tis Peter I love!" she shrieked, digging her fingernails into Cora's arm.

"Peter's not here, and besides, you've got his child within you."

"God, why didn't you stop me?" She flung herself back.

"We've got twenty-five men on this island, and you the only virgin suitable to bear child." Cora slipped her arms about Tatti's shoulders and held her close. "And Lord knows when we're to be rescued, if ever—so I let you go to the gentlest man I've ever knowed, and quieted down them lecher eyes I've noticed on you."

"But I love Peter, not Gordon!"

"Tatti, if a girl can love her father, she can love any other good man."

"What about Peter?"

"Lord Peter can wait, just like Lord Gordon waited—that's what he can do." She closed her eyes and nodded for emphasis.

"Then I marry him in public, forever?"

"Till death do ye part, and I want it writ down."

Tatti slumped back and groaned.

Gordon Wragby dressed carefully that evening. Leslie managed to find a pair of satin breeches and silk stockings not ruined by the storm; and she brushed his finest blue coat until it had an elegant sheen, and helped him club his hair, tying it in a soft black ribbon.

"Really, Leslie," Wragby said, peering into the mirror, "you've transformed me into a captain once more." He nodded at the slender, narrow face and wide frail mouth of his image. "But I think I'm better suited to a straw hat, such as Noello wears."

"Oh, my lord, you're too fine to wear tatters like us common folk." Leslie's soft eyes were wet with love as she ran them over his slender legs where she knelt.

"Leslie." He took her by her hands and raised her before him. "We're made of sterner sinews than our lace and satin covers, but I'm beholden to you."

"Beholden? My lord?"

"For your kindness, dear lady." He hugged her.

"Lord Gordon, every woman on this island

loves thee, and wants thee." Her eyes flooded and she ducked her face to hide them.

"No, I'm frail and lonely, and I live in a world of sorrow."

"We know, your lordship," Leslie said, interrupting Wragby. "Your lady understands you like we could never do, but we still can love you."

"There, there, now." He wiped her short, pert nose and then gently laid the linen handkerchief across her puddling eyes. "I don't understand myself, perhaps no man ever does, and a woman's purpose is to sort his confusion." He held the woman in his arms, knowing he did indeed love Leslie, sorrowful that their world was so complex that he could not take her in love without burdening her with a world of values he upheld, yet did not believe in. "Tatti and I must play a role, which is easy, for we love; yet without it, we all might perish as castaway savages."

"I understand you, my lord. I would only have you know I would love you."

"And I you would love, in honor, dear Leslie." He turned up her face and kissed her salt-wet lips.

Leslie clung about his neck, her ample bosom against his chest, her armpits moist with passion, one leg thrust firm between his knees.

"On your wedding night, I will live on your every breath. 'Tis my secret," Leslie said, releasing him.

"Never was a man more honored on this earth." He pressed her hand to his lips.

"My lord." She curtsied before him, then

went behind him to settle his stockings and fine pumps. "'Tis a wonder I washed out the salt and could save this silk."

Gordon walked out of their thatched cottage, leading Tatti on his arm, and into a gentle night, lit with glowing lanterns set about the tree limbs over their heads, and tracing the green sprays of feathered leaf images from the dark.

"Ah, a wonderland of beauty," Wragby said, looking up, while the whole company of survivors and sailors waited for them to take their seats at the end of the massive table. "Who would imagine we could dare come back to this, this wonderment of living?" He squeezed Tatti's hand.

Tatti nodded, and did not look at him. Noello was seated at the side of Cora, where two places waited for them.

"The Captain and his bride!" The marine shouted, and the company rose, some lifting gourd dippers, others pewter mugs, and some with bottles which had been melted into cups.

"The Captain!" they shouted, and elbows appeared amid the gush of drink, and heavy breath-catching between gulps.

Tatti sought Cora's eye, which searched hers, and saw her quandry. The wedding party was dressed in canvas, skin leggings, leather shoe-packs, tattered frocks. Some of the men wore sleeveless animal-hide vests, with the hair turned in for warmth, and were barefoot.

"And the Captain's lady!"

"Aye, the Countess Tat!"

Tatti slid into her place on the bench, surrounded with beaming faces and bright eyes. The children were seated at their own table in the midst of the adults, and it buoyed Tatti to see them, in their love for her. She avoided looking up at the convivial slurping that followed a round of toasting.

"The King!" Wragby said, raising one of the three wineglasses at the table, which sent the men scurrying to the kegs to refill their tankards.

"Boys, we can't be dry for the King," a sailor cried. "Oh, this Noello wine, it lifts a man's skull."

"Why, it restores my eyesight," his friend said.

After the King had been toasted, Wragby leant toward Cora and said, "I think we'd better eat." He sat back, the marine at his left, and nodded cheerfully to any compliment or word he heard, even when he did not understand.

Along the table, roast saddles of wild sheep were placed, swimming in red gravy and surrounded with fried breadfruit and sweet potatoes. Fresh tropical fruit decorated the steaming platters, and Tatti saw naked, hairy arms reach out with knives and fingers to carve and tear apart the food.

"A hearty appetite serves a happy soul." Gordon Wragby spoke under his breath to her, while they watched the piles of cooked flesh dissolve into shambles, to be washed down hungry gullets with heavy draughts of mango wine.

"I never cared to be a spectacle," Tatti whispered.

"Nor I, yet we must do our duty." He toyed with his food and sipped the last of the Madeira.

Tatti emptied her goblet, and felt the wine sink through her body to tingle between her legs.

"That'll be enough wine, my lass," Cora said, taking the goblet. "Till we have your young'un."

Tatti clutched Wragby's hand, suddenly smitten with a grand warmth of profound love and a sense of well-being in his presence. "Forgive me for being such a ninny—I love you."

"Oh, well, I can always wait till you remember, if you forget."

"Cora, I love you." Tatti whispered to her nurse, who nodded and stroked her hand, out of sight of the company.

Noello's round soft eyes searched the loud, drinking and munching company of men and women, the faces sheening in sweat across the forehead and hair-stubbled cheeks. The women sat among the company, as well as served it, all of them careworn, and occasionally a smile brightened their eyes. Noello turned his face back to Tatti and the Captain, and smiled silently, as if the shift of a leaf in summer light.

"My lady is like a child," Noello said, leaning across Cora to speak, his eyes on Tatti's loose hair that reached to her hips.

"Oh, Noello, you alone showed us the way." Tatti slipped her hand over the rubbery skin of his rough hands, and felt the uneven knuckles and bone beneath.

"I give you Noello!" Caruthers shouted, jumping to his feet.

"No, no, please." Noello shrank down, clutching at Cora's arm.

"There, there now. They mean no harm." Cora set her hands on Noello to reassure him, while a sea of faces beamed at the hermit.

"Perhaps we should dance," Wragby said to Caruthers when it appeared the party had gorged itself on food and drink. " 'Twill improve the digestion."

"My lord, I want the wedding troth pledged," Cora said, leaning forward, and sliding two books before the Captain. " 'Tis time to write it in this book—the ship's Bible. 'Tis water-stained, my lord, but 'tis still the Bible."

Wragby was caught by the dry relentless persistence of the Highland woman. He nodded. "I would not have it otherwise." He lay open the Book of Common Prayer, ruffling past the burial service he had read a hundred times and more over dead sailors who were buried at sea in canvas, with a shot at their feet and the last stitch taken through their nose to be quite sure they were dead. "To be wed is to be whole."

"Man and woman are whole in the Lord." Cora nodded at the Bible.

"No other way, dear Cora." Wragby stood, helping Tatti to her feet, while the whole company fell silent, enveloping the two of them with their riveting eyes which glistened feverishly in the lanterns overhead.

"Hold them for us," Wragby said, nodding

174

at the books. Cora lifted them and faced him and Tatti.

Wragby's quick fingers settled upon the open pages he wanted, and he heard his voice recite the elegant words of English prose, uniting a man and woman into life through marriage. He lifted his eyes, and saw the company of men and women, enraptured by the divine admonitions which he read in cultured words: "to cleave in the spirit as well as the flesh, to comfort in sorrow and to share all joy, and to bless each day as a gift to love," until the flesh would create what the spirit had ordained, and the child was born as visible proof of the holy bond of matrimony.

He glanced at Tatti, and lost the rhythm of his words when he saw the hazel eyes piercing his very being, and caught the radiant love in the exquisite girl.

"Thank you," he whispered. "It was so lonely before I found you."

"Aye, and Gordon, 'twas you who taught me to love." She touched the back of his hand. "When I'd forgot."

"Yes." He nodded, as Cora placed the books upon the table. "I think we must live to remember never to forget we're alive—in thee are God and life, and I would have none else."

"Oh, Gordon." She raised her hand to hide her tears.

"I want it writ down," Cora said, setting her open hand atop the Scripture.

Wragby seized the quill pen and jabbed it into the inkwell, and wrote their names and date and place of marriage. "His Majesty's Isle,

Bermuda." He handed the goose quill to Cora, saying, "As witnesses, Glencora Lundee, of Skarra Firth, and George Caruthers, Royal Marines."

"Three cheers for Lord and Lady Ravendale!" the marine bellowed, and the company stood, breaking into laughter as the music sprang out in a rondel.

"Hurrah! Hurrah! Hurrah!"

Tatti wept into her handkerchief while the quill was scrawled onto the New Testament and handed about. The whole company had shifted into weaving lines and isolated squares with occasional individuals alone, all swaying or dancing to the music.

XVIII

The loud groan of a woman in labor awakened Tatti. She splashed water on her face, and walked out of their thatched quarters, toward the pavilion, brushing her hair.

"It's Caroline, her time's come," a child said.

"Oh, Janie, thank you." Tatti hurried, holding her head sideways to free the length of her hair while she brushed from underneath.

In moments she was in the women's section of the wide thatched building. Caroline's labor had taken her to that point where she alone confronted the massive forces within her body, triggered by some divine ordination, which pinned her to the pallet on the table where she lay.

"Not yet time," Margene said, where the loose-framed Highland woman waited with Cora. Tatti joined them.

"Will she be all right?" Tatti asked.

"Aye, she's gaunt, but she's got wide hips."

The scream commenced as a slow wail, that rose to a high pitch and seemed to satisfy the women who moved about the struggling figure who arched her spine and trembled.

"Born for trouble, we be," Margene said matter-of-factly. "Especially us women."

Tatti saw the triumphant gleam in Margene's eyes as she shared the travail of another woman, and realized the childbirth had united the women with a singular purpose that they alone could share, quite apart from men.

"Everything seems to be done that can be done," Tatti said.

"Aye, in time, 'twill come."

"Cora," Tatti whispered. "Is that—is that what I'll be like?"

Cora turned her by her hand and led her outside. "Nay, lass, you're better nourished and you've had no grief to suffer. And your hips are wider." She set her hands onto Tatti's hips, clucking with approval. "No trouble, my bonnie."

"Thank God for that," Tatti said, hearing the screams coming with a measured frequency.

Tatti went with Wragby as he led the band of sailors and Caruthers onto the savanna. "I'll be back," she said to Cora.

The men were sweating in the morning sun, straining to carry the long pole which

178

slung the cannon. Their legs went in quick running steps to keep under their burdened shoulders that held the sling-timber.

"We'll get our impedimenta onto the building site, then start our dig." Wragby's words were brisk, and Tatti realized the fort was not only a necessity for their security, but also something for him to do.

"That's a marvelous place for a fort," Tatti said.

"We have trees to fell, shingles to split, wood we can soak so it won't burn."

"Burn? From what, Gordon?" The marine waited with Wragby.

"Burning arrows soaked in pitch." Wragby's blue eyes were calmer than she'd ever before noticed. "My love, it is my duty to expect and prepare for every calamity, while we pray for deliverance."

Tatti searched his eyes, and saw the grief that comes with wisdom in middle age, and she suddenly felt sorry for her husband. "There are no Indians, Gordon." She spoke gently.

"Greek fire and the crossbow were used before Christ." His voice was firm.

"I'll come and help," Tatti said, "as soon as Caroline has her child."

"'Twill take us all before we're done," he said, and turned to follow his men out across the sun-burned field.

Tatti watched them move in a group of figures that got smaller until they went out of sight in the tall grass, then walked back to the pavilion.

There was a bond among the women as

they hovered round the table. Margene stood inside the knees, cooing to herself, while Caroline flung her head from side to side, the cords on her neck strained taut.

"Good woman!"

"Here it comes!"

Tatti turned back in time to see a wet, slithering shape swinging by the feet, its head red and mucus-smeared.

"Smack it!" a woman said.

A hand hit the tiny rump, and Tatti heard a mewing sound as the child gasped for air.

"We got another passenger," Margene said, breaking into laughter. "Go tell the Captain."

Tatti walked out into the bright sunlight, knowing they would live, and listening to the excited voices of the women, as they lay the child on Caroline's belly and set it at her breasts to suck.

"The milk don't come down till the third day," she heard Margene say.

"A girl! We've got us another girl!"

The cool air off the ocean restored Tatti, from the sweat and naked travail which had engulfed the emigrant women. "Oh, Lord, I don't want that for myself," Tatti said to herself, shaking back her hair, and ran across the savanna toward where she knew Gordon Wragby waited for her, while he worked with his men. "I've been scared enough already."

Gordon was working with his men at the edge of the pond.

"A girl," she said.

"Good." He nodded.

"Gordon, will you love me when I'm like that?"

"More than now, and now I adore you."

"I don't want to scream, not with all those people around."

"Likely you won't."

"My mother said I came immediately. Perhaps I'll be the same."

"No doubt." He slipped his arm about her and kissed her moist temple where small strands of hair curled on her skin.

"Those women all seemed delighted." Tatti spoke with dismay.

"Yes. Women hold the civilization together in their common purpose to serve life—if they are women."

"And not men?"

"Oh, we serve women—that's our purpose."

"I know you know men best," Tatti said. "But it frightens me to think we should ever need a fort."

"My pessimism." Wragby took a cool drink, and felt the refreshing taste envelop his lungs and body with a kinship to itself in clear water.

Gordon had a vague fear he could not quite describe, of some evil force that might come over the sea and land among this handful of people he had come to love, and desolate them. The fort was his answer to this fear, and he masked his obsession to build it behind his role as a tolerant aristocrat, persistent in his need to command, and to be humored as such.

Gordon sensed that the people respected him, after living with his forbearance and loyalty to them, and his insistence that they respect their ancient values and live despite their sorrow. He knew the survivors saw Tatti as an extension of himself, and in the two of them, their own survival. The fort was his final obligation to life, to England, and to his people, after Tatti. And Tatti was paradise incarnate.

"I never expected my life to be so exciting," Wragby said, walking along the row of holes where they were erecting a palisades, or "stockade" as some of the sailors called it.

The "keep" within the stockade, or the "blockhouse" as those men who'd been to the American colonies called it, was taking shape slowly, rising tier on tier of massive hewn logs, adzed and squared, and towering over the palisaded stockade.

"We'll want gunports at the top of our blockhouse," Wragby said. "I'll want to be able to fire the cannon in any direction."

"Aye, my lord," Caruthers said.

"Yes, I want to be able to lay grapeshot onto the spring, and wherever else we choose." Wragby turned and looked to the distant sea. "And we're out of range of shipboard cannon."

The bosun and the Marine gaped, admiring the shrewd military calculations of their captain.

Wragby settled a drawing board on his

knees and sketched out the details of the fort and the land elevations about it.

"I want you each to understand how the fort is to be defended and how the cannon to be served," he said, not looking up as he sketched out the illustrations. "A fortification slows an assault with an obstruction, leaving the defender a clear moment to fire." He glanced up to see Stowell's brow knit in puzzlement.

"You shoot him while he's trying to climb the wall," he explained patiently.

"Oh, I understand, my lord."

"Good. Now, our cannon is our *pièce de résistance*." Wragby drew flourishing trees about the borders of the plan. "By that we mean, we fire the cannon loaded with grapeshot and canister, like a mammoth blunderbuss, which is absolutely devastating, if we can channel a massed assault we can cover in one salvo——"

"Gordon," Tatti said, interrupting, "you sound as though you enjoy battle."

"Tatti, I was very good at what I never wanted to be." His head tilted quizzically, his lips twisting in dismay. "My lies were my greatest triumph, and wretched slaughter my finest honor."

She searched his face in the stillness of his words.

"I dismissed my duty as folly in private, while I did it in public. Only now that I've lost my ship, and have no future, can I really believe in good—our combined survival. Thus the fort." He waved his hand at the half-finished structure. "Here, study the plans."

Stowell and Caruthers gravely took the sketching from the Captain and studied them.

XIX

Tatti could not believe that she would actually bring forth another life from within her. It was apparent to her—from her labored step, from her difficulty turning over in bed, from the tiredness that sagged down on her legs as she got up—all that was obvious, but she was unable to comprehend it. She had seen and felt the baby kick and move within her womb.

"A lively young'un," Cora said, her head tilted and ear pressed to Tatti's body. "And a boy, I do believe."

"Oh, Cora, how could you know?"

"Lord Gordon, he's frail for a man, but he's fearsome in his manliness. A strong man gets a boy."

"I'll take what comes," Tatti whispered.

"Aye, we takes what the Lord sends, and no questions asked nor no goods returned." Cora drew down Tatti's smock and lifted the light sheet over her legs.

In the last days of her confinement Tatti was swept with moments of doubt, doubt that she had done right. She had led Gordon on, yielded to him to arouse him, and when afire, had excited him ever more, until Gordon had lost his mind to hope and heart to love. Gordon had spent his life, and no great adventure seemed left him, until she had changed that, and brought him back into the world of the flesh and carnal desire. It frightened her in her pregnancy that their love had been so carnal, burning their passion down to a trembling ash; perhaps their bliss was all they had to bind them. It was so absolutely ecstatic, it did not seem possible anything else could exist between them.

"Gordon, I'm sorry if we did too much," she whispered in the hazy light of dawn when she heard his faint breathing at her side.

"Sorry, how?" His voice was gentle.

"Oh, all the doubts—you know as a woman, I led you on."

"Nay." His voice eased. "I followed you, panting for manna from heaven like a starved soul for salvation."

"That's just it. 'Twasn't fair."

"I am well pleased."

"Gordon?"

"Yes?"

"Do you love me?"

"Good Lord, yes—what a question." He

flung his arm out on the bed in mock desperation.

"Well, it's all so different now."

"Tatti—" he rolled up on one elbow to
seek her eyes, laying one hand on her swollen
belly. "When you love a woman, to hear her
breathe at night in sleep is to listen to the
voice of God—that is love."

"Oh, Gordon, I'm sorry I asked." She began
to cry.

"Oh, Lord, no crying now." He rolled
out of the bed onto his feet. "We'll feel better
if we have tea, and watch the dawn come over
the ocean."

"Yes, I'd like that." Tatti raised her hands
to him to be pulled upright.

He slipped her fur-lined sandals on her
bare feet, and leaned down to kiss her child's
distention within her. "My future, my hope, my
love and life, all lie in your womb."

"Oh, Gordon." She reached out to pull him
to her face to kiss him, despite the unwieldy
burden of her pregnancy. "I love you."

By an intuitive sense of the force within
her body, Tatti knew the childbirth was near.
Her thoughts turned from Gordon to her mother, and it was Cora whose voice assured her.
"Dear kin," Tatti would whisper, easing backward in her bed. "How I'd love to see Skarra
once more."

"Bye and bye, we're for Skarra," Cora said.

Her mind was full of Skarra—of her days
with her grandfather, the Earl of Skarra, a very
tall old man who walked with long legs and

187

held her hand when she lost her balance in the furrows of the garden. It was always wet in Scotland, but a quiet wet, not the quick torrents of rain that were carried on the wind, across the night air of the south Atlantic.

"Cora, how nice it would be to put in a garden again," she said.

Cora sat on a rough wicker stool at her side. "Aye, a warm sun and some bottomland, and we'd have a harvest."

Tatti remembered how her father and mother would lie abed at night, talking with the renewed vigor in their voices that seemed to come upon them when home in the old rock and stone country house of Skarra. She would slip into their room, warmed by the gold and red shadows that flickered on the wall from their fireplace, making her parents' bed seem huge in the dark. She would hold up her hands, and her father would drag her up into bed with them and she would lie silent, listening to them talk.

"I do think you can live forever if you can hear love in the voices of your parents," Tatti said. "You know, those low muffled things your parents said, but you never remembered; and all was right on earth from it, and what they said did not matter."

"Aye," Cora said, leaning forward comfortably on the stool. "Like when you could hear echo sounds inside your mother's bosom when she nursed you on her lap, and you could hear her heartbeat when she spoke."

"Oh, Cora, how could you remember when you've lived so long?"

"Tush, lass, a body never forgets." Cora set her hand into the hair at Tatti's temple. "We're all children, forever. We just get better at lying and hiding the tears."

"We couldn't live without the memories of our parents." Tatti was pensive.

"That's why we have parents."

"Without our past, we've lost our future," Tatti said. "If we did not love our parents, we cannot love our children, and we're dead already."

Tatti could remember the spring coming in Scotland, the haunting light that shone down through the mists over the firths, so that a radiant haze softened the air. After the winter, it drew them to the fields, and onto the moors, and into the garden, as if by magic. She could see her grandfather bending over his turning fork, the vast work shoes laced to his feet and his narrow trews giving his legs a stick look.

"The plow bruises the earth," he would say, watching the ponderous Clydesdale horses draw the plow along its furrow. They were so delicate as they leaned backward over their hind legs to turn in the walled garden.

"We all loved the earth in Scotland," Cora said, "likely because we had so little of it."

"Whatever, it was us," Tatti said. She could see her mother and father waiting deferentially for her grandmother and grandfather, who were trudging about the open earth, still moist from harrowing, to say it was fit for planting. It seemed that Skarra was muddy boots and green yew trees among stone, and her grand-parents' labored steps crossing the kitchen garden.

"I believe 'twill bear seed," Lord Skarra would say, and the whole kitchen staff would swarm out like a band of disheveled gulls, dragging sacks and prodding-sticks and striking with hoes, "placing the seed."

As the summer advanced, Tatti walked in the shade of her grandfather, who grew more dour as he aged, offering his opinion to her when no one else listened, not caring any longer to talk to anyone except his grandchild.

"Aye, Miss Tatti," he would say, "if we Scots could stand in our gardens with naked feet, we wouldn't need to beat a damn golf ball around the moor."

Lord Skarra had a great contempt for the native game of Scotland, and hoped they could export it forever to England. "The English should pay for our vices—they've bought everything else." He bent down over his gaunt hips and rustled his gnarled fingers through the leaves of a strawberry plant, and plucked a vast red fruit. "Here, let me see that little red mouth."

When she opened her mouth, he wouldn't put in the berry until she had closed her eyes. "If ye canna' see it, 'twill surprise your pretty tongue with delight when it comes."

Tatti would follow him about the garden, closing her eyes and throwing back her head whenever he came close, always so dour, with hands of bent iron rods it seemed, and yet so gentle she adored him from his muddy boots to his worn face and white-thatched head.

It was a tense, sweet pang that pulsed just under her ribs, it seemed, and toward her back. And she knew of an instant it was the child. "Cora, it's here," she whispered.

"Good. 'Twill come in its own time." Cora's voice was in the form that hovered at the side of the bed, and it reassured Tatti.

"Were you awake?"

"No, but I heard you anyway."

"Gordon?"

"Let him sleep." Cora's bare feet swished on the adzed boards underfoot. "We'll tell him at dawn."

The night lifted with a false haze, and Tatti heard the quick flutter of the small doves scrambling just outside her door. The morning came strong, and Tatti realized the sun was up from the flooding light reflected from the sand of the beach and against the screens of her room.

"How do you feel?" It was Gordon, and she felt his hand across her forehead.

"I'm caught at last by life."

"I'm proud of you." He leaned down and kissed her lips, and tasted the drawn breath where the strength in the woman goes to her womb, while all else ebbs.

She touched his fingers with hers, but stretched up her chin to clear her throat to breathe as a contraction enfolded her belly and enveloped her womb, and drew to a piercing thrust deep in her loins, and she gasped and parted her legs.

"Gordon," she whispered as the spasm passed, to assure him she loved him. Yet somehow Tatti wanted to be alone, away from men, able to be swirled toward the inevitable event that divided her now from all other people.

"So brave," Gordon said, seeing her face break into sweat.

"I'll not scream." Tatti flung her face away from him toward the screen. Gordon sensed her wish to isolate herself, and Cora moved in beside the rough-hewn bed.

All day Tatti lay enduring the pains that came in a regular sequence, and never uttering a sound. People came and went whom she ignored, letting the sweet pain within her belly drive her ever closer to the verge of life. Still she could not imagine what the child would be like, and was content to let her soul follow her body as it obeyed the life forces that gripped it.

Tatti could sense the evening in the cool ocean air playing over her sweating temples.

"Cora, how are things going?"

"The way they should." Cora's voice was both assertive and final.

"Why doesn't it come?"

" 'Twill come—the firstborn always seems to take longest."

Tatti saw the wavering lights from the tallow lamps, and knew the day had passed into night. The pains had become a scarring rack that moved in relentless spasms down her flanks, to make her torso tremble and her bowels strain, and parted her legs.

She felt the wet towels Cora laid upon her lips, to suck the water, and the cooling cloths other hands set across her forehead and temples. Still she would not scream, because her travail was a compact between herself and God and life.

"Cora," she whispered, licking her dry lips, which had cracked in her labored daylong breathing.

"Lass?"

"Have the women wash their hands."

" 'Tis done, Tatti."

Tatti nodded, knowing the child was near. Her legs had drawn up at the knees and parted, and she could feel her whole body heave to turn itself inside out to launch the child at each contraction. Still Tatti could not believe she would truly have a baby—it was much too much to ever dare to see and do. "The impossible," she groaned to herself in a heaving spasm.

"Child?" Cora whispered.

She flung her heaving bosom upward, arching her spine and tearing at the tabletop, digging her fingers into whatever arm or flesh or cloth she could feel, to drive her body to give out the child, and collapsed.

"Try one more time." It was Cora, at her temple.

Tatti flung back her head to get her breath and swallowed, and waited for the next pulsing sweep down her naked flanks.

The pain was on her, her throat seared with flame, and she felt her body rise off the tabletop, arching her spine, and a sweeping sense of time passing out of her belly in a contented warmth between her legs.

"Good girl!" She heard Cora and the excited cry of another woman.

"Ah!" Tatti gasped in a divine sense of absolute triumph at groveling in total life.

"Push! Tatti, push down!" Cora's words fell onto her ears, as though hollow, from another world.

"The head's clear!" A woman who was between her legs spoke matter-of-factly.

"Hold her belly." Cora moved away from Tatti's head to stand between her knees. "I want to suck out its mouth."

The sweep of life out of her loins engulfed Tatti, and she was suddenly breathing full lungfuls of air.

"We have it—a boy!" Cora held up a twisted wet image.

"Oh, Gordon!" Tatti flung back her head. "Gordon?"

"On her belly's where he goes." Cora's hands and the wet child were settled on her stomach, and she heard a small wail.

"Alive!" Tatti cried. "Gordon, he's alive."

Gordon took her hand in his and pressed it firmly to his lips, and hid his eyes. When he looked up she saw the tears. "Tatti—thank you for our child."

"Oh, Gordon!" She smiled at him. "I got you a son, *your son.*"

"Thank you." He hid his face in her loose

194

hair at the side of her head. "Thank you for the life I'd never dared to hope for."

"Put him to her breast, and let him suck," Cora spoke in a loud voice.

"Milk don't come down till the third day," a woman said. It was Margene.

"We suckle the baby at birthing," Cora said, and Tatti felt the life at her breast that she still could not believe was true—that she had actually done it.

"Let me see my baby," Tatti said.

It surprised her to see the small naked human shape with its wet arms flopping over Cora's breast, its tiny face screwed up in wails that came from a wide mouth that was pink gums and no teeth. Cora's hand was wiping dry the small head and body with a soft cloth. "Pretty young'un, he is."

"Put him on me," Tatti said.

She closed her eyes when the slight body was laid on her bosom. It came as a second of divine exultation that she had done the impossible. She had obeyed life, and done her duty, and she had a child to prove it.

"Put him to my breast," she said.

She felt the small body settled at her nipple, and her arms came up to cuddle life into the child by feeding it her milk. She opened her eyes and saw the exquisitely formed little face, with the delicate small mouth open, and the fragile little tongue trembling as it wailed. She nudged the tiny head onto the nipple, and heard the cry stifle, and felt the tongue flutter and press against her distended breast. "Oh, I felt him—Gordon, he's hungry."

195

She turned her head as Gordon raised his face, and wiped the tears from his eyes. "I never thought I'd ever live to see the day," he whispered.

"Did I please you?" Tatti's eyes flamed with an ecstatic light.

"As no woman ever has before, within my ken."

"Aye, next to your mother?"

"Aye." He leaned in and kissed her. "Whatever life I have, 'twas you that brought it back." He stroked her face gently, and kissed her temple, and went out into the first light of the dawn.

BOOK THREE
Bonabombo

XX

Tatti woke one morning nearly a year later to strange cries of great excitement in a foreign tongue. "It's Noello, my lord!" said George Caruthers, popping his head and shoulders into their cottage. "He's gone batty, and there's a strange ship nearing shore!"

"A ship?" Gordon reached for his jacket as he sat up in the dawn.

"Noello's all Portegee and Froggy, and he's crying about death—plumb touched." The Royal Marine touched his temple affably.

"Any colors?" Gordon was out of bed, dragging on canvas breeches and a shirt, slinging a baldric over his shoulder with his massive cavalry pistol.

"Too dark to see yet, my lord."

Tatti was at Gordon's side as the morning came bright on the sea, and behind them, they could hear the forest alive with the flutter of singing birds. On the horizon where they watched was a low silhouetted corvette, glistening in black paint and sinister in its sharp movement over the sea.

"'Tis the *Santiago de Mort!*" Noello cried from the Spyglass Hill, where they had searched the horizon for rescue for nearly two years. "The *Sacred Death!*"

Gordon Wragby kept the schooner-rigged ship in his Italian glass, marveling at her quick maneuvering. Her bowsprit threw a graceful wave to leeward, and she heeled to starboard as her stem came into the wind, and turned through the wind without luffing her sails.

"A corsair," Stowell said.

"Aye." Gordon nodded. "I want our cannons fresh charged, primed, and loaded with canister and grapeshot." He did not take the glass from his eye as he spoke.

Caruthers jogged off, leading four sailors.

"Provision the fort with every variety of fresh produce and meat, and stuff the larders."

The women did not answer him, but stared in stunned disbelief at the marauding vessel now sailing broadside along their coast. Gordon lowered his glass. "Cora, did you hear me? Margene?"

"Oh, sir, right away."

"Get the children, and keep them close."

"Aye, my lord." The women bustled away, their voices hushed in fright.

"Stowell, you will keep spikes in your belt,

200

and a hammer, to spike our field cannons if we fall back."

"Aye, my lord."

"Can't have our own cannons firing on our fort." Gordon spoke to himself. "Noello, who's her captain?"

"Bonabombo, my lord."

"Bonabombo?"

"An Englishman. He killed and skinned a Nigerian king, and nailed his black hide to his masts, and took his name, for luck."

"Remarkable," Gordon said, suddenly very calm, and noticing the black oily sheen on the two masts of the schooner. "Are those human skins on the poles, do you suppose?" He handed the glass to Stowell.

"Wretched man!" Noello danced from one foot to the other.

"I don't know about the hides, my lord," Stowell said, handing Gordon the spyglass. "But he's got a skull for a figurehead."

Gordon took the glass and saw the glaring leer of a skull's teeth breaking in the sea under the bowsprit. "So he has. Brighton?"

"My lord?"

"Run and tell the marine to double the charge of grapeshot."

"Double the charge of grapeshot!" The sailor took off in a hard dash toward the knolls where Gordon had hidden salvaged cannon.

"Thank God the vegetation grows overnight on this island," Gordon said, glancing toward the more prominent knolls where he had spent months dragging salvaged cannons into hidden redoubts. He had buried them in live foliage and fresh vines to cover every likely promentory and cove where a landing party might come ashore near the wreck of the *Daphne*. He felt a surge of triumph that he had not left his people naked before their enemies.

"What will they do?" Tatti said, clutching the baby to her bosom.

"I don't know, my love." He put down the glass, and they watched the slim dark ship schoon boldly along the beach, her men clambering in the rigging and on deck and in the shroud-chains to stare ashore.

"There's a dark evil about that ship," Tatti whispered and shuddered, for the sails were coffee-stained and the deck painted ochre.

"Fit for night attack, my lord," Noello said.

"Fly the Navy Jack of England, Ireland, Scotland, and Wales," Gordon said, nodding toward the pavilion, "but no flags on our fort or arms."

"No colors on our arms!" Stowell cried, gesturing to a sailor to show the Union Jack.

"I want our fortress hidden till we fire," Gordon said flatly. "Twenty-four of us against two hundred, I dare say." He glanced at Stowell for the bosun's appraisal as the marine returned. "How many do we face?" He gestured at the ship that was easing its sails by luffing, to slow the ship.

"I've counted two hundred and eight," Cora said, staring at the ship with her hands over her eyes to shade them.

"Quite sure, Cora?" Gordon said.

"Quite, unless more be hidden below deck."

"The Jolly Roger! My lord!" Stowell shouted as the black flag bearing an immense white skull erupted at the gaff line of her mainsail, and flew defiantly in the crisp morning.

"Well, it's slavery for us, plunder for them and rape for the women, if they prevail," Gordon said, closing his Italian spyglass with a rich popping sound. "It's a pack of wolves in a henhouse."

Tatti felt her intestines roil within her, and she gasped for her breath, even more terrified when she realized how fragile a man Gordon was, and that he had an exquisitely clear picture of what lay ahead. He was so utterly calm, almost insanely calm, because that ship was death.

"All cannons loaded with grapeshot, my lord." The marine saluted.

"Good. Always double the charge of grape when in doubt, Caruthers."

"My lord."

Tatti noticed that the easy familiarity between Gordon and the sailors and marine had suddenly vanished. They seemed swept up in a military esprit, dashing to run, and saluting and repeating commands, and licking their lips while they watched the ship bear down upon them.

Gordon strode down onto the white beach in the broad sunlight, with Caruthers and Brighton at his side, dressed in the grayed remnants of his naval uniform. The Royal Marine wore a red tunic, but walked barefoot, and the sailor was in canvas drawers. They were armed with pistols and cutlasses, and Brighton had two blunderbusses slung on baldrics that cut deep into his naked, muscular brown shoulders. Caruthers had a Jaeger rifle.

"Too lovely a morning," Gordon said, rather more to himself than the ratings. "Much too lovely to quarrel."

They stood in a small group and watched the corvette tack rapidly twice, swinging her booms as she rounded the wreck of the *Daphne*, then luff into the wind with her helm a'lee. They saw her anchor plunge loose into the sea as her sails collapsed in folds.

"A tight ship," Brighton said.

Gordon nodded and watched two small boats flop into the sea, and saw nearly two score men drop into them, feather out their oars, and pull immediately for the beach.

"On the fantail, my lord." The marine spoke quietly.

They saw a group of men aiming a breech-loading carronade toward them. "We've shown no hostile gesture," Gordon said.

An elongated bloom of white smoke puffed out the small cannon and blew sideways. *Whooom!*

"That ain't no peaceful gesture, my lord," Brighton said.

Kawfluff! The cannonball spewed a moist spray of sand that kicked up forty feet short of where they stood on the beach.

"Damn fools," Gordon said. The buccaneers were so contemptuous of them that they had not even landed to parley before falling on them to slaughter.

"They're pulling directly for the cove, my lord," Brighton said.

Gordon watched the rowboats ride up across the combers and beach themselves in a swift motion. A dozen men jumped free and waded quickly through the surf toward them.

"Their powder's wet," the marine said.

"Aye." The carronade vanished behind another blossom of white smoke, and three men fired muskets at them from the second boat. The shot skipped out of the sand in a broad spray that reached Gordon, and richocheted up the beach toward the knolls where Stowell waited at the hidden cannons.

Brighton caught his breath. "They ain't shootin' worse, my lord."

"Aye." Gordon nodded, knowing a small target being fired upon from a rolling platform is really quite safe. "I must discover their intentions."

"Begging your pardon, my lord, but their intentions is clear as daylight to us common folk."

"Quite," Gordon said drily. He wanted to lure the men off the beached cutters to within range of his hidden field guns.

They watched the sea rovers spread out in a line abreast of thirty-eight men, who advanced rapidly toward where Gordon stood. He raised his speaking trumpet, and called out, "Halt, in the name of the King!"

A man dropped to one knee and laid his

arm across his bent leg to steady his aim. The pistol shot whirred the air before Gordon's lips, and it annoyed him that he had risked his life before he could execute his plan.

"Fire your German rifle, and retire as I do," he snapped. He stepped aside as the marine dropped onto his belly, and heard the hammer cock. He watched the eager, tense muscles in Caruthers' calves as his spread-out legs dug in their toes for a rest. "Get the big fellow with the pistol." Gordon knelt at Caruthers's side.

Whoom! The Jaeger rifle thundered across the beach, blasting the sand into a feathery trace, and Gordon thrilled to hear the moist sound of a heavy bullet striking flesh and crushing bone.

"Got the bastard!" Brighton shouted, crouching under the smoke cloud to see.

"Come!" Gordon lifted the barrel of the Jaeger as Caruthers jumped to his feet, and they jogged up toward the knolls, hearing the plop of bullets knocking up sand around them. "That'll slow them, and they'll come in a bunch, I hope," Gordon said, well pleased. He was suddenly aware of how dry his mouth had become.

In moments he had dropped down into a leaf-and-vine-covered redoubt, where Stowell and his sailors waited. "Water," he said to Tatti, taking a gourd to put to his lips. When he swallowed, Gordon realized he was very frightened, for his throat was absolutely parched.

"Thank God we trained the cotters on the cannons." He gasped and looked for the marine and Stowell. "We've killed their officer, so they'll lose discipline and bunch up."

They watched the buccaneers milling about a large man. He was apparently severely wounded, because his legs dangled their booted feet in the sand, dragging furrows as they carried him.

"You got him good," Brighton whispered to Caruthers, who crouched next to him watching from a hiding place in the foliage.

"Dare say he's not their captain," Gordon said. They had only a landing party to deal with, and later they would have the whole ship's company upon them.

"We can fight 'em open," Cutler said, his blue eyes fearless as he stood and stared about at the small band of sailors and cotters who knelt in concealment.

"Down, you fool!" Caruthers said. "You'll betray our hide."

"I ain't afraid of 'em—why, we're twenty-four agin thirty-eight——"

"Down, before I hit ye!" Cora grabbed the front of the skin jacket and dragged Cutler to his knees. When he struggled to rise, Gordon heard a fist smashed into a mouth, making a squishing noise of wet and gristle.

"Cotter, his Lordship gives the orders," Caruthers growled, rubbing his skinned knuckles as the hapless cotter spat out a tooth.

"Dear God, I've got enough to fight, coming up the beach, without another fight behind me," Gordon said irritably, knowing the emigrants and civilians would likely hurl themselves away with impetuous anger, wasting their strength before coming to grips with the massive forces lurking beyond them. He saw the bewildered, lost eyes of Cutler, whom he respected and liked, and he felt sorry for him. "Cutler, dear God, let me fight the battle the way I must, to wear down and kill as many as possible, to weaken their greater strength."

"I thought we could take 'em, my lord."

"Aye, the score or so on the beach, but what of the two hundred on the ship?"

"I ain't afeared, my lord."

"I've never doubted your bravery, but I can afford no losses. The enemy has more men, so they can lose more."

Cutler's eyes softened in comprehension, and he looked down to hide his embarrassment as Cora handed him a wet towel. "Suck it, man, and ye'll have your fight bye and bye."

"They're a'comin', my lord," Stowell whispered.

Gordon swung about. The band of rovers had set down their leader, who was stretched out in the sand, with a man at his body. With a man at each cutter, Gordon saw he had a chance to slay the thirty-four who had reloaded and primed their weapons.

Whoomm! They saw the carronade on the schooner's fantail fire, and heard the shot rip through the thatched roof of the pavilion, erupting an explosion of straw out of the top of the building, though no hole was visible once the chaff had settled.

"Thatching beats all." Cora spoke matter-of-factly.

"Ah," Gordon said. The cannon fire seemed

to give the sea rovers courage once more. They were looking up to the pavilion and the three fortified knolls where he had hidden his guns. He saw them begin walking in a group toward the uncertain silence where all seemed to have vanished. Only the English Union Jack moved, fluttering in the wind that blew through the tree limbs and over the savanna.

"They sense a trap, but they don't know where," Gordon muttered in Brighton's ear. "Now you scurry on your belly to the two other redoubts, and tell them to fire only after I fire."

"Only after us'uns, my lord."

"Aye, only *after* us'uns."

Brighton slipped out, and Gordon turned to watch the band of men come up over the sand.

"A goat, my lord," Higgins said, pointing to a loose goat, running free with a strap about its neck.

"Noello's released all the animals," Tatti whispered.

"Aye, he would." Gordon nodded, glad he'd ordered the children and most of the women into the fort. Some of the women had refused to go and demanded to fight beside the men; Gordon deferred to their request, knowing the men and women would fight more savagely if standing together in the fray. Besides, Gordon had long ago given up disagreeing with women.

The babe at Tatti's bosom began to whimper.

"Suckle him, lass," Cora said, caressing the little boy's body into her arm. The china-blue eyes looked up at Cora, and he smiled, showing his baby teeth. Cora settled his body in Tatti's arms. "Dear little Gordie." Her hand stroked the curls.

Gordon watched the pirates gather together cautiously, their pistols drawn and outthrust, their cutlasses tucked in their armpits. Their eyes searched ahead of them, peering at the silent pavilion and the copse of cedar trees and palmettos that hummed with a gentle wind.

"I don't like it, mateys!" Gordon heard one of the buccaneers say. "Hit ain't natural—swallowed up, they is."

"We seen the women—they got women," another voice said.

Gordon could see the stubble on the faces of the men, and caught the glint of sunlight reflecting in the whites of their eyes. He looked at Stowell who held a smoldering punt in his single hand. "Not yet," Gordon whispered and nudged the hefty naked shoulders of his men to shift the cannon slightly. "A hair and a half to your right." He set his hand on the muscular backs to assure by feel that his men understood exactly what he wanted. The cannon settled in a gritty slurp on the sand, and Gordon looked through the foliage.

"I heard something, matey," a buccaneer said, and stopped, causing the whole company to turn to face him.

" 'Twas your bowels," a swarthy man said, breaking ahead and laughing. The group watched him for a moment, then followed quickly to catch up. "We'll cut their throats and feed 'em to the crabs, and rape their women till they wish they was men."

"*Waa!*" Little Gordie pulled back his head from the nipple at the sound of harsh voices, and Tatti felt her blood freeze in terror.

"Fire!" Gordon's voice was crisp, and he heard his own teeth gnash, which astonished him.

"Fire, goddamn it!" Caruthers shouted as the bosun plunged the punt atop the priming powder.

Whoooomm!

The cannon's explosion blew the foliage clear in a wild shower of spinning leaves, and echoed thunder through their skulls. Gordon's eyes were blinded by the stream of yellow flame spewed out the net of vines, and he heard the third cannon's carriage crash into the sand-bagged stop, where the recoil caught the backward-charging weapon.

"Reload!" Stowell shouted from the midst of the white choking cloud of smoke that swallowed up the redoubt.

"Gordie, dear Gordie," Tatti's voice soothed as the child shrieked in terror.

The volley of grape laid a swath of whipping lead balls that slashed across the bright sand in a massed eruption. Men spun wildly off their legs, dropping weapons and flailing at their bodies or the air as they fell into the disturbed beach underfoot.

The other cannons boomed from the redoubt hidden under the pavilion, whining lead skipping into the air after ruffling the sand as though an invisible flock of birds had taken suddenly to flight. Gordon winced when he saw the cone of spreading shot lash the flesh of men trying to run, crushing those crawling on their knees. They flopped out on their bellies, their limbs contorted or arched, their spines in death throes, and he saw the bodies defecating and staining the sand wet with blood and urine where they died.

"Great Scott, look at that cutlass." Gordon spoke to himself, seeing a buccaneer's sword hit by shot, and spinning into the air in a strange whirring sound.

Two rovers were struggling toward the distant boats, one limping and the other crawling.

"Get them!" Gordon pointed at the figures. "But I want the boats most of all."

"On your feet, hearties!" The marine kicked the sweating gun crew with his bare leg. "After 'em!"

Gordon jumped through the torn vine mat where they'd fired the cannons. The men swarmed out of the redoubt, armed with clubs, muskets, and knives. He was running as fast as he could, but the cotters and sailors overtook him, and he saw desperation flash in the eyes of the two wounded men who saw the wild band in pursuit.

"Capture them!" Gordon shouted. "I need to barter prisoners."

"Rape our women, will ye!" It was Cutler leading the pack, a short club in his hand.

"The boats—dear God, get the boats!" Gordon panted, his breath searing in his windpipe. The three pirates on guard abandoned their fallen leader and seized the oars of one of the boats and began to shove off the beach and into the surf. If Gordon's men could capture and sink the small boats, the schooner would have a far more difficult, if not impossible, time landing a large party of men to mount another attack.

"Men, to the surf!" Stowell roared. "Capture the boats!"

The dozen sailors and George Caruthers swerved away from the two survivors and sprinted for the water's edge.

"Crab feed, was we!"

Gordon heard the outraged cursing of the cotters and the wet thick sound as they splintered the skulls of the two men. Their limbs trembled in nerve signals while their bodies died in the sand.

The single boat, was just beyond the surf. One man stared at the shore, his eyes revealing a determination to escape, while he punted the stern free of the sand, and the other two pulled on the sweeps. Oars were floating loose in the surf where the escaping pirates had flung the surplus sweeps that might impede escape free of the boat.

"Surrender in the name of the King!" Gordon shouted.

The pirate grinned, and made a defiant gesture with his fist.

"Both oarsmen are wounded, my lord," Caruthers said, and Gordon saw the blood oozing from the face of one man on the sweeps.

Gordon caught his breath while his men reloaded their muskets. He marvelled at the courage of the three men; yet he knew they had chosen to live a life that led to death by bullet or hanging.

"Shoot him," Gordon said, and closed his eyes as the marine dropped to his knee and aimed the Jaeger rifle.

Whoom!

Gordon opened his eyes to see the startled look in the handsome face of the pirate who held the punt. He looked down first at the round hole that popped open in his chest, and watched the blood pump into the sunlight in bright spurts, then back at his enemies on the beach. Confusion blurred his eyes, and he slid to his knees and into the sea.

"Wretched fellow," Gordon said, as his men fired into the two remaining figures who slumped out of sight into the bottom of the boat.

Gordon stood in the surf, and watched the waves settle the boat against the beach, then toward the schooner. The ship had hoisted her sails once more, and was underweigh. The glint of the sun reflected in the spyglasses of the men on the fantail; Gordon knew he had outraged angry pirates with a victory that was so stunning they could not fail to avenge its savagery. The cotters had slain all those wounded in the cunning trap of cross-firing cannons loaded with grapeshot.

"Burn the boats," Gordon said, taking the spyglass from Cora's hands. He studied the angry, contorted jaw of the man called Bonabombo, and the silent swarthy men about him. "He now knows how many we are, and he knows we'll fight."

About Gordon his own sailors and cotters were hauling the pirate longboats out of the surf, and he heard the axes smashing them to kindling, to set them afire.

Gordon handed Cora the spyglass and looked up the beach where the bodies of the thirty-five buccaneers lay strewn about in violent death. He was seized with a deep melancholia. Ordinary people see war as a very personal fury directed at them, and have no pity for their enemies, once they are outraged; but Gordon sought to spare himself this emotion, though he understood it. He was a gentleman, who would make killing a sport with elegant rules, because it was so horrible. "I want to see Tatti." He reached for Cora's hand as he waded from the surf. "I never cared for war, and I'll never know why I was ever good at it."

XXI

Tatti scarcely slept in the nights that followed and was at Gordon's side each morning from the false dawn that came before daybreak, to sunrise, watching the sea. The *Santiago de Mort* had vanished over the horizon; but the sea that had brought Tatti and the survivors to the island was the same water upon which their enemies sailed. The bright ocean, over which the clean air blew each day, had become not just a trap that held them in bondage on the island, but also the watery avenue upon which savages might attack them at will, and from which they had no escape. In her realization of their predicament, Tatti understood the immense burden that Gordon had assumed for their combined survival and the

217

incessant need to fortify and defend that had gripped his mind and occupied his days for nearly two years. Tatti saw him now as a strong man, as Cora had, despite his frail body and his impulse to withdraw and contemplate life.

One evening, just after sunset, they heard Noello's cry, and were astonished to see the dark schooner ghosting along their shore in the night air, her sails scarce more than somber shadows over her black hull.

"Night attack ship, she is," Stowell said, and Gordon's face was grim as he searched the silent marauding vessel.

"By God, our longboat!" Gordon turned to them. "Inexcusable folly! I forgot our long-boat!" His eyes flashed in the dark.

The sailors and emigrants stared at him, uncomprehending.

"Stowell, I want the cutter filled with stones, and I want her scuttled in two fathoms of water."

The bosun looked at him a moment, the marine turning his head to search Tatti's face for some clue.

"By Jove, don't you see Bonabombo wants our longboat, our cutter—he'll put swimmers over the side to cut it out. Now quick about it. To the cove, and no light!"

There was a gasp of understanding, accompanied by a cluster of nautical oaths and a scrambling in the dark as they dashed toward the cove where the creek flowed into the sea, where they had sequestered their longboat. Tatti heard the rich clink of steel gun barrels striking each other, as the marine and a hand-picked group of marksmen seized up muskets and followed.

Tatti and Cora hurried across the sand to the cove. Half-naked men were paddling in the water about the cutter while others stumbled down from the knolls in the dark, their steps burdened under the stones they carried.

"Unstep the mast," Stowell ordered, wading in water up to his hips. "Scuttle her a good forty foot out."

Gordon stood on the bank, armed men about him, glancing nervously toward the cove's mouth. His eyes were feverish in the dark, from the pressure of having to think and deal with a nightmare as a rational man.

Suddenly, a single blaze of fire split the night along the beach followed by loud calls.

"A pistol!" someone exclaimed.

"The marine, my lord," Cora said.

Gordon led the band on the shore toward the scuffling they heard. "I want prisoners!" he shouted, waving his younger and quicker men on into the night ahead of him.

An immense wall of flame burst across the dark night on the sea, and they heard solid cannon shot screaming overhead.

"Useless folly," Gordon panted. The schooner had fired a broadside in a desperate gesture of defiance, knowing from the shot seen on the beach that its swimming party was in trouble.

When they came up, Tatti saw eight or nine wet, naked men, some holding the others, their arms pinioned behind them. Two nude men lay at their straining, water-slick legs, one of whom twisted his hands over his bleeding belly. The other's eyes reflected a glassy stare in the night; he was already dead.

"We got two live ones, my lord." George Caruthers voice was loud and pleased. "They come swimming ashore just like you said they would."

The cotters and sailors frog-marched the two nude buccaneers toward them. They still resisted, pushing backward with their muscular thighs as they were shoved from behind.

"His lordship!" Higgins struck a pirate across his bearded face, bursting his lips.

"No, no, Higgins," Gordon said, as the men were brought before him. Their eyes searched his boldly. "Your names?"

One man drew down his chin and cocked a brow at Gordon. "Split-ear and Roo," he said.

"His lordship!" Higgins twisted an ear until the man fell to his knees and cried out, "Your lordship!"

"Let him up, Higgins." Gordon's voice graveled with irritation. "We do not need violence."

The two buccaneers had a majestic dignity about them, in their courage. They faced captors who could make them crawl naked and then slay them, yet they stood composed and unafraid.

Another salvo burst from the schooner, splitting the night with fire and causing a vast uproar among the roosting birds; then there was nothing more.

"Why has your captain come back?" Gordon said.

"You killed thirty-eight of his men—now forty, your lordship." The man called Roo gestured at the two dead bodies at the surf.

"He is Bonabombo, is he not?"

"Aye, Bonabombo, my lord."

"Then he himself, has slain many, and if he is slain, right is done."

"He don't see it that way, my lord." The man called Roo breathed easier, glancing at the women who surrounded them and studied his nakedness. Roo gestured at the women.

"The Spanish Main got too hot for us, and we came to winter in Bermuda—then we saw your women, and that you were just a handful." He searched the eyes of the hushed group of men and women and silent children.

"I want you men to return to your ship. Tell your captain we killed only in battle, and that I want him to sail away and leave us in peace." Gordon could see the relief in the men's eyes. The one called Split-ear smiled, while Roo's eyes searched the women's faces gently.

"Tell him I'll have my glass on him at dawn and to fly any colors except the Jolly Roger if he agrees."

The men nodded as they were released. They bent over, shaking their arms alongside their hips and knees to restore circulation. Roo stooped to run his hands along his flanks and over his loins and down his legs to brush off the water.

"Now return to your ship as you came," Gordon said.

221

"Thank you, my lord, for our lives." Roo dropped to one knee and took Gordon's hand.

Gordon raised him and gestured toward the dark sea. "Now begone. I'll watch for the dawn."

They walked behind the two naked men who waded out into the surf, the iridescence of the sea reflecting in their elegant muscular shoulders and sinuous arms and full buttocks, as they plunged forward and began to swim into the night, toward their ship which loomed in the darkness awaiting them.

Long before dawn Gordon was on the Signal Hill with his spyglass. The *Santiago de Mort* sailed up round the long sand-spit, just after the sun had risen over the horizon. About Gordon was the whole company of castaways. They could see a strange object dangling from the lanteen boom.

"What's he flying, my lord?" Leslie said.

Gordon's blood chilled, and he heard his heart thump inside his ribs as his ears rang with a strange burning sound.

"He's got a dead man a'hanging for a flag, my lord." The marine's voice was matter-of-fact.

"Aye, and he's got the Jolly Roger on the mainmast," Stowell added.

Gordon took down the glass, and they watched the ship sail down their shore, the dead sailor swinging from a halyard, the body hanging out over the water. When the ship was abreast of the pavilion, they heard a cheer

222

swell over the water, and saw the sailor's body cut loose, to fall into the flooding tide to wash ashore.

Gordon swallowed. "Well, he certainly gave us a direct answer."

"No, he ain't a'foolin', my lord," Cora said.

"I wonder which sailor it was?" said Margene. "That Roo was a mighty fine-looking man, pirate or no."

Gordon had spent the day on the savanna in the shade of a copse of cedar trees while the emigrants carried provisions to the fort, and the marine made his round of secret cachements of arms hidden through the forests.

Sometime in the evening they saw Noello driving a handsome naked man across the field before him, gagged and bound with his hands behind him. What astonished them all were the vine hobbles Noello had also used to fetter the man's ankles, so that he could not run. Noello walked behind him and whipped him with a willow switch, saying over and over, "No, I do not like rovers, even good ones."

"Good Lord, it's Roo," Cora said.

They had the pirate unbound in a moment. Noello had only teased him, not cutting his flesh, but the gag had torn his mouth.

"A madman, my lord!" Roo gasped when he could speak.

Noello had found Roo at dawn, spent and lying in the surf on the far side of the island. He had quickly bound his arms behind him and hobbled his legs, dragged him out of the waves, and then had fed him. Gagging him so he could not speak, he then switched him all the way across the island, "to the Captain, for I don't like rovers."

"Will you take me, my lord?" Roo dropped to one knee before Gordon.

"Did you have a choice?" Gordon said.

"I swam against an ebb tide to reach you, my lord, and I almost didn't make shore."

Gordon glanced into the faces of the men and women around him. "Will you accept this man for what he says he is, despite what he's obviously been?"

The man faced the company, and in that moment of eyes that suddenly glimpse beyond the flesh into the soul, and do not turn away in embarrassment, they met, and held. Roo spoke slowly. "You can do with me what you will, but I pray you let me join you." He looked evenly about into their eyes. "I was meant to be with quiet people, and I swam back, just like you seen me swim into the night." He held his arms out beside his shoulders to show himself, his battered but handsome body and smashed mouth, the salt caked in his beard with his vomit, and welts from Noello's whipping clear on his back, from his neck to his thighs.

"Feed him and clothe him," Cora said. "We drug him up from the dead out of the sea."

"Then take him," Gordon said, relieved to have another hand. Gordon knew men well enough to understand a man could change if his life were upheaved and kind folk drew him to their bosom, provided he was a man to start with. "And Roo never cringed, even when he crawled," he said to himself.

Gordon was glad the cotters had accepted Roo, for the man seemed designed to fit in, and be accepted. He had little to say, but leant his hands and bent his body to any exertion, not yielding to fatigue, even when spent and bathed in sweat.

"I ain't never been round folk who kneel in the dirt and work till the sweat runs off their noses," he whispered to Cora one evening.

"Roo, you haven't lived yet," Cora said, "for we've got lots of that ahead of us."

"I'm ready." He glanced at his palms, which were calloused flat into his fingers.

"Eat, man," Margene said, handing him an oiled board-plate heaped with food. Roo had drawn instinctively to the mature grace of Cora and the bucolic self-assurance of Margene, who never blinked her eyes when she spoke or listened. "What's that Bonabombo fellow like, Roo?"

The men and women around the cook-fire became silent, with only a child stirring, as they waited for Roo to answer.

Roo looked slowly about into their faces, then set his plate down on his knees and shook his head. "Bonabombo's got the Spanish rot in his eyes and throat, and he spits it up like he was sick, for 'tis a fact."

"As a man, what is he?" Cora said.

"I ain't sure Bonabombo *is* a man, leastways not like any sort of man I ever knew. He don't kill, but he likes to see death. When we captured vessels, we always shouted "no quarter," because we knowed he'd have what surrendered hung up by their hands, with their bellies stretched taut, and he'd have 'em cut out of their bowels."

"My God," groaned one of the cotters.

"Hush!" Margene said.

"Oh, he ain't like what you ever knew before. He liked to watch the faces of the men when they'd look down and see their entrails splashed on the deck, and still be able to talk."

"Drawing and quartering," Gordon said. "A wretched practice."

"Bonabombo liked to skin folk, too. We was raiding the Ivory Coast and ran down a slaver." Roo toyed with his food in his plate. "We had their treasure, their gold, and we loaded all their ivory aboard the *Sacred Death,* and we thought we was done, because there was too many blacks to mess around with—they was too many to kill, and we was glad, because we was rovers, honest rovers, just plundering. We wasn't murderers."

"But you did kill," Gordon said gently.

"Aye, we did, my lord—but I was a lad of twelve when they took me to sea."

"We ain't judging you," Cora said.

"Thank you, Cora." Roo looked down.

"What did Bonabombo do with the blacks?" Gordon said.

"Why he cut out the biggest bucks on the slaver, had 'em brought over, and stretched out by their arms, and had 'em skinned alive. Lord, i'twas awful. Skinned niggers till he had enough hides to cover his masts, and turn 'em black."

The silence among the listening group was so deep that when Gordon breathed, they turned to see if he were all right.

"I'm well, thank you—and we were right to fight."

"Aye, my lord, Bonabombo knew you'd all come onto the beach for rescue, and when he saw how few you was, with women, he reckoned he'd shoot his cannons to scare you, and then send over a landing party to round you up for a diverting sport, then rape the women."

"A raper, too?" Margene said.

"No, Margene, Bonabombo don't like women. No, he won't touch 'em, but he likes to see his men rape a woman, something of the highlight of a party."

"Well, he got a big surprise then," George Caruthers said.

"Aye, when you killed so many of us, you changed all his plans. He needs you men on his ship."

"Never!" said a sailor.

"Bonabombo don't believe any man is honest, and so he don't understand some men won't go wrong, even when tempted—so he'll not quit."

"Well, thank God we fought." Gordon turned away with Tatti, leaving the stunned cotters and sailors with the grateful Roo.

"Roo, those vittles is cold, and you need something hot," Cora said as she took his plate from his lap.

In the fortnight that followed, the marauding schooner was seen only once, at night, against a full moon. She was close inshore, which alarmed Gordon, not because he felt a landing party was imminent, but because he knew if Bonabombo grounded his schooner on an uncharted or unseen sandbar, he would have the pirates onto the land, despite their wish to stay afloat.

"I have a fool for an enemy, full of cunning and driven by anger with nothing to fear," Gordon observed as he walked the beach with Tatti, his eyes searching the sea, his hands clasped behind him. "It's not so much that wrath kills a fool, it's how many the fool takes with him when he goes."

"He better not trifle with us." Leslie nodded emphatically from where she stood behind Tatti and Gordon, holding their child.

Gordon nodded. "The honors may well be ours, at a price we can't afford."

The nights that followed gave little rest to Tatti, for the preoccupied Gordon no longer sipped brandy or spoke gently with her in the evening, but remained silent.

It was some three weeks after the cutter incident that Noello's wild cries aroused them in the night. "Schooner's aground! She's caught in the lee of the island, heeled over on a sandbar!"

In moments Gordon was up and dressed and armed and into the savanna, with Noello guiding. The old hermit led them in the dark up through the forest until they reached a hilltop. Gordon set his glass toward that dark vista on the beach, and saw the trapped vessel by starlight, her booms hanging out over the water in a futile effort to sail free.

"She grounded in a waning moon," Noello said.

It was the event Gordon had feared. The pirates were now forced ashore. Fighting was inevitable, once they'd walked across the island.

XXII

The castaways carried everything portable from the pavilion and huts up through the knolls and across the savanna to the fort. Their bare feet crushed the long grass into a mat upon which they trekked back and forth all day long. Along the way they set barrels of fresh water, where they paused to drink and pour water over their heads from gourd dippers.

Gordon did not feel any sense of panic. If he bled his opponent by attrition and surprise, he hoped he might dissuade him, if not destroy him. A pitched battle was certainly impossible. He had twenty-five against one hundred and seventy and was impeded by women and children. He could not fight a pitched battle, afield, without losing them as well as his own forces as the battle swayed back and forth. Yet within the fort, he felt he could mount a stalwart defense, as well as preserve the women and children. Gordon had a very clear picture of what he was fighting for: it was life. Not just his, but life as it is lived by all. Remarkably, he felt very calm about the uncertain future.

In the distance he saw Noello running toward him leading his scouts. At dawn, Gordon had sent out men to keep the stranded schooner under surveillance.

"They got men out wading all round the ship, my lord," Brighton said, his tight ringlets stuck to the sweat of his forehead. "And you can hear them cursing."

"Cursing?"

"Aye, they drops everything in the water when they tries to carry it to the beach."

Gordon could imagine the difficulty wading men would have trying to offload a tilted sailing vessel in five to eight feet of water without wetting, molding, rusting, and ruining everything. "Caruthers," he ordered, "I want you to shoot at them to harass them as they try to work in the water."

"We ain't got but two rifles, my lord."

"Never mind. Two well-placed shots are two more dead, and panic for those floundering about the ship."

Tatti was at Gordon's side while he inspected the canvas sails stretched between the blockhouse and the enclosed stockade. Small fires were lit, and the castaways bedded comfortably. Their eyes were feverish, Tatti

232

noticed, when they searched Gordon's face. Their fate on the island was now a matter of life and death, and they all looked to Gordon for guidance.

Late that afternoon he could see the schooner from where he hid with his men. Strung out in a broad front were his dozen muskets, and four blunderbusses. They had slipped and crept among the massive tree trunks and roots, keeping well hidden, until they had the broad beach before them. They watched a disheveled band of buccaneers wading in and out to their stranded vessel, offloading the schooner to lighten her and free her of the sandbar.

"Pick out their leaders," Gordon said to the marine, who snuggled down into the dry punk to get a good rest for his shot.

" 'Tis a good two hundred yards, my lord."

"Aye. Just do your best."

Gordon knelt and waited for the shot.

Whoom!

"The other gun," Gordon said, without waiting to see where the shot had hit. A sailor took the discharged weapon and replaced it with a loaded gun in the marine's hands as he rolled on his side to take it.

"Watch 'em skeedaddle!" a cotter called, and Gordon saw men rushing off the beach and into the water, while others wading toward the beach turned back again to the ship, dumping their cargo into the sea. He could hear the great oaths among the men on the ship, some of whom were jumping into the sea with bare knives and cutlasses.

233

Whoom! Caruthers fired again, and a man up in the rigging with a spyglass collapsed into himself, and fell into the shallow water where the others thrashed about.

"More," Gordon said, slapping the marine between his broad shoulders to show his approval. "I have to reduce the odds."

Careful rifle shots filled the beach and ship, and churning water in between, with human bedlam. Men dashed about without purpose, and nobody in command. Four or five men were stretched out on the sand; two were being carried through the waves.

"Good shooting, Caruthers," Gordon said.

The counterattack came up across the beach, just as Gordon expected and wanted. Wet muskets and flints, against his dry powder and concealed men. And his blunderbusses.

"Do not fire until ordered!" Gordon called up and down the line. Then, kneeling beside the marine, he spoke *sotto voce*. "Caruthers, pick out the officer—he ought to be the most determined."

"Got him, my lord. Has a pistol and cutlass."

"Good." Gordon saw the uneven line of half-naked men, running and halting for the advancing line to catch up, then jogging a few steps ahead once more. They were armed with cutlasses, knives and not over fifteen muskets, which he discounted as being wet. The buccaneers had panicked into attacking before they were ready.

"Say when, my lord." Caruthers held his breath, aiming down the barrel of the rifle.

"Not yet." Gordon saw the rough, turbulent eyes of the buccaneers coming over the beach, as they searched among the trees, and upheaved roots and punk for his men. Gordon swallowed, knowing he'd shortly be at grips with them.

"Now," he whispered, laying his hand on Caruthers's back.

Whoom!

"Fire!" It was Brighton's voice, and Gordon saw men tumble, or spin off their legs onto their bodies.

"Rush them!" A large buccaneer roared, waving a cutlass. "They can't reload!"

Gordon saw the hesitant steps of the slowing line which recoiled around the wounded and dying.

"Rush them!"

The pirates turned their faces toward the trees where smoke lay as a screen, and Gordon saw the forty men running toward him, led by the big man with the sword.

"Blunderbusses!" Gordon shouted, and was deafened by the thunderous roar. *Baalooom! Baabaalooom!*

His eyes hurt and his ears rang, and he saw men fall in the hail of shot. Remarkably, men were dashing past him, their wet legs scuffling in the punk and dry leaves.

"Goddamn you!" The marine had driven a pike through a man's body with such force the point stuck into a tree trunk, while the man with parched leather skin still cursed and swung at him with a cutlass, like an insect thrashing after being thrust by a pin. Gordon closed his eyes as Caruthers collapsed the top of the man's skull with a musket butt.

Gordon had his cutlass in his right hand and his cavalry pistol in his left hand, not sure what to fight as men fought all around him. A musket boomed, and he saw dead men underfoot. He realized the pirates had overrun his position, but hadn't strength enough to dominate.

"There you are!" A tall man with a gashed mouth swung at him. Gordon caught the blow on the bell of his cutlass and recognized their leader. Amazed that the fellow had lived, Gordon parried the heavy blows of the cutlass, which drove him back across a sworling mass of tree roots in a welter of ringing chops.

"His lordship!" He heard distant cries, and he stumbled over the heavy liquid body of a dead man and fell on his back.

"Goddamn you, aristicrats!" The tall man's mouth spat white foam about his blanched face in his fury.

Gordon saw the hate in the eyes as the massive blow of the cutlass came down upon him as a knifing maul. He flipped his light sword up to guard his face, and was blinded in the shower of sparks that rained in his eyes as the swords clashed.

"Oh, God," Gordon murmured, unable to lift his sword, for its point was driven into the earth. His wrist was so weak from parrying the mighty blows that he could not free himself.

The tall man had the cutlass in both his hands, aiming the point at him. Gordon raised the pistol and pressed the trigger.

The massive lead slug struck, enveloping the cool evening air with a shower of blood, brains, and loose patches of skin stuck with hair as the man's head exploded.

"Well done, my lord!" Brighton pulled Gordon to his feet.

"Hey, soldier, you almost lost the Captain," another sailor said.

Gordon could not speak, and looked about for the enemy.

"Oh, they is fled, my lord," Caruthers said.

"Our loss?" Gordon whispered, still unable to focus his eyes.

"One dead, and a few gouges among our sailors."

"Ah, thank God." Gordon took the jug of water from Roo and swallowed, feeling faint.

The daylight attack on the stranded schooner had the effect Gordon hoped it might. It compelled the buccaneers to fortify a sandbagged redoubt on the beach, into which they offloaded, and which was defended by musketeers. The losses of men by the pirates had been so dramatic and the attack out of the forest so astonishing that Gordon's men held the upper hand. Before dawn each day, he posted scouts to harass the pirates with distracting shots, and to keep them under surveillance.

"They ain't landsmen, my lord," Higgins said, "or they'd march straight across the island and fall on us."

"Aye," Gordon mused. Like the Vikings, it was waterborne mobility that made the pirates bold, not any superhuman cunning or bravery. "Their ship is stranded. Pity I can't sink it forever."

It came as a shock that night when Noello and Cutler burst into Gordon's tent on the savanna, waking him and Tatti. "They's marching along the beach, a hundred of 'em!"

Gordon rolled to his feet, seizing his arms. "I want every man and woman out of the fort, and guns at our redoubt!"

He was into the tall grass of the wet, dewladen field, hurrying along with all his men and women. Their bodies were blurred in the moonlight, sometimes disappearing in the sage, and he could hear them panting openly in fear.

"We'll have to move the cannons out of the redoubts, a good hundred yards, and fire them from an unexpected place." Gordon's words were sharp in the cool night air. "They'll come marching up the beach to get our cutter, but we'll have moved our cannons!" Gordon looked into the faces of the sailors about him. "Caruthers?"

"My lord?"

"Grapeshot, all the way!"

"Grapeshot, and double the charge," the marine said.

"Right."

Tatti was among the straining people who heaved against the thick hemp ropes to drag the cannons.

"Quiet!" Stowell hissed as he worked among the men and women who waited in long lines, holding the hemp.

Gordon watched them draw the two cannons up out of the concealed redoubts where they had been fired so effectively, and dragged on dolly wheels across the savanna, carving dark grooves in the earth visible in the moonlight.

"Up the beach, two hundred yards if we can make it."

"We'll make it," Cora said, heaving with a bare shoulder under a gun muzzle. Her large breasts swung free in the moonlight and he realized she had torn off her blouse to make a padding under her shoulder.

"Another surprise for them," Gordon said. The pirates' crew was reduced to a hundred and twenty out of two hundred. If he could wear away another forty, he might induce the band to leave Bermuda. He was caught up in the spirit of the castaways, who moved in a singular purpose. Many of them stripped off clothing to use as makeshift gloves and padding to maneuver the heavy brass weapons. There was an eerie, silent aura about him, of straining legs, bare shoulders, long hair hanging over women's faces, muscular buttocks and knobbled spines, and glistening sweat.

Gordon placed the cannons atop a tree-shadowed knoll that commanded a brilliant white beach, which glared in the moonlight. A silver trickle of breakers licked it in silence.

"They'll be looking down the beach to where we whipped them, not here," he said. "Now load, and keep absolutely silent."

When the cannons were loaded, he had all the castaways who were not actually serving the guns withdraw into a small woods and dig their bodies down into the warm, dry punk. "After we fire, you're all to shriek and yell."

The people nodded and scrabbled down onto the earth, huddling together for warmth.

He held his breath when he saw the dark mob of men moving over the moonlit strand. Their stride was direct, and they had no scouts ahead, but came as a fearful mass who clung close together for courage.

Stowell hid his smoldering punt down in a small depression, his dark eyes afire as they watched for Gordon's signal.

Gordon raised his hand, slipped behind the cannon and lay his eye down its barrel. He watched the mass come under the muzzle of the cannon.

"Fire!" Gordon said, stepping clear.

The cannon roared.

The moonlight split with a yellow ball of fire that spat an orange tongue of flame forty feet across the night, and Gordon heard the whine of grapeshot rain through the men, and slash into the surf.

"My God, Lord Gordon! Look!" The marine turned his shoulders toward a view down across the beach. Dark shapes coughed and crawled and kicked about in circles, while a disorganized and broken column of men ran off, firing their guns toward the island knolls that loomed along the beach.

Gordon stood on the knoll and watched the wounded men struggle and die before sending in his people. "Roo, are any worth saving?"

"Some, my lord."

"Good, save any wounded." He waved the

men and women onto the beach toward the dead and wounded.

"Bonabombo hangs his own men," Roo said, "so taking hostages ain't no bargain, my lord."

"Perhaps, but all the Lord's creatures are divine," Gordon said.

"Pity they forget it, my lord." Cora spoke at Gordon's elbow.

"We'll try to remember it," Tatti said, catching Cora's eye. "For our own sakes."

"Come, Roo, show us your friends," Cora said, leading the sailor down upon the beach.

"Woman, you saved my life," Roo said. "Why?"

"You was naked, and you didn't hide your nakedness with shame. Reckon you was innocent, that's why."

"Thank you, Cora."

"Thank the Lord, not me."

XXIII

After his third devastating attack upon
the buccaneers, Gordon Wragby was swept up
in a profound melancholia. He had walked
among the dead by moonlight, where their
rumpled bodies lay in stark protest to his stunning victories; and he could hear the wounded
groan and cry, gripping their bellies.

Tatti held his arm, and they walked toward
their cottage by the pavilion, followed by Cora
and Caruthers.

"You can't blame yourself," Tatti whispered.

"Aye, we've saved twenty-two wounded,"
Cora said. "And they ain't all gut-shot."

Gordon walked on in silence. After ordering the rest of the castaways to "fort up" for

the night with the wounded, and posting Noello to watch the stranded schooner, he lay in his bunk.

Cora lit a tallow lamp and brewed up a pot of tea, and Tatti poured Gordon a small goblet of brandy that Leslie had brought from the pavilion. "I don't know," he said, sipping the brandy. Taking the cup of tea in both his hands from Tatti, he sat up.

"Caroline nursing Gordie?"

"She's got more milk than I do," Tatti said.

He drew Tatti to him, and held her between his knees and slipped his hands under the loose jumper she wore, and felt her narrow waist, the smooth skin that crinkled under his gentle touch. He ran his hands up over her breasts, and felt her nipples tense between his fingers.

"If I can feel life, maybe it all has some purpose. Perhaps God exists if I can feel him." His voice was more to himself, while the three silent women watched him, and the marine stood discreetly in the shadows behind them.

"We've killed more than a hundred, my lord," Caruthers said brightly.

"George, be still—we know that!" Cora snapped irritably.

"It ain't that we ain't succeeding, it's that we are," Leslie explained to the marine, whose eyes showed his confusion.

The four of them watched him sit down again on the edge of his bunk, taking up his brandy goblet. "Pity the men I've killed, and Lord forgive me. Now Tatti, hold me."

"Gordon, I'm sorry the battle swallowed you in grief." Tatti took his head into her arms.

"You'll feel better, come morning, my lord," Cora said, and turning to the marine, she pushed him out of the cottage. "George, I want you to go get them sailors, and I want every one of them dead men off that beach before dawn, d'ye hear?"

"Aye, dear woman, before dawn."

Gordon's scouts brought him word that Bonabombo had freed his schooner, and had put out to sea.

"They dumped her clean of all her guns and stores to float her free," Brighton said. "We watched 'em by moonlight, and they went out on the tide."

Gordon nodded and crossed the island next morning to inspect the flotsam carried in by the sea from the ship as it was lightened.

"He's got no water and no provisions," Gordon said. "So he's desperate."

The buccaneers had been compelled to heave overboard their sustenance in order to float the ship free. Now they could not leave the island without reprovisioning. "It's water they must have, and they'll come to the creek for it," Gordon said.

Four days later, they saw the pirate ship sailing slowly along their beach. Gordon stood on the shore and watched the men on the decks, who were now driven with no choice. "I was always afraid," he said to Tatti and Caruthers, "that each time we won, we only

245

compelled him to come back—I lack the strength to destroy him for good."

"But Gordon, he made the quarrels," Tatti said.

"And he ain't putting ashore no landing party, my lord," Caruthers said briskly. "You've hurt him bad."

The dark schooner changed her course, her stained sails luffing as she tacked about, and sailed slowly past them once more. "Bonabombo's got sick eyes and throat rot," Noello said.

"Thank you, Noello, but I can't tell him from the rest."

"He's got the Eyetalian spyglass, Lord Gordon," Cora said, shading her eyes with her hand.

"That's him!" Roo ran out a few feet, pointing.

"Alas, they all look the same to me," Gordon said tiredly. He saw the officers standing about her wheel, staring at the freshwater creek. "Water, water they live upon, but it's salt and gall for them." He looked at Stowell. "I'm not going to fight our twenty-five men against a hundred mad with thirst."

That night Gordon waited in the cool air that blew in from the ocean and watched the dark form of the schooner, and he saw the driftwood logs being lifted over the gunwales by its men. "They're going to float in, and no retreat for them."

"They're driven men, now," Cora said. All approved of Gordon's plan not to fight at the water's edge in the dark.

246

That night Gordon waited in the woods above the creek, and watched the men from the ship, who slurped in the fresh water, and thrashed their hands to half-fill the casks which they floated out to the anchored schooner. They moved about in silence, except to drink. Gordon saw the armed guards slip cautiously into the edge of the woods where he hid with Noello, three sailors and Caruthers.

"Far more cautious now, my lord," Stowell said.

Gordon nodded. "Aye, once bitten, twice shy. We've hurt him, but we've got pitch on our hands we can't get rid of."

"Lord Gordon, them men didn't give you no choice," Caruthers said firmly.

Gordon nodded again. The buccaneers had fanned out skirmishers as a screen behind which to work, denying him the bunching-up mass he had had fired upon so effectively with massed grapeshot and blunderbusses. "I'm afraid I've taught him something about fighting."

"We've got muskets, my lord," Brighton said.

"Aye, but they'd overrun us after the first salvo, while we reloaded—one salvo won't do it."

"We whittled down them odds by a half, my lord," Stowell whispered. The twenty-two wounded pirates had died of blood poisoning from the tallowed-greased lead shot fired into their bellies and about their bodies.

"Perhaps, and I'm afraid I made them very, very angry."

As the night wore on, they saw the buccaneers slip along the creekbed toward where they'd scuttled their longboat. The pirates' cunning had increased with their predicament. Men were wading in the water, their half-emerged bodies clear in the reflecting moonlight off the easy flowing creek, while the swimmers broke the surface in obvious disruptions of the water.

"I think we can get in a blunderbuss shot," Caruthers said.

"A good'un, my lord." Stowell breathed through his open mouth as he spoke.

Gordon nodded his head, and heard Caruthers crouch forward, his bare feet rustling in the punk. "No, wait," Gordon whispered.

The men about him turned silently, their eyes puzzled.

Gordon looked away. He knew he must kill again, yet he did not really want to. These were men—coarse, angry, evil, yet men like him nonetheless; and Gordon wanted no part of killing them. "I've never played the Almighty," he whispered to himself.

"My lord," Cora whispered, sensing his inability to order the attack.

"I've killed so many, Cora." He looked into her firm russet eyes.

"Lord Gordon, you didn't make this quarrel."

"Ah, alas, I can wipe them out again, naked, unsuspecting men."

"And what do you think's in store for us, my lord?"

"Where is the milk of human love, may I ask?" He stared into the Highland woman's face.

"Those men love death." Her eyes caught his in the moonlight and held them, while the sailors and the marine waited.

"Order the attack, my lord."

Gordon bowed his head. "Caruthers, the blunderbusses—and God have mercy on our souls."

"You ain't got a choice, my lord," said Brighton, slipping barefoot into the thick brambles after the marine.

Gordon waited with Cora at his side, scarce daring to breathe, for fear of making a noise. Down through the wooded glade they could see the ripples on the pool where the cutter was being raised to the surface. Once he heard a coarse, phlegm-rattling cough, and Noello's eyes flared. "Bonabombo. I can tell his throat-rot."

Caruthers and Brighton and Roo had been gone what seemed hours. A mockingbird began to sing just outside the forest, and the song flooded the moonlight. Gordon knew it was his final act of offense before the initiative passed away from him; and he realized Cora and the common people were right in crushing evil however they could, despite his qualms and the exquisite beauty of the moonlit night and the trilling mockingbird.

Suddenly a glare of orange fire lit the quiet water where twenty men worked about the longboat, stepping her mast and setting oars.

Then a shower of lead slugs rained upon them and sprayed the water, splintering wood as it did.

"*Eeeeyoo!*" Noello broke into a wild scream, and Cora caught her hand over his mouth.

Men were cursing and floundering through the water. "Get the boat, goddamn it!"

A scattering of shots pattered up through the trees where they stood, and he heard his men panting as they climbed toward them in the dark.

"Over here," Gordon called softly.

"We got 'em good," Caruthers said. "Took our time and laid it all over 'em."

"Good, but they got the boat," Gordon said.

Gordon had the men reload, and posted them in a semicircle while he lay down in the dry punk to wait for dawn. He sent off Noello and a sailor to assure them at the fort all was well. He remained to determine what damage he had done and exactly what odds he faced.

In the early daylight they could see that the schooner had sailed away, taking the cutter, and they made their way down to the wide pool in the creek. He saw the quiet bodies of the slain men floating peacefully in the glass-clear water, as though stranded in repose, their hair floating gently free of their calm white faces.

Tatti joined him, with Noello. "Wiped them out again." He gestured at the pool. "It wasn't what I wanted."

"Some of them was good men." Roo spoke at his side.

"Too late now," Gordon said bleakly.

"Gordon," Tatti whispered, "what does a man or woman ever know of what's right or wrong? You had to make death so we could live." She slipped her arm about his waist. "The trees and the grass and the leaves and the animals and worms live on the earth out of love for God. We stand for love and life, like all the Lord's creatures, and it was your duty to defend God and the right."

Gordon opened his eyes, astonished at Tatti's words. Her hazel eyes searched into his soul. "For our children," she said, "the generations to come, is it life or is it death? You said life, and the pirates said death."

"Any woman knows that, Lord Gordon," Cora chimed in. "Now we'll have tea brewed soon as we get to your quarters."

XXIV

Gordon knew he was pitted in combat with an evil force, which had withdrawn merely to lick its wounds. The cotters and sailors, with their strength and their grasp of right and wrong, had compelled him to see the reality of the evil. It annoyed him that he alone, with Tatti, could see the outcome, and it appalled him that a girl should have to face it at his side. He wondered if he had been right to marry her and let her bear the son he adored.

The pirate ship lingered around the island, sometimes disappearing over the horizon for a week, but always coming back. He laid careful plans to defend the fort and he posted lookouts. Noello was his special strength. The little hermit seemed able to smell the wind and predict when and where the schooner would reappear.

"He hates pirates," Roo said, "that little madman."

"Praise be that he does," Cora said. "He don't sleep no more, for coast-watching at night."

One night Gordon was roused from his sleep by Noello and Caruthers with word that the buccaneers were landing in full force from the schooner, on the east bay of the island. He laid his hand on Tatti's sleeping shoulder.

"We're in for a siege." He slipped his pistol baldric over his shoulder and caught Stowell's eyes in the sparse light of their thatched cottage. "Spike all our cannon on the beach."

"Aye, my lord."

Having delayed long enough to hear the brisk hammer blows driving steel nails down into the flameports of cannons, rendering them useless, he turned to Tatti and Cora. "Can't have him bombarding us with our own guns."

"What'll he do?" Tatti's voice caught in her throat.

"Take the pavilion, find nothing, march on to the fort, and lay siege."

"And then?"

"My love, I've done everything I can." He slipped the child up into his arms and went out into the starlit night. It delighted him to feel the live, compact little body against his chest as he walked across the savanna toward the fort. The small round head bathed in curls had the scent of new life. Its fresh, lace-fine hair was clean with hope. He held his son tightly to him.

"So lovely," Gordon said, and breathed into the child's neck and behind its ear. When he looked up, he saw the stars awash against a black sky, with an occasional cloud that moved sedately toward the horizon.

"Gordon, you were right all along," Tatti whispered.

"In marrying a girl so young she was a child to me?"

"I chose you, but I made you think you chose me." Tatti slipped her hand in his.

"Well, I suppose we took root and sprouted wherever the seed was cast," he said.

"Mother said something like that," Tatti said. "Her mother was Russian, you know, and she had to live in the mists and rain of Scotland."

He could see the dark mass of the stockaded fort looming in the distance.

"Tatti, I love you," Gordon said, "and I think the seed is love, and if it will bloom between a man and woman, wherever they live is Eden—the paradise that makes life."

"Will we win, Gordon? I'm so afraid."

"Aye, we'll win."

"And go home to Scotland and England?"

"Aye, we bloom in love, but our roots are buried in the dirt, in England." He handed the nestling child, which cuddled down in his arms content in hearing the quiet words of love between its parents, to Cora, and took Tatti into his arms and drew her to him. "I don't know what exactly will happen, except that the human race is older than evil and wiser than vice, and I do not intend to surrender that ancient order of the race of man."

Tatti buried her head in his shoulder, and felt the iron strength of a man who had grown from calamity and thrived on adversity.

From the savanna, a disheveled mob of strange-dressed men stared across to the fort. A man in a long waistcoat lined with flintlock pistols waved them on, and Gordon put his spyglass on him. A cutlass knocked against his boot heel, and made him tilt when he walked.

"Obviously that's their captain," Gordon said.

As the men neared the fort they spread out into an encircling fan. The marine counted eighty-seven men, some of whom limped. A short, stocky man with a bare chest walked slowly toward the fort, staring up at the stockade and the muskets lying out the shallow embrasures. He was unarmed.

"Parley!" the man called.

"Tell him to speak." Gordon nodded to Caruthers.

"Say your piece!" The muscles in the marine's neck tightened when he bellowed.

"Surrender, and you'll be spared!"

Gordon shook his head, and Caruthers roared, "Never!"

The man walked boldly toward them when he saw they would not fire on a defenseless man. Putting his hands on his hips, he tilted his head and spoke. "We know Lord Gordon Wragby lost the *Daphne*—you Lord Gordon?"

256

"Tell your master to begone," Gordon said, leaning over the edge of the pallisade.

"We ain't got a crew," the man laughed, showing two missing teeth and soft gum as he scratched his naked belly. "You killed 'em, and we need your men."

"Sail on, while you've still got your life." Gordon gestured him away with his hand.

"Fellows, free plunder on the Spanish Main, and enough senoritas to prong your way to hell forever!"

"Avast, you son of a bitch!" Stowell's voice rolled out in a bosun-tone they hadn't heard since the ship was lost at sea.

The man gazed along the top of the parapet at the silent people. He scowled, the face pulling into a dark muscle of anger. "Crab bait —we'll feed you to crabs, damn you!"

One of the sailors leaned into the butt of his musket to take aim at the man.

"No," Gordon said. "Let him go."

"Raid the Spanish Main!" the pirate shouted up at the fort. "All the whores a man could want! Pirates' laws for honest service. Gold and protection." He grinned as he searched the parapet. "Women and rum, enough to make hell a pleasure!" He rocked on his bare heels, secure in the honor of the men he tempted, and under Lord Gordon Wragby's truce.

"You've spoken—begone!" Gordon called out clearly. "Tell your master to depart this island, in the name of the King!"

"I'll tell him!" the man shouted, and turned away toward the encircling men.

They watched him walk toward the armed figure of their captain. "Bonabombo," Noello said, while Gordon looked through the Italian spyglass.

When the dawn came next morning, Gordon saw the raw earth thrown up in gun-pits, situated in a semicircle ringing the fort, pinning it to the creek. All night they had heard the shovels digging. Gordon was relieved to have the enemy visible for his people, the "unknown" clearly in sight.

"Oh, they're just sapping forward to put us under fire." Gordon sipped his tea and watched from the tower atop the blockhouse, as the emigrants insisted on calling it.

"What'll they do, my lord?" Higgins said.

"Annoy us with pestering shots." He shrugged his shoulders.

George Caruthers jogged along the catwalk of the parapet, like a bird dog questing game. Sometimes they saw gun barrels thrust up into sight from the pits, but no heads or faces. Often, they could hear the prying and patting of dirt, by the men preparing for siege.

Once, in a severe rainstorm, the marine asked Gordon for permission to rush the nearest pit, nearly two hundred yards from the fort.

"Powder's wet—we could surprise 'em."

"To kill four or five, and lose you?" Gordon shook his head. "We'd all have to go out to save you when the other pits saw the brawl, and we'd be at a clear loss."

The marine's face fell and he strode away,

squinting carefully out the parapets as he went, carrying his Jaeger rifle.

"Come the rub, a warrior's worth his weight in hope," Gordon said.

"And gold." Cora joined them.

After sharing their intimate lives for two years as castaways on the island, Gordon was confident the cotters and sailors could withstand the assault. The company were camped under tents and thatched lean-tos between the blockhouse and the pallisaded stockade. Cookfires coiled smoke into the air, and the root cellars burst with provisions. Water came from a shallow well within the walls, just above the spring down the hill from them. "We have water, and we can wait them out," Gordon had said.

The next day the people in the fort saw a linkage of narrow trenches tying the pits together, and saw the slotted embrasures cut into the pits for gunfire. Calling Caruthers, Gordon said, "Whenever you can get a clear shot at a face behind a musket butt that's aiming, shoot."

The marine nodded and swallowed.

"But you are never to fire from the same slot in succession. Always change to a new position."

It came as a relief finally when Gordon heard musket shots and felt the timbers thud as lead slugs dug into the wood. All faces turned to Gordon as though he were total deliverance. He carefully sipped tea, ignoring both the shots and the frightened eyes.

"They're getting bolder, my lord," Stowell said, the marine and Roo at his side.

"A clean shot, a clear kill, and duck," Gordon said, without looking up.

In a quarter hour they heard the German rifle thunder among them, and a wild curse float across the no-man's-land.

"He flopped over dead, and his mates stood and cursed," Stowell reported.

"That leaves eighty-six," Gordon said. "Next time, have both rifles ready, and kill two instead of one."

"Oh, aye, my lord," Caruthers said.

The siege lasted for a good fortnight, with the ramparts of the fort echoing to the steady chunk of heavy bullets that sometimes shattered splinters inside the embrasures, but mostly were embedded in the soft palmetto logs.

Gordon's calm indifference to the enemy, and his concern for saving fuel with which to cook, had a stabilizing effect on the besieged. It astonished Tatti to see how quickly the men had reverted to some primordial command to fight. Their entire daylight hours were spent in "peeking" and predicting from where the next shot would come, and trying to kill two men in succession.

"That's eighty-four," Gordon said, when they brought down two pirates with the loaded rifles.

When Caruthers was not able to kill a man in nearly a week, Tatti realized the pirates were learning from their mistakes.

Sometime in the third week Tatti woke, hearing a harsh note in Gordon's voice, and discovered the pirates had dragged a small cannon into one of the pits during the night.

"A carronade, by the looks of its breech-lock, my lord," Stowell said, handing the spyglass to Gordon.

Tension mounted through the day as the cotters realized that any cannonading was bound to slay innocent children in their congested fort.

All through the night Tatti waited at Gordon's side. The keep-tower was crowded as the men loaded their single cannon with a grenade shot, and trued up the muzzle to aim at the distances Gordon had estimated. Below, the emigrants huddled into their quarters, waiting for dawn.

When the first cannon fire rolled onto the savanna, there was a crash of timber and a shower of splinters. A woman screamed.

"My lord, his cannon's exposed!" the marine shouted.

"Well, he doesn't know we have a cannon, too," Gordon said, signaling to drop the broad wooden shutter in the top of the tower.

Tatti, shrinking back against the timbered wall, saw that every man had broken into a wild sweat, naked ribs glistening in the morning haze.

Another blast split her head and the smoke blinded her as she heard the steady, curt commands to the gun crew, and saw the cannon hurtle backward.

"Swab her bore, me hearties!" Stowell cried.

"She's in battery!" Roo called, winching the blocks so that the cannon squeaked forward into firing place again.

She could hear the children crying in the room below their tower, and the shattering of wood as the pirate shots struck their pallisades.

"I'll get him with this shot," Caruthers said, straddling the cannon to ram home the cannonball.

"Good." Gordon nodded. "He'll beat us to kindling if you don't."

The uproar of the crashing shot, out the shutter-port, was cheered wildly by the men, who all began to leap about like delighted schoolboys, laughing and clapping each other on the back. "Got him! Got him, my lord!"

Gordon stepped clear of the cannon and Tatti ran to see. The enemy cannon was tilted straight up at the sky, and men were darting about the open revetment, beating shirts and brooms at small pieces of wood that seemed to smoke in scattered blotches.

"I think he's on fire," Gordon said.

A clear red glow appeared at the side of the upended cannon, which exploded into an orange ball that enveloped the whole revetment in a yellow fire and a thunderous roar.

"We got his powder magazines!" The marine was jumping up and down. "Got his whole gun crew! My lord, look!"

Gordon nodded mutely, and handed the spyglass to Stowell.

They stared at charred sticks twirling overtop the white smoke cloud, and watched the smoldering brands flung out across the savanna. The smoke diffused and cleared, lifting over the dead men sprawled about the earthen revetment.

"We'll have peace for a day or two." Gordon looked for Cora and took Tatti's arm. "It's time for breakfast."

XXV

A relative calm descended over the embattled forces. The emigrants were actually jolly, having shared again a close brush with calamity; having won, they could see the exquisite joy of the simple life they shared as people.

By the dark of moonless nights some of the buccaneers had approached the fort, and called out greetings, and the same invitation to join them in raiding the Spanish Main and the Horn of Africa for the spice and ivory trade.

Sometimes the sailors would glance at Gordon, who had a pallet in the tower, to see his reaction, which was always the same. "If you were meant to plunder and despoil, you'd have long gone your way by now," he said.

The remark seemed to reassure his men; while among the cotters, the idea of abandoning the land for a life of roving sailors was a curse to contemplate, defiling every fiber of their being as husbandmen and farmers.

"Never you fear about our people," Cora had said to Gordon. "We was born to grub in the sod, with dirt a'tween our toes."

"I'll lay my life on that, and the loyalty of my men," Gordon said.

Gordon knew that their "victory" would lead to overconfidence, and he ordered Caruthers and Stowell to make sure the heavy iron-studded gates were slotted and wedged and pegged at all times. It was to Noello that he turned, because only Noello knew how he had dug the tunnel from the back side of the baking oven, under the pallisades and down to the creek, just below the spring. The tunnel emerged in knee-deep water and was concealed by bullrushes; and they could clearly reach its entrance with rifle fire, or grapeshot by cannon, so Gordon had no fear of its mouth being taken by open rushing. The tunnel offered him an opportunity to harass the pirates.

At night, they could often hear the pirates roistering about their beach campfires, just below their abandoned pavilion, and Gordon believed he should create a diversion, if he could induce Noello to conduct a will-o'-the-wisp campaign of strike and flee through the forests when pursued.

"This is your chance, Noello," Gordon said, holding Noello by both his hands. "Only you know the island, and I've armed you with grenades and powder kegs."

The soft eyes searched Gordon's, then looked imploringly to Tatti. "They would hurt her, wouldn't they?" Noello touched Tatti's long auburn hair and she put her hand on his forearm.

"Dear Noello, something must have hurt you," Tatti said.

"Oh, my lady, it did, but I forgot what it was." The soft eyes lit with warmth and adoration as he took Tatti's hands into his gnarled fingers.

"We're all so pressed, and we need you." Tatti closed her slender hands about the knuckles gnarled with age and arthritis.

"My lady, will you come help me?"

"If you need me, yes." Tatti smiled and swallowed, and gripped his twisted fingers into hers. "Of course I'll help you."

Noello breathed through his open mouth, and clung to her hands, tears running over his cheeks from the puddles in the doppled white folds under his eyes.

"Shall we slay them, my lady?"

"If you think we should."

Gordon took both of their hands into his. "I'd like to have some individual scouting done, with a grenade here or a bullet there, for information purposes."

"Aye, we don't want no frontal assault," Caruthers said, grasping Gordon's wish not to send Tatti out with Noello. "We can kill 'em ourselves."

"Oh, of course." Noello bobbed up and down, and he began to giggle. "No, they'll not know who it was, no they won't—and 'twill be me, Noello." He glanced quickly into each of their faces, the eyes ablaze with fear mingled with a mad light. "I can kill them?"

"Aye, but no direct attack—from ambush."

"Ambuscade!" Noello's voice cracked with excitement.

"Aye, that's all." Gordon caught and held their four hands as friends.

"I love you, Lord Gordon," Noello said, and wept openly.

"We love you," Tatti said, and lifted Noello's folded fingers to her bosom and kissed the backs of his hands.

It seemed that every night thereafter was a succession of wild, tormented cries, of a human voice gone mad, and haunted on the wind, accompanied by explosions that shook the island. The wild birds flapped through the moonlight, screaming in protest at the concussions of flaring bombs when Noello tossed grenades into the sleeping camps of the buccaneers, and dropped them from the trees as he slipped away through the forest.

"It's that voice of despair that tears at me here." Tatti held her throat, while the embattled emigrants and sailors listened to Noello's unstable soul go rampant, attacking pirates out of the fantasy world of a childhood that was scarred and had lived on in him as an old man.

"It gives him a chance to work off his oats,"

Gordon said briskly to those who quailed at the subhuman cries that filled the night.

"I think he's likely reduced their number, my lord," Caruthers said.

"Very likely," Gordon agreed. "But I can't risk a pitched battle with all the children."

"Aye, my lord." The marine braced his shoulders in understanding.

In less than a week, the night noise ceased. They wondered if Noello had been slain. For two days they heard nothing, then were astonished to discover Noello standing under their pallisade, looking up and babbling incoherently. The night watch aroused Gordon, who trotted onto the parapet, and could not make heads nor tails of what the hunched little man said.

"Throw him a rope and swing him up, and quick about it."

The sailors flung out a coil knotted to climb upon, and with a bowline bight to sling him up, but he refused.

"Come up, Noello." Gordon leaned over.

"My lady, Tatti, I love her." The eyes flared. "I need her."

Gordon felt the words ensnarl him. Quickly he shouted, cupping his hands about his mouth, "I'll send you Roo."

The wrinkled face knitted in perplexity. "But I love Tatti."

"Lady Tat is suckling her baby just now," Gordon said, gesturing to have him climb the rope.

"No, my lord. I want her." Noello spun about and dashed away into the night. In the distance they heard the call of a pirate sentry, but Noello was gone.

In the morning Gordon sent for Tatti, Cora, and Leslie, as well as Roo and Stowell and Caruthers. He explained that Noello did indeed need company—and as if by invisible understanding all eyes turned to Roo.

"Aye, you," Gordon said to Roo.

The former buccaneer's face broke into an open grin, which even with his short stubbled beard had a jolly boyish look, over his long, sunburned neck.

"He whipped me for half a day, my lord."

"Aye, so he did."

"He's my man, my lord," Cora said, her eyes on Gordon's, taking Roo's hand. "He's an innocent man."

" 'Twas why I sent for you, Cora." Gordon nodded. "I'll read your vows into the ship's Bible, and write them under mine and Lady Tat's." He looked at the rover, and spoke solemnly. "Roo Lundee, do you take this woman, forever, from this day forward?"

"My lord, I was born a bastard and kidnaped to sea."

"Roo, that is not what I asked you," Gordon said, smiling, as everybody breathed nervously, and Cora watched the handsome man she had grown to love. "You now have Cora's name, Lundee."

"I loves her, my lord!" Roo looked astonished that everybody didn't understand the obvious. "I ain't never before had a woman

270

want me naked, without gold in my pockets, who'd feed me and show me how to work without telling me to do."

"Then you take her, forever, in this world and the next?"

"Oh, I do."

"I then pronounce you man and wife in the eyes of God, and before all people." He reached for his goose quill and turned for his water-stained Bible. "Sometimes when the moon wanes, you must slip out to Noello—you'll find him in the forest. Stay off the beaches and the savanna. The pirates fear the forest."

When Gordon stood, Cora's eyes caught his. "Lord Gordon, I want it writ down in the ship's Bible that you swear Roo is a good English sailor, in your hand."

The company of people turned back, watching Gordon, who glanced quizzically at Cora.

"I want it writ out in the Lord's book, or the English will one day hang him." Her russet eyes never wavered.

Gordon took the quill and stroked the bold words: "On this day of our Lord, and in the twelfth year of his Majesty's reign, I did swear in Roo Lundee to his Majesty's Navy as an able and bold sailor." He signed it, "Gordon Wragby, Marquis of Ravendale," while Tatti lit a taper and fired a piece of sealing wax, letting it drip upon the worn pages. Tatti licked the signet ring she wore and plunged the Wragby seal down into the puddle of vaporing wax, filling the room with a pungent odor of incense.

"I'm a royal sailor?" Roo looked at Cora and Tatti.

"As much as any jack tar that took the King's sovereign," Gordon said, standing. "And I'm so glad to have you." He took the man's hand. "Now, I need you with Noello."

"He said he liked me." Roo smiled.

"Good." Gordon handed the quill to Tatti and looked down, embarrassed he had taken so much for granted from a good man.

" 'Tis right, Lord Gordon, that Roo should go," Cora said. "He was spewed up out of the sea to live. I knew it when I claimed him."

"Thank you, Cora."

"I claimed you out of the sea, too, my lord."

Gordon acknowledged her claim. Cora was indeed a treasure beyond comprehension.

The day after Roo had slipped out the tunnel, the besieged sailors noticed a strange wooden contraption come onto the savanna. Through their spyglasses, they could see it was a battering ram, with heavy planking about its slings to shield it from musket and rifle slugs.

The pirates worked all day about the contraption, and an uneasy stillness came over the besieged fort. The sailors and cotters knew they must hold the enemy outside the fort. They could not fight within the fort lest the children be killed in the mélée.

"Obviously they intend to batter down the gates. Well, good." Gordon pounded his fist into his thin palm. "Bring down the tower cannon and set it aside our lower cannon."

"Two cannons, my lord?" Caruthers said.

"Aye, two cannons."

"And double the grapeshot . . ."

"Right, bosun, double the grapeshot."

The men sped off, their voices eager at the plan of battle as they went to work. Gordon set his hands on the open muzzle, guiding the awkward cannon, slung in ropes down the inside of the tower.

"D'you think it will work, my lord?" Cora asked.

"A man's passions forge his fetters, Cora, and Bonabombo is a fool who won't quit while he's yet alive."

"How can you shoot through the gate?" asked Tatti.

"A fool puts his vanity ahead of his life." Gordon tapped his toe, not hearing either Cora or Tatti.

"How's it to work, Gordon?" Tatti said.

"By God, I'm going to slay them. You just watch and see." He clasped Tatti to his bosom, and seized Cora's hands. The Highland woman looked surprised at his sudden emotion. "Cora, I'm not going to give up my life, nor the lives of our people, ever, without a fight."

The day came and passed with many trips by the besieged men and women to the long parapets, to stare off past the enemy earthworks at the heavy wooden contraption that moved on wheels toward them.

"Good Lord, look how it mashes down the grass," Higgins said, pointing at the trail it made across the savanna.

"Aye." Cutler nodded his head. "When you think of what a man could do a'plowing with all that sweat what's gone into that devil's machine, you know something ain't right."

"Cutler, is all Lowlanders dumb? What d'ye think we're doing cooped up in this fort?" Higgins breathed in exasperation at his friend.

"I was just thinking of plowing," Cutler said.

"Well, we ain't out there because they is!" Higgins pointed at the slowly approaching battering ram.

As the night fell, the half moon cast a reflection on the savanna, and Gordon studied his water-bleached Nautical Almanac to find the moonset. "Quarter past one in the morning." He looked up at his men and women. "We'll have them at our gates after moonset. I want all the children up in the tower while we meet them on the ground." The cotters stared at him with round eyes and blanched faces.

"No fear." Gordon patted his almanac. "Now we'll prepare for battle."

It was a relief to have the children up out of the way with those women who nursed them, and with the actual defense of his fort at hand. He walked the wooden planks behind the parapet and caught the reflected starlight, glittering with the moon, in his spyglass. The battering ram had come to an uneven stop, a good nine hundred yards from the fort, and he knew they still feared his cannon.

Gordon could not decide whether to hoist the cannon quickly back to the tower, to fire solid shot at that range, or to wait, as he knew they would hold the ram at extreme range until moonset and utter darkness before advancing. With his cannons double-loaded with spray shot and powder, he was already prepared when they rolled the battering ram up to the fort; and he decided to preserve that posture.

"They may have a *petard,*" Gordon said, turning to the marine and bosun, "a bomb to stick on our gates which goes off and blows in the timbers. Get Brighton right overtop the gates, and Leslie with him, and have a pot fire and grenades to drop. Get him!" Gordon's voice rose.

Leslie and Brighton's faces were stricken with the gravity of what awaited the fort, their eyes bright with a fevered anxiety.

Gordon set his hand on the sailor's shoulder, looking off toward the sinister image looming out of the dark on the savanna. "You are to drop grenades. Leslie?"

"My lord." Her eyes filled with a soft passion as gentle as her voice.

"You light the wicks of the grenades, and hand them to Brighton."

"Yes, I understand," she nodded.

"But you are not to hurl grenades until I order them!" He jerked the sailor's shoulder. "Am I clear?"

"Aye, my lord, most clear!"

A silence came over the party along the parapets, and Tatti spoke. "Gordon, how are you going to shoot through the gates?"

"We're going to open the gates, and fire when they rush into the fort."

"My lord, you wouldn't," Cora said.

"I'll kill another forty—I must!" He turned to the Highland woman. "They have eighty desperate men, and I have a dozen sailors, a marine, and a handful of cotters with broken hearts. I must narrow the odds, or they'll peck us to death." His voice rose as he stared at the men and women.

"Forgive me, my lord," Cora said, curtseying awkwardly before him in contrition.

"Up, up, Cora." He seized her and lifted her up.

As the moon settled through the distant limbs of the cedar forest, they could hear the creak of the wooden wheels on the massive axles as the battering ram was dragged across the grassland once more.

"Lordie, I can hear them," Leslie said. She and Brighton had a tub of coals perched atop the parapet over the gates, and a basket of heavy round grenades, all wicked and loaded.

"The gate is not to open until I order it." Gordon stood in the courtyard, addressing the six cotters who were to lift the slotted beams. "You're to duck behind the timbers as the enemy bashes his way in—and I intend to fire the cannons, full bore, double charged, straight through the open gates."

The men had heard him explain in minute detail, down to the finest maneuver, until they knew it by heart. "And Brighton will hurl his grenades, *after* the cannons fire."

"Right, my lord."

Along the top of the parapets were stationed musketeers who looked down, the fear showing in their eyes. "Now all I want is a harassing fire. Keep your heads down, and just let them know we're helpless."

"Helpless, my lord?" a sailor said.

"Obey your orders!" Gordon spoke curtly. "We're anything but helpless."

The men stared at him.

"I want to suck them in, damn it!" He pounded his fist into his palm, suddenly swept with a great loneliness. It did not seem possible to share his plan of battle with his people, without scaring them to death; and yet he knew only the most daring maneuver would win, using cunning to make up for his weakness. As the battering ram lumbered across the savanna, he could sense the terror rise in the hearts of his people.

"Good lord, if we time it right, we'll win," he whispered to Tatti as they stood together in the dark, between the cannon battery muzzles and the gates. Hovering in the darkness were their men, and behind the cannons in the shadow of the tower were Caruthers and seven sailors.

"We've fought so much, you'd think they'd go away." Tatti's voice was taut.

"This time I'm to put the punt to the touchhole." He spoke more to himself than to her. "I want to have done with them."

"It never occurred to me that killing was more important than living." She sensed his desperation.

"Well, it shouldn't be, but men make it an affair of vanity, and life's the last thing they think of."

"You'd think they'd learn."

"Not that lesson, when it's love turned up-sidedown to death—and it annoys me. I was never a good teacher."

"Gordon, I understand you." Tatti slipped her arms about his waist, and lay her head on his chest. "I want you to succeed so much. I didn't know how we could kill them, through the gates."

"If I told it right off, we'd scare everybody to death."

"I think it's a splendid scheme." She breathed quietly against the bare skin of his chest. "We'll kill forty, at least."

"Pray we do."

"I feel like the people of Carthage and Troy."

"Well, I'd like to have God with us," he said.

"Oh, I've read the Old Testament to Cora all day."

They heard a man call down to them. "It's three hundred yards away, my lord."

"Cora says we're not Jericho," Tatti said.

"We've been decent and we've kept the law." He moved out of her embrace. "Stand behind the cannons and have two extra punts lit in hand, in case I miss the touchhole." He nudged her toward the cannons, and ran to the ladder and climbed to the parapet.

Gordon could scarcely discern the men crowding near the heavy-wheeled machine. As it got closer, Gordon could see the planking, built as a shield, through which the ram was slung.

"Sporadic fire," Gordon said to a man beside him, staring out the parapet.

The man dropped the barrel out the slot and fired into the advancing mass. Gordon shielded his eyes in the glare.

"Fire!" Gordon darted along the parapet. "Fire, but duck!" He stumbled, nearly blinded by the flaring musket shots. A yellow streak flashing out from the oncoming ram told him the rovers had musketeers, and lead slugs smashed into the pallisades.

"They're as blind as we are," he said to Brighton, who was crouching at his knees.

With a crash the great beam rocked the whole stockade of upended pales, shaking the fort. "Hold until you hear me fire!" Gordon slapped the sailor on his shoulder and touched Leslie's forearm, then ran to the ladder, and skidded into the courtyard.

Crash!

The timbers inside the gates were splitting apart from each other as individual boards, showering the six terrified men with chips.

"'Twill hold!" Gordon shouted, and darted to the battery of cannons. He leaped the dark muzzles, and landed in the midst of Tatti and Caruthers and Stowell. His sailors were crouching like eager dogs along the sides and small truck wheels of the weapons. Beside the cannons were his musketeers and the men with blunderbusses.

Crash!

The timbers were splintering, and they could see a flash of fire from outside the fort, where pirates were already shooting through the

279

rupturing boards. Women were crying and children wailing in the night.

"Open the gates!" Gordon yelled.

"Open the goddamn gates!" The marine's voice rolled out like a foghorn.

They saw the six men struggling to lift the crossbeams which held shut the gates, but they were wedged with debris.

"Lift any you can!" Gordon shouted, holding a smoldering punt in his hand.

"Lift all beams, and get clear!" Caruthers bellowed.

Crash!

The gates yielded inward a good yard, but one crossbeam held.

"They'll come through the next time," Gordon said in the awful silence, as they waited for their gates to be torn open.

Crash!

One gate swung back and the other fell flat toward them, torn from its iron hinges, and rolled up a dust cloud as it slammed down.

Gordon could scarcely breathe in the excitement of the moment, where all life hinged on his estimate to fire the battery. He could see men stumbling forward behind the dust, and hear the wailing of children overhead, and he felt instinctively the coiled muscles of his crouching men.

"Through the breach, ye bastards!" A high Midlands pirate accent fell on his ears.

"Not yet." Gordon set his hand on Stowell's shoulder, still unclear as to how many men were in sight.

"Into the breach, ye sons of bitches!"

Gordon saw the slack swing of the massive battering ram, spent as it lunged forward, then swung back.

"We've busted their melon!" The same voice assailed his ears. "The women're in the tower!"

Gordon saw a mass of legs dissolve from around the battering ram and come through the gates stepping cautiously. A face turned up to the parapet, and a bayoneted musket swung in the clear air.

"Rush the tower!"

"Hurrah!" A cheer went up, and Gordon heard a scramble of running bare feet on the boards of the fallen gate, and saw an onrushing mob of armed, half-naked men, their knives glistening in the starlight.

Wham! A blinding stream of fire leaped sideways out the frizzen where the pan of one of Gordon's musketeers fired.

"Tatti!" Gordon screamed. "Fire!" He clapped his hands to his blaze-scarred eyes. "I can't see—fire!"

Tatti froze, horrified at Gordon's fragile hand clapped across his soft blue-gray eyes, chilled with the fear he was blind.

"Fire, dear God! *Fire!*" Gordon shouted, spinning about.

Tatti lunged at the touchhole with her smoldering punt. Its vast orange torch blasted across the courtyard, enveloping a crushing mass of armed men; and she was deafened by the roar as the cannon leaped backward in recoil. Falling on the second cannon, she jabbed the punt into its powder hole, and felt her arm torn backward as the cannon hurtled back on its small wheels, in a searing streak of fire that expoded across the whole fort.

She groaned as she fell over Gordon's foot and grasped his ankle. The blunderbusses were firing, and Tatti saw men falling in parts. Limbs flew over the pallisades and entrails plastered into the timbers as the guns roared into the thick mass.

"Another charge, goddamnit!" The marine's voice rose above the chaos.

"Gordon." She climbed to her knees and clasped hhim to her bosom as the sailors cursed and fired, and she heard them braining a man who had got into the battery. "Oh, dear Gordon, your eyes, your tender gray soft eyes!" She tore off her bodice and plunged it into a water bucket, and set it over his eyes.

"Tatti!" Gordon exclaimed. "Water, yes, cold water." His hands were atop hers. "Fight! Men, fight!" he shouted blindly, while he girdled her waist into his body to steady himself.

"My lord, them grenades is death!" Stowell shouted. "More grenades!"

The cannons roared again, throwing immense flashes of light that spumed out the top of the stockade, from the streaking blasts of powder, and wavered overtop them in strange clouds that reflected down the firelight.

"I can see," Gordon whispered, peering through his fingers and dripping cloth.

"Oh, thank God."

"Bodies, my lord! Bodies everywhere!" Stowell shouted and turned him by his shoulders toward the quivering masses of flesh and bone, and the festooning entrails that hung in uneven cords and loops under the parapets.

"Prisoners, we need prisoners to negotiate with," Gordon said, feeling his singed eyeballs grate with pain. "Cora!" he called, while Tatti held him.

In a moment Cora had jumped from the ladder leading to the tower where she waited with a pistol. "My lord?"

"Save the prisoners! Dear God, spare me some prisoners. I want to talk, not kill!"

Gordon heard his own voice loud in desperation. His agonizing blindness made him despair, for he did indeed want some leverage against the pirate captain, to cause Bonabombo to come to terms, in exchange for prisoners.

"They's all dead men in the fort, my lord," Cora said laconically.

"Well, capture some wounded, dear God!" Gordon shouted as he stood amidst his cheering and cursing men. Then, still holding his hands over his eyes, he wept in despair at the blood-drenched scene of battle.

"We served God and the right, my lord." Cora swept both him and Tatti into her arms, as the men ceased firing and stared in quandary at their troubled captain and the fragile, half-nude girl in his arms.

XXVI

When the dawn came, Gordon lay on his back in the thatched corner of the stockade, his eyes cooled by damp cloths. Leslie and Tatti knelt at his head. He had licked the white dust of the moorish poppy from Tatti's fingers to ease the pain, and sipped it down with brandy, until his burning eyes were numb and he could sleep.

Caroline sat cross-legged at the foot of the pallet, nursing her child as well as Gordon's son; and when he woke, the children were near for him to place his hands upon and feel, since he could not see. "What is it like?" Gordon asked, when his mind cleared briefly.

"'Twas a great victory, my lord," Cora

said, and a silence followed among the men and women who knelt and watched him.

"Tatti?" Gordon reached out his hands to touch his wife. "The fort? The enemy? Where are they, and Caruthers?"

"Gordon, by daylight it looked a scene out of hell—worse than by firelight at night, because the bluebottle flies swarm in clouds for the mangled flesh and blood, and vultures circle overhead in long spirals. . . ."

"Will Bonabombo come in and talk?"

"No, the pits are empty, my lord," the marine said.

"Get the dead outside, before we have pestilence—scatter lye from the soap."

"My lord, they're digging pieces of men out of the gates and untangling guts from the parapets," Cora said. "Takes time."

"Our dead?"

"Two dead sailors and four cotters. They followed them out onto the savanna," Stowell said.

"Damn," Gordon groaned. "Alfred lost at Hastings because his men got overconfident and broke ranks to attack the Normans when they'd all but won."

"Eighteen stout men we got, my lord," Caruthers said.

"Damn, lack of discipline to lose those men." Gordon turned his head away from the voices, intertwining his fingers in Tatti's. "How many did we kill?"

"Well, they's in bits and pieces, my lord," the marine said briskly, "but by counting skulls, we figure we killed forty-two men."

"Oh, God, the stink." Gordon's voice gagged at the sweet, brackish smell of newly killed flesh. "Bury all the dead—pray over them." He reached for his brandy goblet, which Leslie set at his lips. "Morphia, too, please," he said and waited.

Leslie wiped her supple worn finger into his lips and over his tongue with the white powder, and held up his head to drink again.

"Get the dead rovers as far from the fort as you can, and leave them for the birds, but pray over them. Tatti, read the Book of Common Prayer for all the dead. And Caruthers, post skirmishers so you're not ambushed."

"I've got out skirmishers, my lord."

"Good. Tatti, read the words of God that make grief a part of life. Now let me touch Gordie." He sighed and fumbled his hands over his small son's head as he suckled the wet nurse's nipple, and drifted into his morphia dreams once more.

As Gordon's sight mended, it was to Tatti that Caruthers and Stowell reported, and to whom the women came in deference to announce supper and breakfast. It made her childhood slip away from her, and it tired her, so that she remained at Gordon's side, while the bandages covered his eyes.

On the fifth day, Gordon asked for no more opium, and smiled whenever his hand was taken by a child or a sailor or a cotter, as though he was engulfed in a wave of life, simply by the feel of skin and muscle which dispelled the grief of his battle and eased the painful wounds to his eyes.

"I know I'm mending," Gordon said. "Dear morphia not only blinds me, it sweeps me up into huge dark clouds of despair where I tumble end for end, as if in a sandstorm." He patted Leslie's folded knee. "No opium, not when I can see live creatures once more."

When Gordon grew still, he would run his fingers over the pallet, counting over and over, and shaking his head. "By my count, he's got forty men, and I've got ten sailors, a marine, and ten cotters."

"And we've got Roo and Stowell," Cora said. "And Noello."

"Aye. Still not the best odds, but tolerable."

The sunlight glared in Gordon's eyes when he tried to open them, after two weeks of darkness. He knew he would be able to see again, yet his eyesight became an explosion of blinding pain within his head if he actually tried to focus onto some object. If he remained in the shade, or shielded his eyes under a broad straw hat, and refused to look at anything in the full glare of the noonday sun, he could see. And at night, he seemed to have grown better able to delineate what he saw.

"The glare was too much," he said, delighted he could see as well as he could. "It's always the refreshing mist and fog in England anyway, so I don't need to see the solitary flowers; as long as the color's there, and I know it, 'tis still as sweet."

Tatti walked about the fort with him, assuring him all was well.

"No, I must hear from Noello and Roo."

"My lord, we had them with us for three days," Cora said, "but you was lost in your torment."

The savannas were clear of any human life or movement save for the dark shorebirds and vultures that scattered the bones as they ripped loose the flesh. The sun bleached white what had been gnawed upon until the sage grass enveloped once more what lay upon it.

"Incredible that simple grass can wipe out all trace of corruption," Tatti said.

"Aye, we take ourselves so sure," Gordon said. "The grass can't think or care."

Roo came in that night to report on the rovers and Bonabombo. "They's hurt real bad, my lord," Roo said, straddling a small stool and facing Gordon's pallet, as a light rain pattered on the shingled roof of the lean-to. "They was living in the pavilion, until they attacked the fort, but now they've thrown up a small sand fort on the water's edge, and about twenty of 'em stays on the shore and the rest on the schooner."

"A watch at night?" Gordon said.

"A double watch, my lord." Roo ate hungrily out of the oiled plank-plate Cora set across his knees.

"I'm sure he's whipped, but he's mad, and I'm not quite sure how bad he's wounded." Gordon ran his finger along the lower edge of his lip. "Or worse, he may indeed be mortally wounded; and no beast is so savage as man when he sees his mortal limits."

"Oh, Gordon, don't think such things," Tatti protested.

"I'm having trouble with Noello, my lord."

"Trouble? What ails that poor, confused old man?"

"Lives in a world of fancies—when he see'd you'd blowed them pirates to bits, he run through the forest for a day and a night, screaming in Portogee, and scaring every bird into air, agiggling and cursing and shouting about hell and heaven."

"Aye, he's old, and the elderly bear a cross of eternal disappointment."

"That battle took years off his life, my lord."

"Hmm. Deeply hurt by rovers, doubtless, but only God knows how," Gordon said.

"He wants my lady." Roo's eyes settled on Tatti. "He says he wants something pretty to worship, what he never had before in his life."

"Good Lord, not that again," Gordon closed his eyes.

"He's harmless, my lord," Roo said energetically. "He's just balmy as a fruitcake." He drew a circle around his ear with his finger.

"It takes all kinds to get the Lord's work done," Cora said, disturbing the heavy silence about Gordon Wragby, while he turned over the notion that madness knew no victor nor loser.

"We can slip out and rush 'em, my lord," Caruthers said, sensing Gordon's mind.

"Aye, true. Yet 'twas caution that was our

handmaiden to triumph. I'm loathe to risk all in a pitched battle against four to one odds." He turned his face away to the wall, wanting to think. "Let me sleep on it. In dreams I clear the impediment of fear and discover what truly grieves me." He set his hand on Tatti's shoulder, and gestured to be let alone by the others.

When Gordon had regained his strength, he realized his beard had grown, and it astonished him to find it gray. He ran his fingers through it, feeling its sparse growth. "Oh, well, I never liked all that shaving every day."

"I think it's beautiful," Tatti said. They laughed together, one of the rare times they dared to be at ease and touch. "It feels like silken embroidery."

"So now I'm light embroidery."

"No, so masculine." Tatti slipped her palms up across his chin and ran her fingers into his gray-flecked auburn hair. "It gives you an elegant look."

"Lord Gordon, you're beautiful however you are," Leslie said, coming upon them.

Although there was a respite from battle, Noello's wild cry often echoed on the quiet savanna from out of the forest. Frequently incoherent, it always ended with a long-drawn-out wail, "Tátteee!" To keep Noello functioning as their ally, Tatti might have to go to him.

Gordon was not frightened for Tatti's safety. He would send Brighton with her, if she went to Noello; and he was certain the English sailor was a match for any two men. He felt he could not start a day without hearing her voice, or roll from his bed without first touching her hip or feeling her breath come rhythmically against his neck or ear as she slept. Tatti was his life.

"I'll not stay out long," Tatti said. "We'll just slip out the tunnel and through the water rushes, and disappear into the forest, and never be on the savanna."

"Oh, I have no fear for you in the forest," Gordon said. "I just don't know if I could command alone, any more." He shrugged his shoulders as they sat together on the bench in the corner parapet, and watched the sun throw shafts of setting light across the island as it settled into evening.

"Just let me go for a day or two, until I can get him to stop that awful yowling."

"You're right, of course. After all, I have Cora to remind me of my new duties, and Gordie has Caroline to nurse him."

"And I'm almost dry." Tatti touched her breasts with the heel of her palms.

Gordon nodded. "I'll let you go to Noello, tonight—Brighton will go with you, and he'll have diagrams of where I cached the weapons."

XXVII

The dank earth smell of the tunnel filled Tatti's nostrils and lungs as she followed the hairy legs and crouched back of the sailor. The candlelight flung up canted shadows that tilted on the walls, and vanished of a sudden as she crawled behind him. "More light," she whispered.

"Sorry, my lady." Brighton's eyes glistened as he held the light between them.

Tatti nodded, her hair globbed by a streak of mud that clung to it when her head bumped the wall.

"My lady?"

"I'm fine."

She followed his muscular buttocks and mud-stained calves as he half-crawled, half-walked. The tunnel narrowed until she squeezed her shoulders between the vertical posts on which the roof boards lay and felt herself in water to her knees. As she put out her hand to him, Brighton said, "We'll have to crouch when we come out in the rushes."

Her hand on Brighton's shoulder, Tatti waded in mud and slack water to her hips as he led her, stumbling over his feet and legs at every step.

"Air," she whispered. "Smell the fresh air."

"Aye." Brighton blew out the candle. They were wading in open water to their armpits, among bullrushes way above their heads. The stars shone in the utter stillness, and the cool air lay heavy on the slack water.

"We'll wade the creek, and slip out of the water at the woods." He held her arm and watched for the heavy shadow of the trees to cast a gloom over the creek.

Across the savanna, Tatti thought she saw a reflected firelight by the beach which raised shadows in the low scudding clouds.

"Pirates," Brighton whispered. "They ain't got sense enough to quit."

"Well, they're unstable of mind," Tatti said.

"Them's generous words, my lady."

Wading into the gloom of trees along the bank, Brighton half-lifted and shoved her ahead of him out of the water to dry punk and leaves under the trees.

They went quickly into the forest, following the open game trails that led up away from the low ground.

"I grew up from a tad, poaching in the King's forest." Brighton spoke gently.

"I suppose we all must eat," Tatti said to put him at his ease.

"Aye, we allus left seed animals for next year."

"The Lord forgives you, I'm sure, and I hope you said grace, for the sake of the animals you ate."

"Oh, 'deed we did! My father always asked the blessing. We was believing folk."

Tatti was pleased at the confidence shared by the sailor, whom she had grown to admire over the two years of their isolation on the island. He was like a brother to her. She'd nursed him with the vile "spring bitters" Cora and Noello used to purge them or to cool out their fevers when the rains had kept them cooped up in the chilled pavilion about the open fire.

They bedded down in a mass of dry punk and shredded leaves, which Brighton piled atop Tatti, and then snuggled in beside her when she said, "We're wet, and I don't want you chilled in the night air."

The warmth of the dry earth under the cedar thicket eased her, and she let the slumber of quietude drug her mind. Only an occasional leaf crushed as her guardian stretched a foot or moved his shoulder in the punk beside her broke into her reverie, and she fell off into a deep sleep.

The bright call of thousands of birds woke her in the quiet gloom under the woods, and it astonished her to see daylight beyond the limbs.

"My lady?" Brighton whispered.

"Dawn?"

"Aye, but I daren't stir until you'd woke." The sailor got quickly to his feet, bursting loose a shower of leaves.

"My word." Tatti felt her hair matted in a coarse felt of twigs and leaves, thick to touch. "I've got to have a bath."

"When we find Noello, my lady. Lord Gordon said that was our first purpose."

They had come up a long swale that verged on a heavy palmetto grove, and were passing a tangle of roots from a massive tree when they came face to face with Noello.

"My lady Tat." The little man's soft eyes were self-assured. "Oh, look, you're in a ruin." He gestured at her, and turned to Brighton.

"You can't keep clean pushing through the muck all night." Brighton put his hands on his lips and stared impatiently at the little hermit.

"Of course not. Breakfast, then a bath." Noello broke into a shiver of laughter and bounded out ahead of them. "Come."

He led them along a mangrove swamp, out into the high sunlight; and feeling in the water with his feet, he found an underwater bridge that he led them across until they reached a steep bank. In moments they were in the midst of a large copse of trees that shadowed the whole forest in dusk.

Noello's fingers and toes caught into bark notches in a huge tree trunk, and he vanished up into a maze of limbs and clouds of greenery.

"Just follow," Noello said, from somewhere above them.

"Up, my lady." Brighton set his hands to lift her.

"I can manage," she said, climbing behind the splayed toes of Noello, astonished to see the forest floor had vanished the first time she looked back. They stepped out into a roofed platform of palmetto fronds. The cedar buckets formed a wall, alive with scented white flowers.

"I love them," Noello said, plucking a jasmine blossom and coming to Tatti. "A gardenia, the Spanish say." He placed it in the bosom of her jumper. "Wet. Your clothes are wet." He closed his eyes and shook his head. "I'll find dry things for you."

Tatti looked out from under the palm-frond roof and saw the sparkling sea, where the *Santiago de Mort* had doused her sails. A small boat pulled clear of the ship and headed for the beach where a small sand fort had been thrown up.

"Never fear those human devils, not whilst you're in my palm house." Noello's wispy little beard trembled with his quick words.

Brighton's cool, level eyes followed Noello as if seeking to understand how such a human being as he had come to exist. Noello darted, then seemed to flutter about the plants like a small bird, while he set together platters of palm hearts and warm yams baked in honey. These he placed in their hands and gestured for them to squat cross-legged on the woven mats.

"Your clothing." He clasped his hands and

tilted his head. "I'll sew magnolia and palmetto leaves . . ."

"Leaves?" Tatti said, swallowing a mouth-
ful of fried breadfruit covered with honey.

"Oh, yes, I'll hide you here forever, dressed
in nature's purest garments, and hid in the
treetops."

Brighton stopped chewing, and cleared
his mouth. "Noello, my orders don't include
dressing that girl in no leaves." He stared lev-
elly at the little man, whose eyes shifted in a
light of terror.

"Well, it wouldn't hurt to see," Tatti said,
sensing Noello's keen hopes.

"And I have orders for Roo," Brighton said.

"Roo? Oh, Roo, why he's watching pirates."

Brighton nodded and began to eat once
more. After they had breakfasted, Noello led
them down out of the palm house and through
the woods to a shallow, bright creek.

"I have rain ponchos of woven grass," Noello said, leading Tatti out into the ankle-deep
water. "They'll keep us dry, but when we hide in
the trees, we need leaf-clothes for light and
shadow." His large eyes twinkled as he revealed the secret of his phantom escapes from
danger.

"I have diagrams of where our weapons is
hid," Brighton said, squatting on a sunny rock
by the bank, "and I won't need no leaves to
hide in."

Noello lifted a cupful of water and let it
pour over Tatti's matted hair. "Oh, such a
ruin." He talked to himself as he began to wash

298

her hair in a mixture of coconut oil and soap, ignoring the vast sudsing that ran down over her jumper and pantalettes.

"I just got dry," Tatti said.

"Oh, you won't need those clothes."

Tatti felt herself flush, and refused to look at the robust sailor who cradled a musket across his thighs and watched with round eyes.

When the dirt loosened and rinsed out and the fine strands of clean hair lay close upon themselves, she realized Noello was gesturing for her to undress. "We must wash and dry your clothes." He held out his hands to her.

Tatti shut her eyes and reached under the edges of her blouse and peeled the single garment from her wet skin, keeping her back upon the armed sailor on the bank. She handed the jumper to Noello, who crushed it to his chest, then she stooped and ran down the pantalettes from her rump and legs, and reached them over as well.

"Ah, the grace of life in youth," Noello said, his breath coming in short gasps.

He handed Tatti the oil and soap, and stepped out of the creek to a small disguised cache, and returned with toweling. "Bathe and dry, and come." Noello's eyes were alight.

He waited with her, holding the articles for her as she washed her body and he rinsed her, but never touched her flesh. Then he settled the towel about her. "Come, I must dress you."

Tatti spent the morning on the sunny bank, helping Noello fashion long bands of leaves to girdle her waist and to lay as a man-

299

tle over her shoulders. "Soft, soft as feathers, they must be," Noello said. "And warm."

As Noello adjusted and hung the chained wreaths, Tatti noticed he was half-mad with excitement, his soft eyes afire with pleasure as his breath came in hoarse gulps.

"So beautiful, oh beauty of the soul, revealed in the pure flesh." Noello talked to himself as he worked, and Tatti realized he was a well-read man, even perhaps a learned man.

Tatti felt his hands touch her flesh like soft leaves, brushing down her thigh or across her belly and fluttering against her nude breast like a gust of air.

"The image of eternal hope," he said. He tied leaves about her knees, fitting and patting each leaf, where his small hands caressed her skin, worshiping the beauty.

"You must never leave here," he said. "Never grow up."

"Dear, dear, Noello," Tatti said, confident she could contain him. "I must grow up, and I have grown up."

"No." He touched her hips and legs and body to turn her. "No, you are too pretty to live in human squalor." His eyes were aflame as he searched hers. "All I've known is evil, and all my books tell of sorrow."

"Life is more than books," Tatti said.

"If you'll stay, I'll keep you in beauty among my flowers and wild animals. Oh, we'll have a wonderful life."

"I have a little boy," Tatti said. "And Lord Gordon."

"Of course, just the four of us, and I'll never hurt you." He searched her face.

Tatti heard Brighton's worried breathing as he stepped quietly nearer them.

"Noello, every man and every woman must go to the other, someday," Tatti said.

"No, beauty is wasted on youth. They'll rot you with grief—young men are fools, and when they grow old they learn to hate, and worship lies. You must stay."

"Please, Noello." Tatti drew him upright by the shoulders. "You are such a kind man. Let's pretend we're all in love, for now, anyway?"

"Pretend? Love? My lady?" Brighton asked, but they ignored the large young man who towered over them, hands resting on a brace of pistol butts and hairy chest crossed diagonally by a leather musket sling.

"Love is a pretend hope, to start with," Tatti said, smiling into the soft eyes that adored her. "We must start there." She closed her hands over Noello's small gnarled wrists, to make him feel her love and respect for him.

"Oh, yes, tender is the love that lives."

The afternoon with Noello was an absolute delight for Tatti. They had an herb tea, and she glanced at his French novels, climbed out among the giant cedar limbs, fed the hummingbirds he had attracted, played with his huge cat named Coptic, and walked with him through the forest. He gamboled at her side, rustling in leaves, and gesturing at every plant and tree, as though introducing new children to old schoolfriends.

"What a lovely tea," Tatti said, as she sat upon the moss under a cedar copse.

Roo had come in from scouting. The two sailors rested on a small log surrounded with firearms and grenades while they sipped tea from gourd shells and listened to Tatti and Noello.

"My best, a Darjeeling that I saved for this very occasion." Noello poured goat's milk into Tatti's cup until the tea was a light beige.

"I never before drank tea with honey," Tatti said.

"'Tis a natural taste, my lady." Noello's eyes glistened as she sipped.

The two sailors stared down into their gourd shells of tea. Roo scratched his thick beard and glanced at Brighton, then back to Tatti's bare thigh mottled under a wreath of loose leaves.

"We're pretending." Brighton growled at his friend.

Roo pointed at his tea gourd, arching an eyebrow quizzically.

"Drink it." Brighton upended his cup and Roo made a sour face as he swallowed.

"Delicious," Tatti said, ignoring the two sailors, and arresting Noello's eyes with her own, as though he were the only human being on earth. She held out her cup in her slender fingers to be filled once more. Noello got to his knees, and moved about the thick moss to pour.

"If you will live with me, my lady, I'll feed you honey and capture butterflies to cool your brow." He tilted his head and watched her.

"Oh, Noello, I love butterflies, but I love people as well."

"Oh, mortals, that's all they are." Noello sank back onto his haunches.

Tatti set her hand upon his forearm to reassure him. "Noello, the Lord put people here, and we do in our time the days that belong to us, until we have left nothing undone, and we measure it with grief and joy, and sorrow by bliss, until we find a peace in our hearts." She watched the soft eyes that she could feel reach into her soul. "And we must not stop trying until that peace comes."

Tatti decided to stay out in the forest with Noello, after it became apparent that a pivotal issue turned upon her presence. Gordon's shrewd military skill had decimated the rovers; yet still they would not depart. Noello's eager, if unstable mind and his forest skills were indispensable in Gordon's all-out battle against the unpredictable, implacable Bonabombo.

Tatti was torn with an overwhelming desire to see her child, yet she knew Cora would tend her son just as she herself had been tended, and Caroline was a wet nurse who exulted in feeding children at each breast.

The early dawn set a faint light into the forest about Tatti, breaking the ease of her sleep, and she awoke with a wrench. Treetops and green haze settled into her sight, and birds were calling on the cool morning air, giving an unreal fright to her condition. "Cora?" she whispered, for her nurse, and peeked with her eye to see the empty hammock. She lifted her head, and saw she was alone in the palm house. Noello was gone.

She set her hand over her eyes, and she could see her mother sweeping up to the great fires of Skarra to throw up the coals herself, and then hand the poker-iron to the parlor maid to set in the brass andirons.

"I want to hold Gordie," she murmured to herself. "My little boy."

"My lady?" Brighton's voice jerked her into reality, and she was startled to see him hop down from the limb where he'd waited for her to wake.

"Oh, Brighton, you frightened me."

"Noello's off with Roo, all afire to torment Bonabombo." He brought a platter of cold vegetables to her and the inevitable breadfruit, which he had kept hot on heated stones.

Tatti swung out of her hammock, throwing aside the covers, and wanted to shrink back when she realized she was still dressed in what was left of her girdle of leaves and shattered wreaths. Brighton saw her discomfiture at her nudity, and spoke gently as he handed her the breakfast.

"I won't look at you, my lady."

"Thank you, Brighton. It's all rather beyond my control."

"One does what one must, Lord Gordon would say," Brighton said briskly.

After breakfast, Tatti decided Brighton could go in to the fort, to report on Noello and the field campaign he had launched against the pirates with Roo, and to ask Gordon's further directions, particularly as to when Tatti was to return.

"Noello's unstable of mind, but that instability may be the very thing Lord Gordon wants," Tatti said. "Tell him it seems essential I remain." Tatti slipped into her thin white clothing.

"I'll be back in the forest before sunset," Brighton said, and slipped away along the edge of the creek.

Tatti watched the sailor's body consumed in the shadows of the great trees along the waterway, and she turned back to the palm house, where she knew she was safe.

Gordon Wragby perched in a lookout chair atop the wooden tower, with his spyglass on the savanna. He was startled to see the sudden apparition of Noello's distant figure, running in clear view through the long dry grass.

"He's gone plumb balmy, my lord," Brighton said.

"Hmmm, I can see." Gordon frowned at Noello's wild shrieks echoing over the grass plain. "They'll kill him in broad daylight, I'm afraid."

"He's overdoing it," Cora said, her face at Gordon's knee where he stood in the lookout. "First he wouldn't fight, now he's wild."

"Aye, we'll have to get Tatti back in the fort," Gordon said.

He saw a loose squad of buccaneers rush into sight, well behind the darting figure of Noello. They raised their muskets to naked shoulders, and he could see the smoke bloom as they fired.

"If they ain't got rifles, he's safe," the marine said.

"It's his heart that'll betray him," Gordon said, snapping shut the glass. "His mind is already gone."

Booom! Booom!

Gordon jumped at the concussions, and the people in the tower crowded to see great puffs of white smoke explode out of the harmless grasslands, throwing up chunks of sod and clouds of dirt and chaff into which the running men vanished.

"Grenades! Noello's grenaded them pirates!" Caruthers shouted.

Gordon Wragby watched the onrushing men stumble into sight once more, and gather two of their members into their arms who, though wounded, were evidently still alive. The pirates were retreating.

"Well, it's harassment at best." Gordon spoke quietly. "Better than nothing, but grenades and canisters are only effective against bunched-up targets."

"Grapeshot's what we need, my lord," Stowell said.

"The enemy's too wise for that just now, I'm afraid." Gordon turned to Brighton. "Bring in Tatti tonight. Can't risk her."

"Aye, my lord."

XXVIII

The night air was sweet in Gordon's breath as he slept, but from some distant cavern he heard a sharp, discordant blow strike at his slumbers. He knew it to be impossible, that the fort was safe; yet in that flash of truth, his body scorched with the nightmare of another truth: that the probable impossible would prevail. He gasped and clutched in the dark for his pistols as he heard coarse shouting and children crying, accompanied by a woman's shriek.

"Caruthers!" Gordon shook the sleeping marine to his feet. He was alert instantly, a knife glinting in one hand and his pistol cocked.

"My lord?"

"Hush!" Gordon whispered. "Look!"

They squinted down through the cracks in the weathered timbers and beams of the tower where they slept with the cannon and powder.

"Those bastards!" Caruthers croaked. They saw the whole courtyard of the palisaded fort tilting in wild, lopsided shadows thrown from a waving sea of torches carried by strange men who strode about, while cringing children and women crowded into the corners.

"They've breached our defenses," Gordon said, as the flaring images leaped across the stockade. Ugly round grenades were held aloft on the bare arms of the men, still wet from wading the marsh and crawling the tunnel. The wicks were held close to the torches.

"Back, you little nipper!" one of the men shouted, and flung a half-naked child toward a huddling mass of crying people; its tow shirt tore loose, leaving the child suddenly white and nude in the flare-light, in the midst of the skittering figures that were moving from wall to wall of the stockade, trying futilely to escape.

"Huddle, ye bastards!" A coarse voice assailed them.

Caruthers raised the German rifle.

"No." Gordon laid his hand on the marine's arm. "I want you to break from the tower and vault the stockade, and dash into the forest."

"The forest, my lord?"

"Aye, keep Tatti in the forest—you'll have Brighton and Roo, and Noello."

"Noello?"

"My God, he fights, crazy or not."

"Aye, my lord."

"Lord Gordon!" The coarse voice enveloped the fort, and Gordon could see every face turn upward to the tower of the blockhouse. "Lord Gordon, come down, or we'll blow up your children."

A rough man seized a child and held its prone body up over their heads, as another man thrust a torch into the child's face, making it scream and thrash its slender white legs as a small puff of singed hair coiled up out of the swaying flares.

Gordon set his hand up to the marine's lips to still his oath. "He won't kill us all. He needs a crew."

"Where's her ladyship?" A voice rang from below. "Lord Gordon, we want your woman that fired them cannons!"

Gordon heard the clatter of ladders being dropped over the palisades, and he saw a limping man with a long reddish jaw and matted black hair climb into sight.

"Bonabombo!" a rover shouted.

"Somebody betrayed us," Gordon whispered. "Someone told them Tatti was at the cannons!" He walked to the double shutters and flung them open, facing the whole company of pirates and his own people. "Douse your punts, I'm coming down!"

The throng was silent, the children huddled among the women, who were crying openly. He caught sight of Margene, standing alone, her eyes glowering as she searched for the traitor among the upturned faces who looked to their captain. And he could tell his own sailors at a glance, at their sheepish looks of shame in defeat. "My lord," Cora whispered, climbing into his quarters, "I've hid the baby with Caroline's."

"Good, Cora."

Gordon watched Bonabombo, who was on the parapet inside the embrasure opposite him, above the heads of the people and overtop the flares.

"You was the worst man I ever fought!" Bonabombo shouted, clenching his fist over a cutlass bell. He broke into laughter that rose until it began to choke off into an explosion of phlegm, which he wiped from his stubbled lips with the back of his forearm.

The laughter was unsettling, and Gordon noticed a subdued fright in the silence of those who watched Bonabombo.

"I want that bitch that killed forty-two men!" He grinned into the massed company. "And then I'll have my sport." He took a tilting step along the parapet and stopped. "You'll find me a fair man."

Gordon turned back into the dark of the tower where Caruthers waited. "When I walk out onto the drop-ladder, all eyes'll be on me. —I want you to dash across behind me, just as I reach the parapet, and leap the stockade. And don't break your leg—you'll need both legs to run." He grabbed the big man about his shoulders. "Caruthers, you're great. Now be off with you."

Turning to the shutters, Gordon jerked loose the plank that fell out onto the walkway and stepped into full sight. Just as he reached the parapet, he saw Caruthers come hurtling after him. He ducked aside as the big marine bounced on the board, leaped into the air, and was out of sight into the night as he plunged over the stockade and out of the fort.

Boom! A musket ball whistled past Gordon, who stopped, watching the pirates begin to clamber up the ladders toward him.

In the moments that Gordon watched his whole world fall in ruins about his bare legs, he wondered at its purpose. He could see the faces of his people seeking his wisdom and guidance. And he had no answer for them. He had done his best, and still the unforeseen, the impossible had engulfed him. His one consolation was that he'd slaughtered so many of his enemies that they now needed his men to sail their ship. His mind reflected on the irony that he'd likely saved them by doing well what he decried.

"Lord Gordon of Ravendale?" the tilting figure said, stumping along the parapet toward him.

Gordon fixed his eyes on Bonabombo's forehead and waited. He felt the outrage emanate as if it were a smell from the man he had so outwitted in daring and boldness. Hatred glowed from the narrowed eyes of the shrewd, angry man he had not only beaten, but made to look a fool.

"High and mighty!"

Gordon heard the words screamed at the same moment he felt his face slapped sideways. His ears rang and, unbalanced, he slumped into the stockade and slid off the boards of the parapet. He was on the ground, half held in the upraised arms that broke his fall, unable to focus his eyes while his men cursed and flares blinded him.

"You got no respect for human life!"

Gordon could hear Bonabombo's shrill wail, somewhere above him.

"You killed a hunert and sixty brave men!"

"Trash, they was trash!" It was Margene, standing alone, her hands on her hips. "They come at innocent shipwreck folk, and Lord Gordon showed us how to fight—*we* killed them!"

"Kill her!" Bonabombo shouted. "Kill that ugly bitch!"

"That's the cook!" a pirate shouted. "That wench fed 'em out of nothing!"

"Leave her then!" Bonabombo laughed. "Put her in leg-irons and put her to work. A man's belly ain't particular about what bitch cooks the vittles."

The pirates laughed jovially at Bonabombo's humor, and Gordon felt an easing of tensions, though he knew the nightmare of their captivity had just begun.

XXIX

Gordon sensed the main purpose of his struggle would live, even when they had lost the fort, and armed pirates strode about the cowering castaways. He watched as his weapons were collected, and the gates torn asunder, loosing them to fall upon the ground in dust clouds, as the dawn came up.

He remained in the midst of his people, standing outside the gateway as they gathered up their personal belongings and carried them outside the stockade and piled them in the savanna. Bonabombo climbed throughout the fort, exploring its structure, and talking with his men. Gordon ignored the pirates and their chieftain as something which if it did exist, should not exist, and certainly would eventually fail, and he was pleased to see his people take spirit from his composed quietude in their midst.

"We'll burn it, burn her down to her timbers." Bonabombo spoke loudly, letting his voice carry over Gordon and the emigrants.

Gordon ignored the remark as well as the man, holding his hands behind his back and waiting. He knew self-control was the clue to their survival.

As the light came up strong, Margene and Cora came to him followed by Higgins and Cutler. The men had a lost air, but in Margene and Cora's eyes he saw the look of pure cold flint.

"We know who betrayed us, my lord," Cora said.

Gordon looked down at the dust and flattened grass where he stood. About them the emigrants were trekking toward the pavilion once more, under their personal burdens of linen and pots and tubs, and disheveled pieces of clothing.

"It doesn't matter now," Gordon said, not really wanting to know, for it meant more grief.

"The bitch," Margene said quietly. "We'll kill her."

"Now, now, no more of that talk." Gordon looked into the fierce Highland eyes. "Roo turned out true and fair."

"Sheila, the only woman that lost no children," Cora said, "and she denied us her body to comfort the young'uns in the pavilion."

"Aye, a sullen wench," a sailor said matter-of-factly. "Six and twenty men raped her."

"How do you know?" Gordon said.

"Pirates bragged about it," Margene said.

Gordon nodded. It was impossible to get across the savanna unobserved by his watchmen. He grasped Bonabombo's cunning in compelling the surrender of the fort by threatening the children's lives, once inside.

"She flirted with any man," Stowell said.

"Should have married her off," Gordon said.

"Married her! My lord, who'd have her?" Margene cried.

"Lord, I don't know. 'Twas just an idea to avoid trouble."

"That much trouble'd kill a man," Cora chimed in.

Gordon avoided their eyes, knowing they wanted some signal as to what to do. He saw no purpose in revenge, now the fort was lost. The traitor meant little to him. They stopped talking when a small group of rovers came up, shoving a woman in front of them. Gordon saw her face was mottled and swollen by blows. "The bitch," Margene said, clanking her fetters as she turned.

"Take your bitch!" the buccaneer said, flinging the sobbing woman to the dust at their feet. "We done used her."

Sheila's face was bleeding, her hair had been torn loose and her clothing was in disarray.

The buccaneers went off in a clutch, following Bonabombo's loud voice as they lay thatch about the fort to fire it.

"Sheila, go bathe in the saltwater." Gordon spoke quietly.

The resentful eyes searched theirs. "I thought they would love me, but they tore off my clothes and raped me, and they didn't look at me. In a group they did."

"Aye. Go bathe."

"Cut her throat, I will." Margene spat in the dust.

"They didn't want me," Sheila moaned.

Gordon was astonished that the woman was so shallow that all she could see was her rejection at the hands of crude men, when she had brought down the whole world of her friends and kin. "Go bathe your naked body, Sheila. They likely have the Caribbean rot in their privy parts."

Sheila's hands came up to her ample breasts, and her head tilted in sullen reproach.

"You men're all alike. Want our carnal flesh to mock, ye do."

"Slut! I'll kill her!" Margene grabbed her by her hair, and swung her flat before them.

"Hold her, men," Gordon said, nodding to the cook. "Get Sheila up."

"Go wash your face and your privy parts." Gordon spoke without looking at her.

"Oh." Sheila clutched her torn skirt to preserve her modesty.

"Goddamn it, go wash," Stowell said. "Them rovers is rotten where they prong."

"Evil man, I saw you look at me." She flipped her skirt about her legs as she went across the savanna.

"My lord, you done your best," Cora said, laying her hand on Gordon's forearm.

"Perhaps," Gordon said. "They say thirty

pieces of silver is what betrayed Christ, but I've always thought it was vanity."

The cotters and sailors looked at Gordon, their brows furrowed in puzzlement, and he felt utterly alone, in a sudden void of despair. His only consolation was that Tatti was hidden, and his son was disguised at a wet nurse's breast.

After they had got settled into the pavilion, the pirates swaggered with self-confidence. They poked through all the belongings of the emigrants, and they collected the muskets and sharp-edged tools, their hoes and axes and sickles and adzes, as well as their powder. He watched them stagger across the savanna, heavily burdened under the two cannons from the fort that had wreaked such havoc when fired with grapeshot.

Gordon waited in his small thatched hut, watching for another false move by Bonabombo, grateful that Noello and his two men and Tatti had vanished into the silence of the forest. "Tatti's giving orders, at least for now," he whispered to Cora.

The capture of the fort had come so suddenly that he had lost no men, which, though a blessing, impelled Bonabombo to clap leg-irons on the ankles of six of the sailors and four of the most robust of the cotters. It gave the rovers a particular sense of security to have these men in leg-irons, and they stretched a broad tarpaulin on the beach, covering a portion of their sand fortification. They built a large bonfire the night of their victory, and

317

Gordon could hear them singing and roistering as they got drunk.

Gordon walked out and watched the shadowed figures of the pirates breaking into sight about the fire, to vanish into the dark, amidst wild laughter and coarse shouting as their celebration continued. A dozen scowling buccaneers moved through the pavilion, where the children were bedded down, surrounded by women.

"They've always got us blackmailed through the hostage of women and children," Gordon said to Cora, who brought him his supper.

"We women can fight, my lord." Cora watched him as he dabbed at his food.

"We'd all die for you, Lord Gordon," Leslie said, gently settling herself on her folded calves and thighs at his feet.

"No, no, none of that." Gordon speared a morsel and put it into his mouth. "Where there's life, there's hope."

Gordon did not go on. He wanted quiet, a time to contemplate with all human passions held in control.

In the middle of the next morning they were herded onto the savanna. Bonabombo stood on a knoll in the distance and filled the air with shouts and laughter, pointing to the distant logged structure of the fort. Gordon watched the fires lick about the timbers at the corners of the stockade, with a small yellow streak light a single parapet, releasing a shallow plume of smoke.

"Stubborn, them logs is," Cutler said.

"How are you managing with your irons?" Gordon looked down at the naked shanks of the tall, bald-headed man.

"Walking like a pregnant woman, I is, to keep 'em from barking me ankles." He stared pensively at the fetters locked about his legs. "But I ain't no galley slave yet, leastways."

"Have one of the women find out who keeps the keys to the locks on the leg-irons." Gordon spoke to Cora without turning his head.

"Aye, my lord."

The fire had grown about the base of the fort, which, though aflame, seemed to resist its destruction, preserving a hulking image of up-thrust logs. Fires licked along the embrasures, illumining the dark teeth, and sending long columns of smoke up through the distant sun-light, over the yellow tongues of fire. The people watched the fort refuse to yield, smoldering on the savanna.

"He don't know nothing about logs," Higgins said. "They'll rot in this climate before they'll burn."

Suddenly a vast white cloud erupted from within the stockade, hurtling the log tower and the shingle roof upward over a red column of fire that shot a scorching tongue into the air. They watched the shower of glowing red embers rise through the dark tower of smoke, and the heavy logs fell end over end out from the explosion, landing over the walls of the stockade into the savanna.

"Gunpowder," Gordon said. About him the people were very quiet. Their fort had been blown apart, and they watched the dust settle out of the smoke.

"Praise the Lord, the stockade held!" Cora said.

Gordon was astonished to see the vertical timbers tilting ominously outward, like snaggled teeth, yet no longer aflame, and holding fast in a defiant hulk. About him, some of the people grinned in triumph. "Effen we'd not been betrayed, we could'a held out till hell froze over," Cutler said.

Gordon walked back, ignoring the people about him, as he saw Bonabombo heading them off across the savanna.

"Lord Gordon," he called, and Gordon stopped. "You have your pavilion, and we have victuals and fresh water, and we're all hid." He turned out his hands. "Friends in distress, aye?"

Gordon watched the narrow eyes of cunning as Bonabombo wagged his head from side to side. "I don't want no attacks from you, and I want your woman, bye and bye. No woman can kill my men, but I'll wait till she starves out." He laughed, dredging up a chain of phlegm. "And meanwhile we'll camp on the beach."

The women about Gordon glared at Bonabombo, Margene breathing audibly.

"We don't want no women, just men—you women is safe." Bonabombo turned, limping off with his men and leaving guards. "That countess what fired them cannons, that's one woman I do want."

All next afternoon Bonabombo strode about the Signal Hill using a spyglass to study the distant forest. He was deliberate in his plans, sending his men to bring ashore benches and muskets and set up a signal stand, by which a man used flags to send messages back and forth to the schooner which lay just offshore.

Bonabombo lived on the ship, Gordon noticed, yet he had bedded down most of his men ashore—far enough down the beach from the pavilion, however, so that there was no traffic or interaction between captors and captives.

The buccaneers had taken all the weapons and now demanded only that they be supplied with fresh pork, goat meat, and all the whiskey. The cotters watched them drink about their campfires, falling senseless at night after two or three hours of boisterous laughter and quarreling.

"That Bonabombo is a stubborn man and takes no women; he's got evil on his mind," Cora said. "Men who don't want women want what they shouldn't have."

It became obvious to the emigrants that the pirates had settled in for the season. Bonabombo ordered Stowell to lead out hunting parties into the forests of palmetto to shoot wild hogs.

"My men need sport," Bonabombo said, "and they eat, and that one-armed bosun ain't gonna give us no trouble. And if your old madman attacks, we kill your bosun, right off."

Bonabombo leaned forward when he spoke, and winked.

"We have no control over the old hermit," Gordon said, avoiding Bonabombo's eyes. "He was on the island first."

"Then you can say your prayers for your bosun." Bonabombo strode up to the Signal Hill, and took his ease as they watched from the distance.

Gordon considered their situation most carefully. It was obvious they were in no immediate danger, and he was glad no lives had been lost in the fall of his fort. If he played a waiting game, he might eventually be able to strike a balance with Bonabombo, maybe even buy him off with the promise of gold if he would transship them on to any English colony in the Antilles or to the Americas or Canadas.

Gordon had a clear understanding of greed and the role it played in men's lives, and he was ready to deal with it.

"It's time I always play for," Gordon said to Cora while he prepared for bed. "In time all things change."

"Aye, my lord, what's good cures, and what's bad festers to stink and rots away." Cora turned down his bed, for which he was pleased. He was afraid if Leslie tended to his person, it would burden him, for she stared in open adoration of him no matter what he did, even in front of Tatti.

"That Bonabombo ain't changing, my lord." Cora placed his oil lamp by his head as he lay down. "He's got too many guns and men out to shoot a pig. He's hunting Tatti and Roo and that poor little Frenchman, or Eye-talian, whatever Noello is."

He saw the truth of her remark, and turned away his face to the wall. "Keep the baby hid on Caroline's breast."

Cora snuffed out the lamp and whispered, "Do you think he'd harm the children?"

"I don't know, Cora. Knowing grief so close and evil so powerful, I must try for a compromise—but keep the child hidden."

Gordon closed his eyes. Perhaps the night would sweep his body aloft on limbs that were light as feathers, and he could sleep the whole night through. He felt exhaustion press down on him, and he slipped gratefully into the darkness of slumber.

XXX

Hidden in the distant trees, Tatti watched with Noello and the two English sailors, and the marine. It was safe, yet Tatti carried a leaden sense of isolation and dread for the captives of the fort. And riding like a cold stone in the pit of Tatti's stomach was her fear and longing for little Gordie.

"I just wish I could see and hold Gordie," Tatti said while they opened the earth pit where their yams had baked, in preparation for supper.

"That air young'un's safer with Caroline and Cora than you, my lady," Caruthers replied firmly.

"Perhaps, but if you'd ever borne a child, you'd want the child in your own lap, on your own belly, at your own breast." Tatti settled herself, wrapped in a woven mantle of rain-proof grass and wearing chains of leaves over her light garments.

The men were silent, for she had answered them with the longing of life for itself that refuted the men's logic, being obviously right. "Of course Gordie is safer where he is, but I still feel the same way."

Caruthers nodded, while Brighton and Roo were suddenly busy bursting hot potato peels to lard with goat's butter. Noello perched behind Tatti, his eyes searching the forest shadows endlessly and his nose sniffing the quiet air, as though questing a new scent.

"We was supposed to remain hid, till we got contrary orders from his lordship." Brighton spoke gently.

"If they haven't killed him," Tatti said.

"No gunshots was fired, my lady."

Tatti nodded, and began to eat the potato with her fingers. "You said it was me he wanted—the woman who killed forty-two men."

"Aye, my lady." The men were very quiet.

"I had no idea the cannons would do that," Tatti said. The potato tasted warm and crumbled wet in her mouth.

"My lady, now don't you blame yourself." Caruthers turned his sunburned head on his strong neck. "If you hadn't fired 'em, they was a dozen men who would have."

As the night settled over them and Tatti swung idly in her hammock in the frond house, she could hear the men moving among the tree lookouts. Their hoarse whispered voices calmed her, yet even she could see the distant shore where fires rose along the beach.

"Cat and mouse now," Noello said, appearing out of the gloom, still holding the spyglass.

Tatti did not answer, watching the fireflies in small glowing darts that lit and vanished among the cedar limbs. She longed for a woman to talk to, and moved restlessly. "Brighton?"

"Aye, my lady?" a muffled voice carried along a limb to her.

"Will we be all right?"

"So far we're just fine."

"Well, we don't seem to get things resolved. I wish we could all be together."

"We have our orders, my lady." The sailor rocked her hammock gently. "If you can sleep, you'll feel better by morning."

Tatti droused in the slow rhythm of the cradling hammock, until her eyes were heavy and her limbs lifted her weightless into sleep.

At dawn she heard gunfire echo through the forests, and the wild cry of flocks of birds pierced the morning. Coarse voices shouted in the forests.

Rolling out of her hammock to her feet, she realized she was alone. The day lightened, and the sky and limbs and leaves and trees enveloped her. She heard the scattered fire of musketry rattle the air in the distance, and she knew it was undisciplined. The pirates, she thought.

She splashed water in her face to wake her

eyes, and took up a tortoiseshell hairpin to hold in her teeth while she combed and piled her thick weight of hair off her neck and atop her head so it would not be caught in branches and would stay out of her eyes. After she had completed her toilette, she sat cross-legged on a mat, ate cold breadfruit and mangoes, and listened to the distant voices.

By mid morning she heard the crackle of gunfire and men calling from several different places on the island. A long echo boomed through the forest, and she saw a ball of smoke settling onto the water before the anchored schooner in the small bay.

"Oh!" Tatti jumped when Brighton popped into view beside her.

"Sorry, my lady." The sailor settled his hand on her forearm as he knelt, and watched the schooner. "Bonabombo's got thirty men in the forest shooting everything that moves."

"Surely they aren't shooting a cannon at a forest," Tatti said, sliding the bowl of fresh fruit to the man's sinewed knee.

"No telling, my lady. They ain't got good sense."

" 'Twill waste their shot."

"Good riddance." Brighton took up a mango and bit into it without looking, and ate while the juices ran over his fingers and down his arm, and out the corners of his mouth, running in rivulets through the hair on his chest. He cradled a musket in his free arm and had pistols thrust in his belt.

"We 'weren't to fight, I think," Tatti said. She was seeking more to persuade the English sailors and the marine than tell them, because she sensed they were all but possessed by a craving to fight. "We're terribly outnumbered, and his lordship did say he wanted to wait."

"Uh?" Brighton looked puzzled. Tatti repeated herself, and was glad to see the sailor nod. "Oh, we ain't about to fight, but they's killed old Noello's pet goat, and he's all tore up."

"It's terrible when they shoot everything."

"Roo and the sergeant's got him in a tree, yonder side of the woods."

Scarce daring to breathe, Tatti listened to the wide, sweeping line of armed men pass beneath their copse of trees and under the frond house. As the afternoon wore on, they heard the forest silence descend once more, of the still coolness where only the usual singing of the birds was heard among the quiet trees.

"Gone, my lady." Brighton smiled.

"Let's go down." Tatti stepped out onto the broad limb and descended the trunk, her bare toes and fingers clinging to the thick bark.

The forest gloom was a shadowed peace as far as she could see or hear, and she laughed aloud. "Brighton, they've gone—we escaped."

She walked down to the stream bank and perched on a large rock in the waning sunlight, and watched the two distant figures of Caruthers and Roo come across the forest floor toward them. The marine looked worried.

"That balmy Noello, he escaped from us."

"Told you we ought to tie him," Roo said.

"We don't tie up our allies," Caruthers

said, wiping his forehead with his open palm. "Plumb batty."

"Gone loco, over a goat." Roo chewed on a leaf and squatted with the others.

The marine drew in the punk with a stick. "If we fires our guns, they'll discover us by the smoke. So no gunfire." Caruthers searched their eyes, and watched each man nod.

"But Noello's got crossbows and traps hid all over this island. Crossbows don't make no noise."

"Well, I thought they'd given up." Tatti walked over to the three men.

Caruthers stood. "That was before they got Noello mad. He was touched in the head to start with, and now I fear he's plumb daft."

They watched the sun ease onto the horizon, and a gold cape dazzle across the ocean as the shadows of the forest thickened. They each understood they must await the new events, and how far Noello's rampage might take him, and what consequences lay ahead from it.

The next morning began with the heavy thump of grenades from somewhere along the shoreline, and Tatti listened as shouts rose to a crescendo, then diminished.

"They're easy to keep track of, they make so much noise," Tatti said. She felt quite safe, even down out of the tree house.

A fleeting break of light caught their eye, that fluttered in the gloom, then vanished. "Noello," Roo said, as Brighton cocked a musket.

Noello was running in a crouch, looking

up into the trees and behind him as he went. It was hard to keep him in sight among the tree trunks and disguised in his leaf mantle.

"Noello!" Tatti called.

They watched him cut in their direction, and at a distance they could see his soft eyes were afire. Tatti could hear his gasping laughter that came in shivers, making his frail shoulders tremble.

"You can't go back!" He stared at Tatti in proud contentment. "I won't let them have you!"

"Can't go back?" Tatti walked toward the small elderly man who was breathing through his open mouth.

"No. I'm killing them."

"You, Noello?" the Marine sergeant said.

"Oh, easily. They're furious with me. I've killed five already."

"Five?" Tatti said.

"Into the trees, dear friends, into the trees." Noello pointed them toward the forest gloom, and putting his hands together, he laughed. "They'll not defile my lovely." His hand went out to her and fluttered, like a bird's wing brushing her shoulder. "Begone!"

"Noello, we don't need no battle," Caruthers said firmly.

"I have a deadfall waiting to drop on 'em!" He doubled up in wild shivers of laughter, pushing them toward the forest. "I'm leading them to it."

They heard heavy running footsteps crashing in a distance. "Up!" Noello shouted, and broke away from them, filling the forest

331

with a high-pitched scream of triumph and scorn. Tatti could hear the despair of a lost soul who had found its purpose in living, and she shivered.

"Skeedaddle!" Roo shouted, leading them into the thick copses and clambering into the high limbs.

"There he goes!" Tatti heard pirates' voices.

"Fire!"

The noise reverberated among the trees, and the air was wild with the haunting scream of protesting birds that circled against the sky.

"Missed him!"

"Fire!"

Tatti clung to the tree tunk and watched a band of men dressed in pantaloons and sleeveless jackets running aimlessly on the forest floor. They were armed with muskets and stumbled over their cutlasses, and didn't seem to know where to look.

Zing! One of the men grabbed his throat and coughed out a scream, and Tatti could hear him gasping against the arrow thrust through his neck. He flopped in the leaves and went chalk white, and his arms dug light furrows in the brown punk.

"Another crossbow!" one of the buccaneers roared, and the company scattered, hiding behind tree trunks, all looking in different directions. "He's up in the trees!"

A tall man looked straight up at Tatti, his pockmarked face fixing onto her as she lay clinging to the limb overtop him. She quit breathing and closed her eyes, and felt her intestines flop over in fear. She squeezed the rough bark between her knees and silently whispered. "Lord, save me."

"Search the trees!"

She heard their footsteps beneath her. "He's got to be close!"

Zing!

She heard another scream, and heard cursing everywhere beneath her.

"A girl's leg—I see a girl's leg!" A man's voice was calling loudly.

"Shoot her!"

"Can't see! Only her knee and thigh!"

"No, that's the woman Bonabombo wants!"

Zing!

"Get out of here!" It was the loud voice in command. "No, leave that son of a bitch to die!"

Tatti heard running, and saw a man get uncertainly to his feet, and lurch after his retreating companions.

"I tell you, I saw a half-naked woman!" a voice shouted from a distance.

Tatti held her breath when she saw Noello dart up before the wounded man, who had a shaft thrust into his open belly. The man stood upright, his dark eyes round in horror. She watched Noello drop to a knee and aim the strange bow before him. *Zing!* The short bolt struck the man in his chest with a hollow thump, and he fell over.

"God have mercy on us." Tatti closed her eyes. "He's murdering them."

An iron hand grasped her wrist and tore her from her limb, scraping the insides of her knees and her thighs, and swung her on up into the tree.

"You was too low, my lady," Brighton said. "Next time, you climb higher." His voice was grave, and Tatti nodded.

They could hear Noello's shrieking cry of triumph and despair carry through the quiet forest. Later, they heard a deep splintering crash, followed by a heavy thump that made the ground tremble.

"What was that?" Tatti whispered, while the men listened with cocked ears and open mouths.

Screams pierced the distance, gradually diminishing in strength.

"That was his deadfall," Caruthers said. "Use 'em in Africa on animals, they do."

The men looked solemnly at the marine.

"Got spikes in it, it has, to stick 'em."

"My God," Brighton said.

"Bonabombo brings out the worst in a man," Roo said.

"Lord have mercy, we've grown to be what we hated, I fear," Tatti said.

"Oh, you ain't done nothing," Caruthers said briskly.

"I may have caused it."

"A girl? Nonsense." Caruthers dismissed the thought, running his hand fondly down the barrel of his Jaeger rifle.

Bonabombo waited at the Signal Hill, using the spyglass to peer across the savannas at the forests, where he could hear the gunfire, and watch the birds circling overhead, and see the musket smoke rise into sight above the trees. He did not get angry until his search parties began coming in carrying their own dead. They could hear him in the pavilion screaming oaths and swearing revenge, and Gordon walked out to sit on a bench to face the anger when it came.

After the fourth party returned, carrying dead men slung on poles, Bonabombo broke down the hill, cursing every step. Gordon got to his feet, Leslie and Cora standing behind him.

"He's a murderer! Nine men out of my company of forty!" Bonabombo's face was pale with anger.

"Who?" Gordon said, feigning astonishment.

"That crazy hermit!"

"If you'd sail away, you'd not have the problem."

"He's run across the quicksand on bridges hid under water, and drowned men in the swamp! Following him!"

"Quicksand?" Gordon repeated.

"Slings and crossbows hid all through the forest, we've got arrows stuck in half the ship's company."

"I'd keep out of the forest," Gordon said laconically.

"You've got him pretty angry about something," Cora said, her voice bold as she shook her finger at Bonabombo.

Bonabombo's face darkened, his eyes

glazed from the shadow as his face twisted and he ground his teeth. "We saw the woman." He panted. "Goddamn her!"

Gordon felt his heart thump in his windpipe, and he folded his arms across his chest and stared at the unkempt forehead.

"Saw her naked up in a tree!" Bonabombo was struggling for his breath, his eyes glowering on Gordon. "I hate women!"

"Those are bad odds, I'd say." Gordon was pleased to hear the calm in his own voice. "That's one half the human race."

Slap! Gordon did not see the hand that knocked him down. He sat up tasting his own blood.

Bonabombo whirled and went back to the hill as Gordon got unsteadily to his feet.

That night the buccaneers were quiet round their campfires, and the people in the pavilion doused their fires early to retire. Fear escalated among them. It seemed they scarce dared to leave their own company in the thatch village, and Gordon noticed the subdued withdrawal of the children to the corners in their own company.

"Put my pallet in the common pavilion," Gordon said to Leslie. "I'll sleep with our people." He had noticed the terror in the eyes of the cotters and the lost, uncertain glances of his own sailors, as their captors strode among them in growing impatience.

"We know who's got the keys to the leg-irons," Cora whispered as he bedded down, and Leslie nodded.

336

"Not until I say." He closed his eyes. "Have Margene sharpen her knives. We want it silent."

"Aye, my lord," Cora said, and Gordon heard Leslie's breath catch in the dark of his words.

Gordon woke early, when the guards brought up the six hostage children they'd kept overnight to be fed and exchanged for six different children. The women were already up, and brought him fried breadfruit.

He was eating when he heard cheers rising among the pirates on the Signal Hill, and calls from the ship. Gordon walked out to see three men coming across the savanna, carrying a body. "Here," he said to Margene, handing over his plate.

" 'Tain't a woman's body," the tall cook said, as the captives gathered about him. "And it ain't no full-fleshed man."

Gordon and his sailors grew very silent when they saw the dangling body of Noello. He was trussed up on a pole, swinging naked and so scrawny he looked like a wrinkled child with a beard. The head flopped and bled from the open mouth with every step.

"Ambushed him!" Bonabombo shouted in triumph. "Gulled him in with a wounded buccaneer and shot him at ten paces, by God!"

The laughter was general among the freebooters, and Gordon watched as they flung the body to the sand, and proceeded to hack off the head with cutlasses, making wet-gristle sounds against the neck. One of them had the head on a staff in a moment, and set it to face the pavilion. The large circular eyes had a perpetual startled look, and the emigrants went inside to avoid it.

"Now we'll get that countess, and we'll see who plays for sport," Bonabombo said, shaking his finger amid general assent among his followers.

The search for Tatti did not go as easily as the buccaneers had hoped. Tatti and the three men had heard the shot that had broken Noello's leg, and heard him call that he was done for.

" 'Tis our orders not to fight," Caruthers said. "Now into the trees."

They stayed well clear of the forest floor, and up past the green forest leaves. Their cache of fresh herbal foods was large with water stored in earthen crocks, and they hid day and night, always speaking in whispers.

Search parties scoured the forests, time and again passing beneath them, yet Tatti and the three men had simply vanished from sight. After a week the pirates gave up, and Bonabombo grew morose. He dismissed Stowell, and the bosun returned to the pavilion.

All ears listened as Stowell squatted beside Gordon and spoke matter-of-factly. " 'Twas hell, your lordship. Them arrows a'coming at you in front, and them lead slugs a'whistling past the back of your head."

"Aye, you lived," Gordon said.

"They was too sudden scared to remember to shoot me, and I always flopped on my belly, first arrow zing or shot."

"Noello knew you and liked you," Cora said.

"We was both cripples, I reckon. Leastwise he thought so."

"Noello's wound was in his heart, and yours is just an arm." Gordon lay his hand about the bosun's shoulder and drew his head into his neck and spoke gently. "Cups, you're a brave Englishman."

"Your lordship." Stowell began to weep. "Ye called me by my childhood name." He hid his face in Gordon's chest.

"Now, now, Cups, chin up." Gordon held the sailor with his other hand in the back of Stowell's head until the man got control of himself and stopped sobbing.

"Ye need vittles," the woman said, kneeling to hand him a platter of food and wiping his face.

Bonabombo lay in his hammock slung in the Signal Hut, sipping rum and shading his face beneath a wide-brimmed hat. He stayed that way three days.

"Of course, the children. We'll trap her." He sat upright; and Gordon, who was watching from the shade of the pavilion, knew of an instant they were all in much trouble.

XXXI

That night Gordon fell into a sleep of despair. His mind kept erupting against his soul, and his rest was a burden as he slept. Sometime in the very pitch of darkness he felt a woman's fingers across his lips and her hand on his chest as he lay on his pallet. "Sshh."

Cora and Caroline had come to him with his sleeping child in their arms. The women laid the child's quiet form against him, cradling its head over Gordon's shoulder.

"You was fitful," Leslie whispered, and Gordon smelled the rich scent of new life in the child Tatti had born; and in the dark, he could discern the exquisite symmetry of the fine, parted lips and small teeth, where the little

341

boy breathed. The head was a mass of curls, and an arm with alabaster smooth skin moved fitfully against Gordon's sparse beard.

"We knowed your sleep's a burden, my lord." Caroline snuggled against the baby's other side.

Gordon stroked the child's head, his fingers drifting through the fine hair, and he felt a purpose to life. His heart lifted, and he breathed easier. "Thank you," he murmured.

"We'll take him when you feel easy," Leslie whispered. Gordon lay on his back a long time, listening to the life-force in his child, until a peace insensibly engulfed him, and he could drowse.

The next morning the buccaneers entered the pavilion with their muskets at the ready, and herded the fifteen children out onto the beach, and up across the savanna which lay against the cedar forest. The emigrants were quite still, looking toward Gordon for guidance; yet he gave no indication of resistance, nor of outburst. He avoided their eyes, watching the children walk away, staring back at the adults with lost eyes.

"Get on there, little nippers!" the buccaneers called out good-naturedly.

They watched the children move across the long savanna of tall grass, the tops of the small heads brushing in and out of sight, up to the edge of a dark mass of trees. They heard the distant calls of the buccaneers who shot their muskets into the trees, and then herded the children back into the midst of the sun-burned savanna; and they watched the children

342

tied loosely by foot in a roped group that could not run, and made to sit down. Three men remained to guard them.

"Mine and yours is too young to be there," Caroline said, and the gaunt woman with large swinging breasts walked toward the cluster of small figures in the distance.

Gordon was silent as the guards drove her back. He was joined by the survivors, who watched the children all morning, mumbling words of dismay, but not talking or looking into each other's faces. They realized Bonabombo was holding the children hostage to the bonds of love within a woman, to ransom their freedom with the ruin or death of that woman. Instinctively, everybody understood the nightmare ahead, and refused to show it on his face, for fear it might come true.

"I think I could kill him with a rock," one of the sailors whispered to Gordon, looking up to Bonabombo who had watched through the long spyglass.

"Aye, so you could, but can you tell me how we kill the other thirty, with all but four of our men in chains?"

"I'm sorry, my lord," the sailor whispered.

"No—gallant notion, but I need time or more power."

All afternoon they watched the distant figures on the savanna, and when the afternoon air blew toward the sea, they could hear the faint crying of some of the children.

"Slow but sure remedy," Bonabombo called toward the pavilion.

When Cora walked up to bargain water

rights for the children, Bonabombo laughed uproariously. "Let 'em drink rain water." He looked back to his grinning men. "They ain't going to die, woman, unless that girl don't come in." Cora watched in silence as the men broke into guffaws. "Your wench told us the girl saved the children and one of the sucklers is hers. Now, we're going to find out which baby goes to what tit, right lads?"

By the next morning the pavilion was taut with mad schemes to rush the pirates. The buccaneers, anticipating the awful tension, were armed with cutlasses and dirks, and pistols. "No, they're mean and they're smart," Gordon said.

At noon they could hear the children, still held captive in the savanna. They were crying and calling openly to the adults they could see in the distance.

"He's got her," Gordon said to Cora. "She'll come in. It's not a woman's nature to hold out against life, and he knows it."

"Aye, got us where the hair is short, my lord." Cora shaded her eyes with her hand. "Do you think he'd take me, or any other woman instead of her?"

"No. The battering ram was his supreme achievement, and just when he'd won, Tatti fired the battery and wiped out half his men. He was done in by a frail woman."

"Any of us would've done it, my lord."

"Perhaps—but Tatti did it."

"He could've sailed away," Cora mused.

"Dear Cora, human nature is vanity, so in

love with victories that it risks the only victory that matters—life." He put his hands behind him, and glanced at the sandy flecked face. "You taught me that, on this island when I lost my ship."

"Tush, my lord, the tempest swallowed our ship."

"The Admiralty won't see it that way." He tried to jest, but he felt the leaden despair weigh in his bowels. "They've got Tatti, and I fear for her."

"My lord, I'm sorry." Cora slipped her arm about his waist, and held him.

Early in the afternoon Gordon saw movement at the edge of the forest, and saw Tatti's lithe step and slight figure emerge into the sunlight of the savanna.

"It's the girl," a sailor said, and in silence they watched her walk toward the crying children. One of the guards fired his musket into the air, and on the Signal Hill, the buccaneers whooped and howled, as though in competition with each other in a rite of masculine bravado.

"Let's go," Gordon said, walking rapidly, and leading the survivors. Cora strode at Gordon's side with Stowell. Behind came those clanking in their leg-irons.

Tatti was amidst the children, and to his left the pirates were moving through the long grass. In moments, they were each running, and he could see Tatti taking up children into her arms, and others swarming about her waist, raising their arms to touch and be picked up.

"We've got her!" a buccaneer shouted, as the two groups engulfed the children and the girl. The women swept up the scattered, weeping children and the buccaneers circled to stare at Tatti, who ignored them.

"There's your mother," Tatti said, letting a small child slide down her thighs to the ground.

The child ran to its mother, leaving Tatti with Gordie in her arms, to confront the men who had grown desperate to capture her. Gordon set his hand at her back and girdled the little boy's body in his arm as she held him.

"Mama?" Gordie pulled back his head to look at his mother, and then at his parents together. Gordon did not look into Tatti's eyes, knowing that each understood no emotion was to be shown, though Tatti crushed the child into her bosom, pressing his face into her flesh and feeling him squirm delightedly against his mother.

They heard Bonabombo walk behind them, rubbing his stubbled chin and grinning at his men. "Now we know which young'un goes on which tit, eh men?"

The buccaneers ran their eyes slowly up and down the girl's body, searching her face, greedily staring at the wreaths of intertwined leaves that girdled her waist and knees and lay over her breasts.

Cora was at Gordon's side with Caroline and her own child. "You were brave to come in," he whispered. She looked away, shaking her head imperceptibly, in anguish and torment.

346

"King Solomon would'a cut a child in two to find its true mother," Bonabombo laughed, glancing about at his quiet men, who stared in transfixed silence at the women and child and the tired, slender officer in a tattered navy tunic.

"Bonabombo, he was smarter than Solomon!" Bonabombo shouted, circling the small group. "I didn't need to cut no child in two to discover its mother."

There was an unearthly silence as the enormity of what had occurred became apparent to every eye.

"Trash!" It was the raucous voice of Margene, sucking in her hollow cheeks and spewing out her words. "No, you was trash that'd kill fifteen children to torment one woman—no, you ain't no King Solomon."

"Bitch!" Bonabombo knocked her to the ground and hurled himself on her, clawing at her face and tearing out her hair, while she dug grooves of flesh from his face and spat foam from her lips and shrieked foul oaths.

Gordon winced when he felt the spell broken by the awful fight sprung by Margene, and was relieved to hear his men and the buccaneers pull them apart. Margene got to her feet, her leg-irons clanking, still defiant.

"No wonder we couldn't discover her in the trees," said a short man with a mustache. He reached out and touched a leaf on Tatti's breast.

"Shall we divvy up the flesh, mates?" Bonabombo said. Gordon caught the glint in the bright eyes. "You bastard," he said, care-

347

fully clenching his fist into a hard ball. He slipped his hand from Tatti's back and aimed the fist at the man's nose. He felt the ecstatic crush of cartilage that broke flat under his knuckles against the lips, and saw the blood run out the nose and mouth to mat a pool of gore that spumed blood on Gordon's fist.

"Gordon!" he heard Tatti scream. He did not feel the blow that knocked him senseless at her feet.

Tatti let Cora have her child to hold, with Caroline's, to save its life as she faced the violence.

"Been a long time since we had a pretty woman, mates?" Bonabombo said.

"No need for that," Stowell said. "A white woman of breeding's worth five thousand pounds on the Spanish Main."

"Divvy her up!" A rover laughed in a high-pitched voice and ran his arms about the waists of two of his companions, who giggled hoarsely.

"Maybe the Englishman has five thousand quid?" Bonabombo's right eyelid dropped to a slit as he faced Stowell.

"Maybe," Stowell said.

"Got to see what you're buying," Bonabombo said. He set his hand at Tatti's throat and jerked off her leaf mantle. As it fell, he raked her waist bare, until she stood naked before them. The buccaneers laughed nervously at the nude figure, one voice going high.

"Show us what you're made of, girl." Bonabombo's laughter was wild, dragging up chunks of phlegm that clung outside his mouth in his stubble.

The English sailors and Stowell watched while the survivors shrank backward with the children. Tatti's eyes were blank, seeing but blind, and fixed above their heads.

Gordon moaned at her feet, where Leslie had his head in her thighs where she knelt, trying to lift his waist at his belt to help him breathe. "Dear, dear man," Tatti said, dropping to her knees at Gordon's side.

"He ain't hurt. Just put him to sleep—got too many fine airs for rough company." Bonabombo laughed.

"Five thousand pounds sterling," Stowell said evenly, avoiding Cora's eyes. She knew they hadn't a tuppence on the whole island.

"Well, let's sleep on it," Bonabombo said. "I'm a patient man."

They walked slowly across the hot savanna toward the pavilion, the naked girl in front. Stowell walked just behind her. The small of Tatti's back had burst into sweat in her fright, the cheeks of her full buttocks slipped past each other in the rivulets of sweat that ran down between them. He was embarrassed that he had noticed her intimate fear. Her skin was slippery wet where it pressed against itself between her thighs and along her armpits, and that her body made a small squishing noise when she walked.

"So the Englishman wants to buy her?" Bonabombo chuckled to himself.

Stowell did not answer. He listened to the

people's bare feet crushing in the dry sage grass as they followed. They were carrying their captain, who still was not coherent and could not keep his balance. "He tips over, he does," Stowell heard Leslie say. "That beast hit him with a musket."

When they got to the pavilion, Stowell brought canvas pants and a jumper to Tatti, who was still surrounded by buccaneers. "No need to parade her like a savage," he said, ignoring everybody. "Put them on."

"That's what I like, a gentleman," Bonabombo said.

"I'm all right," Tatti said, looking to Cora after she was dressed, and allowing leg-irons to be clamped to her ankles.

That night the rovers kept Tatti at their own beach fire. After Stowell was certain they were quite drunk, he walked down to be among the pirates, some of whom were already sprawled in stupor. Bonabombo was stretched out on a wicker lounge, warming his body, his eyes closed.

"We're hostage to our children," Stowell said.

"Aye, every man's got his price." Bonabombo sat upright.

"Send the girl to us for the night. She won't run."

"To you, Englishman?"

"You've got us by the short hair."

Bonabombo toppled over backward, laughing. "Take her. I told you, I was a patient man—but mind you, if she's gone by morning, we chop up the children." His eyelid fell to a slit. "I can do what King Solomon didn't have the grit to do."

"Come on, girl." Stowell pulled Tatti to her feet and kicked the iron fetters between her ankles. "Free her leg-irons." Stowell stood with his back to Bonabombo and waited that deathly moment to see if he'd win.

Bonabombo stood, running his eyes over the sailor, who kept his face on the heavy lock.

"Aye, free her." Bonabombo snapped his fingers, and a buccaneer dropped to his knees with a key to unlock her bare feet.

"Woman, you can't hide in the forest with a crying child, and you can't leave it, because I know which one it is." Bonabombo walked in close to face her. "Bible kings don't mean nothing to me." He grabbed her by her chin and faced her to him, and gripped her flesh when he saw her eyes were fixed above his eyes onto his forehead.

"I understand." Tatti spoke slowly, without looking at him.

"Then go."

"Come, my lady." Stowell turned her away by her arm and walked into the night from the pirates' camp, hearing Bonabombo laugh to himself. "Lord Gordon's got a big headache tonight."

That night Tatti lay her pallet by Gordon's side. His form thrashed feverishly, and his voice was unsettled. "He ain't come round yet, my lady," Cora whispered from among the slumbering figures within the broad open building.

"Cooling his temples." Leslie spoke in the

351

dark, and Tatti was glad to have Stowell near-by.

"We'll just wait," Tatti said.

"Aye, we'll play for time, as his lordship says," Stowell said, adjusting his canvas pallet next to the moving forms around the stricken captain.

XXXII

Stowell's arm throbbed with pain just beyond the stump where it was cut off, it seemed, and he woke. He felt his heartbeat striking the wound, and he blew out his lungs, trying to exhale the pain. He knew it came from the great doubt in his soul as to how to handle both his fear and his quandary, and he was uncertain about himself and what to do.

Through the long night he had listened to Gordon Wragby struggle to regain consciousness, and heard the women ministering to his restless form. He was leaderless at this critical hour. Tatti could direct him, both in her sublime youth and self-assurance born of her class and education as a woman, to save the whole company of them, lost on the island shipwreck. But not now.

Tatti was the very thing he could not save from the sorry things he suspected, as a man of the sea, that lay ahead. He felt small and powerless, and never more the Yorkshire plow-boy who went to sea. "Good God, I don't know what to do," he whispered to himself.

He heard the birds begin to sing and knew the day was not long off, and he felt no pleasure in his life. He loved Tatti more than himself. And there was no way he could die to save her.

The day started easy enough with breakfast, and daily housekeeping chores were done in silence. Gordon's mind cleared, and his fever dropped, but he was still off balance when he tried to stand, and toppled over. "So far, so good," he whispered to Stowell, when the bosun reported. "Stay with her and take your men."

"Aye, my lord." Stowell turned away.

Around noon two buccaneers came to get Tatti, and they walked down to their campfire where they had spread an awning. Stowell walked partway down to keep her in sight, and squatted on the sand. Bonabombo had come ashore from the anchored *Santiago de Mort* where he slept and was waiting to talk to Tatti, and Stowell was glad to see her return in about an hour.

"They want me to sing and dance," Tatti said. "Sheila told them how I entertained the whole pavilion."

"Not bad," Stowell said.

"To hear 'Froggie Went A'Courtin,' " Tatti said.

"Aye, then let them," Stowell said matter-of-factly.

Gordon's mind was clear, and he sensed the excitement in the buccaneer guards about the pavilion, and a certain assured lack of caution. "Get one of the women into the forest," he whispered to Cora, "and have the marine and Roo and Brighton come in, hid, with their blunderbusses and grenades."

Cora closed her eyes, nodding in assent, then whispered, "Margene's baking loaves of bread, to fill with powder."

"My God, she'll blow us all up!" He lay his hand on Cora's fingers and let his head drop back. "Inside a loaf of bread, a grenade might work."

"Ahh," Cora exhaled. "We got the grenades, we didn't know how to fix them. Like big French cakes."

"Cakes?" Gordon said.

"So glad your fever's broke, my lord." Cora bathed his temples with a small towel, while Leslie smiled and cooled his wrists and ankles.

Gordon felt his brain seem to swoop from side to side within his skull as he turned his head. "Lord, he almost brained me."

At sunset Stowell followed Tatti down from the pavilion to the buccaneers' fires, and he sat in the sand, quite out in the gloom, where he could watch without being noticed.

As the dark came, his men joined him. Bonabombo was in his wicker chaise, drinking rum
and watching good-naturedly as his men
roistered about their fires. They ate with their
fingers, which shone with grease in the dark,
as they held chunks of pork to their mouths
and cut them short with their knives. They did
not spill their rum as they washed down their
meat, Stowell saw.

Tatti sat across the fire from Bonabombo,
her hair piled atop her head and her knees
drawn up within her clasped arms, and waited,
ignoring the whole company. The men moved
about behind her, and Stowell heard their
voices getting louder in oaths and jests as the
night darkened. He could see their faces
flushed in the open fires, although no fight had
yet erupted among them.

"It's not natural to be drunk and not fight
by now," Stowell whispered.

"Scurvy lot," one of the four sailors whispered, a small man not considered fit to put in
leg-irons.

They saw Bonabombo get up and walk
aound to the girl, and the buccaneers fell silent. "A little hornpipe, for my brave lads?"
They heard the flute break into the lively notes
of the sailors' dance, and they could see the
uncertain glance on Tatti's face as she got to
her feet, licking her lips and breathing through
her open mouth.

"The sailors' hornpipe!" shouted a rover,
eyes glinting in excitement.

Tatti commenced uneven steps to the

quick notes, gradually getting her hands and legs in unison to the flute and fife, so that in what seemed seconds she was dancing about the edge of the fire in the rollicking notes of the hornpipe, climbing a fantasy ratline and sheeting in the sails, and heaving around the anchor.

"Bravo!" The buccaneers shouted their approval. Two short men squatted into a variant hornpipe, and broke into wild laughter as a third man fell into the edge of the fire.

Stowell watched the enchanted shadow of the girl's body and thighs, thrown up against the awning, and followed the graceful steps of her elegant legs, the rapid movement of her hands and the swaying of her long neck in time with the rushing music. It pleased him to see she had cast a spell of beauty that for a moment transfixed the roistering company into silence as they watched.

"Faster!" Bonabombo shouted.

The flute picked up in a mad wail of rhythm, and Stowell could see the lost expression in Tatti's face as she circled and the fire reflected in her frightened eyes.

"God, 'e don't quit," said a sailor at Stowell's side.

The whole band of rovers seemed to find release in the chaos of Bonabombo's cheering, and began to imitate the girl in gross exaggeration, tilting their hips and leering at each other.

"Enough!" Bonabombo cried out, and the music stopped, leaving Tatti to halt in mid-step, gasping for air from her throat and heaving body. "Little merriment after supper, eh hearties?"

The men laughed delightedly and one fellow grabbed another man between his thighs, causing the man to whoop and jump forward to more happy shouts.

"I like it not," Stowell said.

They sat in the sand and heard Tatti's voice singing the nursery rhyme of Scotland, about the dashing froggie who would marry but could not, courting as he went, sword and pistol by his side. Stowell was blissful as he listened, and was startled to hear it stop. Bonabombo was in front of Tatti. Stowell got up.

"Shall we divvy up the girl, lads?"

"Youh!"

"Hurray!"

"Stay," Stowell said, walking into the firelight. Bonabombo whisked a knife down the length of Tatti's jumper so that it fell open, leaving her white breasts alight in the reflection. In another motion he had her stripped from head to foot.

"Hold it!" Stowell shouted.

"You've brought five thousand pounds sterling?" Bonabombo leaned forward, the mouth ajar and one palm up. "Everything's for sale."

Stowell strode up to the fire, where a lank man had picked up the shreds of Tatti's clothing and had stepped backward, giggling.

"Don't touch her!" Stowell's words choked him.

"Five thousand pounds ain't too much."

"So far we've done naught but fight a fair battle." Stowell glowered at the men. "But this is death or hanging, by God's teeth."

"That ain't nice talk," Bonabombo said, staring over his men in the silent moment that followed.

"By God's teeth, you'll die!" Stowell was blind with rage and he swung his balled fist into a pirate who set his forefinger on Tatti's nipple.

"Take her lads, that's the lady!"

The buccaneers did not move, and Stowell reached his single arm to encircle Tatti in the moment of confrontation. "Men!" he shouted, and was satisfied to see the diffused images of his men running toward him.

Bang! A pistol shot blazed and one of his men grabbed his leg and fell to the sand. The buccaneers swarmed toward them, and cursing figures scuffled about each other.

"Take him!" Bonabombo's voice was clear above the fight.

Stowell had Tatti by the back of her neck to guide her clear when a hammer blow jolted his skull, and his eyes blazed many lights.

He was down on the sand under the awning, his mouth full of grit. About him lay his men on their bellies with their arms being trussed behind them. "Don't hurt 'em, me hearties, we'll need 'em as fresh hands to ship on the *Santiago de Mort!*" Bonabombo shouted.

"You'll hang!" Stowell spat his words.

"That ain't sociable." Bonabombo stepped over Stowell's body and set his foot on the stump of his arm. He settled his full weight on the wound, driving the arm into the hard sand.

Stowell screamed in the blind fire that shot up his shoulder, to envelop every quivering nerve of his body in scourging pain, and turned his right arm into a clot of flesh that wanted to die, but could not, and he fainted. He could hear Tatti screaming, "Don't kill him!" It surprised him to realize it was he that she meant, and he focused his eyes on her.

"That's a tame Englishman." Bonabombo turned to the girl. "Take the lady, boys, and teach her what a woman is!"

Two men swept her up off her feet by her thighs, and her torso fell backward and was caught by two more men. They spread her thighs until her pubic region was open and her crotch unfolded to the buccaneers, who laughed nervously and pulled back.

"There she is, boys, a real lady!"

The men shoved each other forward, their glowing faces fixed on the faint hair of the girl's private parts and soft lips held up before them. The men who had her thighs and buttocks laughed, and shook her hips up and down. "Come on, mates, let's see a real prong!"

Tatti gasped and arched her spine. "Wait!" she screamed. "What is my body to you?"

The question deadened the faces which had been alive with expectation at her nude flesh.

"If you tear my body limb from limb and break my bones and spend your passion, in my life or death, you will not touch me." She stretched her hands out toward them. "I live in the spirit of God just as you see me, naked or covered."

"Damn her!" Bonabombo roared, spittle flecking his lips as he saw his men pause. "Take her, damn ye—she's the enemy of all of us men. Take her while you have her!"

Tatti writhed and kicked her small feet in the air. Stowell sensed a delicate honor to her, an integrity that struggled in its bare flesh to preserve its sanctity, even when hopeless. He could see her twist her white flanks and watched her breasts tremble as she arched and turned her spine.

"Hang it out, mates!" Bonabombo roared, and Stowell heard the men shout and push forward.

One man lunged ahead of the group, his pants dragging over his heels, his urgent buttocks gone flat and muscular. The men cheered, and he heard Tatti scream as the man plunged into her, the buttocks rutting into the soft crotch. He listened to her scream and closed his eyes.

"That's it, matey, a real ride!" The buccaneers were shouting and clapping each other on the back.

Stowell watched the ravishment, man following man, nervously holding back until a fellow had gone on ahead of them, then rushing into the girl's crotch to plunge it as quickly as possible, as if only in the full presence of the other men could it be done, and not alone.

He could hear Tatti screaming until his

ears were split by her voice, and watched her writhe, once tearing loose a hand which struck blindly into the face of her captor.

"Spirited little wench," said the man, catching the hand again and grinning.

"This ain't natural doings, as God is my witness," Stowell said to the sailor trussed at his side.

"My God, Bosun, what's got into these people?" The sailor had his head up watching.

Each man trembled above his tautened buttocks, leaning between the soft thighs, and in turn slid backward to his knees to crawl away, to the encouraging words of those who held up the girl's body.

Tatti's screaming never slackened, and her leg, when it got free, kicked spasmodically at whatever she could reach, once striking a buccaneer in the chest who was roping up his pantaloons and stretching his legs, making them laugh.

"A great prong, Bonabombo!"

"No, thank you, mateys, no women for me." Bonabombo winked.

The fire in Tatti never slackened, and she fought savagely against her assault, so violently that the whole clutch of them had the wild appearance of smooth white skin and soft flesh that undulated in a staggering group of men, who struggled to keep on their muscle-knotted, hairy legs.

"Filth! Ye filth!"

Cora was in their midst. She had a rover by the long hair of his head, twisted back, and a knife lay over the soft skin of his throat. "Drop the girl, or I'll cut his throat!"

The struggling mass spilled Tatti out of its midst to the sand; and a silence gripped the men. The knife was already edged with a sliding bead of blood that trickled off its point.

The man's eyeballs were white, as they implored his mates and Bonabombo.

"Ach!" A guttural noise behind Stowell, and he saw Leslie had a second man on his belly, his face shoved down into the sand, and his neck over a butcher knife.

"We cut their windpipes!" Cora's russet eyes flamed as she searched the silent throng of men, who did not move a muscle.

"Like a hog's windpipe!" She wrenched back the man's head. He began to vomit, and her hand reddened with a film of blood that ran down the thick muscles of her forearm.

"There's a good sport, woman," Bonabombo said, taking a step.

"No more!" Cora said, as her man screamed over her knife, and the man on the sand pleaded for his life.

Tatti was lying naked on the sand in front of Stowell, and he got to his feet. "I'll take her," he said, as the rovers shrank away from Cora.

"Take her, we've had our sport, eh, hearties?" Bonabombo grinned about his men. "And his lordship could hear her scream. I had my sport with a gentleman's lady."

Stowell slipped his hand under Tatti's armpit where she huddled, and lifted. "Up!" His voice was stern as she broke into sobs and hid her face with her hands. "Pick her up, men!"

He led the limping and weeping girl across the sand toward the pavilion and saw Margene come out of the gloom. "Bad, Bosun?"

"The worst. Get me rum."

"I know'd it."

"Get him rum," Cora said.

"Never seen the likes before, 'cepting the rector of the parish talking hell. 'Twas God amok—my arm, get me rum, woman."

"God amok?"

"Aye, woman, amok. What e're we thought we were as men and women, they proved we ain't."

"Not to me," Margene said indignantly. "I told you they was trash."

"Oh, God, woman!" Stowell took the full cup of Jamaican rum that a woman fetched him from the shadowy figures who greeted the band. He gulped and felt its heat down into his belly. His eyes watered, and he stopped before the ashen-faced figure of Gordon Wragby, who was supported by two cotters. The Captain's eyes were a cold fury in the gloom.

"Bosun, get her up to the saltwater pools, where the sun and the wind evaporate the high moon tides until it's salt brine left." Gordon's voice was icy calm, and clipped in perfection. "Turn her upside down, and flush out her privy parts, and keep at it even when she screams." He waited, the fierce eyes on the sailors.

"Aye, my lord."

"Then purge her with brine until she vomits and until her bowels run off."

Cora flung the rover at Gordon's feet. "Why, my lord?"

"The Caribbean love rot. Now move on." Gordon turned back toward the pavilion where the rover guards had disappeared in the chaotic night.

XXXIII

The rum roared about in his chest, lighting a fire which cleared his mind of doubt, and numbed the throbbing pain of his arm. Behind him, Stowell could hear the sailors carrying the girl, and the footsteps of the emigrants in the sand, and it startled him not to hear the clank of leg-irons.

"The fetters? What happened?" He gestured to the gaunt figure of Margene, who strode in a loose Highland gait ahead of them toward the salt-brine pools.

"Knifed the keeper of the keys," Cora said laconically.

Three shadowy figures dashed past the walking band, going the opposite direction, and Stowell saw the marine sergeant and Roo and Brighton. They clanked with heavy grenades strung around their belts, and slung firearms across their naked backs, as well as carried weapons in their hands.

"Killed him?" Stowell said.

"Margene got him in the heart with the pig-sticker. He never felt a thing."

"Maybe I ought to go back and help," Stowell said.

"Cups, we got our work here."

"Aye." Stowell stood in the thin mooncast of the high water tideline as his men came up. "Get her upside down and get the saltwater down her."

The sailors looked uncertainly at him. "The love rot putrifies a woman's privates. Now get her upside down." He sipped his rum, and watched the sailors flip Tatti's legs into the air and drop her head. He heard her gasp.

"We have no choice, my lady," he said.

"No more," Tatti shrieked, reaching up to protect her privates with her hands.

"Lord Gordon's orders," Cora said, and Stowell nodded to see her hands pulled free so that her pubic region was uppermost and her thighs wide parted.

"Please! I beg of you!" she cried, and Cora turned away.

Stowell nodded to Margene who had dipped up a bucket of harsh salt water and filled a bottle. "Get it down her," he said. The woman hesitated, then poured the bottle into the open flesh that was before her.

Stowell watched the water run over Tatti's

white belly and rush down the crevice between her buttocks, making her cry out, "It burns!"

"Down her privates," Stowell said, taking the bottle from the woman and putting it under his armpit. He set his hand into the soft folds of her crotch that were faint under the moonlit shadows of fine hair, and felt his fingers slip down through her private parts. "In there," he said to the woman. "Put your fingers down it so I can find it."

She slipped her hand atop his, and he carefully set the top of the bottle of salt water into the parted opening. Upending the bottle, he heard it gurgle and flood into her body as Tatti screamed and struggled wildly.

"You're killing me!" Her legs stiffened and trembled in the sailor's arms, who clung hard. "I'm on fire!"

"Hold her head," Stowell said matter-of-factly, as she flung her body back and forth, and Cora knelt to support her head and shoulders.

"Please, I beg of you! Please!"

Stowell moved at his own pace, ignoring her cries. "I'm sorry, my lady, but if we don't, you'll have no chance of a life of your own."

"Your husband ordered it," Cora whispered.

"But Gordon can't feel it!"

Stowell doggedly flushed out her privates while she wept and cried out. When the men looked at him to set her upright, he shook his head.

"Get her up—I've got to purge her."

"Bosun, 'tain't decent," Margene said,

while the emigrant men and women watched in transfixed silence.

"Never said it was. Got to do her mouth as well, now her backside." He upturned his pewter mug of rum and felt it bolster his purpose with an absolute deliberation.

"I want her backside." Feeling for her vent, he motioned for the woman to pry it apart so he could set the bottle neck into it. "It's worse if I don't," he said, and pressed the bottle past the woman's fingers and into Tatti, causing her trembling body to convulse in their midst.

When they had got her upright in their arms, he took a scoured bottle and set the top inside her teeth, which fought to spit it out. "Hold her head, men," he said quietly. "Drink, my lady, t'will puke you." He watched her nose and mouth explode in a spray of salt and vomit, her jead jerking out of their hands and heaving the mixture onto all of them.

"Let her down," he said, "so she can empty herself."

They eased her onto the warm sand and watched her body contort in cramps as it voided itself and listened to her cry out that she was dying and afire.

"We'll carry her to the creek and wash her good when she's done." Stowell walked over to the small keg of rum and poured himself another tot, and downing it, he looked back at the wretched figure lying out on the sand, vomiting and running off at the bowels, and crying that her privates were in torment. He loved her in her courage and ravishment.

"Somebody's going to hang for this night," Stowell said, feeling a great anger rise in his gorge for the cotters and survivors of the shipwreck. It was a cotter who had betrayed them. He glowered at the emigrants. "'Twas one of you who turned traitor."

"They ain't all bad," Margene said, bringing two pails of freshwater to where Cora knelt at Tatti's shadowed form in the faint light.

"Aye, and you've been mighty free with that girl," a woman said, "taking liberties with her body."

She was a big woman named Ada. Stowell was so furious he did not answer.

"'Twasn't not decent, 'twas carnal."

"You bitch!" he said. "Talk about her body, you lice sold out her soul to that goddamn trash, out of jealousy."

"Never saw a woman so ill-used by a man," she said self-righteously, snuffling.

"Woman, I've heard you sing your hymns and read your Bibles, them that can, and I'd say you've mocked everything you've worshiped. You betrayed her, damn you, out of envy." He glared at the emigrants, and pointed at the retching girl. "There's your pride in the sorrow of a child. For shame, you bastards." He spat mightily into the night. "You people wouldn't know God from Adam's off ox."

The big woman bridled and backed away with the cotters, leaving Cora and Margene with Tatti. He sat down with his men to wait for the purging to spend itself, and handed round the rum.

Sometime past midnight they got Tatti up to the freshwater pool and bathed her, and wrapped her in skins and bedded down in the shadows of a cedar thicket overlooking the beach and pavilion. Stowell let his hand lay along Tatti's temple, and when he felt her move, and her eyes focus onto him, he whispered, "I love you, oh, I love you, Tatti."

Tatti slipped her hand out from under her covers and drew his fingers to her lips, and held them there as she kissed them.

"People ain't all bad, Bosun," Cora said.

Stowell looked away. " 'Twas what I felt when I said it."

"I'm going to kill Sheila," Margene said, her eyes gleaming at him in the dark. "She brought us all to ruin. Just like Lord Gordon's got to kill that Bonabombo man—but we ain't all that way, no we ain't."

Stowell lay back, his mind dragged down into a sense of futile hopes, and his sleep was a gross burden that exhausted him.

XXXIV

Gordon Wragby knew he had reached that particular moment in life where, catapulted over the crest of an onrushing wave and engulfed, he could never turn back, but must swim onward in the great tide of water that seized him, not knowing how it would end, only that he must go forward.

He waited on the sand outside the pavilion wrapped in a blanket, with Leslie and the half-grown boy, Silas, whom they had sent into the forest to find his Marine and Roo and Brighton. He used his Italian spyglass to see by starlight that the cutter was still beached in the white lip of foam at the water's edge, and he knew Bonabombo was ashore for the night.

"I'll have to kill him," Gordon said.

"He's not worth your life, Lord Gordon," Leslie said, sensing the iron purpose, and the finality that told her Gordon doubted the outcome. "You have Tatti and little Gordie to live for."

"Aye, the fruit of love from a great woman, as is every child." He lay back as Leslie and the boy steadied him.

Gordon's men found him waiting for them, and dropped to their knees around him, unrolling grenades and laying out blunderbusses in a motion of brawn-sinewed arms, their clear eyes searching his as he huddled in the blanket.

"They're unnerved by their own debauchery, and I think we can strike," Gordon said.

The marine and the two sailors nodded in assent, but yet seemed puzzled.

"Life is cured by living it, not by debauching it. Though the act of passion may appear the same, 'tis not." Gordon drew the blanket about his throat. "What's in the soul determines the purity, not in the flesh."

The people kneeling about Gordon quieted their breathing in an effort to understand.

"These men have betrayed their own divinity in their cruel passion, and this should be punishment enough, but they can't admit it, so 'twill get worse until we kill them."

"Aye, kill them," the sergeant snarled, and Gordon heard the others ball their fists and pound the sand at his feet. "I always know'd we'd have to."

"I'm always mystified why men will slay

each other when they can live in paradise—vanity, alas." He shook his head and avoided their eager faces.

"What is the plan, my lord?" Caruthers said.

"The plan?" Gordon was surprised at the question. It passed him again into a role of violence he truly hated, and yet which fate had put upon him. "Aye, the plan." His head cleared, and he looked into the questing eyes that glinted in a rising moonlight. He lay his hand out atop a grenade. "I no longer know what to tell you, except they'll be shamed and irresolute, and they'll be bunched up, for misery loves company."

They nodded their heads eagerly, grasping his understanding.

"Use the blunderbusses and grenades and stuff the muskets with stag-shot to get the cripples."

"Ooo, clever, my lord," the marine said. "Who'll give the order to fire?"

Gordon shook his head. "You will. I can't tell you any more. You must fight this battle alone—I can't walk yet. But I want Bonabombo."

"I can kill the bastard," Roo said.

"No, he's mine. His crime was against all people who live and do not ruin." Gordon looked away. "That man's evil is pitted against life itself." He felt the wick in the grenade, and heard himself say strange words he'd never said before. "He attacked God, when he attacked the cotters." He looked up at the three men and the boy. "Perhaps we can expiate our crimes against our cotters on the moor, this once, at least."

The sergeant nodded, his burly neck plain in the rising moon, and Gordon saw Margene had joined them as well as other cotters.

Gordon lay back, after hearing Margene report on Tatti's condition. Leslie had vanished, along with his three armed men, and Higgins and Cutler and some of the robust cotters had joined the Royal Marine.

"Well, Silas, I suppose we're alone," Gordon said to the half-grown boy when Margene disappeared into the night to join the attack.

"I'd like to go, my lord."

"No!" Gordon put his hand onto the boy's shoulder. "They've got thirty men to kill, and three to do it."

Leslie MacIntosh had grown to girlhood in the Scottish Highlands, and she had married a gentle kinsman, and together they had lost three children in infancy. When uprooted off the moor, she had one child in arms and a husband who was in shock at leaving the glens of Scotland. In the storm, what she loved had died; and yet, in the storm, she had discovered another man who reminded her of her husband, in Gordon Wragby, and in tending him, she could live once more. She knew he was expecting to die, and she knew she could not again find a purpose to life, if Gordon died.

"Let me carry the grenades down to the rovers," Leslie said, her calm eyes searching the hushed group in the pavilion. "Cook has them disguised as hot bread."

"If you run, they'll know it's a trap, and scatter," Roo said.

"I'll stay."

They watched her for a moment. "'Twill kill you."

"I know." Her calm face settled on their eyes, moving from face to face. The men averted their faces from her.

"If she dies, I don't want to take no prisoners," Margene said.

The seven men nodded, still avoiding the eyes of the women who watched them. "All right," Caruthers whispered.

They watched the lonely form of Leslie MacIntosh walk toward the broad awning of the pirates, where an occasional figure could be seen moving before the dying fire. When she vanished inside the sand fort, Caruthers jumped forward, leading the men and women, each carrying a single grenade or weapon so that they did not clank.

Inside the open revetment, they saw Leslie smiling, and lifting the linen covers of the basket she carried slung on an arm. Her face was radiant as she looked at the sleeping men, and called to them.

"Hot bread, dear friends, sweet rolls and a dawn breakfast for gentlemen!" She turned gracefully on her bare feet and pretty legs.

Men were getting up, out of awkward slumbers and too much drink.

"Sweet rolls and hot bread!" She smiled and lifted the white linen and sniffed inside. "So warm." Her eyes turned back to the waking pirates.

"This is the one we should've pronged," said a man, freeing his pantaloons caught in his buttocks as he got up. "Broad hips."

"Sooo delicious, after a night of pleasure." Leslie smiled at him. At least a dozen men surrounded her.

"My belly's growling," a voice said.

Leslie slipped her hand into the basket of five grenades and took the smoldering punt, and jabbed it into the white wick thrust out each loaf of French bread, and stared at the men who had casually destroyed her whole purpose to life. She waited for a merciful God to forgive her act of unspeakable savagery against all she'd been taught on earth.

Whooooom! Whoooom!

For a split second Leslie saw the great light that blinded her eyes and numbed her body's nerves. There was an eruption of sound and strange broken objects that vanished into night, and she saw no more.

"Get 'em!" Margene screamed, as the men dashed forward, carrying their blunderbusses and muskets.

Gordon Wragby saw the night split in yellow bursts of fire that hurled up timbers and towers of sand, and he could see the streaks of red flame where the hand weapons were fired.

Then a concussion rocked the whole beach and turned the night suddenly day, and Gordon saw his own people falling backward from it in the series of quick explosions along the sand.

"Sounds like a keg of powder," Gordon said, getting unsteadily to his feet. "Come, boy, let's go see how much we damaged the enemy."

He met his people retreating in awe before the towering pire of erupting debris that rose in spewing waves out of the pirates' fort.

"My God, Margene rolled in a keg of powder!" Brighton galloped up, looking backward. "It set off the whole fort!"

"No Bonabombo?"

"No, my lord, we didn't see him."

"The longboat! Look in the longboat," Gordon said, veering toward the white image of the beached boat.

"Leslie killed herself with the grenades, my lord." Caruthers dashed up, smoke blackened.

Gordon heard his soul resound with grief for a tortured woman who should have had peace and given love but was denied. A sudden strength enveloped his body as he tasted brass in his throat.

He saw a tilting figure splashing down the surf, his legs heavy in the running tide. "Bonabombo!" Gordon sprinted to head him off, his people running after him.

"I want you!" Gordon shouted, as the man turned, a pistol leveled at Gordon's belly.

"I'll shoot!"

"I'll kill you anyway." Gordon waded out, and heard the hammer fall, and the flint misfire in the wet sea water.

Bonabombo cursed, flung the pistol at Gordon and reached for a second weapon.

Gordon leaped through the knee-deep

water, alive with a hidden strength he'd never felt before. "Bastard! You fouled us!" he yelled, clutching at the retreating figure in the water.

Boom!

Gordon grasped his fragile hands about the throat under Bonabombo's red-stubbled jaw and closed his fingers over the cartilage in the man's throat, hearing it crush under his grip.

"Vile wretch!" Gordon gasped, aware of a pain in his belly, so trifling he could scarcely feel it. At last he had his hands upon the evil force that had attacked his dream.

The pirate's eyes grew large, the lids rolling backward, and his arms flopped wildly at his sides.

"Die, vile bastard!" Gordon was engulfed with an immense need to kill, and have done with evil. His fingers crushed the windpipe and choked the whole neck and throat.

The tongue thrust out the mouth as Gordon squeezed with every fiber of his body. The man flailed uncontrollably with his legs, leaping out of the waves, and the tongue swelled red and the nose bled down over Gordon's slender wrists.

Gordon was not certain how long he strangled Bonabombo, but he could not let go, even when the body was still and the legs dragged lifeless with the flowing motion of the surf. His mind began to clear when he realized his people were all around him, and had watched in silence while he strangled the pirate. Their amazed, clear, living faces reassured him.

"My lord, he's dead," the marine said.

"Oh, yes, of course."

Gordon looked back at the vile thing he held up, and it astonished him he could not free his hands. "Oh, Lord, he's got me."

"Nay, my lord."

The men leaped forward, and ran their fingers under Gordon's fixed, rigid hands, and eased them upward, while he stared at his own numb fingers.

"Curious. I can't even feel my own hands," he said.

"You're wounded, my lord," Cora and Margene ran their arms about his waist as the body slipped under water, knocking awkwardly against Cutler's knees as it went out with the tide.

"Yes, I suppose I am. Where?"

"Your belly, my lord." Cora's face was grave in the rising moonlight, and a gasping hush settled over the cotters and sailors who stood in a group about their captain.

"I don't feel a thing," Gordon said, as they picked him up and carried him out of the surf. In that split second, Gordon knew he would die.

"Get me Tatti," he whispered, and let his head fall back.

XXXV

Gordon lay in their big, rough-hewn bed, under which the ticking had been puffed to ease the quiet pain in his stomach, and to keep him cool. Tatti sat beside him, their child in her arms. Men and women hovered outside their thatched hut, speaking in a hush, fear in their eyes.

Cora and Caroline were in and out every moment, and Margene came and stared at him and walked away, muttering to herself.

"Now, now, I'm perfectly comfortable," he said to Tatti. "And I feel just fine."

Her eyes flooded with tears, and she hid her face behind one hand while she held Gordie in her other arm.

"Now, now, no emotion." He ran his hand

over the little boy's slender foot, and felt the refined bones move with grace within the firm, elegant flesh. "Ah, such a marvel is a child's foot." He caressed it. "We mustn't frighten him." He eased his hand onto Tatti's hip and let it slide down her thigh along her frock, and drew her against the heavy bed frame.

"You brought me life," he whispered. "You brought me God, when I was too genteel to find Him."

"No, Gordon, don't say it."

"Aye, too genteel for the Almighty, too sophisticated to lead rebellion, and too wise to be cynical, and then you changed it all. One naked girl running up and down the decks of a foundering ship, who dragged children and shouted to live." He folded his hands over his chest and looked up at her, his eyes gone soft with release from worldly care and concern for trifles. "You did the impossible."

She smiled at him, and Gordon felt a great warmth sweep through his bosom, an enchanted spirit that stopped time altogether in that moment, as if the second were eternal itself. "I love you," he whispered. "I love you in the dawn, love you in the night as you sleep, and I feel you breathe in my arms, love you when I hear your feet brush the boards of our grass cottage." He glanced up at the peaked thatch. "I loved this hut."

In that moment he knew she understood he grasped his mortal limits. He did not care, he wanted to tell while he could that he loved her. The pain in his stomach came and went. At first it was a round hole that went through the skin and light hair on his belly, and had a dark red tinge of flesh that turned violet in the middle. "The bullet's in my bowels."

"Gut shots are fatal, my lord." Cora spoke with ashen gravity.

"I know."

"And they're painful."

"Aye. How's the morphia?"

"Plenty, my lord." Cora looked at Margene and Tatti, who wept in silence. "The Turkish poppy. When the pain comes."

"Aye, when the pain comes." Gordon looked up at the woman. "Just now, I feel great. Tea and brandy, please."

"Nay, my lord, no spirits," Cora said.

"Then just tea. I daren't mix brandy with opium."

Gordon was determined to die with grace and leave his people with a courage to cling to their lives as they watched him give up his. It was the last thing he could do for them. Yet deep within his soul he knew he did not want to die, that he wanted desperately to go on living, that he wanted to see his son grow into a little boy and on into manhood. He wanted to hear him laugh and enjoy the confusion and exultation of young men and women in their teen-age years when they richochet from absolute bliss to despair, to wild conviction, to obedient faith. He wanted to stand firm as a man and parent, present and waiting for the children to grow on into men and women. Gordon wanted all this, desperately, but he knew the pistol shot was fatal in his bowels.

The pain was a sweet ache, that grew to a

piercing stab, just occasionally, and he'd raise
his arms for the women to turn him slightly,
to ease the rotting wound within his body. It
hurt, but he refused the opium.

"No, not yet. When it's unbearable, I'll
ask for it."

It was Tatti he wanted to see as the pressure of shortened time rose under his heartbeat
against his every breath.

"I want you to take my son home, to
Wragby Hall," he said.

Tatti sat on the edge of the bed and
nodded in silence.

"You'll be alone, but you'll still have the
land and our families."

"I have Skarra," Tatti whispered. "All of
Scotland's behind me."

"Aye, but he's still my son." He lay his
hand on hers.

"Gordon." She searched into his eyes, past
the veil of what hides the soul of people from
each other. "I have one purpose in my life—
you."

He smiled at her words.

"And that purpose lives in our son, in Gordie. 'Twas my Russian grandmother who gave
me strength to endure in God, and my mother
who made me want to live. I loved my father
and old Lord Skarra, and so I loved you." She
set her hands atop his slender, dessicated
wrist. "And when I loved you, all that I had
loved came again out of me in our child."

Her eyes were clear in calmness of her
words.

He nodded, and looked down, knowing

he wanted to be with her. "How much I want to live. Strange, at middle age, life has become so sweet."

Tatti did not look at him, because she knew she would weep at his wish that was to be denied him. "I'll make him strong, our son, with the creeks and glens and the moors of Scotland a part of him."

"You won't turn your back on England?"

"No. But Scotland's stronger."

"Our past is our children."

"I know, he'll be you, but he's us both. I'll never let you die." Her fingers closed over the back of his hand, and they sat that way a long time, breathing in the absolute quiet of a timeless love as the sun settled onto the ocean and dazzled the shore with light.

Gordon slipped off into sleep at odd moments, when the day was clear, or even when someone was speaking to him. He was conscious only of Tatti's voice, coming through to him, and it alone seemed able to call him back.

He was in occasional pain. Tatti had wiped the bitter white taste onto his tongue to quiet his torment, and his mind was cooled by the constant touch of wet cloths on his temples.

"Oh, it's no bother," Gordon kept trying to say, and it astonished him to see the wrenching anguish in the faces that occasionally came into focus.

He thought he saw himself standing at the foot of his bed, as a little boy holding his father's hand. The two of them stared at the man in bed.

387

Gordon woke up, and was delighted to see Tatti standing at the foot of his bed, holding Gordie by the hand.

"My word, I saw you as my father, and Gordie as myself."

Tatti laughed and walked to his side, carrying the child. "Tea, time for tea."

Gordon nodded, knowing they only put the teaspoon to his lips, and that nothing went into his stomach.

"My parents," Gordon said. "I want to see my parents, and when I sleep, they come." He closed his eyes and felt himself waft away into an ether that had no limits.

He saw the hunting field sweep into sight, the horses thundering across the green sod as they crashed through the top of a hedge, and he heard the French horns sounding the glorious call of "full cry," and he saw his mother, bolt upright in her sidesaddle, and his Great-aunt Betsy, who hunted all day at eighty-four, and had to be lifted into a special saddle and lashed into it—they all raced past him, calling his name. "Gordie! Gordie!" His mother smiled at him, under her flying veil, and he was afraid her horse would fall, and he panted for his breath in fear.

"Ah, my horse," he said, when he saw the empty saddle with its flopping stirrups. He recognized Pericles, his seventeen-hand hunter. The horse seemed to change gait, and he was astride once more, racing to catch up to his father, whom he had seen rein up. "Halloo! Halloo!"

French horns were sounding all across the

field, and he was riding in the midst of his people, flying over ditches and leaping walls and hedges—and the music was all French. His father hated English horns. "Too barbarous to salute the quarry."

Gordon could hear himself laugh outright, and feel his mother lay her hand atop his, as their horses raced along behind his father.

"Gordon, it's me, Tatti."

The vision of his mother vanished, and he saw Tatti, the delicate blood-red lips and full teeth.

"I was hunting with my mother." He took her hand. "I want to go back."

"All right." Tatti's voice was soft, yet firm.

"My son?" Gordon said.

"As God is my witness, I'll raise him as an Englishman," she whispered.

There was a little boy in his arms then. Gordon knew the end was not far off.

"Pray the morphia outlasts the pain," he whispered.

"Does it hurt?" Tatti kissed his parching lips.

"No, not at all. The opium kills the pain, and all I do is go off with Papa and Mama. They're all there.

"Wragby Hall, take Gordie to Wragby." Gordon was clutching the child into his chest, and drifting off to his nursery, where he could see the warm fire his nanny had lit, and immense gold and red shadows flung themselves against the headboard and leaped up and down the Italian silk wallpaper of ancient Rome.

He smiled when he saw his father and mother at the side of his crib, and his father reached into his bed, and lifted him against his massive chest, and he heard the deep resonance of his father's voice, and his mother smiled and kissed the back of his neck.

"Gordie dear, dear little boy, we've waited for you," his father said, and Gordon snuggled into his father's great arms and lost himself in the huge strength of his father's body, while he felt his mother's hands gently ruffle through his hair, and go softly up and down his back.

Gordon lifted his mouth, and kissed the stiff bristly ear of his father, and snuggled down again as his father carried him. "I love you, Papa," he whispered, and reached out and touched his mother's face, as her hand held his, and Gordon Wragby knew he did not want to go back, once he'd found his parents again, and that he'd crossed into death.

XXXVI

In Gordon's death Tatti felt sorrow fracture her soul, with nobody to spare her, only Cora, her nurse, to help bear it.

Gordie was an endless demand, and her salvation. As a running toddler, he was never quite settled, and always hungry. His resemblance to Gordon both shocked her and filled her with a poignant grief at what had been between them, what might else have been, and what was forever broken. The beauty of their love lived on in their son.

Tatti sat on a rough bench within the shaded courtyard, and let Cora and the women lay out Gordon's body. The men had withdrawn well out of earshot of the pavilion to build a cedar coffin for Gordon, even before he had died. Tatti had chosen the copse of cedar trees on a knoll between the savanna and the beach where the graves were dug and Leslie already buried.

"Side by side," Tatti had said. "If I can't lie· by Gordon's side through eternity, then I want another good woman. Let it be Leslie."

The sailors and Cora did not look at Tatti when she spoke. It surprised her that she could function at all, after his death and her rape. She knew she owed her endurance to her mother and her grandmother. "We were beaten a thousand times, but we never lay down and quit," she thought.

Before Gordon had died, in a lucid moment, he had directed all the men to give Tatti their allegiance, with her in final command, and charged the Royal Marine and the bosun to see her decisions fulfilled. "Bye and bye, the Admiralty will send ships to seek us out, in a lull from the wars with France and Holland and Spain."

Tatti had listened to the men in silence, and nodded to their daily words. The cotters seemed frightened, and she realized how much they had depended on the frail Captain.

Tatti walked in that night to Gordon's bier in their small grass-thatched cottage. She was pleased to see the candles standing at the corners of the catafalque.

Tatti stared at the waxen face of the man she'd loved, now sunk in at the cheeks, with his lips a fragile white as though paper, and his dark thick eyelashes the only color on his face. His hair had been tied back with a clubbed black ribbon, and then she realized he was in his uniform.

"We'd want him buried proper, my lady," Cora said, as Tatti's eyes searched the elegant remnants of his formal naval uniform, the tarnished gold lace and the water-stained sash of silk crossing his slight chest and bearing the decorations and honors of his rank.

"Knight of the Garter." She touched the knee of the satin breeches and ran her hand down the white silk stocking. "Knight of the English Realm, and perhaps the only thing of England that will live—oh, I adored him."

Tatti put her hands to her face and wept until she felt drained of tears and remorse that she had lived when he had died and her outrage that a man of peace should die in a world where violence was tolerated as normal.

"There, there." Cora brought her a wet cloth and helped her wipe and cool her face.

"Whatever I am, that man made me," she whispered to Cora. "He spoiled me for all other men."

"Bye and bye, the grief will ease."

"Perhaps, but never the loss." There was a book lying under the hilt of Gordon's elegant dress sword upon which his gloved hands were folded.

" 'Twas my Bible, my lady, under his sword."

"Gordon would like that."

"I wanted the holy script over his heart."

"We'll keep the ship's Bible and the ship's log, to return them to the English," Tatti said.

"Oh, indeed yes, Tatti. It's writ out plain

who was married and who was loyal to the Crown." Cora nodded.

That night Tatti asked Cora to sleep with her on a pallet at the foot of the catafalque; and she slept fitfully, occasionally waking to see fresh tapers burning around the elevated body. She always fell back to sleep, assured by the watchful eyes of the cotters who sipped a hot drink of parched cocoa beans, and waited for the dawn to come.

At mid morning the cotters came with the coffin. Tatti waited outside with Gordie while they laid Gordon into the open cedar frame. "I want it Russian," Tatti had said to Cora. "I want him carried open to the grave as my grandmother's people did."

She watched the barefoot sailors emerge slowly into the bright sunlight, the open coffin on their shoulders, carrying it into the pavilion. Tatti heard the spontaneous prayers of the cotters, spoken in their native dialect, while the other mourners listened with bowed heads. Then came the gentle voices singing the old country hymns of the Low Counties as well as the Highlands. She held their son and waited until Cutler and Higgins turned to her and looked to see if she was ready.

Tatti walked up to the bier and stared again at what she'd loved and lost, then swung up the child to her breast and said, "Papa."

"Papa?" The bright eyes settled on the lifeless statue of Gordon. The little boy reached for the hilt of the dress sword.

"To protect us." Tatti held the child's face into her shoulder and wept. "Kiss your father."

Cora lifted the child to Gordon's lips and the child shrank back.

Tatti leaned over and kissed the figure. "Do what Mama does." She held her son over his dead father's face. "Kiss your father."

The child put his bowed lips to the pale hollow cheek, and scuffled in her arms as he both kissed and pushed away from the figure of death.

"Someday you'll know," Tatti said, swinging the little boy to her breast, glad she had stood at her son's side to honor his father. Someday he'd remember and be a part of all that Gordon was.

When Tatti stepped clear of the bier, the sailors picked up the open coffin and carried it out into the sunlight toward the grave. She walked slowly behind them. Gordon was going relentlessly away from them. In the bright day she could see the soft wind stir his hair, and in it she saw the gray.

"He was a great man," she said to Cora. "Too fine for life. I had his love, and I have his son, and I am his life," Tatti said, turning back to their quarters. "That is my purpose, that and dear, dear Skarra."

"Scotland," Cora said.

"Aye, that we be." She led Gordie away by the hand.

BOOK FOUR
Skarra

XXXVII

The bright days on the island passed one by one and settled with each starlit night, yet they could not reach Tatti. She could draw her breath at dawn watching the changeless grandeur of the sea, and walk the sun-struck beach at evening, always hearing the deep rumble of the ocean, and somehow, she was alone. It was Gordon she missed, and even in the midst of beauty, her days had a poignant grief to them.

The schooner had a fortune in pirates' gold bullion and sterling plate stored aboard it, in five heavy chests. Stowell and the sailors offloaded the treasure and brought it to Tatti, who looked at it, nodded, and said, "Put it over there, in the corner, so we don't stumble over it."

Tatti was aware of the tension to leave the island, once they had the captured schooner. "Charles Town, in the Carolinas, is due west, my lady," Stowell said. "And 'tis a fair west wind, all the way."

"Soon, I'll make up my mind." Tatti was swept away in a lassitude that she sensed she must live through, as the emigrants had done after the shipwreck. "I know the Admiralty seeks us."

The sailors and cotters saw the veil of protection fall over her eyes shutting them out of her soul where she grieved, and they withdrew, one sailor saying, "There 'tis, boys, her ladyship ain't made up her mind yet—so we can dig taters and eat fish and hunt hogs till she does."

Tatti knew they did not really mind, and took long walks, leading Gordie by the hand, and carrying the great heaps of sea shells the little boy gathered and brought to her. Cora walked with her, and never pressed her, as they all waited.

Tatti lived in her grass-thatched cottage with Cora and Gordie and mended, really having quite forgot the turmoil of their battles and ravishment, feeling only her loss.

In the pavilion, well after midnight, Stowell heard a voice call him.

"Bosun," the voice whispered.

He groaned when he rolled up onto his elbow and saw the eyes of Margene.

"Come, Mr. Stowell. It's Sheila."

"Sheila?"

Stowell got to his feet with the aid of Margene and another woman, and they walked outside, and down onto the beach.

"My God, what have you done?" Stowell saw a woman's naked body lying in the moonlight. He could see the eyeballs in as dead reflection as the knife blade that stuck up out of her breast. The fingers of the hands clutched the blade, fresh with blood.

"She fell on it," Margene said, and Stowell noticed vague figures of other women in the distant moonlight.

"Great God, 'tis murder." He shook his head.

"She fell on it."

"Get her down the beach, and slip her into the ebb tide."

"Aye, Bosun." Margene sucked in her cheeks and puffed her toothless gums. "We wasn't going to have no killing while Lord Gordon lay dying. But once we'd buried his lordship, we wasn't going to take no traitors back to England."

"You didn't need to kill her." He turned away toward the pavilion.

"She ruined us all," Margene said.

"She wanted to show ner naked body." A woman's voice spoke from the group. "So we stripped her naked before we killed her."

"My pallet," Stowell croaked, "and don't tell her ladyship."

"We want it official that she drowned," Margene said.

"Aye, 'tis official. She drowned."

The women helped him back to his pallet, where he fell into a deep, spent sleep, astonished at human nature. All he could think of was the battles, the storm, his love for Tatti, and his sympathy for Tatti's grief.

It was a bright morning, and Tatti felt the wind blow her hair free as she walked toward the pavilion with Gordie. "Parched corn and honey," she said, smelling of breakfast. "We must hurry, Gordie."

Tattie came into the midst of the happy, breakfasting band, some at rough tables, others sitting cross-legged on woven mats, while one or two wandered out into the dawn on the beach, to eat their breakfasts.

"Oh, my, such an elegant repast." Tatti's eye fell onto the hot trays of thick roasted oats that had been rolled and parched with honey and shredded coconuts. "Oats are the strength of Scotland." She took a bowl and held it while one woman dipped out piping hot spoonfuls and another poured goat milk.

"We'll feed Gordie," Cora said, nudging the little boy along at her knee, "and make him tall like a Scotsman."

"Incredible, the English." Tatti swallowed a moist spoonful, and munched more crunchy flavor in her mouth. "They feed oats to their horses, which are the finest in the world, and eat bleached flour themselves, till they're spindly and winded." She swallowed again.

"And they laugh at us for eating our oats," Cora said. A cloud passed over her face. "There's exceptions, my lady."

"Oh, Lord Gordon would be first to agree." Tatti took her nurse's arm, and they walked through the happy eating company to watch the early sun throw a broad spangling cape across the white caps on the sea.

Tatti was eating her second bowl of parched oats and honey while the little boy played in the sand at her bare feet when she heard a wild cry.

"Sail ho!"

Cora stopped eating, her mouth half ajar as she munched, and the cry rolled down from the Signal Hill.

"Sail Ho!"

"A sail, man-o-war, and to the north'-ard!"

The bosun rushed past them, followed by the sailors and the marine, some of the men already armed.

Tatti set down her bowl as the women came up and stood with her to watch the approaching ship, and the men dashed up into the pits and redoubts, preparing to fight.

"This time it's slavery or England," Tatti said. "Perhaps we should pray the ship has civilized colors, any flag will do."

"Even the French," a woman said.

"Pray it's French, they love their children," Tatti said.

They could see the ship grow in size, and catch a glint of sunlight sparkle on her tall varnished masts that stood among her towering white sails.

"English, she's English," Stowell said, moving quietly to Tatti's side. "But I can't convince the marine."

"He's fought too many battles to believe anything, poor man," a woman said.

The ship lay onto her port beam, driving her bow deep into a quartering sea under a full spread of sails. Her topsails fanned out like white wings on which her gallants spread wide above them, and overtop all were her royal gallants and her skysails, drawing the ship across the sparkling ocean as though a delicate cloud.

"England!" Stowell shouted, running down across the beach, waving his arms, and followed by his sailors, their shirts tied to their muskets to signal.

"A lovely sight," Tatti said, watching the ship. She glanced toward their pavilion, where George Caruthers had raised the crosses of England, Ireland, and Scotland in the Union Jack.

Ballooning her white sails in the wind before the long masts, the brig careened westward along the shore of the island. Her stern rode easily above her graceful overhang, following the long, easy swells her bow drove through.

On the island they stood in a transfixed group, with only Stowell down in the surf to his knees, and watched the ship cast her bow into the wind, letting her sails luff, and the ship leave to in the water. They saw the immense colors flying at the mastheads and the jib sprit.

The Cross of Saint Andrews flew at the mainmast, the Cross of Saint Patrick at the foremast, and the British Jack at the mizzenmast. "Only a Scot would fly the flags in that order," Tatti said.

"It couldn't be." Cora shook her head. "Not Peter!"

"A very stubborn boy, he was," Tatti mused aloud. "And alas for us." She looked down at her curly-haired child, and saw Gordon Wragby; and knew she could never love a boy, whoever he was, not after loving a man.

They watched the brigantine fall off across the wind, fill her sails once more, stand down the beach out of cannon range of the anchored schooner, and heard her anchor let go into the sea with a large splash as her sails collapsed into their varnished spars. Then they saw the men.

The rigging, ratlines, and yardarms of the ship were crowded with men who were cheering in great hurrahs.

"Thank God, they found us," Tatti said, and was astonished to see all the cotters down on their knees, weeping and praying in grief and thanksgiving.

Tatti felt too spent to join them. She crossed herself in the Russian manner, and whispered, "Thank thee, Lord, to stay our tears, and grant us peace once more in the bosom of our families." She led the child toward the shore.

They could see a longboat slung over the brigantine's side, and a boat crew clamber into sight. Moments later, the men were rowing the boat boldly toward the shore, as though on parade, flying an immense red, and white, and blue flag of imposed crosses.

"'Tis Lord Peter," Cora said, staring through the spyglass.

"The long glass," Tatti said, and saw the blood-red lips on the pallid skin, and the graceful body slouching at his ease in the stern of the boat. "Aye, Peter. He found us." She closed the spyglass with a rich popping note. "I always knew he would."

The people were harrooing along the edge of the surf, and sailors were out in the water to their armpits. A boat had already boarded the schooner when Tatti heard the brisk command, "Lift oars!" The boat rose onto a rushing breaker, and hurtled through the surf, skidding bow first up onto the dry sand, while the castaways went wild, swarming over its gunwales and seizing the men into their arms, pulling them over to kiss, making the disciplined oars tilt askew and rattle against one another.

Tatti waited up the beach with the child and Cora, and watched the naval discipline dissolve behind the pale young officer who skipped across the thwarts of the boat, and leaped out onto the sand, his eyes onto her.

"Tatti!" he shouted in the bell-clear voice of youth. He ran toward her.

"Oh, Peter." Tatti went toward him, holding the child, then letting go to fling herself into his arms.

"I swore to God I'd find you." He crushed her into his chest against his white waistcoat.

"Peter, we waited."

For a blind second, it was as if they were alone again on the Scottish moor, hopping from stone to stone in the midst of a shallow river, with white water swirling past their bare toes that gripped the moss-covered rocks. It was the feel of childhood all over again, a glimpse into the past that declared the future to be pure bliss, and forever.

"The French." Peter put his mouth to hers, and pressed past her teeth. In that moment Tatti knew he'd discovered it was not the same because her mouth would not lie to him. "We had to fight the French." He pulled his face back to look into her eyes and understand what stood between them.

"Your lordship," Cora said, leading up Gordie.

"My child," Tatti said, putting her hands onto the boy's shoulders and setting him in front of her.

"Yours? Tatti?" Peter's face showed unbelief, and absolute calm, born of generations of self-control. "Pray tell me why?"

"Love, Peter." She stared quietly into his soft gray-blue eyes.

"Love? For whom?"

"Lord Gordon Wragby."

"The Captain, I see." Peter's eyes went down the beach to the ribbed hulk of the *Daphne,* which loomed up as a relic of a distant age. "And you fell in love?"

"I grew to adore him."

"She be a widow," Cora said firmly. "We lost Lord Gordon six months past—died a hero's death, he did. Died in our arms."

"Dead?" Peter said, looking back to Tatti.

"Aye."

"She's free, when the grief passes." Cora held the child's hand. "And this be Lord Gordon of Ravendale."

Peter looked down at the child, then up at Cora, and settled his puzzled eyes onto Tatti.

"The young'un needs a father, and Tatti owns the gold, pirates' gold."

"Gold?" Peter said.

"Lord Peter, 'twas a long story," Cora said.

"Peter, I grew—we all grew up or died when the tempest swallowed our ship." Tatti spoke quietly, and led him toward the pavilion.

"Tea and cakes for his lordship," Cora called to two women, who scurried up the beach ahead of them. "And the finest French brandy!"

Tatti walked slowly with Peter toward the broad table the women had carried out into the open shade of the trees, where they had a clear view of the anchored ships and the ocean and the happy men and women.

Peter unslung the baldric of his sword, which a woman took, curtseying as she did; and he sat alone with Tatti and the child, while Cora stood in earshot. "The tempest? Shipwreck? Survival, and then siege by pirates?"

"We endured, then prevailed," Tatti said, sipping her tea.

"But you don't have any men, to fight off hundreds," Peter stared at the distant shipwreck and licked his tongue along the edge of his brandy goblet.

"We had a marine and some sailors——" Tatti was cut off.

"Lord Peter," Cora said, "we had a wise captain and brave men, and we had women who weren't afraid to die."

"Women?" Peter looked into the russet eyes of Tatti's nurse.

"'Twas the women who went to the foot of the cross at Calvary, when the Savior's disciples turned rabbit-hearted and fled."

"Peter, later." Tatti laid her hand atop his. There was still so much boy in Peter.

"We have five chests of gold," Cora said briskly. "Her ladyship's gold."

The first days after the arrival of Peter's ship, HMS *Hyperion*, were a time of great elation. The sailors who came ashore to help gather up the castaways were swept away in the delight of being accepted not only as long-lost relatives, but as saviors as well. Nothing was too good for them. Peter's officers accompanied him ashore. They toured the island and studied Gordon Wragby's slow, relentless defense of his people and repulse of the enemy at the fort.

"Lord Gordon Wragby had a dreamer's name with the English," said a tall Irish officer, Sean Finucane. "Never fit for court functions and Admiralty politics."

"My husband loved his duty," Tatti said, as she walked with Peter and four naval officers, "but he loved life more."

"And he died not knowing we'd captured gold," Cora said.

"I think the thought of it might have bothered him." Tatti saw a look of dismay pass over Cora's face. "But it doesn't bother me."

"Well, we'll have to follow Admiralty law, to see how it's disposed of," Peter said.

"As long as them Admirals know it's our blood money," Cora said, "the law's just fine."

"That's why we have laws." Peter spoke without looking at either Tatti or Cora, and studied the flotation and pulley problem of dragging the salvaged cannons out from the revetments where Gordon had hidden them, down the beach, and out onto his ship for return to England. "Can't understand how a handful of men and women put up what I'll need a hundred men just to drag to the water's edge."

"My father said they built the great cathedrals of Europe and Britain with men who couldn't read or write, and used plumb-bobs, right-angles, and dishes of water to raise them." Tatti clasped her hand behind her back as she spoke, and avoided the officers' curious glances at her, as though she were something more than the Countess of Skarra and Ravendale.

"Ah, yes, Sir Jonathan, the Edinburgh lawyer." Peter looked at the distant shipwreck. "You've lost Skarra, you know . . . ."

"Lost Skarra?" Tatti whirled on him. "Impossible!"

"No, afraid not," Peter said briskly. "Skulduggery, of course, between the Earl of Argyle and the Westminster government. Your father's pleading his case in Lords."

410

"But we've always lived on Skarra."

"We still have Fendrath," Peter said.

"You bought Fendrath. We grew out of Skarra!" Tatti's voice was fierce with outrage that anybody would dare to touch her beloved Skarra, her Scotland and her moor.

"It's just a matter of money—buy off Lord Cecil, that simple."

"*Nouveau riche*," Tatti sneered.

"Aye, they bought their titles with their climb, but they are a fact of life." Peter's voice was pleasant and assured.

"Then I suppose it's money," Tatti said.

"Regrettably, yes."

Tatti knew she would never surrender the gold. It had been no more than an object to stumble over in her grass-thatched hut but it was now her ransom for Skarra.

"I'll never surrender Skarra," she declared.

Peter strode through the open sunlight on the beach, where his men were strung out in file heaving on long hawsers that inched the cannons out of their firing pits.

"Hid them in shrubbery," Sean Finucane said. The big Irishman shielded his eyes as they watched the cast bronze weapon emerge into sight, like a strange beast struggling through a mat of vines. "Gordon Wragby was a natural warrior."

"Well he died," Peter said. "They would never have believed how he lost his ship."

"He didn't care," Tatti said, annoyed that other men who lived could speak about a man she loved and who was dead. "The Admiralty, the government, they were nothing to him—he was a gentleman."

"A Christian gentleman," Cora chimed in.

"My lady." Finucane lifted his velour hat as he turned to Tatti, sensing her annoyance. "If I didn't know otherwise, I'd swear to God that Lord Gordon Wragby was Irish. Only a saint and a scholar could fight as this heroic man did against the elements and tyrants and yet prevail."

Peter looked at Tatti and, in that moment, saw that childhood was now gone in the rush of the awful facts imposed by life on grownups. He saw her as a woman, assured and loyal to a man he'd never known, widowed with a child, and commanding respect from other men as a woman alone.

"Thank you, Mr. Finucane." Tatti spoke quietly.

"A gallant horse and a great man are rare, my lady." Finucane dashed the crown of his hat atop his knee and bowed.

"No, dear sir, the Irish never bow." Tatti gestured upward with her hand.

"With her ladyship's permission, the Irish always bow to beautiful women."

Tatti smiled quickly at the lively compliment of the handsome man, while Cora and Peter exchanged glances, and looked solemn.

Tatti turned across the sunburned sage grass and went toward her child. She would always love Peter as a boy, but that was then—he had to grow to be a man before she would love him now. Until then, she loved only Gordie and Skarra; and she would use her body or her wiles of flesh and grace of manners to win and hold these two things. It rejoiced her heart to know she had captivated a man as bold and witty as the Irish officer. But her secret love was Gordon and Skarra, and she was determined to win, law or no law.

XXXVIII

The anchored brigantine rested on the water like a glistening swan. All afternoon the laden small boats had beat their oars frantically in the surf, ferrying the emigrants and their provender out to the ship. Tatti watched from the pavilion as the skin-wet sailors heaved the stems of the small boats seaward off the beach, and afloat beyond the breakers.

"I'll stay one night alone on the island," she had said to Peter. "Just Gordie and Cora and I."

Peter nodded and rowed out in his gig to the ship with his officers and men.

That evening as the sun settled onto the ocean and paused above the glinting edge of

415

the sea, beyond the proud ship, Tatti walked to Gordon's grave.

She held the child's hand, and Cora was beside her, each woman silent while they listened to their bare feet rustle in the soft sage grass. The thicket of cedars was cool, and deeply shadowed as the sun grew huge and eased out of sight to the west.

"Likely I'll not come again to his grave."

"'Twill be known to God," Cora whispered.

"Aye." Tatti knelt and pressed her forehead into the earth at the edge of the grave that lay hidden under a punk of dry evergreen needles. "Forgive me for living and wanting to live," she whispered into the dirt, feeling the moist humors of the earth on her lips. "O Lord, preserve him and all he loved, sustain him in the hours beyond time, keep Gordon, O Lord, till I come to him—and Lord give me strength to keep his faith, now and forever." She touched her forehead into the dirt and rested it there, until she felt her burden ease.

"He'll wait." Cora's voice was scarce audible, as the little boy watched his mother and the older woman who stood behind her.

"Gordon, I love you." Tatti came upright and dug her hands down into the earth through the dry leaves and needles. She waited until she could feel herself cry, and in her tears taste her release from Gordon, to pick up their burden of living, and to go on. "You, and none other," she whispered, and stood.

Cora embraced her gently to her bosom, holding the child between them, and they stood that way in silence, on the island alone, until it was dark.

"He lies beside a good woman." Tatti could taste the salt of the sea and the ease of her soul as they walked back to the grass-thatched hut.

At mid-morning Tatti waited on the beach in glaring sunlight while the boats came ashore for them. Peter was silent when he came up, and Tatti looked at the bleaching wreck of the *Daphne*, still fluttering a torn remnant of sails and a tattered flag. The gaunt hulk thrust her bow into a shallow sea, while sand now filled in to her broken sterncastle.

"Burn it, Peter."

Peter looked at the shipwreck. "Very well."

"It's the last thing I can do for Gordon." She burst into tears, heaving again and again in spasms of sorrow, until she was spent with grief.

Later, alone with Stowell and Cora and her child, she watched the pyre of smoke rise up from the shipwreck, unfurling a long feather into the clouds. In less than an hour the blazing wreck collapsed into a sizzling ember at the water's edge.

Watching the ship die and vanish, Tatti sensed a release of Gordon and his ship to her, and she turned to Cora. "He and his ship are mine forever."

Waving aside the sailors who would have carried her through the surf, Tatti waded out to the Captain's varnished barge, her child in her arms. She was wet to her hips and felt the light frock lay about her legs, and saw the barge come alongside her, while a forest of bare arms and hands reached out. She was pulled out of the sea and into the air in a shower of white water, and swung into the sternsheets, as the child broke into tears.

"Good show," Peter said, nodding to the coxswain, and they heard the sailor cry, "Out oars!"

"Give way together!" the coxswain shouted.

Tatti looked back at the island, then toward the waiting ship. Cora settled her hand on hers as they rowed toward the *Hyperion*.

Tatti, Cora, and little Gordie shared Peter's cabin with its varnished fretwork doors and bookcases. The brigantine followed a long, slow plunge under an easy spread of canvas, her course set to the northeast. "To Cherbourg," Peter had said. "I have sealed documents for the Duc de Guise." He pointed at a small locked desk. "He's the bastard brother of the Dauphin."

The sea was still tropic, and they opened their casement windows across the fantail of the ship to let the fresh air blow through. In less than a week, the old ways of intimate respect and good humor for their mutual confinement settled upon them. Peter sipped lime juice in his bunk during the heat and wore only his linen breeches that ended just below his knees.

"Any Stuart court would be jolly," Tatti said. She wore only her camisole and pantelettes. She pressed a cool cloth over Gordie's forehead while the child dozed in a small hammock.

"I can say one good thing about these ships," Cora said firmly. "That wind that blows first hither then yon, till a body's face is scorched, is the wind that sweeps away them pesky flies."

"No flies!" Tatti nodded, and Peter dangled out a slender white foot to flip the Spanish lock on one of the five stacked chests of treasure.

"Aye, as long as we sail, we're free—not till land do we face chaos and human evil."

Peter flopped backward into his bunk, flinging his forearm across his temple, and showing a patch of fine dark hair in his armpit. Tatti saw it, and immediately blushed across her neck and cheeks in embarrassment, because she had licked her lips, and Cora had seen her.

" 'Tis an ill wind that blows no ship," Tatti said, and blushed again when she realized how empty her words sounded when she spoke to hide her embarrassment.

"Thy thirst is right, my lady." Cora laid her hand on Tatti's forearm and spoke in spiritual intimacy.

"I must turn in the gold." Peter did not look at them as he spoke.

"Lord Gordon said it belonged to us," Tatti said.

"Laws of the Admiralty and salvage," Peter said.

"We're Scottish," Tatti answered quietly.

"Aye, so we be, in the rub."

"The gold is ours," Tatti said, carefully modulating her voice to silence any hint of determination from arousing Peter. She noticed, however, that Cora's bosom heaved as she listened.

"'Tis an English ship, flying the Union Jack of the Royal Navy."

"I'll need the gold to save Skarra." Tatti lay her hand on the ropes of the sleeping child's hammock to give it motion. "I'll have to buy off Lord Burghley and the courts of law, in London—and buy the Scots in Edinburgh."

"What about my naval career?" Peter said sitting upright.

"You won't need a naval career with that much gold." Tatti let her eyes travel across the ironbound, brass-studded chest upon which their hand basins set, and their teakettle rested. "Lord Gordon was wasted in the Navy."

"Perhaps, but he died true to his duty and his breeding."

"This is his breeding." Tatti looked at the touseled hair of the sleeping child. "And to that I'm true."

"Now, now, Lord Gordon bloomed wherever he was cast," Cora said, wanting to encourage a romance, out of necessity to circumstance, regardless of the pull of the hearts involved. "A good tree casts its fruit to flower, even in a desert."

"Aye." Peter dropped his chin onto his bare chest, in thought. "Yet, we'd be stealing."

"Everybody gets to steal except us," Tatti said. "We're supposed to be above it, the ruling class."

"It's not our class. It's the law."

"They can rape us on the moor, and kill us, and uproot our tenants, and ship them into slavery, and burn up our whole nation, calling it freedom and liberty and union, but we can't steal."

"Oh, God, such logic." He swung his bare shanks from the bunk. "I'll have another lime juice."

Cora reached out a red graveled arm and hand, tinkling a tall spoon in a glass as she did. "Your lordship."

As Peter put it to his lips, the fine sweat beaded his forehead. Tatti wrung out a small towel and spread it, to cool his bare torso in the heat. "We'll be into the cold weather, soon enough."

"Aye." He looked into Tatti's face, the corners of his mouth crinkling upward in a smile. "I never before knew temptation, because I had no such opportunity. But we could put it into Hanseatic thollars with the Dutch— t'would all be paper money then."

"Paper money?" Tatti said.

"Oh, yes, paper notes. You can't carry a million pounds sterling without an oxcart or wagon, so you use paper notes." He stopped talking when he saw the two women had held their breath in absolute silence, and had closed in on him.

"Yes, Peter? What else?" Tatti whispered.

"Oh, nonsense!" He fell back into his bunk in mock dismay. "Naval officers don't steal."

"No, of course not." Tatti was amazed at the hoarse note in her words and swallowed to hide them when she saw a look of alarm sweep Peter's eyes.

"I'd say the gold belongs to the Indians," Cora said briskly, "and if there are no Indians to give it to, then it belongs to us."

"Cora always sees it the Lord's way," Tatti said.

Peter rolled his head from side to side on his pillow, as their broad cabin followed the pitch of an easy swell on the ocean. "Paper money. You can carry it anywhere to trade, and nobody can rob you—but, no, I've got to turn it over to the Admiralty."

"Of course we can't steal it," Tatti said, idly swinging the child's hammock once more, her mind racing into a thousand schemes to steal the gold. She blushed when she saw Cora's eyes studying her face, and she knew Cora understood her intention when she saw her eyes grow round with dismay.

"We be Scots and kin, my lord," Cora said, attempting to ease the grand theft that tempted them.

"I'm a King's officer."

"I married an Englishman, and I have his child," Tatti said. "I agree it is English gold."

"Oh, well, then it's all settled," Peter said, swinging out of his bunk. "I need a breath of fresh air."

"Of course, it's all settled," Tatti said.

As the *Hyperion* sailed northeast, skirting the Azores and heading for the Bay of Biscay, north of Spain, Peter took more to the open deck, where Tatti often joined him. The weather cooled, and Peter wrapped his neck in mufflers, pulled heavy leather sea boots onto his legs, buttoned his heavy coat to his chin, and watched the quick-running slate sea.

Tatti girdled her waist in layers of skirts and drew thick mantles over her cloaks when she stood at Peter's side on the windswept deck.

The ship moved in grace, almost a thing alive under her broad spread of canvas, crashing from wave to wave.

"There's a pure sweep of clean air about the ocean under sails," Peter said, "that fills a human soul with hope that all life is this way." He looked back into the white froth traveling across the gray sea.

"It's like fishing on the River Dee and along the creeks of the Scottish moor." Tatti felt her boots balance her legs beside him as they stood together on the slanting deck. "I love it."

"Ah, those were good days."

"Childhood. Peter, we were meant for each other out of a happy childhood."

"Aye, the soft haze of Scotland and the gentle light we played in and grew from."

"You found no other?"

"No, only you." He glanced at her quickly. "Only you would unhook a fish and not kill it."

" 'Twas more than fishing," she said gently.

"Aye, 'twas love," he mused. "Tatti, why did you marry Gordon Wragby?"

"The world turned upside down with death at the shipwreck, and he was a man like my father, and I knew I had to start life over."

"That's profound." He touched her hand.

"We were Scots—listen to yourself." She felt him draw close, and hugged his hand to her waist, while she rested her eyes on the white misted sea.

Peter nodded. "We'll have a jolly dinner with the officers."

Tatti held his arm as his fingers entwined hers, and felt the fresh wind blow across their faces while they stood together.

That night Peter invited his officers to dine with Tatti and Cora and him. The finest plate and dishes were set and port and Madeira wine stood in crystal decanters. Tatti enjoyed the company of the bluff officers, particularly the Irishman, Sean Finucane.

Finucane flourished his goblet and called, "A toast to the rose of Scottish heather!" He turned to the head of the table.

"Mr. Finucane, in Ireland the enthusiasm for beauty knows no bounds," Tatti said. "The rose is English, the heather Scottish, and the shamrock Irish."

"My lady, to love one flower is to love all flowers, for beauty belongs to itself."

Tatti shook her head slowly and smiled, lifting her glass. "To Ireland, eternal parent of Scotland, as my father says."

"Hear! Hear!" Peter slapped the table with his fingers as the exclamation was taken up, and the officers drained their goblets.

The dinner went well, exquisitely served by Hindus while a Scottish piper played light airs from the companionway. After dinner Tatti walked with Peter onto the raised poop deck of the stern. She watched the troubled white wake reflect in the gold light from their taffrail lantern, following their ship out of a stormy night.

"It makes me shiver," Tatti said, drawing her cloak about her. "A hand's throw away lies the indifference of the ocean, and death, while here we stand, warm and aglow with good friends and human love."

"Love is sweeter when death is apparent and life itself seen so fragile."

"Peter, oh, Peter." She took his hand.

"Perhaps I fished and trekked the moor to escape Mother."

"Dear Lady Mary."

"A marriage of 'old money.'" He nodded.

"Think of those five chests of gold and silver, Peter." She felt his fingers twitch in her palm, and he withdrew his hand.

"Peter, I'll need some money to buy clothes in Cherbourg. I haven't a thing to wear." She shook her head vigorously. "Not a thing."

XXXIX

The elegant fields of France, divided by tidy white walls with small cottages nestled at the corners, passed before the quarterdeck as the brigantine tacked back and forth into Cherbourg. "'Tis as if all of France is a vast garden," Tatti said.

"The richest soil in Europe, and the brightest minds." Peter nodded. "Astounding they're given to so much chaos."

"Father always said human thought led to insanity if pushed to its ultimate conclusion."

"That's a good Englishman for you," Peter said. "Brilliant lawyer, Sir Jonathan Hogarth."

The moist air bathed the countryside, and wet the stone quay. Scrambling Frenchmen in knit stocking caps rushed aboard the ship.

"*Arrêtez! Arrêtez!*"

"Stop, stop," Tatti said, watching the hubbub of the French, laughing and gesticulating among themselves.

Suddenly, their attention was drawn to a heavy, mud-splattered coach that clattered into sight behind four matched horses.

"Le Duc de Guise!" cried a postillion rider. Outriders had drawn up at their gangway, swords unsheathed to salute.

The liveried footmen had leaped down, and flung open the door, as a small, handsome man stepped into sight.

"Pierre! *Mon Dieu!*" The man said when he saw Peter and came toward the ship.

"Phillipe!" Peter called, and went down the slanting ladder to the wharf.

Tatti watched the two young men stop, and talk intimately; and in a moment, she saw the Frenchman look over Peter's shoulder, his eyes searching the ship until they came to rest on her. The eyes smiled, and he looked back to Peter, and Tatti heard him. "Her complexion, so fair and her chin so elegant." He seized Peter's shoulder. "Lucky young dog, you."

Peter turned, laughing with the young Frenchman. "No, not what you think."

"All men think the same." He looked at Tatti again.

Once on deck, Tatti saw that Phillipe de-Guise was indeed an elegant, composed, and absolutely assured young man, and quite fair. He bowed to her, and Tatti curtseyed.

"Your grace." His light Norman eyes were bright as they traveled under her throat, and she instinctively put out her hand to touch his fingers when he gentled her balance on the deck.

"The honor of France to be the first to welcome home the rose of unrequited love," Phillipe said.

"We all adore France," Tatti said. The heavy coach standing on the quay caught her eye, and she knew she had found the vehicle in which to carry the gold to Holland. "We're so starved for gallantry in England—the weather makes us phlegmatic."

"Phlegmatic?" Phillipe turned to Peter.

"The Marchioness of Ravendale means dull, staid, fox-hunting, country churls," Peter said.

"But of course." Phillipe's well-bred mouth bowed, and he took Tatti's hand into both of his.

"I shall love traveling through the small villages of France—oh, the geraniums and fuchsia in the courtyards. Truly, mosaics of living color."

"Well, after the ball, we'll go coaching!" Phillipe waved his hand.

"I'd love that," Tatti said.

The Château Carteret was aglow in the distance, filling the soft night with a luminous radiance in the green forest. Tatti's carriage drew up to the porticoed gallery. Through open doors of glass, with Palladian arches, candelabras of brilliant crystal shone out.

"Your château, so lovely," Tatti said, stepping down before the duke.

"Oh, our country place." He took Tatti on his arm. "The mud we grew out of."

"Carteret?"

"When we grow bored or sick of Paris, we always come home to Carteret."

"How wise." Tatti entered the great hall where liveried servants took her wraps and she was supplied with a mask through which only her eyes would show as she flirted, which was the purpose of the ball.

The English officers were outstanding in their dark hunting-blue coats among the satin breeches and rich silks and yards of lace and puce that moved in a stately minuet across the ballroom. The music swept Tatti into its elegant three-quarter time, with the contradance swirling the costumed dancers into dashing flowers that whirled round and round each other. Her hand was out and caught, and she turned time and again, in curtsey to another masked figure, or slipped her own mask to smile in response to a stranger.

"Not French," one young man said, his eyes bold upon the back of her upswept hairdo when she turned.

"How can you tell, monsieur?"

"Your swan neck is English—how I'd love to see your underlimbs."

"My legs, monsieur?"

"Ah, you are English—so direct."

"No, Scottish." She lifted her mask.

"Mmm." He kissed her fingertips. "How I tire of the short necks of Brittany."

"I love to go coaching."

"Oh, alas, I lost my coach at the gaming table."

"Alas, misfortune." Tatti smiled and was gone into another man's hand.

Tatti enjoyed the ball. Each dance opened on the delicate notes of the flute, and swung out on the violins, dashing the refinement of Versailles across the ballroom; and when she danced, it seemed she had danced forever through her life, and that all life was truly a graceful pose at an endless ball. When the music paused between dances, Tatti was surprised to find herself among so many perspiring temples and loose flowing tresses of hair, straying from high-piled hairdos, and back in the world of reality.

"Oh, I do love to dance," she whispered to Sean Finucane, whose auburn red hair framed his Irish face and whose eyes alternated from pathos to anger to merriment.

"Jolly way to meet each other with no claim nor obligation."

"I want the gold," she whispered while the couples strolled together between dances, and men in satin brocades stooped to help ladies find their lost combs on the parquetry or knelt to free a high heel from a hem.

"And Lord Peter?"

"I have to save Skarra."

"You'd trust me?" His eyes pierced hers.

"Aye, Ireland's the thrall of England."

"You'll get me hanged, my lady." Finucane threw back his head and laughed.

"I'll need the Frenchman's coach."

"Oh, I wouldn't miss it!" Finucane began to cough as he laughed. In a moment he stopped. "I'll not shed blood, my lady."

"No, of course not." Tatti set her hand on his cuff, nodding genteely to a dark French couple, the young man's brocade coat showing crescents of sweat in his armpits.

"Your price? Do you have a price?" Tatti spoke without moving her lips.

"My price?"

"Yes. Gold, or love?"

"My lady, I don't buy love and I'm not for sale."

"Thank you." Tatti's eyes caught Finucane's, and she saw a direct man who was grand enough in his soul to understand her task as a woman, and to take no offense nor advantage of her. "A man like you would be easy to love."

"Ireland's my love, Tatti."

"A rare man indeed." She squeezed his large muscular hand.

Tatti went over her plans a thousand times. All she needed was Phillipe de Guise's Norman coach and horses, and to get Stowell, Caruthers, Roo, and Brighton to lower the gold out the sterncastle windows into a small boat to be rowed down the quay to the waiting carriage. Then it was a long gallop to Holland and the Dutch bankers.

"It's not only illegal, it's immodest," Cora said, gulping, when Tatti explained it in her bedroom of the château. "How can you seduce

432

two different men in one night, and steal a King's ransom?"

"I can do anything if I have to," Tatti said. "And I mean to have the gold Gordon left me, to save his son and keep Skarra."

"Oooo, to think I raised thee from a babe."

"Good, now you can share the sin." Tatti spoke crossly, annoyed that her nurse had raised the specter of Puritan morality.

"Thou wouldst shame thy mother and thy father." Cora's voice trembled in passion as she undressed Tatti.

"Father's in Westminster talking law."

"Lord Gordon never meant for his beloved to use her body . . . ."

"Cora, my God, what else has a woman got to use except her body?"

The robust Highland woman shuddered.

"Oh, Cora, where's your common sense?" Tatti turned to her old nurse, her arms outstretched. "The spirit of love is not the flesh— to use the flesh is no more than that, but love is divine." She hugged Cora into her body. "Whatever man I seduce is to win a respite so what I truly love will flourish."

"I do not understand thee, yet I will abide."

"Good, Gordon Wragby I adored, Peter is yet a poetic boy, and I love the sailor, Stowell, for his loyal courage."

"That Yorkshire plowman?"

"Aye, and I'll have any other man I have to have, to keep my true love."

"And when do we do these things?"

"When the moment is ripe."

With resignation Cora turned Tatti round, tied the ribbons of her nightgown over the small of her back, and pulled down her bed.

It was easy to convince Peter she needed to remain in the fresh country life of Château Carteret, when he returned to the ship. Tatti even brought along Margene and Stowell and the marine, as outside servants. "It's not just loving two men in one night, it's coordinating their seduction to the stealing of the gold and loading the carriages—and I'll need two."

Cora nodded.

"I've promised to run off with Phillipe on a grand tour to visit his kin—every château north of the Loire, he said." Tatti's eyes lit with excitement. "He can't get his breath when I kiss him, and I won't yield until he takes me away, even when he has me half nude."

With four Spanish doubloons, Margene procured from the apothecary the opium sleeping potion Tatti needed to quiet Peter. Then Margene carried Tatti's instructions to Roo and Brighton at the ship as to how the treasure was to be stolen.

Tatti had never expected she might have to use her wiles and her body as a deliberate ploy to have her way; yet never before had she ever truly wanted anything. It never crossed her mind that there was anything wrong with her plans. She was sure her mother would approve. "Just as long as your heart's pure," as her Russian grandmother would say; and it pleased her to know Cora's loyalty to her was

434

stronger than the Highland code of Puritan morality. In her heart, Tatti sensed, as did her father and grandfather, old Lord Skarra, that morality was often a form of intellectual passion that grappled with the flesh.

"Thank goodness I've got my mind separate from my flesh," Tatti said to herself, as her light carriage drove her through the French countryside of hedgerows, down to Peter and HMS *Hyperion*. Tatti eased against the padded velour cushions, and smelled the perfumed wild roses that banked the roadbed. All was ready on the brigantine.

That night Tatti dined alone with Peter. She noticed he was disturbed, because he avoided looking at her while he ate and sipped wine.

"What is it?" she said.

"Phillipe. You stayed at Château Carteret a fortnight."

"Civilization. I need it."

"And not Phillipe?" His eyes met hers. "Gallant, suave, extravagant, so French."

"Oh, Peter." Tatti rose quickly and came around the low table. She ran her hand down his temple and let her fingers play down his neck, rooting through the folds of his stock until she felt the light hair verging across his chest. "Only you."

She put her mouth atop his when he raised his head, and slipped her tongue past his teeth, making him catch his breath, as his arms gripped her legs and his hands seized her. She sucked in her breath, and felt Peter rise onto his legs, as if her mouth held him captive by his tongue and soul, which she now held firm in her mouth.

"Tatti," he choked.

She had her hands inside his unbuttoned waistcoast and shirt and her fingers playing in the fine hair in his armpits. She felt him lunge into her arms and body, suddenly possessed.

"Get them off," she whispered, helping Peter jerk out of his elegant uniform and rip loose the buttons of his shirt, until he was nude from the waist up. His hands were snatching clumsily at her garments, and by pulling a ribbon here and loosing a button there, he detached articles of finery and lace and strewed them about the cabin. She was nude, down on her knees, pulling free the satin breeches until the fine-boned young man was naked—white once more, as she'd seen him in childhood, and on the moor—and she knew she could love Peter again, if she did not have to seduce him so outright.

"Lord, forgive me," she whispered. She thrust her breasts into his lips, and felt ecstacy engulf her as his tongue caught the budded nipples and caressed them against his firm palate. His hands pulled her into his body, and he gasped. "Tatti, I love thee."

"And I thee."

His arms went all to iron, and he tilted her down over her back, into the bunk, and his arms and legs swam as they pressed her limbs apart. She clung to his mouth in wet passion, and felt her own knees rise to let him strike his way up her body until she felt his iron manhood press at the gorged folds she raised for him at her loins. She heard him gasp as she clasped what he lunged to press into her and enfolded his whole body in her arms and legs. He was a prisoner to her life and need for him, and she knew she would devour him with the bliss he could not live without.

She felt his spine arching and every muscle in his back rippling in ecstasy as he trembled in undulating waves, then he sighed and lay still, every nerve, muscle, and bone utterly spent.

"I love you," Tatti whispered, her own body quivering in joy from her legs, up over her belly, to her breasts and her mouth as she felt him sag into a deep sleep of absolute rest.

Tatti was up early to admit the sailors and Caruthers. She had lifted Peter's contented torso as he slept, and had put the crystal goblet of sherry laced with opium to his lips.

Cora covered Peter's drugged body carefully. "Good, he mustn't get a chill," Tatti said, as the men tiptoed about the Captain's cabin. "Thank God, we can blame the French for stealing the gold."

Tatti watched the heavy, iron-strapped chests being lifted. Caruthers's massive biceps and shoulders bulged as he and Roo eased them out the slanting casement windows of the overhanging sterncastle of the ship. She heard the muffled voices on the water and the deep thud on wood as the chests were loaded into the waiting longboat.

After everyone except Cora and Caruthers

437

had climbed down the Jacob's ladder to the boat, Tatti went to the hatch leading up to the quarterdeck and called, "Mister Finucane?"

The big Irish officer filled the room, taking in the situation at a glance.

"Now you're to leave me to explain to the English how an Irishman let the French steal their gold."

"Oh, Sean, dear man." Tatti slipped her arms about Finucane and drew down his strong mouth and kissed him, tasting the bristling strength of his shaven lips and muscular jaw, and held him for a moment, seeking to touch his teeth with her tongue.

She heard a harsh noise behind the man's head, and felt him drop out of her arms as the marine and Cora caught the large body, and the head fell forward.

"God, not so hard!" Tatti gasped.

"The English would hang him as a lying Irishman," Cora said, stretching out the semiconscious body on the deck by Peter's feet, "unless we cracked him on the head honest."

"I never hit an officer before, my lady." Caruthers's eyes were struck with uncertainty.

"Never mind." Tatti covered Finucane's body with a heavy robe, and saw the bleeding wound in his scalp.

"He'll mend, my lady."

"All right. I don't want him hanged."

"Come, girl, we just saved his life." Cora led the way down the swaying ladder where sailors' arms drew them into the longboat.

Tatti saw the two angular shapes of the

heavy coaches waiting down the quay. The oars splashed in unison, spilling small cascades of water each time they surfaced to reach for another stroke. "In time, I could love either of those men," Tatti whispered to Cora.

"Never mind now." Cora looked ahead. "We can't turn back, and we've made our thievery look real—the English will hang anybody over gold."

"So will the Scots," Tatti mumbled into her cloak.

"Mayhaps, but we ain't had enough gold yet to murder over."

"Aye, just religion."

"Ease your heart, daughter, we ain't stopping."

Cora's resolution cheered Tatti from the grave misgivings that welled up in her.

The boat was at the stone steps, leading out of the water to the dock, and Tatti followed the men, who seemed almost to run with the treasure chests.

Phillipe was dressed in a white cloak and light brocade hat. "Ah, Tatti, you'll love France."

Tatti saw the eager, expectant eyes burning in the dark, and it stunned her that in the world of reality her plans were coming true. Her decision to seduce two different men in one night was not the exciting adventure she thought it might be, but a voyage to the edges of a nightmare, into which she might tumble forever.

"Phillipe, the night was made for us." She

came up to him as his eyes traveled to the five chests of treasure being lifted atop his two coaches.

"Mon Dieu, who owns that money?"

"We do."

The young Frenchman's face hesitated, then broke into a wide smile. "You stole it from Peter?"

"Our expenses," Tatti said, climbing into the luxuriously upholstered coach.

"Bravo!"

Tatti smiled and licked her lips as Phillipe stepped into the coach behind her, and she heard Cora say outside, "Drive on!"

The coach lurched ahead on its wheels, and the body began to swing and plunge independently of the axles, suspended on its leather straps.

"Sherry?" Phillipe said.

"I'd love some."

Phillipe pulled open a traveling credenza, containing cold meats, cheeses, and several varieties of wine and loaves of French bread. "We'll feast through Normandy."

Tatti gulped down her wine, feeling it raise a warmth within her soul, and she smiled at Phillipe. "Ah, Phillipe, the future is ours."

"And not now?"

"Now! As I promised!" Tatti threw back her head, knowing Gordie was in the following carriage, and laughed a slow, throaty sound as Phillipe's hand felt into her bosom to loosen the buttons at her throat.

The coach was dark, yet by moonlight Tatti could see the smooth white flesh, not certain

440

whose it was, of elegant legs and arms and twisting bodies that seized and lost each other, of torsos that slipped against each other's skin in a film of sweat, until she had Phillipe locked between her legs and gripped into her bosom, while his wet mouth went from her neck to her breasts, and his hands clutched at her long hair, and he swallowed for his breath that she drew from his lungs with her mouth.

The coach swung in a rhythm all its own, plunging along behind the horses, and Tatti felt the rapture of being in a swing, with the graceful body of a man caught between her thighs, within her, and unable to get away. She was engulfed in delight, and she gripped Phillipe's body into thighs and arms as he trembled and sighed, and trembled again, then slipped out of her limbs and body into a crumpled heap of spent white flesh on the floor between her knees.

She rested a moment, and then lifted his head whispering, "Dear Phillipe, such wild love." When he could not speak coherently, she drew down the silk-quilted coaching wraps over his body, and reached for a small sip of wine.

"Mon Dieu, in a carriage it is worth one half of eternity." He smiled contentedly and lay his head across her bare knee and fell asleep.

XL

The panorama of gentle green shadows and pink blossoms, mingled with the plunging reds of geraniums, rolled across the windows of their coach as it swept along the French countryside. When Phillipe ordered his coachmen to turn southeast toward Caen and Paris, Tatti laid her hand on his forearm. "Oh, Phillipe, please, let's drive along the Norman coast— I've grown accustomed to the ocean."

"*Mais oui*, but yes."

Phillipe waved his hand in the fair morning light, directing the coaches to skirt the untraveled side roads along the English Channel.

Tatti smiled as they breakfasted together and watched the distant sea roil easily beneath a counterpane of soft clouds. "I adore it."

"We'll need fresh horses."

"Anywhere—buy them." Tatti touched her purse which jingled with gold coin.

They trotted into a small courtyard of an inn where the flowers burst in color from tubs and windowboxes and clematis climbed across the doorways along the windows and atop the gate. Hostlers were swirling about the coaches, and Tatti noticed Phillipe's face cloud when he saw Stowell's hooked arm and the Royal Marine's short jacket pull up, to reveal three flintlock pistols.

"We have so many," Phillipe said, glancing at his body servant, Hypolette, and his four coachmen.

"Oh, we don't want your kinfolk to think we're poor country cousins."

Phillipe's expression eased as Tatti, holding Gordie by the hand, led the way into the wood-paneled, deep-scrubbed dining room of the inn.

Settling herself at a round sunlit table, with Phillipe on her left and the child on her right, Tatti ordered truffles rolled in an omelette of goose eggs, with French bread and bacon.

"Scottish salmon," Phillipe said to the waiter, who bowed and withdrew backward, not turning his back on the honored guests.

Outside, in the bright, flowering courtyard, Tatti saw her men moving about the fine coach horses that were being brought out and hitched into the leather tugs and doubletrees of the vehicles. Roo was eating a joint of mouton, held in one hand, while hooking up a haines with the other. A long knife was sewn into its scabbard at his collar.

"They were Lord Gordon Wragby's men," Tatti said, sensing Phillipe's apprehension.

"Ah, the Marquis de Ravendale."

"Absolutely trustworthy."

Tatti leaned back into the coach as it swung out of the courtyard and onto the high road once more, while the whole staff at the inn came out to stand and wave. "Nothing like a little money to ease things," she said, playing with Gordie's hair.

Cora sat opposite her and Phillipe sprawled at his ease shading his eyes to look at the sea.

"Thank the Lord you're more loyal than moral, dear Cora," Tatti said, closing her eyes.

"Well, I think the Lord meant for us to live before he put a judgment on us."

They were crossing the Pont du Sud in Dieppe, where the high road turns south off the bridge, before continuing on up the coast to Belgium, when Phillipe sat bolt upright.

"Enough!" he said. "This isn't the way to the valley of the Loire."

Tatti looked deep into Phillipe's pale Norman eyes. "No, we're going to Amsterdam."

"Amsterdam! *Mon Dieu!*" Phillipe's head popped upright.

"Aye, Amsterdam. I have two million pounds sterling to put in Dutch bank notes."

"The treasure?!"

"My money."

445

"And what about our beautiful love?"

"Phillipe, I loved you with every fiber of my soul and body as I'll do when I love again, but a woman loves forever only the first time. After that she loves only for the moment."

"*Arrêtez! Arrêtez!*" Phillipe thrust his head out the coach window, ordering the carriage halted.

"Never mind," Tatti said, tugging at his thigh to pull him back to safety as he clung half outside the vehicle. "My men are in control."

Phillipe slid back to his seat, ashen, his eyes unable to focus.

A bald head peered down outside the window at them, and Cutler said, "My lady, what do the Frenchy want?"

"He said drive on to Amsterdam." Tatti did not look at the cotter as she watched Phillipe.

"Thank'ee, my lady," Cutler said, and slapped the reins over the horses' backs."

"My coachmen?"

"Prisoners. They're all my prisoners." Tatti watched Phillipe's eyes.

"And me?"

"Caruthers!" Tatti called, rapping at the window. In an instant the Royal Marine was in their midst, cramping the elegant coach with his size.

Tatti nodded at Phillipe.

Caruthers pulled a jangling set of hand-irons from his belt, and hesitated before he reached for Phillipe's small wrist.

446

"Gently," Tatti said, as Caruthers took the elegant, small hand into his rough fingers and clamped the iron hoop over Phillipe's wrist, then in a flip, clamped the other shackle over his own massive, bare forearm.

Phillipe stared incomprehending, first at the hand-iron, then at Caruthers, then at Tatti, at Cora, and at Gordie who smiled at him, and climbed between his knees to reach the new iron toy.

"Jezebel!" Phillipe hissed. "Betrayal of our sacred love."

"Phillipe, you're shackled to the Royal Marine who stood at Gordon Wragby's feet when he died—you've been honored to have him by you, as was our Captain." Tatti watched Phillipe carefully.

"But why?" Phillipe put his face down into his hands. "Such love, it was worth a lifetime of bondage."

The people in the coach were silent as they looked at the young Frenchman.

"Phillipe," Tatti whispered, winding her hand into the hair on the crown of his bowed head. "Louis, the King of France, is guarded in his palace of Versailles by the Scottish Guard of Highlanders who stand at the right of the throne of France." Her voice was soft, and yet carried a resolute note to every word. "The French king cannot trust his own life to his own countrymen, and 'tis we, the Scots, who guard the King of France."

"But our love?" He raised his face and threw open his hands.

447

"Divine," Tatti said.

"Ah, a blissful desolation of the soul, and a peek into heaven."

"Shouldn't we be happy then?"

"Why not?" Phillipe's eyes lit with good cheer, and he raised his arm, clanking the chain to the marine's. "Oh, the English and their duty."

Caruthers looked to Tatti, his brow puzzled, and then to Phillipe. "Your grace, it ain't personal, you understand."

At Calais Tatti drove straight to the docks, where she found a small Dutch coasting schooner. It was dawn, and an ebb tide was sweeping down the channel, out to sea.

"Amsterdam," Tatti said, stepping among the sleeping forms who stretched and scratched and yawned.

"Amsterdam? No, my lady, I'm waiting my consignment at noon, to carry to Antwerp."

Tatti thrust her hand into the folds of her cloak, and reached out a fistful of gold doubloons. "Amsterdam! Now!"

"Amsterdam it is!" The broadfaced Dutchman whirled, nudging a slumbering figure with his booted foot. "Avast, ye lubbers, and set sail!"

"Set sail?" a figure croaked.

"Amsterdam! And out on the tide!"

The Dutch were silent when they saw the laden coaches looming above the ship on the stone quay, burdened with people who seemed to swarm down, bearing trunks they

448

staggered under as they carried them on quick-running legs.

"Klas Norlund," the Captain said, as Tatti handed him four large pieces of gold. "More at Amsterdam."

The waking Dutch sailors stood apart from the group of English who had suddenly appeared among them.

"Cast off!" the Captain shouted.

Tatti dashed back up the steps to the coaches, where Phillipe watched. "Phillipe, if I did not love you, I would not use you. But here." She thrust a purse of gold in his hand. "A bliss it was for me, to go coaching with a man who loved love more than life." She caught his face in her hands and kissed the well-formed mouth, tasting Phillipe's forgiveness in the foggy dawn. "But I love life enough to want that more. Love will come again—later."

The broad-beamed Dutch coasting smack sailed stolidly up the English Channel, never out of sight of the Continent, and took the heavy seas over her port bow. Tatti watched from behind the steering tiller where Klas Norlund guided the ship's course. The man's red-cheeked face wore a perpetual mist of water droplets, as though being wet were a part of his normal living.

"Your ship doesn't plunge." Tatti spoke approvingly.

"Nay, my lady. We heel on our beam end, and we let the waves break over us."

"Quite apparent."

" 'Tis safer in rough water to schoon your bow at all times."

"I would never question the Dutch about seamanship," Tatti said agreeably.

The Captain nodded, moving his eyes from the taut canvas of his mainsail to his jib-sheets, then to amidships where Tatti's men had joined the Dutch sailors whenever an extra hand was needed. Tatti could see it unsettled the Captain to know her men could sail, and she gestured to Cora and Caroline and her little boy, settling Norlund's anxiety. "Captain, I wouldn't undertake piracy with an empty coasting schooner and women and children."

"Aye, my lady. You have enough gold to buy the Royal Dutch Bank of Amsterdam." He glanced about his ship. "I love this ship, but it's nothing to what you already own."

On the third day Tatti saw the flat land of Holland rimming the slate sea which beat against the Dutch polders. The windmills turned in ceaseless motion, pumping out the water, and it astonished Tatti to find the bright city of Amsterdam rise straight up off the dikes that ringed it on all sides.

"A marvel of engineering," Tatti said, and Norlund nodded, calling out his commands in Dutch to bring the ship quite against the quay.

Sailors in wooden clogs caught the ropes flung them, and the sail slid down the main-mast as the men warped the schooner sideways into her berth.

The Captain put his hands onto his hips, and cocked his head. "Amsterdam, my lady." He nodded down the brick-paved street, lined with neat, compact buildings, all scrubbed and gleaming beneath the overcast sky. Tatti saw the quay and the streets were alive with men, wagons, carts, and live produce as well as timber and coal.

"Is it safe?" Tatti said.

"Safe?" Norlund threw back his massive head. "Of course it's safe. We Netherlanders have fought the sea so long to live, we're as honest as our noble enemy—we do not steal." He walked to the gunwale where his men had run out a brow to walk upon, and gestured with his open hand. "Take your gold to the bank."

"Thank you," Tatti said, reaching out a small pouch of gold florins. Norlund took them, and chucked them in his palm to weigh them. "Too much, my lady."

"No, divide it as you see fit."

"Aye." The Dutchman nodded formidably, and walked toward the Englishman. "Down the street is the Royal Dutch Bank. Follow."

Norlund in the lead, they picked their way past the piles of cheese, gaggling geese, swinging baskets of fish, and tulip bulbs. Tatti had Cora and Gordie with her, and the motley throng of unkempt, barefoot sailors followed, leaning out as they struggled to keep their footing on the wet bricks as they carried the heavy chests of precious metal.

"The treaty with England carefully protects the sanctity of the banks, Peter said." Tatti saw the great banking house lined with marble arcades.

"That's because the English can't get their hands on it," Cora said dourly.

451

"I want to bank my gold, in trust," Tatti said to a thin, ascetic-looking man in a white ruff and Van Dyke beard. "In your bank."

"This bank? That much gold?" His lips pressed into a slit and he swallowed.

"Of course, this bank, Soren," said a florid man in Calvinistic black, with a vice-president's silver chain about his neck.

"But whose is it?"

"Soren, you never question a customer." The large man beamed. "Obviously a lady of breeding."

As if by invisible signal, the bank was full of smiling men who gathered about the chests, among the sailors who stared at them with silent, incredulous eyes. "To us 'tis blood, to them 'tis gold," Stowell said to the Royal Marine.

Some of the bankers were speaking to Klas Norlund, and looking sympathetically at Tatti and Gordie. "Awful how the Spaniards robbed the Indians," said one banker. "Well, it's in safe hands at last." Men nodded resolutely around him, and Tatti discovered she could say nothing wrong. They closed the bank for the rest of the day and called out their armed guard as they counted the doubloons and florins and weighed the bars of solid Inca gold melted into squares stamped with the Royal Spanish Crown.

There was a clatter of hoofs on the brick outside the marble arcade girdling the bank.

"Her Van Wykoff!" a small clerk cried. "The President of the Royal Dutch Bank!"

"Good Lord, I thought he was on his death-bed," said the florid-faced vice president.

The armed soldiers in visored and crested

steel helmets opened the iron-grilled doors. A slender man was carried in, his eyes sunken back in his skull, his thin hair still askew from his pillow. He caught his breath when he saw the piles of gold and silver stacked all about the marble floor of the counting hall.

"My God," he cried, struggling out of the arms of those who carried him. "Solid gold— money. The bank is solvent! Saved!"

"Praise God." The vice-president nodded, closing his eyes.

"My lady," Herr Van Wykoff said, turning to Tatti, "you have saved my bank and your country, which we underwrote." He breathed. "Witlessly, I might add."

Tatti searched into the deep-set eyes of the sick man.

"My lord, I hadn't thought of that."

"And I feel well—I'm well!" The bank president turned to his clerks and officers and soldiers.

The whole room broke into applause and jolly laughter, except the florid-faced vice-president who looked a bit pale.

"I'm so glad I helped you," Tatti said. "Now, we need lodging."

"Name it! Name anything in Amsterdam, my lady, and it's yours." The bank president clapped his hands, and two secretaries darted up to his side, pen and parchment in hand.

XLI

The small trunk was stuffed with paper bank notes, bearing the watermark and seal of the Royal Dutch Bank of Amsterdam, as well as sealing-wax imprints on each note. It served as a sturdy footrest in the floor of the high-wheeled coach Tatti had hired in Dover for the gallop to London. She sat back and smelled the rich scent of hawthorne and wild-rose along the English post road, and saw the lilacs growing beyond the churchyard wall.

"Ah, Cora, England! To smell the air is to coach through heaven." Tatti's eyes settled on Gordie. The little boy smiled at her, in his hands a small sailboat that her man had whittled and rigged as a schooner. "Just like your noble papa's," Caruthers had said.

Tatti's first act on landing at Dover was to buy out the remaining years of service of the Royal sailors and the Royal Marine, so that they were no longer considered deserters. In the heavier coach that followed were her clothing and other servants. She had glanced back once, and the vehicle looked more like a boarding-party of seamen, perched atop a boat drawn by horses. "They was not born to gentility, Tatti," Cora said, sensing Tatti's thoughts.

"Thank heaven they weren't, or we'd all be slaves on the Spanish Main," Tatti said.

"I'll put that Roo to work in the moor," Cora said.

"Do you love him?" Tatti said.

"He's gentle." Cora smiled. "And he's ardent."

"Well, what more can a woman want?" Tatti watched the wide green field sweep by, filled with Hereford cattle that browsed along a creek bank in the shade of sun-dappled elms.

"He's like having a boy to raise, a grown boy between my sheets and at my bosom, who can't do enough to learn things my way."

"That's good, for now at least."

"Aye, I pushes him free at every chance, but he wants my way."

"Aye, Lord Gordon sensed it—gave him your name, Lundee."

"I'll make him a Scot, I will."

"Better for him."

"Innocent, he was, and I knowed it. That's why I took him."

Tatti ordered her coaches to the Godolphin Arms in the City of London, and sent runners to the Temple Bar and Saint Paul's Cathedral, to enquire for Sir Jonathan Hogarth, King's Counsellor. Within an hour, the young man had come back and was panting out his story. "Sir Jonathan be at the Pembroke Inn with her ladyship and Lord Skarra of Scotland."

Tatti paid off the boy, who was hostling while he read law at night.

"We'll bathe, and go," Tatti said.

"'Tis evening," Cora said.

"I want to see my mother and father, and I want to show them my child."

Cora stripped the little boy and shouted at the serving maids. "Hot water and tubs, and quick about it!"

Tatti felt every breath she took rise with excitement, pure, absolute hope and exquisite joy. She was going with their grandchild, to see her parents. She had done something perfectly right; and she had carried their faith, and not only endured, but prevailed.

"Oh, I want to see my mother!" She hugged her arms together between her breasts. "Oh, I want to be with her."

"Child, eat and bathe." Cora was peeling clothing from her body, while handing Tatti a small loaf of bread, stuffed with chicken and watercress.

"I feel like a schoolgirl coming home."

"Aye, eat, ere ye faint."

Tatti wrote a small note to be delivered

by a runner, ink staining her fingers and a taper alight to melt sealing wax. "Take it!" she shouted at the boy, thrusting a crown into his hands. "To Sir Jonathan!"

Her coach clattered through the narrow streets of London, the hoofs echoing with a mellow clop in the light evening fog, while she clutched a French hanky in her fingers, and held the little boy's hand. Cora sat opposite her, holding the ship's log and Bible of the *Daphne*. They did not speak, so intense was the excitement.

She heard the hostler running in the dark, beside her horses, and was astonished to see her door pulled open and footmen standing under flares at the door of the Pembroke. "My God, we're here!" she gasped.

She saw a middle-aged man, a flat lace ruff spread on his shoulders and under a salt-and-pepper gray beard. "Papa!" she cried.

In moments she was out of the coach, shouldering aside the footmen, and swinging her child clear of the door.

"Tatti, we waited," Lady Frances said, and Tatti glimpsed her tall, slender mother for but a moment before she was swept into her arms and cloak, and felt her father's arms about the three of them. "Mama?" the child's voice trembled from the midst of them.

"Home," Tatti gasped, and began to laugh as she wept and held her parents. "No, don't move." Tatti put her face into her father's shoulder and did not raise it until she had wept out her stifling sobs, and had regained her composure.

They walked slowly out of the evening fog, and into the inn that was ablaze with a great log fire, and glowed with lanterns and candles along the walls.

"Lloyd's tolled the bell for the loss of the *Daphne* five days ago," her father said, "when Peter landed at Falmouth from France."

"Peter? Is he all right?"

"Aye. Some trouble about gold, but we know now that people survived the shipwreck." He gestured at the festive lights.

"It was as though the sea had swallowed you up," Lady Frances said.

"Oh, such a storm devoured us."

"Aye, hurricanes, they call them," Sir John said.

They sat at a table before the fire, spread with a rich damask tablecloth and laden with partridge and venison decorated with green sprays. The stews and individual meat pies filled Tatti, but she ate on, caught in one of those eternal moments of sublime grace that sweeps a family together as a body in peace and love.

Gordie fell asleep in his highchair at the table, but Tatti would not let him be put to bed. "No, let him sleep tipped over in the swaddling robe," Tatti said, "and sleep where he can hear our voices as a part of him."

"Poor dear." Lady Frances let Cora put the child into her lap where she held him in his sleep.

At the foot of the table sat a young barrister, Thornton McAlister, who was reading law under her father.

"The money?" John Hogarth asked, dipping his fingers into a bowl and wiping them on a napkin. "You obviously have plenty. Where did it come from?"

"Bequeathed me, Father." Tatti exchanged glances with her mother.

"Lord Gordon Wragby was a gallant man," Frances said, smiling at the sleeping child's face, and Tatti heard Cora breathe audibly.

"Lord Gordon was impoverished," her father said.

"He left me Wragby Hall—I have the deed." Tatti looked up hopefully.

"Wragby Hall never minted gold," her father said. "Lovely estate though it may be."

"A French nobleman left it to me, Father." She looked into her father's eyes.

"I dare not trespass upon the circumstances, daughter," Sir Jonathan said, toying with his Italian fork.

"Thank you, Father."

"A nobleman?" her mother said.

"Aye. Friend of Peter's, bastard son of the King of France."

"In France, they're all bastards, I think," Sir John said. "It's the only place a bastard can live in dignity and grace with honor—in England our bastards are all mean and sullen."

"So right, John, look at the Duke of Monmouth," Lady Frances said.

460

"Aye, and Archie Campbell, the Earl of Argyle."

"He got Skarra?" Tatti said.

"Bought off Cecil, but I'm to argue the case in Westminster."

"Papa, I have gold." Tatti laid her hand on her father's fingers, and felt the skin looser with middle age than she'd known it in childhood.

"How much gold, Tatti?"

"More gold than I can ever spend." She leaned into her father's face. "I can buy Skarra," she whispered.

"The Dutch bank drafts?"

She whispered into his ear. "Over two million pounds sterling."

"Good Lord!" Sir John faced her. "Was that Peter's gold?"

"No, Father, it was never counted. Nobody knows how much, except me."

"Oh, thank God you told me. I'll have to defend Peter at Falmouth."

"The French stole the gold, Father."

"The French?" her mother said.

"I see we're going to be in court." Sir Jonathan ran his fingers through his beard. "An illusive shipment of gold that vanished."

"No corpus delicti, my lord," said the young lawyer, speaking for the first time.

"Excellent, no receipted count." John Hogarth said to himself.

"And I want to see the King, at court," Tatti said.

"The King?" Lady Frances said.

461

"Yes, the King. I'm the Marchioness of Ravendale, and I'm rich."

"Daughter, you're changed," her mother said.

"Mother, I had to."

"Oh, I'm glad you did." The slender lady rocked the sleeping child in her lap, and Tatti saw the fragile look about her mother's mouth. "John, we did not fail."

"Aye, but we have work to do."

Tatti shoved back her chair as a footman ran to ease her free of the table. "I want to see my grandparents."

Tatti moved over to the Pembroke Inn, to be closer to the Court of Westminster and Saint James's Palace and Hampton Court and to be with her parents and family while she determined her next move. Tatti's father now wore the wondering look of a sensitive man in his maturity who has come to realize there is a higher law than man's law, based upon forgiveness. He was as eager to ferret out details as if he were a doctor scribbling endless notes of the symptoms of the patient's disease to put off diagnosing a malady he knew would be fatal. As a very successful lawyer, he had slipped behind the mask of endless details that kind men wear to avoid grief.

"Papa, I have gold," Tatti said to him, when he had come into the large front suite of rooms Tatti had taken. "I can buy the law."

"Let me argue the case, first, to satisfy the vanity of the law."

"Thank God, there's a corruption to the law, so we can have justice."

"As long as you practice that, and never truly believe it." John Hogarth warned. "Thornton McAlister is writing three different legal briefs." He went down the hall, calling "Thornton!"

All his life John Hogarth had glimpsed a wisping shred of another law—a law beyond the letter of what he practiced, a law that served life and not thought: where God was an infinite spirit, and the human mind anarchy. He felt that man had to pay homage to the spirit, or perish altogether.

"That's what happened to the French," he said. "The human mind ran amok with logic."

"I beg your pardon, my lord?" The large burly young Thornton startled him, and he jumped.

"Oh, talking to myself. Best person to have an argument with."

The deep chuckle of the young man pleased him, and he led the way into his temporary office where papers and books scattered the broad tabletop.

"Lady Frances will be here shortly for tea."

While Tatti waited at Pembroke Inn for the proper formalities to be exchanged between her father and the equerries of the court at Hampton, to announce the availability and wish of the Marchioness of Ravendale to attend the court, Tatti enjoyed her grandparents.

"So ye foxed 'em all, eh, lass?" old Lord Skarra said, his light blue eyes sparkling, under the loose folds of his eyelids, and the dessicated skin wrinkling on the collar of his Melrose jacket.

"Aye, Grandfather." Tatti sat on a stool between her grandparents, before the fire. "Actually they fooled themselves. I just waited them out."

"The mustard seed will not perish from this earth," her Russian grandmother said, perching her embroidered slippers on a stool. She had become quite Oriental in her aged years, with her dark wrinkled skin and blue eyes. "So womanly of Tatti."

"And you brought home a little boy, I see."

"Aye, Grandfather."

"Have to take up gardening with him." Old Lord Skarra's lips compressed and eased.

"Bruce, no more mud holes for you. Not at ninety."

"Tush, Lydia. I live out of your control."

"We'll see." Lydia touched the toe of his shoe under his Stuart trews with hers.

Tatti sent for Stowell, Caruthers, and the other men and women she had acquired in her entourage, and presented them to her family.

Old Lord Skarra walked slowly down the line of servants, taking each by the hand, saying to each man and woman, "Well, now that you've had an adventure that brought you to the edge of eternity, you know what every soldier knows."

"Your lordship," Brighton said, bowing.

"You can never taste a delight until you swallow and it's gone." He patted the backs of the hands he held, then walked slowly back to his wing chair by the fire.

"Grandfather, we might go mad if the bliss did not end," Tatti said, nodding jovially and dismissing her retainers.

"That is only for men." Lydia's eyes were enveloped in wrinkles as she smiled to herself. "A lady in bliss is eternal."

"Aye, you win, my lady." Old Lord Skarra settled himself, raising his feet atop the padded stool.

Tatti's carriage galloped along the graveled roads that wended through the willow-lined lakes of the great park of trees outside Hampton Court. Three swans broke into flight, beating their wings in quick succession on the water and honking as they went.

"Ah, a good omen, my lady," said the lady in waiting who accompanied Tatti in the swaying carriage.

"An omen, Lady Maud?"

"Yes, the swans fly only for his Majesty. They circle and reel in great rings of birds over his head, then they all swing in to light on the water once more."

Tatti nodded, seeing the deer and Irish elk browsing along the edge of the forest. "He doesn't hunt?"

"Oh, no, the King is French. The bon mot, the witty, charming thought, rule the English court."

"So glad," Tatti murmured as the carriage

clattered over the brick paving to a stop before the Tudor doors of the wing where she would stay. Only Cora was with her. Gordie remained at the Pembroke Inn with her family and Caroline.

"All sobersides are banished from Court."

The liveried footman let down the carriage steps and opened the door, standing back to guide the ladies' feet and to assist with a brawny arm their stepping down.

Lady Maud set her hand on Tatti's wrist to hold her a moment. "All the court knows of your travail, of the gallantry of Lord Gordon Wragby as he fought and died, and of your loyalty to him."

"Thank you, my lady."

"Nothing boorish about money. King Charles's father lost his head over money and our greedy merchants."

"Thank you." Tatti listened as the lady in waiting instructed her on the court's mores and tastes.

"He'll love your lips and teeth."

"Me?"

"Oh, yes, the King loves beauty. Keeps a little spaniel in his arms at all times just to stroke its silken coat."

"Indeed, my lady."

"No preachers. He enjoyed the preachers and diviners who argued at Westminster for seven years about the new republic for England—used to visit them as a prince to see the sport of 'the fighting wild asses of Araby,' he called it."

"The word of God seems usually to be the

size of the mouth of the man who mouths it," Tatti observed.

"Bon mot!" Lady Maud touched Tatti's arm with her fingertips. "The King will love you—we all will."

The great ballroom of Hampton Court was ablaze with a thousand reflecting prisms of light, that glittered over the costumed men and women who moved to the graceful measures of French music. Pilasters of fluted columns stood in rows on all sides of the ballroom. Some bore classic images of Rome and Greece and others cascaded long green tresses of shrubbery. Tatti felt transported into an Italian garden, through which lovely women with half-nude breasts festooned yards of silk wandered like walking flowers, followed by gallant men in rich satins and taffetas.

"The Duke of Rutland and her ladyship, the Marchioness of Ravendale!" The major-domo's voice rolled across the flagged hall leading to the ballroom; and Tatti was swept out of reality as the elegant men and women paused in their chatting groups and posing figures of the minuet to glance at her. In fantasy, she alone existed on earth, and it thrilled her.

"Thank you," Tatti whispered, feeling the gloved hand of the duke press upon the back of her fingers, leading her slowly toward a brilliant archway where everybody was in white satin and dripping yards of lace.

"The King?" she whispered.

"Aye, lass. He wants you."

467

"Wants me?" Tatti swallowed in her whispers, nodding to each side of her as she walked.

"Oh, not to seduce, to look at." The duke chuckled and patted her hand. "He loves Nell Gwynn."

"His mistress." Tatti nodded.

"The Queen's delighted. Her Majesty loves the King and all he loves."

Tatti glanced into the urban, compassionate eyes of the civilized man on whose arm she walked. "We exported our Puritan fever for judgment and lucre to Boston," the duke said.

Tatti glanced ahead and saw a small man dressed in radiant white taffeta with elegant diamond-studded buckles at his knees and brooches pinning the ribbons that tied his silken shoes. He wore an auburn wig, and gestured with his open hands as he spoke. All the people about him smiled at his words, and dancers who stepped to the measured minuet bowed to him as they swirled past.

"King Charles?" Tatti said.

"The King," Rutland said.

"Ah, I knew it." King Charles turned his slender body and smiled at Tatti, his genteel mouth and frail jaw alight with pleasure. "Gordon Wragby's only solace."

Tatti folded down into a deep curtsey and bowed her neck so that her coiffure touched the parquetry at the King's feet, as her Russian grandmother had taught her to do.

"My word, lass, you didn't learn that in Scotland," Charles said. As he reached down and seized one of her hands to raise her, Tatti saw the profound sorrow in the King's eyes.

The white was below the blue, and his eyelids sagged in delicate rings.

"At Skarra, your Majesty." Tatti stood and smiled.

"Aye, Skarra and Princess Lydia—those Russian tsars live in terror and tyranny."

"I adored her," Tatti said.

"Here, you may be French, but not Russian. We exiled our fanatics and Protestants to America. England is too composed for revolution and tyranny."

Tatti took the slender fingers of the King's hand and walked with him onto the ballroom where the music suddenly stopped. The elegant aged monarch bowed to her as she curtseyed; then he stepped forward, his hand elevated, as the strains of the minuet swept alive once more.

"So divine, that Wragby found you," Charles said, setting his extended toe in a gentle tap to the hem of her skirt. "You had a son."

"Indeed, your Majesty."

"What a gallant sailor to have lived and died, and had a child to love."

Tatti turned under his hand, feeling Charles's eyes run over her narrow waist and across her small breasts that were upthrust by French netting, and caught just below the nipple to leave a faint shadow at the edge of her peach gown.

"To have had a woman to love." Charles smiled softly at her.

"After true love, all other love pales, your Majesty." Tatti spoke, caught by the suffering eyes of the English King, and emboldened to speak by her glimpse into the man's soul.

"Take good care of his son, my lady." The King stopped dancing, drew Tatti's hand into his waist, and walked from the parquetry, gesturing for the other dancers to resume the minuet.

Lackeys served iced fruits and wine which Tatti took and held without eating.

"I have the complete report of the *Daphne*," Charles said. "And I know you want Skarra."

"Indeed, your Majesty."

"The government sold it to Argyle in Edinburgh." The King tasted an iced lime.

"I can buy it back, your majesty."

"Argyle will object."

"My lord, the Stuarts, not the Campbells, are kings of England and Scotland."

"Salisbury," Charles said, gesturing toward a large man with an Elizabethan ruff and heavy gray beard, "give the girl back Skarra."

"Difficult, your Majesty."

"She'll buy it, and Campbell does want the crown. Think of a way, Lord Salisbury, as a form of life insurance at my death."

"Oh, your Majesty, don't!" a lady said, and a hush settled over the elegant company.

"Oh, come now, I'm lively enough." King Charles thrust out his slender stockinged leg, and put his hand onto the arm of the lady in waiting.

"Skarra is Stuart to the end," Tatti said.

"So you want that mud hole in the moor," Charles said.

"We grew out of that mud hole, your Majesty, all of us." Tatti smiled serenely.

"Home, bonnie Scotland, where we lived in our rock communes with our shaggy cattle." Charles had a lost look for a moment. "Then the throne and the riches of England." He patted Tatti's hand. "Robert Cecil, Lord Salisbury himself, will find a way—he loves his head on his shoulders."

"Your Majesty jests too severely," said the Lord of the Privy Council.

"No, when I die, 'twill be your head or Campbell's that falls on the block under the axe. Now think of a way, a loyal girl in the Highlands or a cunning traitor in Edinburgh."

"Your Majesty's wisdom will prevail," Robert Cecil said, and Tatti watched the most powerful man in England bow before her and the monarch, a cold, savage light glinting in his blue eye.

"Ah, the tedium of politics," King Charles said. "Without the monarchy all they do is hang and murder each other."

"Your Majesty," said the lady in waiting, curtseying; and the whole company went down, each man touching a knee to the polished floor before the King of England.

XLII

The heavy parchment deed was delivered to Tatti complete with the Royal Seal, Lord Salisbury's signature, and the royal "Charles II, Rex." Tatti was blinded with delight and excitement, and could not read it except for the word *Skarramus*.

"Mine?" she said, thrusting it at Thornton McAlister and her father.

"Aye, lass, all yours." Jonathan smiled.

"Mine!" Tatti crushed the parchment to her bosom, and dashed off to wake her grandparents. "We own Skarra!" she shouted.

Old Lord Skarra was being adjusted into his bed and nightcap as Tatti burst into the room, waving the parchment. "King Charles and Robert Cecil signed it! Grandfather!"

"Daughter," Skarra's voice cracked with age, "Campbell's got our land, and possession is nine-tenths of ownership." His voice came stronger as her grandmother and parents came in. "Raise the clans, but do not fight. The Stuarts, the MacLeans, the Gordons, the Fraziers, the Rosses, and confront him with your deed." He cleared his throat. "He's a stealthy thief and he'll run before an open equal."

"Thank you, Grandfather." Tatti looked at her parents. "I'll do it, Cora Lundee and I —I grew up with cotters."

"I have no doubt," said her father, tugging fitfully at his graying beard.

"She'll do it?" Thornton McAlister asked, his eyes rounded in disbelief.

"Of course she will." Her father turned. "Now let's get on with Peter's case."

Tatti could see the placid moonlight flood the plains of the countryside as her carriage traveled north. Against the deep ruts where the wheels rolled, the coach swung from side to side in a ponderous rhythm, and sometimes she could see the carriage behind hers, carrying her valuables and retainers.

She had left George Caruthers and Roo at the Godolphin Arms, with enough money to discover and hire the famous Yorkshire highwayman, Shade Turpin. Tatti put a thousand pounds on Turpin to ride into Scotland to see her. She was determined to rescue Peter and Sean Finucane, should Sir Jonathan lose his case in the court of law. "King Charles would understand," Tatti said to Cora, who sucked her lip and frowned at Tatti's plans.

Traveling north through Cheshire toward Wragby Hall filled Tatti with gloom. She had decided to stop off on her way into Scotland to visit the country seat of the Wragbys and to visit Gordon's sister Nellie.

The country inns were a respite in the Lake Country where Cheshire and Lanca verged, and Tatti could scarcely drag herself to push onward each dawn.

"'Twould be easy to retire with a fortune," Tatti said, as she stood on one foot in her morning tub and sipped tea. Cora was piling her hair atop her head, gathering loose strands to tuck under the tortoiseshell combs.

"Nay, lass, ye reap what ye sow. Even Charley Stuart said we was better suited to rock huts and kin than prancing in London."

"Aye," Tatti said, easing herself gingerly into the hot water.

"Well, he's the King, and the King ought to know." Cora gathered up the loose nightclothes over her robust forearm in a deft sweep.

The square towers of stone loomed at the end of a long valley, through which ran a quiet stream lined with rushes and willows. Cattle grazed in the rich dark bottom meadow, and a vast park of trees surrounded the hall. "Wragby Hall, my lady," announced her driver.

"Stop!" Tatti cried, and when the coaches halted, she climbed atop to the footman's seat with Gordie and Cora. "I want him to see what his father loved."

The fresh English air bathed their faces as they galloped down the valley and entered the massive wood where ancient trees laced their broad tops and cooled the forest roots. "To think, Gordon played among these trees, and waded these brooks." Tatti hugged the little boy to her. "Oh, Cora, I feel close to him."

At the vast double doors of Wragby Hall, their footmen pounded on the oak, and the echo rumbled through the silent house. The gray, forbidding pile was utterly quiet except for the song of birds in the adjacent forest.

" 'Tis your estate, my lady," Cora said, and gestured for the others to follow.

They circled the great house along a graveled path between well-clipped hedges of holly. Within, Tatti saw the roses and vast banks of lilacs.

"I see the lilacs," Tatti whispered.

The path ended abruptly, and they faced a sunken square garden filled with bright flowerbeds. At one end sat a lady in a wide straw hat and white gloves to her elbows, having tea. Behind her stood footmen in livery, and three maids served her.

"That be Lady Nellie." The coachman spoke to Cora.

Taking Gordie's hand, Tatti walked slowly through the garden.

"Oh, Mama! Rabbits!" The little boy pointed at the tame rabbits that grazed about Nellie's slippered feet and frisked into the air in successions of joyful hops. Lady Nellie was having tea with her rabbits, and a large white cat that shared the marble bench. Then Tatti saw the pug-nosed little lap spaniel at Nellie's knee.

"Just in time for tea, my dear," Nellie said, putting out her hand.

"I'm perishing for tea," Tatti said, quickening her step.

"And the little boy?"

"Tea, please."

"Your little boy."

"Yes, Gordon's and mine."

"Well, I have my animals," Nellie said, plunking cubes of sugar into the teacups.

"Gordon loved animals," Tatti said.

"Yes, you know Gordon?" The face stopped moving, and Tatti saw the deep blue eyes rivet onto her.

"Yes, I married him. This is our son." Tatti moved the child toward her.

"That child? Gordon's?"

"Yes, my lady."

"Gordon's dead. He died many years ago."

"I made him live, my lady."

A dark, sane shadow of insight passed across the powdered white face of Nellie Rush. "You gave him a son?"

"Aye. I'm the Countess of Skarra."

"Well, he can learn to play with my rabbits." The old lady broke into delighted laughter. "A man that's kind to animals will be kind to children, and the boy is the father to the man." She clapped her hands together, tipping her teacup. Two maids ran to blot up the tea.

Tatti sipped tea and ate small cakes until

Nellie fluttered her fingertips, signaling to the servants the tea was over.

Tatti followed Lady Nellie as the liveried footmen darted about the flowerbeds, capturing the rabbits, and Nellie led the procession of maids and men and struggling rabbits into the great home.

That night Tatti dined alone with Nellie, in the formal dining room. "Every greedy cousin has come to tell me either that the servants are poisoning me, or that my girth was cut to throw me from my horse."

Astonished at the sane grasp Nellie had of reality, Tatti listened very quietly.

"The King sent an equerry from Westminster a fortnight ago with a scroll of honor at Gordon's death, and the details of his marriage and his son, our son."

"Our son?" Tatti said.

"My word, yes. The boy is as much me by blood as he is Gordon."

Tatti caught the cool reasoning that Nellie's insanity had kept hidden for a lifetime.

"Now, my lady, you see the boy is ours, yours and mine."

"You jest," Tatti said, cocking her head to peer past the banks of candelabras.

"I never jest, dear girl."

"You had them all foxed."

"Tatti, my daughter, I had to outwit them, for Lord Rush, my late, unlamented husband, was a goring bull."

"A bull?"

"Not a nice bull like Europa rode—a mean bull, and he should have stayed off horses. His

478

horse broke his neck." The old lady laughed. "I have Cribbage grazing in the park before Wragby Hall. My champion."

Tatti nodded. "We saw the stallion, my lady."

"And now I have little Gordie, and he has me."

"Gordon Bruce Wragby," Tatti said.

The next morning was sunny, and Tatti had breakfast on the terrace of Wragby Hall. The park was alive with the call of birds, and she heard the sweet pining notes of the nightingale that turned her heart toward Gordon. "The very songbirds he listened to," Tatti whispered to Cora.

"Likely, my lady, or their kin."

The butler moved sedately about their table, which was alone on the vast Italian gallery overlooking the park.

As Tatti sipped her tea, she noticed a vine with a light gray trunk, so thick it seemed a small tree, climbing up the side of the stone wall to the third story, and clustering with a rich verdure at one of the windows.

"Look, wisteria, growing up the house, and into the window, I do believe." Tatti gestured down the terrace.

"Lord have mercy, a body can't close the window," Cora said, rising and walking purposefully down the terrace to stare up at the huge wisteria vine.

"Ahem, my lady. 'Tis the rabbits' room," said the liveried butler.

"The rabbits' room?" Tatti looked at the

large man, who bowed in response to her direct look.

"Lady Nellie keeps a huge bed in that room, where her ladyship sleeps, and the rabbits play about the floor, they do."

"Good Lord." Tatti gulped her tea, and called Cora.

A saddled pony had been led to the terrace for Gordie to ride after breakfast. Gesturing for Stowell to come, Tatti called, "Cups, lead the pony with Caroline and the boy—your hand on the bridle at all times."

"Aye, my lady."

"Cora, come!" Tatti went to the French doors of the manor house. "That huge wisteria vine goes to her window, and enters the house."

Cora nodded. "We ain't here to judge, my lady. They said her man was a beast, and a beast will ruin a woman."

Tatti ran up marble flight after flight of stairs, the servants standing back against the walls as she passed, until she was on the third floor. "Down this way," she said.

The double doors burst open before her hands, and she entered a room jammed with living wisteria, from the ceiling to the walls, and vines looping across the floors, while rabbits scampered away from her.

"Good Lord," Tatti said, and saw three squirrels dash out the window, along a thick vine.

"My living conservatory," Lady Nellie said as she walked out from the midst of greenery. "Most people have theirs in a greenhouse. I have mine where I can enjoy it." Her large eyes smiled like an ancient fairy lady, who somehow had not vanished with the dawn. "Are you astonished, my dear?"

"Well no, I just hadn't expected it," Tatti said.

"Come." Nellie led Tatti to the heavy twisting vines that climbed in her window sill.

"So massive," Tatti said.

"Gordon climbed this wisteria to see me, when we were children, and every night I listened to him coming up the vines to visit. In the wind, his soul comes, and we play with the rabbits again, just as we did in childhood."

"Oh, dear, dear Nellie." Tatti broke into tears and hugged the elderly lady to her bosom.

"I lived, Tatti," Nellie whispered, "on my brother's love and my insanity. When you're rich and alone, you have to play at being crazy to keep your cunning relatives at a distance, and stand off the insolence of strangers."

"Oh, Nellie, we have the little boy—you needn't be crazy any longer."

"Aye, I sent for the pony directly as the King's message came." Her vast blue eyes fairly radiated in lights. "I saw him riding in the park. And we'll have dogs for Gordie."

"We must call him Gordon Bruce," Tatti whispered, taking the hanky that Nellie handed her.

"Oh, we'll have a grand time." Nellie hesitated, her eyes sweeping inward again for a moment. "But I may play crazy from time to time, just to confound my servants." She broke into delighted laughter, and caught Tatti by the hands. "Now I have Gordie again."

XLIII

Her coaches had traveled deep into the Highlands of Scotland, and Tatti clothed herself in a scarlet riding habit, to go sidesaddle. She was wrapped with an immense Stuart tartan that swathed her from her high-piled hair to the hoofs of her white horse, and she cantered with her gillies ahead of her vehicles.

"Skarra," she said, "we're bound for Skarra."

Tatti enjoyed the startled look in the eyes of the cotters she met on the moor, and when Keith, Laird of Blair Castle, rode out with his retainers to see for himself, she called for the parchment.

"The King's signature!" Her triumphant

voice swept the reluctant cunning from the face of the Scottish chieftain.

"No trick, lassie—they behead all rebels in Edinburgh."

The thin, sinuous man read the parchment. "I canna read Latin, but I can see Charley Stuart's hand, and that o' Salisbury."

Tatti struck the top of the parchment. "I want back our mud hole, as the King called it."

"Did he now?"

"Skarra!" Tatti took the parchment and galloped on. "Tell it on the moor!"

"My lady, we're among the MacLeans!" The outrider galloped up to their carriages that night.

The coaches were pulled into the courtyard behind the small country home on the moor, as a light drizzle began to pulse in sheets of water. Tatti and Cora picked their way across the cobbled and brick court, behind servants who held torches and younger people who scampered past them in the gloom, carrying their trunks, and children.

That night, before a roaring fire of peat, Tatti faced the Fraziers, the Gordons, the Stuarts, and related clans. The heavy parchment lay on the broad table. Rough men, swathed in tartans and plaids, some in kilts and others in trews, read and fingered it. "I call on all the clan chiefs, in the name of the King," Tatti said.

"Parson," one of the chiefs said, nodding and stepping back for a lank man with deep-set eyes and wearing black.

The Presbyterian clergyman fingered the deed and title as though it were a little unclean, sniffling with his wet nose, while the whole room watched.

"A trick, Parson?" a clansman said.

The lank neck and thick mop of wet hair moved slightly. "Nay, no trick—'tis Latin and Popish but signed by Charles Stuart and that Englishman, Salisbury."

"Before I raise my clan, I want an officer of the King to tell me," said Ian Stevenson.

"I'll raise the Gordons, regardless. There's no guile in the heart of a woman who loves her parents, her child, and bonny Scotland," said the Earl of Badgenoth, a short, thick man in kilts, rattling his claymore on the tabletop. "The lass has English money. What more proof d'ye folk want?"

The roomful of men stared at Tatti, as though reassessing the whole venture.

"I want Skarra back, and Robert Cecil's afraid of the Earl of Argyle," Tatti said. "He fears Edinburgh at the King's death."

"Aye, there's your motive," said the parson. "And the English money in the hand of a Scottish lass is your proof." His hawklike eyes scoured the Latin document. "Popish, and I like it not, but ye have your truth."

"*Aaheeeehah!*"

Tatti was gripped in a wave of panic and seized Gordie to her bosom as the clan chiefs raised the ancient war cries of Scotland. She pressed her head down atop the child's, realizing the weather-stained and robust Highlanders were swept with the old frenzy once more, to attack the enemy and drive him from the moor.

"No, no! No war." She tugged at the surcoat of the parson, and shook Stevenson's claymore to get their attention.

Finally, quieting the clan chiefs once more, Tatti said, "No bloodshed, dear God." Tatti searched their faces and hugged her child into her bosom. "The Campbells are kin, regardless of fault, and the King wants Scotland for Scots, not death."

The men stared solemnly at her, then glanced at each other. "The lass talks wisdom," a voice said.

"I want to raise the clans and confront Argyle at Skarra Castle." Tatti spoke softly. "In his shame he'll depart before all Scotland."

"Her Rooshian grandmother confounded us all," said James, Earl of Badgenoth, and began to laugh. "That suffering Christ we never had the patience for."

"I like it not," said the parson, his eyes following Tatti with renewed interest. "Ye pray, then ye smite with the sword of the Lord."

"I ask it for Skarra, where Scotland began."

Tatti's eyes searched the lined faces of the coarse men with hair tufts poking about their rough-skinned ears. Some had wet beards running up over their cheekbones from which their blue eyes searched hers in beds of weather-wrinkled skin.

"Aye, for thee, lass. Thy grandfather could raise a nation to war, but he loved Scotland before his vanity."

"Thank you," Tatti said.

Her horse's hoofs cantered over the wet moor beneath her, the dawn mist cool on her cheeks, as Tatti looked down on the Firth of Skarra where the rock castle fit into the lea of the glen. The wet nest of green yew trees and rhododendron seemed to spill about the keep tower, and soften the edge of the battlements and the Italian piazza.

"Skarra," Tatti whispered, reining in her white horse and feeling a thrill run through her. Her eyes glanced out onto the North Sea toward Norway and Jutland, then looked behind her.

"The clans have risen, my lady," said Lord Eric of Strathdane.

"Oh my, so they have," Tatti said. She let her eye travel up the mountainsides, down which moved long streams of armed kilted men, hairskins about their torsos. She could see their naked arms, bare for fighting, slinging great swords and shields, with muskets and bows and pics thrust up at random as they marched toward her. And she heard the whole dawn reeling to the skirl of the war pipes and drums.

"Out of the earth they came," said Lord Eric, his accent revealing his English education.

Wherever Tatti looked, she saw the relentless motion of shaggy, half-naked men moving up the glens and down the firth, and she saw the Rampant Lion of Scotland, carried on their banners, as well as the cross of Saint Andrew.

"Do you suppose I can hold them?" Tatti was swept with a sense of terror, and looked for Cora.

Cora was mounted on a gray Highland

pony, being led by a gillie and following a piper. Stowell led another pony, with Gordie on its back and glanced nervously at the great throngs of armed men marching in a route step over the moor toward them. "They's long columns coming from all directions, my lady," Stowell said.

"Takes a man to stop a fight, dash it all!" Lord Eric said, biting his lip. "Scotland and Ireland bear a thousand wrongs that cry for vengeance."

"Ride out, Tatti, and canter along before them," Cora said. "Assert the right of your cause with no wrath in your heart."

Tatti whipped up her horse and dashed out along the crest of the knolls that rolled down to the firth. She let her horse run, heading off the lead of each column, crying, "The King wants the moor for Scotland, and we're not to fight."

The men stared at her as they marched relentlessly toward the stone fortress held by Argyle. The clan chiefs seemed unable to arrest or divert the silent men who followed the banners and the war pipes, despite Tatti's Stuart tartan flying from her throat and hand before the oncoming men.

Tatti galloped back to the knoll overlooking Skarra, where she could see the battlements were bristling with armed men, and the cannons run out of fire.

"Even I can see it's a fight," Tatti said.

"You've got him outnumbered," James of Badgenoth said. "And 'tis kin in the castle that

488

betrayed them." The Earl shook his head. "They see Argyle and his men with the mark of Cain."

"Oh, that wretched Bible fury," Tatti said.

Cora waved her hand, shouting, "Look, Tatti!"

The mounted nobles and chieftains about Tatti turned to see a small cavalcade of horsemen coming at a gallop across the moor, with trumpeters sounding a call to attention.

"English, by their breastplates and plumes," Strathdane said.

Past the confusion of galloping men and the Royal Standard of Scotland, Tatti saw the face of Peter.

"Peter!" Tatti cried, whipping her horse out to meet him.

In moments the two mounted groups had met, and Peter was standing in his stirrups to size up the impending clash, his hand on Tatti's arm to calm her, and nodding perfunctorily to the Scottish nobles and officers.

"They're about to assault Skarra," Tatti gasped.

"The officers have yet to dress the battle lines," Peter said. "We have time, but barely." He spurred his hunter toward Skarra, Tatti at his side.

"Father won your case?" Tatti shouted over the galloping hoofs of their two horses.

"No, lost it—too much money stolen. Court-martial ordered me to the Tower."

"The Tower?" She had trouble holding her seat in the sidesaddle, as the ground shuddered under the hoofbeats of their horses.

"Aye. Ruined my career, but Robert Cecil doesn't give a hoot in hell for money he never saw."

"That crafty Salisbury."

"All is forgiven if I can hold the Highlands." Peter was galloping toward the drawbridge of Skarra, gallant in his navy hunting blue coat and gold buttons, with Tatti at his side. "You're the mother of Gordon Wragby's son and his true love. And if you love me, then Cecil reckons we're English enough to trust, and Scottish enough to hold Scotland and threaten Argyle in Edinburgh."

"The web of kinship suffered us to endure." Tatti clung to her horse as Peter reined up before the stone walls of Skarra, and their horses' hoofs scattered in showers small stones against the heavy battlements.

A sandy-faced man with thin hair and wearing a breastplate looked over and shouted, "Who goes?" It was Archibald Campbell, Earl of Argyle.

"Officer of the King!" Peter shouted. "In the name of his Majesty, Charles Stuart, open your gates in peace."

"Ye call that peace?" The man gestured at the long columns of men forming into battle lines of dress to the loud commands of their officers and the rattle of snare drums. "War pipes, d'ye hear?!"

"Argyle!" Peter stood in his stirrups, snatching Tatti's parchment deed from her hands. "In the name of the King and the Royal Seal, I bear you this order. As Peter Alexander

Frobisher-Barrett, surrender Skarra! If they take it by force, they'll take no prisoners."

"Peter, you knave!"

"Campbell, I can't hold them." Peter waved at the advancing Highlanders. "Open Skarra and ride out at my side!"

The English escort had cantered up, and were sounding their trumpets just under the battlements of the old manor house, now bristling as a fort.

"Campbell, ye damn fool!" Lord Eric of Strathdane shouted, cantering up. "The girl bought back the title to Skarra, and the lady's in the King's service. One day your greed will lose you your head."

The sandy-faced man looked out along the knolls where the war pipes sounded the charge, and he heard the wild cries of old hatreds rise like specters from the onrushing men. "Strike the banners!" he shouted.

Tatti's horse was enveloped by a swirling mass of men who dashed past her and over the ballustrades, and up to the moat, where they fired their guns and shot arrows at the suddenly empty battlements. Broken spears fell about her horse, and lead slugs splattered into the stone beyond her head.

George Caruthers had Tatti's horse by the bridle, leading it toward the drawbridge which was slowly cranking down where Peter and the nobles waited.

"Argyle's surrendered!" The officers were shouting. "Argyle struck his colors!"

Tatti saw the great mob of sullen Highlanders gathering about the drawbridge, beyond the Scottish officers and chiefs.

"No treachery!" Lord Eric shouted at the resentful eyes of his own men. "We'll march them barefoot back to Edinburgh, but no killing!"

The Earl of Argyle rode out to face Peter. He was a middle-aged man, whose eyes were so full of craft that he obviously could not see the second convolution where the cunning led only to his own grief.

"This time you're saved," Peter said, raising his hand in salute.

"How much money did it take?" Argyle said, glaring at Tatti and the parchment, then at the Scottish nobles.

"My God, man, you got off free with your life, and yet you prattle about money." Lord Eric laughed harshly. "Someday they'll have your head in a sack not worth a twopence."

Tatti sat her horse at Peter's side all day as Argyle's men were disarmed and headed barefoot across the moor toward Edinburgh. "All of Scotland will laugh," Badgenoth said.

Peter nodded, and led Tatti's horse toward a quiet knoll in the distance, where a red and yellow tent and small encampment had been erected.

"I have some questions I'd like to ask you," he said.

"Questions?" Tatti said.

"Yes. You stole the gold?"

"Yes. You told me how, but I knew you lacked the nerve." She took his hand as they rode along toward the tent, where she saw Gordie and Cora waiting with Stowell and Caroline and her little girl.

"You almost had me beheaded."

"No! I had Father to lawyer in the courts, and money to buy off Robert Cecil. I'd even try to seduce the King to save you, and I hired Shade Turpin . . . ."

"Oh, yes, that Highwayman will be here tomorrow for his second thousand pounds."

"Good. I'll pay him."

"Why, Tatti?" His eyes searched hers deeply.

"Because I loved Gordon Wragby and the son he gave me, and because I loved Skarra, and the old stones, half buried in moss and ferns."

"And me?"

"I loved you first when we were skinny, naked children in a creek, remember?"

"And Phillipe?"

"Please, Peter, as a woman, I should have some secrets. After all, I needed the gold to corrupt the law—to have justice."

"Oh, Tatti." Peter broke into laughter as they rode into camp. He jumped down from his horse and helped her out of her sidesaddle.

She came up in his arms, measuring his eyes softly. "Peter, the human race is older than evil and wiser than vice, and that's all I was trying to do—love it so it could live." She slipped her arms about his slender waist. "Kiss me, Peter, as you did when we were children —only differently, now that we're grown up."

Peter drew her mouth into his and tasted the truth on her lips. His own lip bled where her teeth grazed his mouth with passion. When he pulled free, he took her hand, and they walked inside.

"Peter, I love you," she whispered, "but it's so hard to grow up."

"I know. I had to lose you to find you." He slipped his arm about her waist and hugged her hip to him as he walked, feeling their bodies move like one person together.

THE MAGIC OF
AOLA VANDERGRIFF

DAUGHTERS OF THE SOUTHWIND
by Aola Vandergriff   (92-042, $2.25)

The three McCleod sisters were beautiful, virtuous and bound to a dream — the dream of finding a new life in the untamed promise of the West. Their adventures in search of that dream provide the dimensions for this action-packed romantic bestseller.

DAUGHTERS OF THE WILD COUNTRY
by Aola Vandergriff   (82-583, $2.25)

High in the North Country, three beautiful women begin new lives in a world where nature is raw, men are rough . . . and love, when it comes, shines like a gold nugget. Tamsen, Arab and Em McCleod now find themselves in Russian Alaska, where power, money and human life are the playthings of a displaced, decadent aristocracy in this lusty novel ripe with love, passion, spirit and adventure.

DAUGHTERS OF THE FAR ISLANDS
by Aola Vandergriff   (81-929, $2.50)

Hawaii seems like Paradise to Tamsen and Arab — but it is not. Beneath the beauty, like the hot lava bubbling in the volcano's crater, trouble seethes in Paradise. The daughters are destined to be caught in the turmoil between Americans who want annexation of the islands and native Hawaiians who want to keep their country. And in their own family, danger looms . . . and threatens to erupt and engulf them all.